Up Jumped

A Crescent City
New Orleans Mystery

Martha Reed

UP JUMPED THE DEVIL
A Crescent City New Orleans Mystery

Copyright © 2023 by Martha Reed

All rights reserved. No part of this book may be reproduced in any form or by any electronic or mechanical means, including information storage and retrieval systems, now known or hereinafter invented without the prior express written consent of the author unless such use is allowed under federal copyright law or in the case of brief quotations embodied in critical articles or reviews.

This book is a work of fiction. Any references to historical events, real people or real locales are used fictitiously. Other names, characters, places, dialogue, and incidents are the product of the author's imagination. Any resemblance to actual events, locales, or persons, living or dead, is entirely coincidental.

Trademarked names may appear throughout this book. Rather than use a trademark symbol with every occurrence of a trademarked name, names are used in an editorial fashion, with no intention of infringement of the respective owner's trademark.

First Edition
ISBN: 9798870202402
Published December 2023
Cover art by Karen Phillips – www.phillipscovers.com
Printed in the United States of America.

Also by Martha Reed

THE CRESCENT CITY NOLA MYSTERIES
Love Power (#1)
2021 Killer Nashville Silver Falchion Winner
Best Attending Author
2021 Killer Nashville Silver Falchion Finalist
Best Mystery

THE JOHN AND SARAH JARAD
NANTUCKET MYSTERIES
The Choking Game (#1)
The Nature of the Grave (#2)
Independent Publisher IPPY Book Award
Mid-Atlantic Best Regional Fiction Honorable Mention
No Rest for the Wicked (#3)

Acknowledgments

Cheryl Hollon for sharing her writing craft wisdom
when I was mired knee-deep in a Gordian Knot middle muddle
during our carpool drive to SleuthFest 2022.
"Start at the end and work backward."
The Florida Gulf Coast and
The Mary Roberts Rinehart Pittsburgh Sisters in Crime, Inc.
My crime writing enablers. Guilty as charged.
You know who you are.
Sheriff Randy Smith and the
St. Tammany Parish Sheriff's Office
for providing Major Crimes Investigation procedural details.
Dru Ann Love of Dru's Book Musings and
Kristopher Zgorski of BOLO Books
for your munificent support of our community.
The welcoming librarians and staff at the
Cooper-Siegel Community Library, Fox Chapel, PA.
Thank you.

Chapter One

Sunday, February 12, 2017
11:58 PM

There he goes. Jane's palms hit the gravel as she skidded to one knee on the pebbly ground. Scrambling up, she ignored the burn from her scraped skin as she raced along Parallel Alley No. 1. Hooking a left around a parapet tomb, she ran down the darkened tunnel of St. Louis Alley. The slim hooded vandal, obviously a kid and impressively nimble, jigged sideways between two bricked up burial vaults before melting into the shadows.

Recalling the cemetery's grid-like layout, Jane increased her speed. *The Basin Street exit is locked. Cut down Alley 7-R and head him off.*

Sliding to a halt in the middle of Center, she scanned the area, alert to any flickering motion. The hazy cloud cover slid off the moon, flooding the white tombs with ghostly light. Holding her breath, Jane cocked her head, listening intently and catching the merest whisper of rolling pebbles under a pair of speeding sneakers. *He knows his ground,* she grudgingly admitted. *You can run, buck-o, but you can't hide. Tonight's the night this shit stops.*

Speeding down an alley lined with bricked-up oven tombs, Jane glimpsed the hooded figure. Clutching a section of decorative iron fencing, he swung into the open grassy Protestant section.

Got you now. No way you get out of there without going through me. She skirted the shattered marble angel lying in front of the Fontayne mausoleum before turning into the cemetery's walled western corner.

"Give it up," Jane shouted as her pulse hammered her eardrums. "Don't make this harder than it needs to be."

The hooded vandal slowly raised both hands. Spinning on his heels, he sprinted for the mottled wall separating the Protestant burials from the Catholic believer super majority. Leaping like a New Orleans Saint's running back, he hooked both arms over the wall's upper edge. His sneakers scrabbled against the coarse-grained limestone as he scrambled up. Backlit by a streetlight and balancing like a circus tightrope walker, he rose to his full height before aggressively flipping Jane off and nimbly dropping over the wall onto Treme Street.

"Fuck!" Jane spat, bending to catch her breath, her bellowing lungs on fire. *This needed to work. I've only got forty-five days left.*

Her leaden footsteps ticked like a metronome as she returned to the Basin Street guard station. *I can't lose this gig. The money's right. I'm catching up on the back rent I owe Leslie and Ken.* Jane's nose twitched as she caught a whiff of smoke from a Newport menthol cigarette. *Great. Just what I need. Mose is checking up on me.*

"There you are." Mose Gallier, the NOLA Catholic Cemeteries' Deputy Director of Operations and her immediate supervisor pushed off the wall. "Thought I'd stop by. See how it's going."

"Almost caught him tonight, sir. Cornered in the Protestant section." Jane indicated an inch between her finger and thumb. "Came this close."

"How'd the gutter punk get by you this time?"

This time? Jane bristled. *Is that a dig?* "Climbed the rear wall like Spiderman. It was impressive …"

"Still confident you can catch this asshole? Stop the desecration?"

"I could've stopped him tonight, sir, with a sidearm."

"You know the board has forbidden the use of firearms in the cemeteries."

UP JUMPED THE DEVIL

"Or a Taser."

"The city has banned stun guns. Jane, we've discussed this. The board will not turn a blind eye on using an illegal weapon and potentially opening the door to a lawsuit."

Crissakes! Will you get outta my way and let me do my job? "The taser ban is under review, sir. I mentioned using one in my original security proposal. I carried one at Guardian Self Storage."

"What you did at your last job is between you and your previous employer. It has nothing to do with us." Mose smoothed his seventies porno star mustache. "Jane, these vandals are damaging the tombs and disrespecting the many important New Orleans families interred here."

"Sir, most of the graffiti is coming from the registered tourist groups. They're the ones handing out boxes of chalk with their admission tickets."

"You let the maintenance crew worry about the chalked XXXs and any lipstick kisses. Those are easy enough to remove. You were hired to provide security. This *petit con* desecrated Marie Laveau's tomb using pink latex paint."

Dropping his cigarette, Mose stepped on the butt before stooping to retrieve it. "You need to remember St. Louis Cemetery No. 1 is still in use. Families visit us to pay their respects and to grieve. They get upset when they see vandals damaging their private property, and then they call me." Slipping the spent butt into his cigarette pack's cellophane sleeve, Mose slid the pack into his pocket. "Do I need to mention the board didn't guarantee your contract renewal? We need to see results. Your limited contract expires in two months."

Jane registered an acidic ripple of anxiety. "I'm aware of the timeline, sir."

"I put my neck on the line when I recommended you for this position." Mose cracked his knuckles. "This heightened security idea needs to work. Seeing a successful result soon is personally important to me."

A-ha. Jane hid her smile behind her fingers. *I heard the Executive Director is retiring in May. Sounds like Mose is angling for a promotion.* "How about hiring me some backup? I outlined that in my proposal."

"You can put that idea right out of your mind." Mose spun the UNO class ring he habitually wore on his left pinky finger. "Catholic Cemeteries operates as a non-profit on a restricted budget. The only way I got you approved was because you came cheap."

Don't blame me. Jane bit her tongue. *I'm not the one putting stress on your budget. I'm sure the legal fees defending the Archdiocese against those fresh sex abuse claims are the real culprits. And that money should be going to the victims.*

"As you recall," Mose heedlessly continued, "we went through these details before you signed your security guard contract."

"It's Chief Security *Officer*. Sir."

"Whatever. Are you still confident you can do the job?"

"I never quit," Jane stated. "How about my suggestion to install infrared game trail cameras? They're inexpensive, only about sixty bucks apiece including a SIM card." She circled her finger. "Someone could hide in this cemetery for a week, and I'd never see them patrolling alone on foot. Any word from the board on that idea? We could scope everything inside the perimeter wall for under a grand."

"I'm responsible for more than just St. Louis Cemetery No. 1." Mose smoothed his tie. "I oversee twelve others. All in, you're suggesting an exorbitant unplanned budget expense. I can tell you now, that's not going to happen."

Thirteen cemeteries. Jane added this data nugget to her knowledge base. *Good thing Mose isn't superstitious about unlucky numbers.*

"Besides, video surveillance got voted down at the last board meeting. Families might consider it an invasion of their privacy during a difficult personal time. Many are still *trop chaud* that the *Easy Rider* movie got filmed here – illegally – in 1969." Pulling out his phone, Mose typed a memo. "Thanks for the reminder. Before my time and those actors were trespassing, but I still get blamed for it. That movie's fiftieth anniversary is coming up in 2019. We can anticipate even more tours and visitors."

"Let's hope they're not all dropping acid."

Mose looked up, obviously puzzled. "What did you say?"

"Have you ever seen *Easy Rider,* sir?"

"I'll check Netflix." He frowned. "So? What's the next step for your heightened cemetery security plan?"

"I'm developing another key strategy."

Mose looked doubtful. "Care to share it?"

"No, sir. It's still preliminary." Jane coughed into her fist. "Tentative."

"I want to see this new key strategy outlined on my desk by mid-week. And I expect to see specific tactics outlined with solid anticipated results."

"Not a problem, sir." Jane lied.

Chapter Two

Monday, February 13, 2017
7:28 AM

Jane jogged around the classic red Cadillac Eldorado convertible parked crookedly in the driveway. Pulling the sweat-soaked T-shirt off her sticky skin, she bent down and unsnapped Piddles' harness. The black standard poodle happily trotted away to sniff the brick courtyard. *Give him a minute to enjoy the morning before we go in.*

When they'd headed out for their regular 6:30 a.m. run, Jane had noted the persistent ticking as The Boat's big V-8 engine had cooled. *Gee stayed out all night again.*

Before they'd reached the street, she'd also discovered Ken Pascoe, Gigi's father sitting in his rocker on the front porch. She had caught Ken's deep inhale as he'd savored his first fat spliff of the day.

"Don't know how you do it, Ken." She'd jogged in place. "If I got baked before breakfast I'd forget how to breathe."

"Wake and bake takes practice." He'd chortled. "Don't give me that look. It's medicinal. Eases my arthritis."

Eager to get to Crescent Park, Piddles had yipped.

"Hush, dog!" Ken had hissed. "Don't wake the house. Gigi just got home."

"I noticed."

"Sorry for the reason, but I like having her home again," Ken had stared at the vacant house across Plessy Street. "This neighborhood's been too quiet lately. Feels empty. Unnatural." He'd shuddered. "This much silence gives me the weebs."

Ken had flicked the spliff into the shrubbery. "How's Gigi doing? I know she's got that Mardi Gras krewe thing filling her days but is she okay? She say anything to you? Should her mother and me be worried?"

"Gee seems chill. We've been hanging out as much as we can with our schedules."

"She still dating that FBI fellow?"

"No. There's been a glitch. He got recalled to Boston on special assignment. You know Gee. She likes keeping life more in her face, more ... immediate."

"Sorry to hear that. I hoped this time it was going to work out." Ken had absent-mindedly massaged his strangely splayed thumbs. "I'm sure Gigi's missing her friends. She's gonna need us now more than ever."

Ken was right. Jane agreed, startled off the fender as Piddles cold-nosed her hand. *I need to make more time for Gee. Be a better friend.* She paused again as a random childhood memory bubbled up from her blistered brain.

When she was nine, a savage spring storm had rolled across Nantucket Island during the night. Walking to school, Jane had discovered a baby owl huddled in the seagrass, all terrified and unblinking dark eyes, and downy feathers. Cupping the owlet in her hands, she had raced home. Her dad had immediately driven them to the island's bird sanctuary with Jane feeling the tiny creature's wildly thrumming heartbeat against her palms the entire way. She vividly remembered the omniscient feeling of overwhelming compassion as she'd murmured, "Don't be afraid. It's okay. You're safe. I've got you now," for a full hour until she'd handed the owlet over to the sanctuary's caregivers.

I used to care a lot about a lot of things. Whatever happened to that yes, I do give-a-shit version of me. Jane stumbled as sudden insight flooded her mind. *Crissakes. I haven't checked out. I feel that protective about Gee.*

Chapter Three

Same Day
7:52 AM

As she crossed the courtyard, the scent of country smoked bacon wafting from the Big House's kitchen window tempted her nose. *Ah, bacon. The finest of flavors. Although Vermont Grade A Amber maple syrup might give it a run for its money.*

Since she'd moved to NOLA Jane had learned to revere its multi-cultural cuisine. The chalky 20-gram carob protein bar waiting on her kitchen counter suddenly seemed like a pitifully uninspired breakfast choice.

The screened porch door swung open.

"Jane? We're fixin' to eat." Her landlady Leslie Pascoe winsomely smiled. "Care to join us?"

She bounded up the splintery steps, Piddles at her heels. "You don't need to ask me twice." Leslie prepared luscious Creole dishes. Jane's empty stomach gurgled in anticipation. *Please, NOLA food gods. Be good to me today. What are the odds Leslie made her famous buttermilk biscuits and red-eye gravy? Look out, carbos. Here I come.*

"Gigi, put down that phone." Leslie shooed Jane toward the kitchen table. "We're havin' a meal. Hand Jane a plate while I fix her café au lait."

"I'm expecting an important email today." Gee flipped her phone face down on the tablecloth. Her chair cracked alarmingly as she tilted backwards, stretching one arm over her head, and reaching toward the cupboard. "Morning, Jane. Get ready to dig in. Maman's been cookin' since dawn."

UP JUMPED THE DEVIL

"Needed to do something useful since I can't sleep." Leslie gave the contents of a cast iron skillet a ferocious stir. "Never did sleep much anyway. Sleeping even less now with this *chose irritante* hanging off my leg."

Pointing her toe, she hiked the hem of her gauzy floor length boho skirt, revealing a black GPS monitor strapped around her right ankle. "I loathe this *fou* shackle. Feels like I'm someone's house slave."

"House arrest is onerous." Jane laid a nubby homespun serviette over her lap as her mouth watered. "And don't I know it."

Gigi's Aunt Babette tugged a palm-sized red flannel cloth bundle from her cardigan pocket. "Before I forget, Jane. I made you something."

"What's this?" Jane cautiously poked the colorful thread-wrapped gift.

"Voodoo." Ken huffed. "She made one for each of us. Nice thing to find sitting on your breakfast plate."

"It's a good luck *gris-gris*." The elderly voodoo queen's dark eyes shone. "To break the chain of evil luck we're traveling through." Repeatedly snicking her tongue against her front teeth, she separated the strands of the tightly knotted tie with her pointed fingernail. "Purple thread for justice. Green for faith. Gold thread for power. I made yours extra potent, Jane, because I sense the *Ghede* are watching you."

Jane shivered. *AB is a generous soul, but she knows I hate this voodoo shit.* She plucked the *gris-gris* by its zig-zagged pinking shear edges. "Should I open it?"

"No! Never. It must stay sealed for the *juju* to work."

Jane felt the odd lumps and bumps through the cloth. "What's in it?"

"Good things. Lucky things." Aunt Babette resettled the seven silver bangles on her left wrist. "Cowrie shells, stripy beads. A lock of your pretty yellow hair I found on the floor when Leslie cut it. Tuck that *gris-gris* in your bag," Aunt Babette directed. "Carry it with you wherever you go for protection." She cocked her head like an alert sparrow. "Any more questions?"

"I've got one for Jane." Gee stopped picking her nails. "When did you get house arrest?"

Chapter Four

Same Day
8:02 AM

"I was never ... sentenced to house arrest," Jane stammered. *I've never told anyone this before, but if not now, then when?* "And I didn't need to wear an ankle monitor. I was forced to surrender my passport and my service weapon." She firmed her lips. "The Court ordered me to stop presenting myself as a law enforcement officer pending the outcome of the civil trial and reinstatement."

"You were on trial?" Ken lowered his coffee mug. "Christ! I hope I never go through that."

Leslie stopped whisking the eggs. "You never told me you went to jail during our interview for your apartment."

"No." *I should've kept my mouth shut.* Jane desperately tried to halt the slippery slide into misinformation. "I never went to jail. I was placed on paid administrative leave while I.A., uhm, an independent commission investigated for Internal Affairs." A PTSD tremor sparked her spine. "I.A. thought they had enough evidence to charge me with illegal use of lethal force. They raised it to a grand jury. That's when I got moved to extended unpaid leave." She laughed bitterly as the memory twisted her gut. "What nailed me was John's affidavit that I skipped the verbalization warning. Level 2 on the Use-Of-Force Continuum."

"Who's 'John'?" Aunt Babette picked up her tea.

"My Nantucket force commander." Jane faced the aching betrayal. "We grew up together. He was my best friend. Loved him like a brother." She swallowed hard, twice. "The short answer is the grand jury dismissed the charge against me. They found I was justified in using lethal force against Mason Hollister."

Gee stared. "Hollister was the man you shot."

"He was." Jane felt queasy. *I need to own this and tell them the full truth.* "Mason Hollister was the man I killed." She swallowed again, her mouth tasting like bitter ashes. "Because of John's statement that I never verbally warned Hollister to stand down, his father found a shyster lawyer who was willing to take the case. The Hollisters sued me in civil court." The memory still felt so raw that Jane itched. "The civil trial took three years. Drained me dry. Cost me eighty-two thousand dollars in legal fees. I sold my house, my car, pretty much everything I owned to clear the debt."

"You lost your home?" Aunt Babette clutched her robe at her throat. "We're not gonna lose the Big House over our troubles, are we, Leslie?"

"No, dear." Leslie calmly carried the platter of warm vanilla crepes to the table. "We don't need to worry about that."

"Enough jibber-jabber." Ken stabbed the stack of paper-thin crepes with his fork. "Do we really need to talk about this now?"

"House arrest is still better than sitting in the Orleans Parish Prison, Maman." Gee teased Piddles with a fatty bacon scrap. "Remember when they left those prisoners locked inside during Hurricane Katrina to fend for themselves?"

Aunt Babette shuddered. "Imagine facing a Force Five hurricane locked in a prison cell without food or water."

"At sea level." Leslie agreed. "And knowing that bitch Katrina was coming right at you."

"And no air conditioning," Gee added.

"Enough!" Ken roared. "Will you goddamned women please shut up?" He rested both fists next to his plate. "You're worrying this fucking thing to death. Just leave it the fuck alone. Stay in the day. Wait and see what tomorrow brings tomorrow."

UP JUMPED THE DEVIL

"Ken's right." Leslie calmly distributed portions of the leek and cheddar cheese omelet. "We can be patient one more day."

"*Bebe*." Aunt Babette sniffed before smiling apologetically. "This smells *exquis* but I can't eat a bite with tomorrow being such a big day." She stroked her wrinkled neck. "I'm so nervous my throat's closed up."

"Eat what you can, dear. We'll have two good reasons to celebrate tomorrow since it's also St. Valentine's Day." Leslie coyly gave Ken a wink. "A day made to celebrate true love."

"Don't remind me." Gee scowled. "Love stinks."

"J. Geils Band," Ken automatically replied around a mouthful of egg.

"Getting this shackle off my leg is the only present I want." Carrying the skillet to the sink, Leslie left it to soak. "I'm gonna dance through Mardi Gras this year a free woman again. Best present I could get."

"Yah, you right about that, *sha*. Imagine walking down the street tomorrow night with no one bothering us and no never mind. I'm gonna be *si joyeux* I'll fart confetti."

"Goddamn, Babette." Ken choked. "You're insane."

Jane lowered her fork. *No wonder NOLA is the murder capital of the universe. Louisiana homicide laws are wacked. Never heard of the 60-Day Rule before. Had to toss everything I knew about Massachusetts law out the window.*

NOPD Detective Dupree sure as hell jumped the gun when he formally arrested Leslie and Aunt Babette in December without having sufficient evidence. What was Dupree thinking? He had to know their Louisiana arrest warrants would permanently expire in sixty days unless they were formally charged with a crime.

"Only one more day to go." Aunt Babette lightly clapped her hands. "Unless that *maudit* District Attorney charges us today, tomorrow is our Freedom Day."

Talk about working an investigation against a ticking clock. Jane returned her knife to her plate. *Unless the D.A. files manslaughter charges against Leslie and Aunt Babette today, they'll both walk. And the D.A. won't file formal charges until the Medical Examiner determines Marianne Tanner's official cause of death. And the M.E. is refusing to be more specific than official cause of death: Undetermined because of the condition of the skeletonized remains. What a cluster fuck.*

Jane snorted. *And no D.A. or prosecuting attorney in the world is going to carry a homicide case to court without knowing the victim's confirmed cause of death.* Her mind raced ahead. *Did Leslie kill Marianne Tanner using blunt force? Or did Aunt Babette bury Marianne alive? Crissakes! The trial would open under a cloud of reasonable doubt from the get-go.* Jane slowly folded the serviette into neat thirds. *The kicker is that if their arrest warrants expire today, double jeopardy comes into play. Neither one of them can ever be charged with Marianne Tanner's death again.*

Ding, ding! Jane sat back, considering her own grimly checkered past. *Let's welcome two new members to The Murderer's Club.*

Chapter Five

Same Day
8:47 AM

"Listen up." Ken stared down his fork. "Everyone needs to shut their yaps until we put this cluster fuck behind us. No one volunteers one more word until we know those charges got dropped. Jane? You listening? This includes you."

Gee toyed with her toast. "We are talking about murder, Pops."

"I know that." Ken snarled. "But your mother's facing forty years in prison. We'd never see her again. Is that what you want?"

"Only if I get charged with second degree manslaughter." Leslie blanched.

"Which is why," Aunt Babette quickly interjected, "We should go with me for involuntary manslaughter. I can survive twelve months and probation."

"I'd still be facing aggravated 2nd degree battery for hitting that woman with the shovel."

"Which is still better, *sha*, than forty years."

"Stop this!" Gee leapt to her feet. "I can't stand this conversation."

Everyone jumped as Gigi's phone trilled. Striding back to the table, she snatched it up. After swiping the screen, she yelped, "Yes!" as her face filled with glee. "Pops, good thing you're sitting down. You ready for this?"

"Why?" Ken looked wary. "What have you done?"

Gee smirked like a gargoyle. "I emailed a producer to see about working on your new album. This is his answer." Clenching her fist, she pumped her left arm. "He wants in."

"I never agreed to that. What new producer?" Ken repeatedly blinked. "Who'd you pick?"

"You are so gonna die when I tell you." Gee looked up from under her mascaraed eyelashes. "Frankie Malcolm."

Ken's jaw dropped open. "Frankie's still alive? I don't believe it. How'd you find him?"

"Used this dope thing called Google search," Gee sarcastically replied. "Found his website." Rereading the message, she smirked. "Seemed like the right place to start since he worked with you and the original WarBirds."

"Smart ass. That was thirty years ago. Where are my cheaters?" Patting his pockets, Ken stood and squinted over her shoulder. "Let me see that. What did Frankie say?"

"He must be serious. He's willing to fly here and discuss the idea with you in person." Gee's thumbs hovered over the keypad. "Okay if I say 'yes'?"

"Say 'Hell yes!'" Ken nervously chewed his lip. "Frankie Malcolm. I'll be damned."

"Done. I'll keep my eye on this, Pops. Let you know what he says." Gee flicked her fingers. "Damn, it's nice working on something positive for a change. Been a lot of closed doors and negative energy lately." She turned. "Speaking of which how's the new cemetery security job working out, Jane? All good? I've been meaning to ask."

"One small hitch. I need to catch a spook and I'm running out of time. He's proving … elusive."

"Spook?" Aunt Babette looked up expectantly.

"A human spook, Aunt B. A trespasser vandalizing some of the tombs." Jane blindly stared out the window. "What I'm doing now isn't working. I need to develop a capture strategy. Maybe set a trap."

"Need help?" Gee raised one eyebrow. "Need some … backup?"

Jane admitted the truth. "I could use some assistance."

UP JUMPED THE DEVIL

"I'm in." Gee slipped her phone into the back pocket of her ripped jeans. "I'm working my shift at Club Oz tonight from eleven to four, but I could give you an hour before my shift, if it helps."

"I'll take it. That would be great." Jane relaxed. "Meet me at the cemetery when you can."

"Trust me with your Ducati and I could drop you off and swing by after your shift to pick you up. Save on gas."

"Nice try." *Gee's been trying to borrow my bike for a month.* "I've already said that's not going to happen until you learn how to ride Monster properly first."

"Look who you're talkin' to." Gee cocked her hip. "I've had tons of practice. I've been riding monsters improperly since I was sixteen years old."

"Gigi!" Leslie dropped the spatula into the sudsy sink. "Honestly! The things you say."

"Honestly," Gee parroted. "How hard can it be?"

"Hard enough to get you creamed if you don't know what you're doing."

"Fine." She surrendered. "I'll take The Boat tonight and meet you at the front gate." Her eyes twinkled. "When's my first lesson?"

Chapter Six

Same Day
10:17 PM

"Jane, you do this for a living?" Gee whispered through the wireless Bluetooth headset. "It's *rampé*. Doesn't it creep you out?"

"Nothing to be scared of. Everyone's dead."

"Says you." She inhaled. "I'll need to leave soon for my shift."

"That's okay. I usually see the spook closer to midnight anyway."

"I'll come back." She exhaled. "Until we catch him."

"I appreciate your help. Got your pepper spray handy?"

"S'right here. Next to my knee."

"Remember, it's only for self-defense. You are not to engage. Leave the capture to me."

"We've been over this. I got it. I chase the spook to you and then skedaddle." She inhaled again. "I liked using my baseball bat idea better."

"Let's avoid you getting charged with A&B and trespassing tonight. You're not even supposed to be in the cemetery grounds after open hours."

"Not an issue. My BFF's head of security." Her voice turned squeaky. "She approved of me being here."

"Okay. I have to ask. What are you smoking?"

"Nothing."

"Liar. I can hear you toking through the mic."

"Technically, I'm vaping. Chanel from the club gave me some cannabis oil. Want to try some? I'm willing to share."

"Crissakes, Gee, stop it. I can smell the stink from here. If I can smell it, the spook can, too."

"Fine." She paused. "Jane? You seeing orbs?"

"What?"

"Orbs. Little yellow orbs floating around the tombs. There's another one! S'weird. Anyway, Aunt Babette says orbs are pure energy. Spirits are attracted to them if they have unfinished Earthly business. I think these orbs might be Fancy and Dee-Dee trying to help us tonight."

"More likely methane from the decomp."

Gee strangled a snorting cough. "I liked my answer better."

Jane resettled her headset. *NOLA burial practice is odd. I get that you can't plant a coffin six feet deep when the water table's only a foot down, but not embalming the bodies and using tombs as personal cremation ovens seems flat out bizarre.* She swallowed drily. *Don't know what I'll do come August when it gets super-hot. Mose said the escaping gasses sound like a row of beauty parlor hair dryers.* She shuddered. *I'll need to bring some Vicks VapoRub to smear under my nose to mask the stink. And CSI training be damned, I do not want to be here when they reopen a tomb for a new body and use a ten-foot pole to push the bones into the caveau underneath. Crissakes! Who wants that crap job?*

"Jane? Where's your family buried?"

She refocused. "We've got a plot in a Quaker cemetery on Nantucket."

"You're a Quaker?"

"No, but my family was, back in the day. The plot is already paid for."

"We could ask Maman about you using our Broussard tomb, if you wanted to stay in NOLA with us."

"Thanks, Gee. Appreciate the offer, but I should probably go be with my parents. You know, wrap it up, since I'm the last one."

"That's so sad." There was a static burst. "Does your Quaker cemetery have nice tombs like these ones?"

"No. Quaker cemeteries don't even have tombstones. Just grassy hills."

"No tombstones?" She doggedly pursued. "Why?"

"They were considered too worldly."

"Then how do they know where the bodies are buried?"

Honest to God. Jane massaged her temples. *When Gee gets stoned it's like dealing with a nosy two-year-old.* "They use longitude and latitude off a chart."

"Shhh! Hold up. Someone's scrambling over the gate."

"Showtime." Jane's heartbeat accelerated until it drummed her ears. "Make some noise. Drive him toward the Protestant section. If he turns or if you see any type of weapon other than a paint can, back it down, Gee, and I mean it. This ain't your fight."

"Got it, yo. Here I go."

Jane heard a distant gong-like sound like a tipped over metal trashcan. A split-second later the echo repeated in her headset.

"That got him. He took off running. Heading for you along the Conti Street wall. Wearing jeans and a silver hoodie."

"Keep your distance. Remember what I said. No contact."

"*Merde!* He's a fast little fucker. Just passed the big Portuguese tomb."

Fingering the handcuffs clipped to her duty belt, Jane settled her stance. The open Protestant section at her back was eerily silent except for the distant buzzing murmur of Interstate 10. Straining her ears, Jane caught the repeated crunch of running shoes on pea gravel. Rising to her toes, she leaned forward as a hooded figure raced around the corner of a marble tomb.

Crissakes! It's just a kid. She leapt.

Spinning with preternatural ability, the trespasser pivoted left. Jane grabbed a handful of silky fabric that slipped through her seeking fingers. Off-balance, her bad left knee locked. She tripped, crashing hard onto her right elbow. Rolling off her shoulder with the momentum, Jane scrambled to her feet as the vandal raced for Treme Street.

Not now! Not again. Not when I'm so close.

A second running figure closed the gap.

"No, Gee! Don't!" Jane shouted into her headset.

Arms outstretched like a gigantic crab, Gee launched into a magnificent flying tackle.

"Surprise, motherfucker!" She shrieked. "Hold still you little pissant. Ow!"

"Goddammit, Gee!" Jane limped toward the struggling huddle. "I said no physical contact."

"Let *go*!" The vandal struggled to bury her thumbs in Gee's eyes. "Get offa me!"

"*Merde.*" Gee rolled off and away. "It's a girl."

"Stay put." Jane raised her pepper spray. "You're under arrest."

"You cain't arrest me." The trespasser crouched, glancing for an exit like a trapped feral cat. "You're no cop, bitch."

"I'm all the cop you're gonna need."

"Fuck you." Warily rising to her feet, the girl looked to be roughly fifteen years old, a rail thin five-foot-three with a headful of unruly ringlets. "I didn't do nothing."

"You're trespassing. And vandalizing these tombs."

"Wasn't me.' She spat. "I was takin' a shortcut home."

"Climbing two eight-foot walls is a shortcut?" Gee challenged.

"I don't hafta answer to you."

Spinning on her toes, she kicked Gee squarely in the groin. There was a hollow 'pock' sound. Gee's eyes turned glassy, and she slumped to the ground.

Jane froze as the girl sprinted for the Treme Street wall.

Do I chase her? I can't leave Gee just lying there.

"Fuck!" Rolling back and forth, Gee squinted in agony. "Motherfucker. That hurts."

Jane knelt, feeling helpless. "I told you to stay out of it. This was my fight."

"Too late now. Needs to pass." Gee repeatedly coughed. Pushing off her knees, she shakily stood, gasping like a tide-stranded fish. "Need to call Club Oz. Not swinging off any pole tonight."

Jane grasped Gee's muscular bicep. "Is it getting better?"

"Won't get better 'til I sit on a bag of frozen peas. *Merde.*" She huffed. "Been awhile since anyone rang my bell. I'll be pissing blood tomorrow."

PTSD distortion buzzed in Jane's ears. "You'll never have to do this again. It's my problem. I can't be responsible for you getting hurt."

"We won't hafta do this again." Drawing another shuddering breath, Gee straightened. "Because I know where that bitch lives. And I know exactly how to draw her out."

Chapter Seven

Tuesday, February 14, 2017
6:38 AM

Hitting Monster's kill switch, Jane rolled the silent Ducati motorcycle up the driveway next to The Boat. She was surprised to see Gee leaning against the fender, thoughtfully smoking a cigar even as dawn brightened the horizon.

Jane slung her helmet off the handlebars. "How you feeling?"

"Sore." Dropping the cigar, Gee carefully crushed it out. "One of the girls sold me a Tramadol. Took the edge off."

"You went to the club anyway?"

"No. Chilled with Krewdio-54. We're finishing our costumes for the Mardi Gras parade."

"All night?"

"Pretty much. Most of us don't get off work until four anyway. Kick a double espresso and carry on." She scratched her jaw. "Should be my motto."

"Ken!" Leslie's voice rang across the courtyard. "Why didn't you tell me this?"

"Pops is in big trouble," Gee sadly stated. "It's bad. Maman's really upset. They've been at it as long as I've been home."

Jane scanned the still shuttered ground floor bedroom window. "What are they fussing about?"

"Just wait. You'll hear."

"You're worrying over nothing," Ken rumbled. "I'll go to One Stop as soon as they open and see about getting your bail bonds dissolved after your court appearances today."

"And there goes another fifteen *thousand* dollars we'll never see," Leslie acidly protested. "It's not just the bail bonds, Ken. You never should've signed that promissory note without talking to me first. The Big House isn't yours to use as collateral. Pied Stan is a viper. Now he has a hold over our *home*. You weren't supposed to access this house or my money until *after* I died."

"Did you want to stay in jail?" Ken's voice rose. "What else was I supposed to do? Stan was the only one willing to loan me fifteen grand in cash. Besides," he sputtered, "Louisiana's a community property state. Stan said so."

"He's wrong. And this property is protected. It's set up usufruct. You have the right to live in the house and get Jane's rental income after I die, but the property belongs to Gigi after you die or if you remarry. Trust me." Her voice trembled. "I worked with my lawyer plenty to make sure of it."

"Usufruct?" Ken sniggered. "Sounds more like 'I so fucked'."

"Don't you dare try to joke your way out of this. I made very certain there will be no questions about my estate. This house has been in the Broussard family for seven generations. Not many families can say that anymore. I meant to keep it safe for Gigi's inheritance."

There it is again. That weird wrinkle Leslie has about holding onto things.

"And since it's come out that your girlfriend Marianne Tanner is Gigi's birthmother, I wanted to make sure that Gigi stayed my legal heir – not you – since she was never formally adopted."

"Dammit, Leslie. I've never known you to be cold. That almost sounds heartless."

Gee restlessly shifted. "Do I need to update my birth certificate? It's still got Maman and Pops listed on it."

"That's a question for an attorney," Jane said. "I don't even know if you can update a birth certificate."

"Sweetheart, I'm not sure I'm happy with this new Will idea of yours. Maybe you should've talked about it with me first."

"Too late. It's already beyond an idea, Ken. I inherited this house from my parents when I turned eighteen *before* we were married. I needed to do what I think is best for the property."

"I'm tired of fighting. It'll be fine." Ken surrendered. "I'll go back to stocking shelves at the Dollar Store. Earn the money to pay Stan back that way. Let me do the worrying."

"It will not be fine. Paying Pied Stan back will take years, Ken – with interest. And this new worry will be hanging over our heads the whole time." She sobbed. "I can't forget you did this behind my back. I think, I think you should sleep upstairs in the spare room from now on."

"On the third floor? Across from Babette?"

"Yes."

"Leslie, we have shared the same bed for thirty years."

"Thirty-three. Maybe you should've thought of that before you levied a lien against our home. Think of it, Ken. If we miss one payment, just one, Pied Stan can evict us. You, me, Gigi, Aunt Babette. We'd be homeless. Living on the street."

"Sweetheart, please."

"Don't sweetheart me, Ken. You have broken my trust. And I made such great plans. You have ruined St. Valentine's Day."

"Like I said before." Gee pushed off the Cadillac. "Love stinks."

Chapter Eight

Same Day
6:11 PM

Gee shook the greasy paper sacks she held in both hands. "To catch the right fish, you need to use the right bait."

"Is that why you ordered double onions?" Gripping the halogen flashlight, Jane nervously scanned the Poe Street warehouse's dankly crumbling corners. "Crissakes. Anyone in here could track us by the smell."

"Not for nothing, Sherlock, but that's the idea."

"Not sure why I needed to shell out eighteen bucks buying fancy hamburgers," Jane grumbled, navigating around a loose pile of shattered bricks.

"With cheesy tots and orange Nehi. We're offering a full meal deal." Gee shook the sacks again. "Quit your bitchin'. I'm helping you keep your job."

She cautiously stepped through an open doorway that retained its twisted hinges but no door. "Street people want three things: hot food, whatever drug keeps them healthy that day, and a roof over their head when it rains."

"This is NOLA. It always rains." Jane avoided an oily black puddle. "How d'you know she lives in this warehouse?"

"Fancy and me stumbled up on her and her brother once when we scoped out using this place for our pop-up disco." Gee ducked under a loosely looped cable. "A bunch of homeless use this warehouse for their crib. No electricity, but it's still got running water. That's key. Keeps the toilets working."

"Where do you stand with that?"

UP JUMPED THE DEVIL

"Stand with what?" Gee looked confused. "Running water?"

"No, sorry. Your disco idea."

"I think that big dream died." Gee's shoulders drooped as she climbed the grimy staircase. "Not sure I want to do it anymore without Fancy and Dee-Dee. That was our big dream. It's not the same dream doing it alone."

"Sometimes dreams change." Jane keenly felt Gee's sorrow. "But maybe it's only on hold. I mean, look at your dad. He's working on a new album, and it's been thirty years. He's chasing his big dream again." Jane switched the flashlight to her left hand. "Don't give up on your disco idea just yet, Gee. If you want it bad enough, you can make it happen. Just let me know what I can do to help."

"I appreciate that." Reaching the landing, Gee turned. "What's your big dream?"

"I don't ... think I have one."

"Gotta have a dream, Jane. Gotta have something to hang your hat on in the future to keep you moving ahead, even if it's not your final big dream. Like me working on the choreography for the Mystick Krewdio-54's Mardi Gras parade unit this year."

Turning, she trotted up the next set of iron steps. "Still need to find a space for the krewe's after party. We're running outta time. Trying not to panic. Wanted to use Club Femme du, but they don't take private parties during Mardi Gras, and even if they did, we don't have the kinda dough they'd charge us." She paused. "That's a laugh. We don't have any money. I'm thinking now we could use this space."

"An abandoned warehouse?"

"Why not? It's free. Got plumbing. Bring in a car battery, string some lights, get a sick DJ, call it a rave. Parking garage right next door, three blocks from the St. Charles streetcars." She stepped into a dim cavernous room lit on one side by a row of opaque windows. "It could work."

"Until the cops show up and shut you down."

"That would add to the fun." She grinned. "Everyone likes a little late-night scramble. Adds more drama."

Jane's eyes watered as the acrid stink of piss burned her nostrils, the tell-tale scent of human occupation. Studying the gloomy space, she noted black trash bags piled against one wall next to folded bundles of dirty quilts and soiled bedding. She ran the halogen flashlight over the floor. Despite the filth, it looked like the warehouse squatters had identified their own individual and private territories.

"Shit, Gee. You'd need a firehose to clean this place. Or a fire."

"We'd hold the rave downstairs. No need to come up here."

Jane flinched as a crusty bundle shifted.

"Hey there, brother." Gee walked over. She carefully crouched, peering at a rheumy man sitting on a bed made of flattened cardboard boxes. Avoiding a puddle of burned out candle wax, she extended a paper sack. "Brought you some supper."

He straightened his grimy knit cap over wisps of his scraggly white hair. His face was sunburned brown, but the inside of his wrists revealed his naturally paler skin tone. *This man's been living outdoors for decades.*

"Bless you, sir." He snatched the sack with a gloved hand that had the fingers cut out of the fabric. "What've we got?"

"Hamburger, cheesy tots, and an orange Nehi."

"Next time bring eggs." His snarl revealed his gray toothless gums. "Meat's too hard on my mouth."

"Anybody here with you?" Gee slowly rose. She shook the second sack. "We brought more."

Gooseflesh prickled Jane's forearms as she heard a sibilant whisper of movement from the shadows.

"*Sak pase?*" The girl stepped around a concrete pillar. She gripped a section of metal pipe. "What you want, bitches?"

Assuming a defensive stance, Jane settled her weight on her heels. "We just want to talk. Nothing more."

Pointing at Gee, the girl snorted. "That scene queens still limpin'. You didn't get enough from me last night?"

"I know I did." Gee shook the bag again. "It's a shame these cheesy tots are getting cold. You look like you're one meal away from starving to death."

"Tots?" The girl sniffed repeatedly. "What else you bring?"

"Hot food. Why d'you care?"

"Gimme." She slid the pipe into a shoulder-high cinder block hole. Warily stepping forward, she snatched the sack, stuffing a handful of tots into her mouth with her dirty fingers. "Needs hot sauce."

"Keep chewing," Jane said. "Last night you said you weren't in the cemetery to vandalize the tombs."

"Ain't no liar." Tearing the paper wrapper open, she wolfed down a mouthful of hamburger. "You're the swamper works there, right?"

"Swamper?"

"Maintenance man." She savaged another bite.

"I'm head of security. Why were you in the cemetery?"

"Looking for my 'bro." She vigorously chewed with an open mouth. "Been missing a week. Ain't like Rex. Usually finds his way back to me stone blind unless he's drinking lean."

Gee looked uncertain. "Lean?"

"Purple Drank," Jane explained. "Prescription-strength codeine and promethazine cough syrup mixed with soda and hard candy."

"Sizzurp." Gee shuddered. "Nasty ass shit. It can seriously fuck you up. Rots your teeth."

"I get so mad when Rex do lean." Balling the wrapper, the girl dropped it to the grimy floor. She concentrated on scooping up the remaining tots. "But he be that way sometimes. Rex gets *couvon* when he pick up the cup. Couple of times a month I hafta go find him. Fetch him back." She smeared the greasy corners of her mouth on the back of her hand. "Granny Duchamp lived in Iberville before she died. Rex gets confused. He forgets we live here now."

Jane looked at Gee. "Iberville?"

"Public housing. Torn down four, five years ago."

"That's right." The girl dropped the empty sack to the floor. "You work in that cemetery. You seen Rex around?"

"Maybe. Has he been painting the tombs? Painting over the graffiti?"

"Maybe." She mimicked, wiping her fingers on her silver hoodie. "Rex's mental. Thinks tagging tombs is disrespect. Wants everything looking nice for the dead people like they give a fuck."

"I might have seen Rex," Jane said. "What's he look like?"

"Suppose he looks like me." A sudden and surprising smile illuminated her face. "Since he's my baby brother."

"He might be the one I saw last Sunday."

"You saw Rex on Sunday? Good to know. Means he ain't so gone. I'll steal a cigar for Baron Samedi asking for his help."

"If your brother's missing, you should file a police report."

"Surely not." She scoffed, sucking on the straw, and finishing the soda. "Like the po-lice care when homeless go missing. Cops don't give a shit about us. They like keeping us invisible, keeping us in line."

Gee looked troubled. "Couldn't social services help? Some kind of foster care?"

"Ha! Fosters wanted to bust us up. Send Rex away." She crunched some ice between her molars. "Not gonna happen. I promised our mama I'd watch over Rex. Keep him safe." Proudly raising her chin, she met their eyes. "We been independent since we was eleven. We doin' alright."

"Is Rex's last name Duchamp, like your grandmother's?" Jane asked.

The girl looked startled. "What's it to you?"

"We can file a missing person report on him."

"We know just who to talk to." Gee agreed.

"Don't you do that, bitches. Don't sick no po-lice on us."

"Take it easy." Gee fluttered both hands, palm side down. "We're trying to help. You gotta phone in case we need to reach you?"

"A phone." The girl gave Gee some serious stink eye. "And who'd be paying for that?"

"What's your name, then?" Jane asked. "How do we stay in touch?"

"That's easy." Cubed ice spilled across the floor as she dropped the Styrofoam cup. "We don't."

"What if we find Rex?" Jane called. "What if we find your brother?"

The girl pointed to a heavily graffitied brick wall before lithely slipping down the staircase. "Leave me a note."

Chapter Nine

Same Day
7:14 PM

"I'm taking N. Rampart to avoid Decatur." Gee caught the red light at the Canal Street intersection. Reaching down, she pressed The Boat's in-dash cigarette lighter before flicking her index finger dead ahead. "Traffic backs up when it rains heavy like this."

It feels odd to have The Boat's canvas top up, and not feel the wind on my face. The windshield wipers smeared the lurid neon French Quarter bar signs into rainbows. The lighter popped. Gee lit a cigar, squinting against the pungent smoke.

"What do you do on your bike when it rains?"

"Get wet."

She snorted. "At least now you know Rex Duchamp is your vandal. You got a name. That solve your problem?"

Jane stared into the wet night. "Mose won't be satisfied with a name. He'll want an arrest to prove the cemetery's secure again, to make himself look good to the board." Jane's head snapped back as the stoplight turned green and Gee floored the accelerator. "I'm torn. I need to stop the vandalism, but I don't want to get that kid Rex into more trouble. Sounds like he's had it rough enough already."

"I'm with you." Gee repeatedly puffed the cigar. "I'm feeling itchy, like I need to do something. I keep remembering what Pops said about Marianne hanging out with The WarBirds because she had no place else to go." Cranking the steering wheel hard right, she turned down St. Claude Avenue. "What d'you think about asking Detective Dupree for advice? Maybe he could hook us up with somebody in Social Services. Set something up. Somebody must have a program to help get these kids off the street."

"Detective Dupree is with CID Homicide. We should ask him who took Detective Bordelon's job. Missing Persons and the Juvie Section would be a better place to start," Jane suggested, as another thought crossed her mind. "Speaking of Marianne Tanner, has the Coroner's Office contacted you about releasing her ... remains?"

"No. Haven't heard a peep."

"That's strange, Gee, if you're officially listed as her next-of-kin."

"The D.A. had until the end of today to decide about charging Maman and Aunt Babette. Maybe that's hanging things up."

"Maybe. Are you planning on holding a memorial service?"

"Now that's a topic I haven't introduced to the family yet." Gee puffed. "I can just imagine the look on Maman's face if Pops is ever dumb enough to suggest putting Marianne to rest in the Broussard family tomb. *Merde.*" Pulling The Boat into the driveway, she stubbed out the cigar. "I'd better warn him. Maman'd go full on nuclear. Millions of innocent civilians could die."

A low lamp was burning on the screened-in back porch, shedding warm yellow light over the courtyard. The wavering notes of a jazz clarinet shimmied as Jane popped the passenger door. The clarinet was answered by a snapping snare drum and a brassy warbling trombone. Ducking her head, Jane hunched her shoulders to avoid the spitting rain. "Sounds like someone's having a party."

"Hey, girls!" Leslie called. "Come join this *fais do-do* we got going on."

"This sounds like trouble." Trotting up the splintery steps, Gee snatched the screened door open. "What are you two doin'?"

"Celebrating!" Aunt Babette raised her champagne flute.

"The D.A.'s office called." Leslie looked triumphant. "They've declined to press charges."

"Against either one of us. It's official! We are free!"

Raising her pants' leg, Leslie displayed her ankle monitor. "This shackle comes off tomorrow."

Gee cocked a wary eye. "Where's Pops? How long have you two been drinking?"

Leslie laughed. "That grumpy old man's gone to bed."

"You two need some coffee."

"Only if it's Irish." Leslie giggled.

Aunt Babette reached for the sparkling pink champagne bottle. "Why ruin this lovely buzz? Join us, girls. Grab a glass."

"You go ahead," Jane said. "I still have my shift tonight."

"Gigi, here. I know you'll have some. It's delicious."

Gee sipped the champagne before studying the floor. "I'm glad to hear that news, I really am. But that means we'll never know how Marianne died."

"Oh, honey." Quickly setting her glass down, Leslie crossed the porch. "I know how hard this must be, but we need to put the past in the past. All of this happened so long ago when you were just a *bebe*." Clasping her hands, she looked hopeful. "There's nothing we can do to change the terrible thing that happened. We need to live with it – and we will for the rest of our lives, but it's time to let go and move on. Life is for the living."

Gee's brown eyes grew even darker. "I know that, and I'm trying to move on, but there's been so much death lately." Setting the champagne flute on the table, she pressed her fingers to her brow. "I've been missing Fancy and Dee-Dee, and now there's this." Her shoulders drooped. "When will it stop hurting?"

"Sweetheart." Leslie wrapped Gee in a gentle hug. "I know you're missing your friends. We just need to step through this, one day at a time." Stepping back, she held Gee at arm's length, looking up into her eyes with concern. "You won't believe me now, but I promise it will get easier. Yes, we will remember Dee-Dee and Fancy with love in our hearts, but you need to remember you are not alone. You have this family to help you get through this."

"We're here for you, *sha,*" Aunt Babette agreed.

Dropping her arms, Leslie stepped back, smiling with a desperate kind of brightness. "Where have you girls been? What've you been up to tonight?"

"Gee helped me track down the cemetery's spook," Jane said. "She ID'd a person of interest and got us a name. It was good detective work. A solid lead."

Leslie nervously twined her fingers together. "That's good news, right?"

"It is, but it's sad." Gee drained her champagne. "We found a couple of kids living rough on the street."

Aunt Babette looked perplexed. "Why were they messing with the St. Louis Cemetery?"

"They grew up in Iberville. The boy keeps going back there. He forgets they don't live in the projects no more."

Aunt Babette tsk-tsked against her teeth. "That land got bad *juju* ever since the gov'mint shut down Storyville. They never should'a been allowed to do that. Run us out and stole our good businesses."

"Storyville?" Jane wondered. "Was that some kind of urban redevelopment plan?"

Gee refilled her glass. "Storyville was the old vice district. Had the brothels, dance halls, saloons, gambling houses, vice dens."

"Great marble palaces of joy," Aunt Babette corrected, proudly raising her knobby index finger. "Some of the finest houses in the city."

"Babette." Leslie looked nervous. "Not everyone had a marble palace. There were plenty of nasty ten-cent cribs."

"Storyville was where an independent woman could get herself rich," Aunt Babette argued blindly. "'Specially women of color."

Jane felt confused. "It's a good thing they tore Storyville down, right?"

"No. It was not," Aunt Babette vehemently stated. "Storyville was the heart and soul of N'awlins, the birthplace of blues and jazz music." She pointed at the record player. "Billie Holiday, Jelly Roll Morton, Louis Armstrong all worked in Storyville's sporting houses and cabarets."

"Babette, I'm not sure you need to share this much detail with the girls," Leslie worriedly interjected.

Gee suddenly looked devilish. "Aunt Babette? You ever work in a sporting house?"

"Don't you sass me, Gigi Pascoe. I'm too young for Storyville and you know it. Besides, who are you to trash talk me? Sex trade is sex trade, and it's still going on with you dancing half-naked down at that Bourbon Street club of yours." She raised her chin. "But Grand-mere Arsène Fontaine sure had herself a good time in Storyville for those few years she could. Listed in the Blue Book and all with her name in big capital letters."

"Capital letters?" Gee gaped as fresh knowledge dawned in her eyes. Turning, she stared at her mother. "You never told me Grand-mere Fontaine was a Storyville madam."

Aunt Babette resolutely reached for the champagne. "Then maybe it's time that I did."

Chapter Ten

"Arsène Fontaine was only sixteen when she knocked on the door at Miss Lulu White's Mahogany Hall. Wore her best dress." Aunt Babette studied the sparkling bubbles rising in her glass. "The only dress she had. Filled her cardboard suitcase with magazines and crumpled newspaper to give it weight, so no one would know it was empty."

She settled in. "Lulu White made her wait two hours for her interview, with her empty stomach growling for a nickel bowl of milk and cornmeal mush the entire time. Set the tone for their relationship." She chuckled knowingly. "But Arsène knew she was exactly where she needed to be because she had plans and ambition. Only the most beautiful octoroon entertainers worked for Miss Lulu White. Arsène was determined to start her career at the very top of the profession."

"Octoroon?" Jane wiggled uncomfortably. "I don't think you're supposed to use that term anymore."

"It was *supposed* to mean someone descended from slavery," Leslie offered. "Someone seven parts White to one part Black."

"Say mixed race," Gee suggested.

"In any case, it was the product of slave rape coming down through the generations, from having enslaved Black mothers and White fathers. Sometimes, the White owners freed these women, sometimes the women earned enough money to free themselves. That's what I meant by saying octoroon."

"Arsène couldn't have been a slave around 1900," Jane protested.

"Arsène was never a slave." Aunt Babette sipped her champagne. "She came from the Fontaines, a free Creole family, *gens de couleur libres* from the beginning."

"Then why did she call herself octoroon if she wasn't one?"

"Because." Aunt Babette drawled. "It added allure to her value in the Storyville market. Lulu White advertised octoroon girls because their exotic background and beauty attracted wealthier clients. Attracting rich and powerful men was always the goal."

"Nothing new there," Gee stated. "We're still doin' it."

"Let me get this straight." Jane felt confused. "Arsène invented an octoroon background to work as a prostitute?"

"So she could work as a top-ranked prostitute and build an important clientele." Aunt Babette emphasized her point. "Jane, what Arsène did wasn't wrong. Sex trade in N'awlins was legal. Storyville's *dames de joie* were world famous. Visitors coming through the Southern Railway Station saw Storyville first thing on purpose. They called it the Tenderloin District or the Queer Zone."

Gee grinned wryly. "Sounds like my kind of place."

"You, *sha,* would've loved Storyville." Aunt Babette tapped Gee's knee. "The music, the dancing, the cabaret, the finest restaurants, the gambling dens. Brrrr!" She laughed merrily. "Don't you just love that last one? Sounds like a cave full of naughty bears."

"Sounds like Vegas," Jane said.

"Pretty much the same idea. Jus' like Vegas, the Storyville party never closed." Aunt Babette adjusted the faded pillow at her back. "Tom Anderson ran the place. They called him the mayor of Storyville." She settled both hands in her lap. "He produced a Blue Book listing all of the sporting houses and the services rendered." She playfully cocked one eyebrow. "And where to find the best music from the 'Southern darkie orchestras.' What we now call blues and jazz music. Can you imagine?" She laughed. "That guidebook cost a quarter, back when you could buy a good time for a dime. Oh my, yes." She rocked gently. "Those Storyville folks had themselves some fun. Jane? You look shocked."

"I'm having a hard time unpacking this." Jane squirmed. "On Nantucket I arrested prostitutes. In Massachusetts, it's a crime."

Gee looked up. "Did you ever arrest their johns?"

"No." Jane blushed. "We never really went after them."

"That hasn't changed," Leslie said. "Women pay the price and men pay the money."

"It wasn't always women prostitutes we arrested," Jane added uncertainly. "But the johns were always men."

"It's universal." Aunt Babette's bright eyes darkened. "Sex is a strategy powerless people use to survive. *Honi Soit qui mal y pense.* Shame on him who thinks evil of it."

"I'm not sure what you mean."

"Humm. How do I explain this?" Aunt Babette fingered her gold, green and purple beads. "Do you girls remember the fairy tale, Beauty and the Beast?"

"Yes," Gee slowly replied.

"What's it about?"

"From what I remember." Gee rested her elbows on her knees. "A girl gets trapped in a castle, but because she's beautiful and kind she makes the Beast fall in love with her. The evil spell is broken. He turns into a handsome prince. Did I get it right?"

Aunt Babette rapped the side table with her knuckles. "That's pretty much it but think about what the fairy tale is really saying. Beauty survives by making the Beast fall in love with and protect her. It's a survival tale, a blueprint of what to do when the worst thing happens."

"What's the worst thing?" Jane wondered.

"It's survival instructions on what to do if you get enslaved."

"Say again?"

Aunt Babette firmed her wrinkled lips. "Say your village gets overrun by a group of raiders. A girl gets taken captive, which is a *genteel* way of saying she becomes a sex slave, sexually available to anyone who wants her. She gets no say in the matter. As a slave, she has no power. The fairy tale tells her to submit and to make the scariest, most powerful monster fall in love with her because then she will have power over him. She turns the table, and she wins."

"Crissakes!" Jane gasped. "I'll never look at the Disney princesses the same way again."

"And the story is directed at girls because they're seen as property and objects even when they're not captives or slaves." Aunt Babette's necklace of gleaming beads puddled on the table as she leaned in. "You'll notice we never direct survival tales to our boys like this."

"There's Jack and the Beanstalk," Jane countered. "He runs into plenty of trouble with that giant."

"True, but Jack never *submits*. He outsmarts the giant until he figures out a way to kill him. That's the difference. Jack's fairy tale is about taking active action versus staying passive to survive."

Gee crossed her legs at the knee. "That's because boys get choices girls don't get. And I know what I'm talking about."

"*Exactement.*" Aunt Babette sat back. "So don't judge Arsène Fontaine for doing what she did to survive." She thoughtfully wove the beads around her fingers. "She had her reasons for never marrying which was her only other economic option. As a young, single woman alone in the world she made the best use of the choices she had at the time."

Jane's phone chimed. "Shoot!" She sprang to her feet. "I'm going to be late for my shift. Good thing I don't believe in fairy tales since I'm a single woman."

"The hell you don't." Gee scoffed. "You're Sleeping Beauty. Still waiting for a handsome prince to ride by, give you a kiss, and wake you the fuck up."

Chapter Eleven

Wednesday, February 15, 2017
11:10 AM

Gee slid into a rare open booth at Café Irene. "I'm surprised Dupree agreed to meet us."

"Don't be." Jane carefully sipped her brimming mug, the café au lait so blisteringly hot it deliciously scorched her lips. "I've never known a detective turn down free coffee."

A tinny bell pinged over the door. Jane looked up to see NOPD Detective Antwon Dupree ducking his bullet-shaped head as he entered. Unzipping his navy Criminal Investigative Division windbreaker, his eyes scanned the room. *Is he looking for us or checking for exits.* Dupree still displayed his Hurricane Katrina Survivor lapel pin on his starched collar with his brass Star and Crescent badge clipped to his belt. *I can't get used to seeing him with white hair.* Crossing the café, he loomed over their table.

"You two been staying out of trouble?"

"And why would we do that?" Gee sassed, sliding across the bench seat to make room. "Weren't you bringing someone?"

"Separate cars. She's still parking. This neighborhood's tight." He waved the server over. "Two espressos, please. Add it to their check." He settled his hands palm-side down on the Formica. "You two been keeping well?"

"Well enough." Gee's face tightened. "After losing friends."

"We all been doin' that." A burred edge roughened his voice. Straightening, he cleared his throat. "Detective Trahan's joining us. She's with CID's Missing Juvie Section." He flicked his fingers in

Gee's direction. "From what you said on the phone, she's the right contact."

Jane leaned on her elbows. "How's it going, breaking in a new partner?"

"She's alright." He shrugged. "Kinda chipper. Bordelon was a grumpy old fart, but we worked together a lotta years." He studied the ceiling. "A new partner takes some getting used to." The bell rang again, and he dropped his chin. "She's got modern ways."

An obvious law enforcement officer marched straight down the narrow center aisle. *Mid-thirties.* Jane estimated. *Five-foot-six and a solid buck fifty.* She wore a crisp white pocketed dress shirt tucked into belted black trousers. Her medium brown hair was wrapped into a tight bun at the nape of her neck. She had softened the cop look with feathered blonde highlighted bangs, and she wore rose-colored lipstick. Jane felt surprised. Most woman detectives she had known eschewed makeup.

Jane slid closer to the wall as Dupree, hampered by the tabletop, half-rose.

"Detective Shelli Trahan, NOPD CID. Shelli with an 'i.' These are our concerned citizens, Gigi Pascoe, and Jane Byrne."

"I've heard of you both." Studying Gee, she slid onto the bench seat next to Jane. "You were involved in that FBI white supremacy serial killer takedown."

The server returned. "Two espressos. Can I bring y'all anything more?"

"I think we're good," Jane said. "Thank you."

"So, catch me up." Squaring her tablet against the table edge, Detective Trahan twisted the curled lemon peel into her cup. "What have you got going? Why are we here?"

"We found two kids living rough on the street as part of Jane's job." Gee returned her coffee cup to its saucer with a ceramic click. "The girl said her brother's missing."

Trahan swiped her tablet to life. "And your job is?"

"Head of security at St. Louis Cemetery No. 1. The boy's been vandalizing the tombs. That's what caught my attention."

The detective cut her eyes sideways. "You have anything to do with him going missing?"

"Of course not," Jane retorted.

"Had to ask." She started tapping the keypad. "Two juvies, one missing. Got it."

"They're squatting in the Warehouse District," Gee eagerly offered. "The girl's name is Cleo Duchamp. Her brother Rex is missing."

"I know the Duchamps," Dupree rumbled. "They work as a team. Rex Duchamp's been tagged for shoplifting, pickpocketing, minor assault. Mostly from popping drunk tourists in the Quarter." He unconsciously twisted his serviette between his fingers. "Cleo's down for selling stolen credit cards and phones plus she's got prostitution charges against her, if I'm remembering right."

"I hate hearing that," Jane frowned. "She's just a kid."

"Some Johns like 'em young," Dupree brutally stated.

"No age limits I've ever seen outside the club," Gee agreed.

"I'm not surprised Rex Duchamp's missing." Detective Trahan toyed with her spoon. "We've been seeing an uptick in missing homeless people this time of year. S'been increasing steadily since I started tracking it."

"Winter's over," Jane suggested. "Maybe they're leaving NOLA for work."

"These aren't people with significant job skills. We used to see an uptick in the *incoming* transient population before Carnival season, but that's been reversed."

"That makes no sense." Gee fanned her fingers. "Why would anyone leave NOLA *before* Mardi Gras and miss the parties?"

"The increase is odd. And the missing homeless demographic is skewing younger."

"How young?" Jane probed.

"Really young. The average median homeless life expectancy used to be fifty years old with deaths linked to overdose, suicide, or long-standing health issues like untreated diabetes. Lately, though, we're seeing more missing homeless in their teens and early twenties." Her eyes grew unfocused. "I can't explain it. And the increased casework lands on my desk."

"Runaways, maybe?" Jane suggested.

Detective Trahan delicately finished her espresso. "Possibly."

Jane squinted. "Sex trafficking, out of state?"

"More likely," she agreed.

Gee frowned. "What makes you say that?"

Detective Trahan neatly returned the cup to its saucer. "Because we never find their bodies."

Chapter Twelve

"How many people disappear during Mardi Gras?" Jane wondered.

Detective Trahan thoughtfully tapped her empty cup with her fingernails. "Missing tourists, missing homeless, or in general?"

"All of the above. I eat data."

"Generally, two or three tourists go missing during the Carnival season. With the homeless population, we officially register a dozen to fourteen, maybe as many as eighteen each year. Like I said, we see a significant annual spike."

"Homicides have leveled off," Dupree smoothly inserted. "Overall, the number is surprisingly low, considering we get more than a million visitors, and everyone's binge drinking." He tugged his earlobe. "The only uptick we've seen lately is drunks getting killed by parade floats."

"The crime stats do pop around Fat Tuesday before Lent," Trahan agreed.

"Nothing good ever happens after midnight," Jane joked.

"Actually, the highest hourly crime totals fall between five o'clock and 10:00 p.m."

Gee looked surprised. "That can't be right. The club scene doesn't even get lit until ten."

"True," Trahan said, "but law enforcement starts moving the tourists off Bourbon Street at midnight, which flattens the curve."

Dupree chuckled. "Can't resist the midnight march."

"Midnight is when most people realize they've lost their wallets or their phones." Trahan paused. "That Bourbon Street stretch between St. Louis and Toulouse is a howling bitch. Even the patrol horses get nervous, and they're bred for it."

Dupree straightened. "If you really want to take your life in your hands, tackle the Iberville and Bienville corner."

"How about Rex Duchamp?" Gee testily interrupted. "Jane? Maybe you should call Win Carter. See what he thinks."

Detective Trahan turned sideways. "Who's Win Carter?"

"NOLA FBI." Jane picked at a scabby epoxy patch on the tabletop. "We worked with him on our last case."

Gee brightened. "Now we have cases?"

Yes, I guess we do. Jane gripped this new idea afraid it might slip away.

"It's too early to involve the FBI." Detective Trahan swiped her tablet. "I'll reach out to the bureau as part of our NOPD response when the time comes. First off, though, someone needs to file an official missing person report on Rex Duchamp." She studied Gee. "It doesn't need to be a family member, but we do need a case contact."

"Use me." Gee sadly volunteered, tucking her hair behind her ears. "I've filed these reports before. This is starting to feel like *déjà vu*."

"I'll need your name, relationship to Rex Duchamp, his approximate age, any identifying characteristics, a street address so we can interview persons living at that address and conduct a search, and the length of time he's been missing. I can email you a fillable PDF form if it's easier."

"Yes, do that. Ready? It's GoYouBadGirl69@gmail.com."

"We'll start there." Detective Trahan tapped Gee's contact information into her tablet. "Once the preliminary report gets filed, I'll be assigned as the Handling Officer. I'll need to determine the cause of his disappearance: runaway, abduction, or cause unknown. We will need a family member or next of kin to authorize the release of his medical or dental records." She looked dubious. "Does he have anyone?"

"His sister Cleo is the only relative we know of. Right, Gee?"

"And she doesn't trust the NOPD. We had to bribe her to talk to us."

Dupree perked up. "Bribe?"

"Hamburgers, orange Nehi, and cheesy tots."

"Let's cross that bridge when we get there." Detective Trahan kept pecking out letters. "As we work through this, if we suspect foul play, we'll bring in the District Investigative Unit."

"Meaning me." Dupree tapped his chest.

"And once the report is filed and verified, I'll notify the Medical Examiner's Office and enter Rex Duchamp into the LACMEC/NCIC missing person database to initiate the investigation and trigger an AMBER Alert since he's younger than 17."

"What's LACMEC?" Jane asked.

"Louisiana Clearinghouse for Missing and Exploited Children. It's just one database we use. I'll also file a report with the National Missing and Unidentified Persons System (NamUS) and NLETS, the International Justice and Public Safety Network to alert state, regional and federal law enforcement agencies. We'll cover the bases."

Glancing at her phone, she picked up her tablet, and stood. "I'll provide an update in thirty days. Hopefully, if Rex Duchamp is found, we'll be in touch to conduct a recovery interview." She hesitated. "I have another idea. There's a woman I know at DCFS." She slid her phone and the tablet into her bag. "Department of Children & Family Services, Orleans Parish. Nice woman. Covers exploited children or kids without proper custody or guardianship. I'll run this by her. Explain the situation. See what she suggests."

"Thank you," Gee simply said.

"Sounds like a ton of work," Jane commiserated.

"Getting one homeless child off the street is a win." Detective Trahan's bright eyes saddened. "Only there's always two more ready to take their place."

Chapter Thirteen

Same Day
2:45 PM

"Hope nothing's wrong." Gee leaned over The Boat's steering wheel. "Aunt Babette's sittin' on the porch. Why is she home this time of day?"

The elderly woman waved. "You girls want some herbal tea? Help you relax. Come on up. I'll pour."

"I was considering another herbal option, but I'm game." Gee trotted up the steps, politely holding the screened door open with her square, masculine hand. "Aunt B, why aren't you at work?"

"*Sha*, I'm not sure I'm working anymore." She raised her cup. "Delilah's family is closing *Le Maison Gris*. None of them wants to continue the business." Pursing her lips, she sipped her fragrant peppermint tea. "I do not understand why anyone would give up such a profitable shop but that's their decision to make, not mine."

"What are you gonna do?"

"I could give Tarot readings off a TV tray in Lafayette Square like some of them others." Settling her shoulders, she smiled with secret amusement. "Who knows? I'm still wrapping my mind around the whole 'not working in the shop anymore' part of things. It might be nice to have a break. I've been working since I was ten years old." She gently smiled again. "As long as Leslie doesn't mind having me around the house."

Picking up a plastic bear, Gee squirted clover honey into her teacup. "Where's Maman?"

"She's at church, helping set-up the Lenten pancake supper."

"And Pops?"

"He went out, carrying that *maudit* guitar."

"That's a good thing," Jane said. "Maybe Ken's working on the songs for his new album."

"You keep believing that." Wincing, Aunt Babette massaged her arm. "Those WarBirds songs are jinxed. Nothing good will ever come from them. Every song Ken Pascoe touches is cursed."

"Aunt Babette, you can't seriously believe that." Gee stared. "Marianne was a genius. Her songs deserve to be heard."

"It's to your credit you're defending your biological mama, *sha*, but I will keep my doubts. That woman left this world *furieux*. Her anger still holds the power to harm the living. That past has not been settled yet."

"Speaking of the past." Jane lifted the soggy lemon teabag from her cup. "Whatever happened to Arsène Fontaine?"

The older woman looked pleased. "You want to hear more about our family?"

"It's got me curious. That whole Storyville thing is a part of history I've never heard before."

"That's because it's herstory." She cackled. "I'm sure they didn't teach herstory at any school I imagine you went to."

"Was she an orphan? How did she end up alone at sixteen?"

"Jane's right." Gee hooked her elbow over the back of her chair. "Where was her family? She was Creole. She must've had a billion cousins. Everyone in NOLA's related."

"Arsène had plenty of family. That wasn't it." Raising the lid, Aunt Babette checked the teapot. "Her father kicked her out of his house."

"That sounds harsh. What'd she get kicked out for?"

"Because Arsène fell in love with one of her cousins, Roark Fontenot." Aunt Babette refreshed her cup. "It was a terrible scandal. Roark was handsome as the devil, and Arsène fell hard. They had a torrid affair, flaunting their love in public, throwing it in everyone's face. They even sat next to each other in the same pew at Mass in St. Louis Cathedral. Stopped just shy of taking communion together."

"Was the scandal because Arsène was only sixteen?" Jane asked.

"No. It was because Roark was married, and his wife found out. *Merde*. She started spreading the most vicious gossip through town, and it all fell on Arsène for tempting Roark away from his legal wife and their children. Arsène's reputation was ruined in Creole society."

"And that's why her father threw her out of the house."

"No." Aunt Babette vehemently shook her head. "Not for love. Her *papa* threw Arsène into the street because he considered her a headstrong, disobedient, and rebellious daughter. Roark Fontenot did the honorable thing. He offered Arsène a *plaçage* arrangement, and she refused."

"*Plaçage*?" Jane wondered, confused by the term.

"I get it." Gee snapped her fingers. "Roark asked her to be his mistress, his *placee* and she rejected him."

"*Exactement*. They would have had a *mariage de la main gauche*." Aunt Babette stirred her tea. "A left-handed marriage. Arsène would not be recognized as Roark's legal wife, but she would have retained her social status. Plus, Roark would leave Arsène one-third of his estate and recognize any children as his."

"Hold up." Jane still felt puzzled. "This Roark guy would've had two families going at the same time? Isn't that bigamy?"

"It wasn't uncommon, or unlawful. It was legally recognized."

Gee grinned wickedly. "You can still see some of the *placee* homes on Rampart Street. Some men even kept more than one *placee*."

"They must've had deep pockets and a helluva lot of stamina." Jane protested. "But if Arsène loved this guy, and the arrangement was acceptable like you say, why did she reject him? It sounds like that would've gotten her out of trouble."

"Because of her rebellious pride," Aunt Babette said. "Arsène refused to be Roark's mistress. She demanded that he get a divorce and legally marry her. She insisted on becoming his legal wife." She smoothed her collar. "And that could never happen because the Fontenots were a devoutly Catholic family. They still are. That was the sword Roark's legal wife held over his head. If he divorced her and remarried Arsène, he'd commit a mortal sin and lose his soul."

"Let me get this straight," Jane sputtered. "So, instead of becoming Roark's mistress, Arsène become a prostitute? Is that what you're telling me?"

"Arsène decided to create her own destiny." Aunt Babette stoutly raised her finger. "She was going to show them all, and she did. Built her own fine mansion on Basin Street in the center of the sporting life traffic. Danced with New York high society. Traveled to Europe many, many times. Arsène had it all until the U.S. gov'mint shut Storyville down in 1917."

"I know this part," Gee said.

Jane grasped the significant date. "They closed Storyville because of the war?"

"The gov'mint never liked N'awlins having a legal vice district." Aunt Babette looked ruffled. "They'd been looking for an excuse to stamp it out for years. During the war they found one. N'awlins was an important port. Lots of shipping and ordinance came through here."

"With lots of horny sailors on shore leave." Gee grinned.

"And that did us in. The Navy prohibited prostitution within five miles of a military site, and that put Storyville smack dab on their radar. The city fought back as best we could. Storyville business owners took the fight to the Louisiana Supreme Court." She sighed. "We lost. They sent the NOPD into Storyville and shut it down. Can you imagine? Those same crooked cops who'd been taking Storyville graft for years. It was the end of an era." Her voice grew soft. "End of Arsène's business, and her independent way of life."

The chair cracked as Gee sat up. "If Arsène never married, how're we related?"

Aunt Babette cackled again. "She's my grand-mere. Even though Arsène shunned marriage, she had two natural daughters. My mother, Marie-Claudette, was born in 1921. My *Tante* Marie-Justine came along in 1923." She rattled her beaded necklace through her fingers like a rosary. "From what I remember, I believe everyone was happy enough. I know they had enough money to be comfortable. Grand-mere Arsène retired to a nice little house in Faubourg Treme. We used to visit her for Sunday dinner after Mass. She fed me ginger snaps. To this day, when I taste ginger, I remember her."

"All of that changed when I was thirteen." She dropped both knobby hands into her lap. "My papa, Honore Phillipe Broussard was a proud man, a successful Creole businessman, well-respected, very proper, *corriger*. Papa frowned on *Tante* Marie-Justine's side of the family because although she never married, she also had a natural daughter, Melanie." Aunt Babette's face grew troubled. "*Life* magazine published an article about Storyville that everyone read. I think Cousin Melanie reminded Papa too much of our Storyville *histoire*. He discouraged Melanie from calling on us. He was rude to her when she tried."

Picking up her teacup, she found it empty, and returned it to her saucer. "I don't know where Melanie Fontaine is now. Eventually, she faded away."

Chapter Fourteen

Thursday, February 16, 2017
11:20 AM

Gee scanned the lively packed-to-capacity crowd. "I know Café du Monde is a tourist trap, but their beignets are the bomb."

"I hope Detective Trahan's still here." Jane time-checked her phone. "We're twenty minutes late."

"We're fashionably late. I see her." Gee led the way, nimbly dodging between the many wire tables and chairs. "Sitting in the corner with that couple."

"There you are." Detective Trahan smiled tightly. "I was about to give up on you."

"Trouble finding parking," Gee lied. "You know how it is."

"Shelli, I'll get going." The man half-rose. "Good catching up with you."

"No, Cuddy, please. Finish your coffee." She turned to the next table. "*Pardon.* We need another chair. Could we snag this one?"

"*Certainement.*"

"*Merci pour ton aide.*"

Jane shivered as the detective dragged the wire chair over the concrete floor. Catching the alert waiter's eye, Trahan held up two fingers before pointing at their table.

"*Ms.* Gigi Pascoe and *Ms.* Jane Byrne." She emphasized their titles. "This is Ms. Graceland Cuddy, the DCFS Child Welfare worker I thought you should meet. These two ladies," she tripped over the descriptive gender-based word, "initiated Rex Duchamp's missing person case."

"Graceland?" Gee cocked her head. "That's an unusual name."

"Mom was Elvis' biggest fan." She resignedly shrugged. "Call me Grace."

"And *Mr.* Calhoun Cuddy." Reaching into his breast pocket, the man pulled out a handful of ivory business cards. "A pleasure meeting you both."

"You two married?" Gee asked.

"Oh hell, no." He chuckled. "Cousins is all. Same last name. Call me Cuddy."

Jane studied his name in raised black ink on the obviously bespoke card. **Calhoun Cuddy, Heaven Sent Mortuary Services. Licensed Funeral Director. Affordable Cremation Services and Whole-Body Donations.** *He even looks like a funeral director with those fancy cufflinks and that sober navy suit.* "Whole-body donations?"

He eagerly pulled his chair closer. Jane stiffened as their kneecaps touched.

"It's a special mortuary service option we offer families who can't afford to pay for their loved one's final disposition." His fingers checked the part in his carefully styled hair. "They donate the remains for scientific research, and the donation covers the cost of cremation. Of course, any remaining cre-mains," he smiled gently at his own jest, "are returned for internment. We consider our clients as family. The service is very much appreciated by the community."

Their waiter, wearing a crisply ironed and spotlessly white knee-length apron, swooped in carrying a tray with two café au laits and a plate holding four golden brown beignets sprinkled with sifted powdered sugar. Jane's mouth instantly watered as she smelled the hot sweet fried dough aroma. Setting everything on the table with a flourish, the waiter slipped the tray under his arm before gliding away toward the kitchen.

UP JUMPED THE DEVIL

Gee cupped her coffee in both hands. "I left Cleo Duchamp a note, asking her to meet us here. No go. Her note to me said Jackson Square at noon. It's not easy reaching her. She doesn't own a phone."

"She's not dumb." Jane studied the wide open plaza across the street. "She picked a public space with multiple exits."

Grace glanced over her shoulder. "All we can do with these homeless kids is try."

Cuddy studied Detective Trahan. "You said this girl's brother is missing? What happened? Where's he gone?"

Trahan dusted powdered sugar off her fingertips. "We don't know yet. But we're going to find out."

"Evidently," Jane said, "Rex Duchamp has a lean addiction. Forgets himself and wanders off."

"It's an epidemic." Trahan scowled. "What I want to know is where's he getting that stuff? Prescription cough medicine isn't ask-and-have. Someone is supplying him."

Cuddy finished his coffee. "I give y'all credit for trying to help. You are earning your way into heaven." Pushing back from the table, he stood. "Now, if y'all will excuse me, I need to go meet an electrician."

Grace blinked. "Cuddy? What're you up to now?"

"Expanding the facility." He slyly winked. "Can't complain when business is this good. Need to make room for more customers."

"It's getting on to noon," Detective Trahan noted. "We should probably be going."

Opening his wallet, Cuddy neatly covered the check with two twenties. "I'll get this. Nice meeting, y'all. See you later, 'cuz."

"See ya." Grace hobbled like she had sore heels as she followed Gee to the sidewalk. "Damn planter fasciitis. Very nearly cripples me." She winced. "What made you decide to get involved with the Duchamps? You're not a blood relative, are you?"

"No." Patting her pockets, Gee shook out a cigar, tucking it between her teeth. "I feel like I need to do something. Not just ignore the situation." Flicking her lighter, she repeatedly puffed. "Maybe it's because I was adopted. I keep wondering what might've happened if my parents hadn't taken me in. Given me a safe home. What would my life be like? I'd probably be living in a warehouse, same as them."

"Is that where they're living?" Grace limped for the curb. "Which warehouse?"

Protect your intel. Jane's instinctive caution flared. "I don't recall the exact address."

"Halfway down Poe Street." Gee checked for traffic.

"We should use the crosswalk." Detective Trahan hesitated.

"No time." Gee waved at the braking drivers as she herded them across Decatur Street. "I see her." She pointed as they passed through the plaza's wrought-iron gates. "She's crossing the barricades in front of the cathedral."

Chapter Fifteen

"That's her?" Grace squinted. "In the silver hoodie?"

Detective Trahan slowed. "I suggest you two make first contact since she already knows you. Explain who we are, and when she's comfortable, wave us over."

"Got it." Gee skirted a flowerbed overshadowed by the cathedral's towering black spires, walking so quickly that Jane had to trot to keep up.

"Remember, Gee. Don't take everything at face value. She could be working a con."

"So could they. Jane, where's your faith in humanity? What makes you so distrustful?"

"Practice. I'm not saying we shouldn't help. I'm saying let's keep our eyes open when we do."

The slim feral girl spotted their approach. Keeping her back to the open gate, she turned.

"You ast me to meet you here, and here I am." She buried both hands in her hoodie pocket, looking ill and defensive.

"It's Cleo, right?" Jane asked. "Cleo Duchamp?"

"How d'you know my name?" Her dark eyes widened. She rose on her toes, poised for flight.

"Be chill." Raising both hands, Gee made a calming gesture. "It came up when we started looking for your brother, Rex."

"You find out where Rex is at yet?"

"Not yet. We filed a missing person's report. There's no news, but we brought a couple of people who can help." Gee pointed across the plaza. "They're standing by the statue."

"You put a cop on me?" Cleo's voice rose to a squeak.

"You need to meet her. Detective Trahan's in charge of your brother's investigation," Jane said.

"The other lady is a child welfare worker," Gee added.

"I seen her before, talking to some others." Cleo pulled her hands from her pocket. "How do I know this ain't some kinda trap?"

"Why would we trap you?" Jane angrily replied. "We're trying to help."

"People been helping homeless get off the street before. Some never get seen again."

"For this to work, you need to trust us." Gee rested her hands on her hips. "And we need to talk to them. Can we bring them over?"

"I guess." Cleo looked sullen. "Like I got a choice."

Gee flicked her fingers. The two women walked over, Graceland Cuddy taking the lead. Stopping roughly six feet away, she folded her hands and adopted a carefully passive posture.

"Cleo Duchamp? No need to be nervous. I'm Grace Cuddy with the Department of Children and Family Services. This is Detective Trahan. We're here to help you."

"Say what you gotta say." Cleo cocked her hip. "I'd rather work with them two. Them, I trust."

Grace smiled. "Everything works better when we work together as a team."

"And I want to help find your brother." Detective Trahan hooked her thumbs on her belt. "I checked the warehouse address this morning, looking for witnesses. It was empty. No one was there."

"Of course, they wasn't there. They saw you comin' and took off out the back door."

"So, who can I talk to who might have information about your brother?"

"Ask her." Cleo pointed at Jane. "She's the last one who seen him."

"That so?" Trahan turned. "When was that?"

"Sunday." Jane scrambled to recall the exact date. "The twelfth."

"No activity from Rex Duchamp since then?"

"Not that I'm aware of at the cemetery."

"Let's stay on task and focus on helping this young woman." Grace pulled out her phone. "Ms. Duchamp, I can get you into the Rainbow House Crisis Center. You could have a warm bed and a roof over your head tonight."

"I ain't goin' there." Cleo mulishly refused. "Nobody is lockin' a door on me or tellin' me what to do or when to do it."

"Don't you want free hot meals, a shower, clean clothes, and medical attention?"

"I just said I ain't goin'. I'd rather stay independent. On my own."

Grace stepped back, frowning. "There's not much I can do if she's not willing to work with the system."

Stand-off. What do we do now? We can't arrest her and make her go.

Gee rolled up on her toes. "How 'bout living in a regular house?"

What regular house? Leslie is going to purely freak out if Gee brings Cleo back to live with us.

Cleo's shoulders rose. "You teasing?"

"No." Reaching into her pocket, Gee pulled out a key ring. "A friend of mine left me in charge of a house in Faubourg-Marigny. You could stay there until things get sorted out."

Jane blinked. "Fancy's place?"

"Why not?" Gee dangled the keys. "It's sitting empty. Probably be a good thing having someone living there, taking out the trash and turning on the lights."

"Gee, Fancy's Will hasn't been proven yet. Cleo could get arrested for trespassing."

"Not if I give her permission to stay there. Fancy made me her executor. Who's gonna object to this besides me?"

"You need to follow the rules," Jane argued blindly.

"Rules are made to be bent."

"I might do that." Cleo looked skeptical. "What's it gonna cost? Nobody gives away free cribs."

"Not a dime," Gee expansively stated. "Utilities are covered by the estate. Don't you see? This way we'd know where you are, so when we do hear something from your brother, we can get it to you quicker. This has to be better than chalking notes on a brick wall." She glanced at Grace. "Would that work?"

"I've presented my option." She held up both hands. "This is strictly between you two."

"I'll need a street address of record for my report," Detective Trahan said.

"5602 Dauphine Street." Gee automatically rattled it off. She turned. "We could help move you in tomorrow, if you like."

Cleo's eyes flared. "So quick? How 'bout Saturday? That'd give me time to get the word out in case Rex comes looking for me."

"Saturday is good. How 'bout noon?"

Cleo swallowed. "I could do noon."

Jane's conscience gave her a nudge. "I'll pay for a pre-paid phone."

"I get a phone?" Cleo's amazed look quickly turned darkly suspicious. "Why y'all doin' this for me?"

Gee's sculpted biceps bulged as she confidently crossed her arms. "Because we can."

Chapter Sixteen

Friday, February 17, 2017
2:27 PM

Repeatedly glancing up and down St. Claude Avenue, Gee shook out her hands. "I'm so nervous I can feel my heartbeat in my throat."

"I'll get going then." Jane stood. "Leave you people to it."

"No, Jane, please stay." Leslie twined her fingers. "You're part of the family. It would be good to have a buffer."

Gee laughed. "Or an independent witness in case somethin' goes wrong."

Ken finally stopped pacing the splintery porch boards. "Don't know why I'm so nervous about meeting Frankie. It's not like I haven't done this before."

"Sure, you did, Ken." Aunt Babette steadily rocked the wicker chair. "Thirty-five years ago. Way, way, way back in the day."

"You're not helping." He scowled from under his bushy eyebrows.

"Sweetheart, she's teasing." For the sixth time, Leslie squared the legal pads stacked on her lap.

"Leslie, you've got the songs. You're sure? You've checked?"

"Who are you talking to?" She laughed. "I've triple checked, Ken, honey. Will you please relax? This can't be good for your blood pressure."

Leaning over the railing, Gee hissed through her teeth. "I think this is him. He said two-thirty."

A heavily tinted black Cadillac Escalade pulled up in front of the Big House. Swinging into the patched gravel driveway, it halted under the spreading live oak tree.

"Oh, shit." Ken flexed his fingers. "It's happening."

The driver's door popped open. A trim, tanned, well-preserved middle-aged man dressed in black stepped out. *He's short, about five foot six. Those ostrich quill cowboy boots give him a boost.* His medium brown hair was fashionably clipped into parallel lines over his ears. Pausing in the shade, he stripped off his gold aviator sunglasses, tucking them into the breast pocket of his pressed Oxford cloth shirt.

"I don't believe it." Ken's voice cracked. "Frankie? Good to see you again, man. How long has it been?"

"Ken-ny Pascoe, you dawg. Thirty-four years." His gold Cuban chain bracelet shone as he turned back to the Escalade. "Let me collect my partner. We'll be right up."

Tracking around the hood, he opened the passenger door, offering his hand to help a brunette woman from the car. *Crissakes!* Jane blinked. *She's gotta be six feet tall.* Ducking her head, the woman stepped into the sunlight. Reaching up, she resettled her overlarge black framed sunglasses before smoothing the lap wrinkles from her belted cherry red linen business suit. Her strappy black stilettos matched her wristwatch and her ebony alligator leather briefcase. Jane felt a ripple of green-eyed jealousy. *Her accessories must have cost thousands.* A heady cloud of gardenia perfume wafted over the yard on the breeze.

As she drew near, Ken Pascoe sucked in his gut. Jane sneezed.

"Why, Jane! Look at her." Aunt Babette trilled. "She looks like the dark version of you."

Frankie paused at the base of the front porch steps. "I thought it best to bring my legal counsel, Serena Melnyk in from the get-go." He toyed with his sparkling diamond pinkie ring. "Serena's also my scribe."

"Scribe?" Leslie stuttered. "What do we need a scribe for?"

"We're just talking about Pop's new album, right?" Gee added.

"Why stop at one?" Smiling warmly, Frankie escorted Serena up the steps before tapping his temple. "My memory's not what it used to be. Spent too many Saturday nights in Studio 54 during the eighties. Serena keeps me legal, on the rails."

Ken swept his right arm forward. "Frankie, Serena? I'd like you to meet Leslie, my wife. Aunt Babette, my daughter, Gigi, and her friend, Jane." He pushed the front door open with one huge paw. "Let's go sit in the living room. Got more chairs."

"Nice to meet you," Serena politely offered, ducking her head.

Aunt Babette quickly scuttled for the kitchen. "I'll fetch sweet tea."

"Unless, Frankie, you'd like something stronger?" Ken suggested.

"Day drinking, Ken?" Leslie frowned. "It's barely half past two."

"Iced tea is perfect. Thank you." Frankie sat, elegantly crossing his legs at the knee. "I've sworn off alcohol."

"What?" Ken gasped. "Cut out the rocket fuel?"

"Apparently," Frankie straightened his cuffs, "according to my doctors, I've already drunk my share."

"There's a share?" Gee squeaked.

Squeezing onto the loveseat next to Jane, Serena extracted a chrome laptop from the briefcase. "I'll set up a Zoom recording. Do you have WIFI? No problem, if not. I brought a mobile hotspot."

"We do now," Ken bragged. "Gigi insisted on it."

Leslie nervously toyed with her necklace. "I'm still not convinced we needed that extra monthly expense."

"I'm paying that bill myself, Maman."

Holy crap. Serena's overpowering perfume flooded Jane's sinuses. Her eyes itched and her nose began to run like a faucet. *Can't she smell how strong that is?* "Excuse me a minute." Jane stood. "I'll grab a chair. Give you more elbow room."

"So, Ken. Let's jump right in." Frankie carefully uncapped a pen. "We've got thirty years to cover. To start, how many songs are there? Enough for a full album?"

"There are eleven of them," Leslie interjected.

"Eleven? Fully complete, polished, and done? Are some only tracks?"

Leslie looked confused. "I'm not sure."

Ken crossed his beefy arms. "Eleven finished songs with instrumental and vocal tracks. All of them polished to perfection."

"Excellent. Have you given any thought to a playlist?"

"Some." Ken massaged his thumbs. "But it's meant to be a solo album, Frankie. My own work. The WarBirds are gone. You know that, right?"

"I get that. I do. Still, such a tragedy. We'll never know what might have been." He sighed. "It would be nice to mention the boys in the marketing and publicity campaign and such. You know, as a tribute. There's still a cult WarBirds fanbase. Especially with the recent resurgence in vinyl 45s."

"Not that *we* ever see any money from 'Love Power,'" Leslie acidly stated. "Ken sold that royalty to a bunch of New York crooks."

"My new album is not *Blood Sport*," Ken quickly inserted. "This is something new, something completely different." He rapped his knuckles against the coffee table twice. "I'm launching a whole new mojo."

"Are any of these eleven songs the ones you originally recorded during the *Blood Sport* studio sessions?" Frankie pointed at the legal pads Leslie gripped. "You know, with the boys? Songs that were on the original master tapes that got burned?"

"No, I won't be re-recording those songs. These eleven new songs were never recorded. It's all new material. I want to record them, fresh. They're that good. They deserve to be heard."

UP JUMPED THE DEVIL

"I'd love to sing backup tracks on Pop's new album," Gee brightly announced. "My goal is to be a lounge lizard someday."

"Keep practicing your scales," Serena offered, without looking up.

Ken guffawed.

"Here's the tea." Aunt Babette backed through the swinging door. She carried a black toleware tray piled with a stack of vintage rainbow-colored aluminum tumblers. "Sorry it kept me. I decided to brew a fresh pot for our guests. Had to ration the ice. I hope it's cold enough."

"Aunt Babette, let me help you." Gee leapt up.

Halfway across the room, the elderly woman suddenly stood stock-still. "Shhh." Pulling the tray closer to her chest, her eyes widened. "Did you feel that?"

"Feel what, dear?" Leslie slowly rose.

"An energy pulse. A brilliant flash of light. For a moment, everything stopped."

"Gigi, take the tray. Maybe you should sit down, dear. You've been doing too much."

"Leslie?" Aunt Babette continued to stare vacantly into space. "Someone has crossed one of the seven gates of Guinee to join us."

"I'm sorry." Serena's hands hovered above her keyboard. "What's going on?"

Aunt Babette cocked her head, her voice a low monotone. "I'm not sure what this is. It has to do with the songs. It has a very strange energy. It feels malicious, but there's an odd warmth at its center. What is this thing? I'll need to consult my Tarot deck. We may need new protective *gris-gris*."

"Does this happen often?" Frankie whispered.

"Often enough," Jane admitted.

"Too goddamn often," Ken emphatically stated.

Leslie nervously poured out iced tea. "Once everyone gets resettled, I'd like to go over the royalty agreement to make sure Ken doesn't get scammed again."

"Good idea. Let's stick to business." Frankie smoothed his silk tie. "First, Ken, let me say that you're not going to believe how much the music business has changed since the last time we worked together, and not just the technology. I'm more than just a beatmaker these days." He placed his hand over his heart. "These days I put the ideas together, hire the session musicians, suggest changes to arrangements, supervise the audio mixing and the mastering, and mix the final record formatted for both vinyl and digital downloads."

"Digital downloads." Ken tasted the words. "I'm not sure what that is."

"What's your cut for doing all those things?" Leslie shrilly interrupted.

Frankie checked on Serena's progress. "After we sign our contract, I get three points of the album's royalties." He shifted on his seat. "It's an industry standard that hasn't changed."

"How much is that in real money?" Leslie demanded.

"Each point is one percent of the revenue earned in total album sales," Serena smoothly explained. "Net, not gross. Based off the price that is yet to be determined."

Leslie continued to stare. "What's Ken's advance?"

"Nothing up front since this is a private capital risk venture," Serena continued. "He'll earn eight percent off the net album sales plus, as the singer/songwriter he'll a earn a mechanical royalty of roughly nine cents every time a song from the new album is played on terrestrial broadcast radio, in a live performance venue, or on an online streaming service." She ticked the points on her manicured fingers. "He'll also earn an extra performance royalty if he decides to tour."

"Nine cents?" Aunt Babette squawked. "Ken only gets nine cents from every album?"

"Nine cents multiplied by the number of times each new *song* gets played." Serena neatly tucked her dark hair behind her ears. "Ten million annual downloads per song on a new hit album, especially one with an established cult fanbase like the one The WarBirds has is not outside the realm of possibility."

"That's too many zeros for me." Leslie looked bewildered. "What does that mean in cash?"

"It's simple enough." Serena slid her index finger along the touchpad. "Ken's projected cut would be approximately ... eight hundred thousand."

Ken gaped. "Eight hundred thousand *dollars*?"

"That's what I've been telling you, dawg. Just on plays." Frankie shared an oily smile. "*A month.*"

Chapter Seventeen

"Sign me up!" Ken roared.

"Sweet mother of God." Leslie held her fingers to her mouth.

"Hold on, Pops." Gee leaned forward. "You need to talk to a lawyer."

"Gigi's right." Aunt Babette set her tea on the table. "And I need to ask the spirits for guidance."

"To hell with that." Ken stabbed the air with his finger. "This is *my* new album, *my* new songs. *My* decision to make." He turned aside. "What's our next step, Frankie?"

"I'll need a copy of the eleven songs to preview a playlist."

Leslie clutched the legal pads to her chest. "We don't have a copy. All we have are the originals."

"Are those the songs?" Serena reached into her briefcase for her phone. "I can snap a picture and upload them to Google Drive, granting everyone access permission."

"I don't know what that means," Gee whispered.

"Me either," Jane said.

"How do we know you won't steal Ken's songs?" Leslie glowered protectively. "Steal his ideas?"

Frankie toyed with his pen. "No worries there. Ken's songs are automatically protected by copyright from the minute he wrote them. If I, or anyone else tried to produce one without his express permission, we'd get sued."

"Honestly?" Serena added. "In the few cases I'm aware of where copyright theft has occurred, the songwriter made more money from the lawsuit than from recording and releasing the song. Generally, everyone settles copyright claims before they go to court."

"No one enjoys paying exorbitant legal fees," Frankie insisted.

Leslie carefully placed the legal pads on the coffee table. "It's your call, Ken. Are you comfortable sharing the songs with these people?"

UP JUMPED THE DEVIL

"I was born ready." Ken rubbed his hands together. "Frankie, I trust."

"Fantastic." Frankie brightened. "Any thoughts, Ken, on the new album's title?"

"Yes. I want to call it *Street Angel*. That's the theme."

"Interesting title." Serena's fingernails clicked as she typed. "Are you open to calling it something else if our marketing team thinks that title's too controversial?"

"Yes, sure, yeah, well, maybe." Ken looked flustered. "I'd really like to use that title, Frankie. It is a rock 'n roll album. It represents my artistic expression. My creative juices. My flow."

"I'm sure Ken can work with whatever those people like," Leslie said.

"Pops wants to name the album after my mother." Gee crunched an ice cube between her teeth. "Since she wrote the songs."

"Since she … I'm sorry. What?" Frankie turned pale. "I'm confused." He pointed at Leslie. "I thought she was your mother."

"Maman is my mother. I'm adopted," Gee easily agreed. "Marianne Tanner was my birth mother. She wrote all of The WarBirds' songs. Even 'Love Power' was hers."

"Ken?" Frankie's voice rose to a higher pitch. "I thought you wrote The WarBirds' songs. Your name is listed on the discography. You know, the fucking copyright?"

Ken stared miserably at the floor between his feet. "No, Frankie. I just transcribed them."

"Are you shitting me?" Frankie leapt up. Elbowing the side table, he nearly tipped his tea. "Those songs." He pointed to the legal pads. "Right there. Tell me straight up you didn't write them."

"Frankie, I didn't write them," Ken repeated, looking ashamed. "Marianne Tanner did." His shamed look changed to a sulky and defensive pout. "It wasn't a secret. We all knew it. Scottie, Mick, Lemonhead. Even Marianne was in on it. Fuck, Frankie. You remember how it was. We were keeping our heads down trying to hook the gravy train."

"This is a cluster fuck." Frankie pressed his temples. "No, it's more than that." His head snapped up. "It's fraud, and you're a liar." The veins stood out in his neck. "Do you know how much effort I've already put into this project? How much billable time's been wasted? First you burned the session tapes, and now you're telling me this?"

Extending both arms, Ken obviously appealed for sympathy. "Frankie, we just wanted to get *Blood Sport* produced. We wanted to be rock stars like Ozzie, like Judas Priest. We were making shit up as we went." He collapsed against the cushions. "It was part of the game. Part of the big show." Folding his arms, Ken looked defensive. "We weren't the only ones doing it. A lot of people cut corners back in the day."

"A lot of people did not fuck with copyright law," Frankie shouted.

"I don't understand." Leslie whimpered. "What does this mean for Ken's new album?"

"It's a fucking dealbreaker is what it means," the producer snarled. "Serena? You want to weigh in on this?"

"Obviously." Her tone stayed reasonable. "We'll need to determine who owns the copyright on the songs as our next step."

Leslie snatched up the legal pads. "What do you mean who owns the songs? We own them. We've kept them safe for all these years. They belong to us."

"Not necessarily. You may have possession, but you may not own the copyright." She scanned her notes. "Where's Marianne Tanner now?"

"She's dead," Aunt Babette trilled. "We buried her in the back yard under the chicken coop."

"Pardon?" Serena blinked.

"The short answer is yes," Jane inserted. "Marianne Tanner is dead. That's been determined."

"You're certain of it?"

"The Coroner's Office has her skeletal remains."

Serena typed another note. "Who are her heirs? For the estate?"

"It's me. I am," Gee said. "I'm her daughter. Her only child."

"Is there anyone else out there who might dispute ownership?"

"No," Ken firmly stated. "Marianne was an only child. I'm sure the uncle she lived with must be dead by now."

"How about Marianne's parents? Her mother, her father?"

"Both dead. Her mother died when she was a kid in grade school. I remember that much. Her dad was in prison for burglary last time I heard, but Jesus! That was forty years ago. He's gotta be dead by now."

"That leaves Gigi as next of kin, right?" Leslie hopefully asked.

Serena looked intent. "What was Marianne Tanner's state of domicile?"

"Hell if I know." Ken looked befuddled. "Not sure she had one. She lived on the street."

Serena glanced at Frankie. "This might still work. We'll need to ask Legal to research homeless person probate law. Do you know, did she leave a Will? Where does her probate currently stand?"

"We haven't asked about her probate, what with concentrating on our own troubles," Leslie slowly stated. "Gigi? Have you heard anything?"

"No, Maman. They've haven't even emailed me about making the funeral arrangements."

"Another red flag on the play, Frankie." Serena tapped her laptop. "If these people haven't been contacted about Marianne Tanner's estate, there could be someone else, another family member already actively acting as her executor or personal representative."

Gee gaped, dumbfounded. "What do you mean someone else?"

"Another family member more closely related to Marianne Tanner than you are."

"But I'm her daughter."

"How do we determine that?" Jane asked.

"If she died in New Orleans, the local Coroner's Office may be able to assist you." Serena checked her wristwatch. "This needs to be resolved before we can move forward on drafting a contract."

"Kenny, I hope this works out for us." Frankie stood. "We're staying at the Frenchman's Inn through Mardi Gras. After that its sayonara." He snapped his business card against the coffee table. "I'll be waiting for your call."

Chapter Eighteen

Saturday, February 18, 2017
10:17 AM

"If you ever need a break." Jane rested her elbow on The Boat's channeled white leather seat. "I can drive, you know."

"I do know that." Gee gripped a slim brown cigar between her eyeteeth. Reaching over, she popped an 8-track tape cartridge into the built-in dashboard player. "I like driving. Calms my nerves." She spoke around the cigar as Barbra Streisand's mesmerizing voice filled the air partnered by Donna Summer's sassy three octave plus mezzo-soprano. "Helps me think things through."

"When did you start thinking things through?"

"Ha-ha, funny." She flicked her fingers at the disco tape. "Enough is enough. Just so you know, I'm ghosting your boy, Cesar Mayas. Texted him: 'Bye, Felicia,' on Wednesday. Decided it was a bad romance."

"Maybe he's super busy. It was a special FBI assignment, a career builder. Tough to turn down."

Gee settled the cigar in the ashtray. "It's really cute that you're defending him, Jane, but maybe he's just not interested."

Jane slumped. "I'm sorry."

"Sorry for what. This was between me and him." She shared her elfin grin. "Not the first time the rocket failed to launch."

"You don't have time to date anyway." Jane rubbed the gooseflesh off her arms as The Boat slipped through a chilly patch of shade cast by the overhead Pontchartrain Expressway. "Rex Duchamp is still MIA, and we need to figure out who Marianne Tanner's new 'closer relative than you' is."

Gee cut her eyes, grinning. "Now we're detectives?"

I'm not a detective anymore. Jane hid her wince at Gee's use of the title. "Let's say private investigator. And why not? We successfully solved our last investigation."

"*Mais yeah,* we did." Tossing her head back, Gee laughed. "Just never call me a private dick. But," she snorted, "we'll need to figure out a way to make some money. We'll never see a dime outta Cleo Duchamp."

"Agreed. And I've got a bad feeling about her brother, Rex."

"You think he's dead?"

"Seems most likely, don't you think? Why else would he drop out of sight or not contact Cleo if he's holed up somewhere safe."

"I hate thinking that, but I bet you're right." Gee stubbed out the cigar. "And my unknown new family member? Pops came up blank when I asked him about it at breakfast." She tightened her grip on the steering wheel. "I checked the songs for any hints or liner notes. Nothing there, just lyrics."

"The songs are written in Ken's handwriting?"

"No doubt about it. Pops handwriting and original blue ink."

"That might help with the copyright dispute. Let's think about this, Gee. Ken's the only one who ever said Marianne wrote those songs. Other than his word, there's no other proof."

"Nice try." Gee wryly smiled. "Pops might be a stoner, but grifting is outside his wheelhouse. This morning he swore to me that he's never lying about writing those songs again, even if it costs him the royalty money."

"Leslie might have something to say about that."

"I know, right? But Pops is genuinely spooked about recording those songs. He said The WarBirds' music has an active evil juju attached to it. He wants to record those eleven new songs and move on as quick as he can, and he never talks like that. Usually, I get that kinda hoo-ha juju outta Aunt Babette."

UP JUMPED THE DEVIL

Pulling The Boat into a municipal lot, she slowed, searching for the largest space. "Maman wants that royalty money bad. I get that. Must be tough losing the same Easy Street gravy train twice in one lifetime. But she wasn't there when the songs were written. She came later, after the fact."

"Exactly. That's what I mean. Everything Leslie knows is hearsay, and the other WarBirds are dead."

"*Merde*." Gee's eyes went wide. "What if their families want in on Pop's royalty money?"

"Then you can kiss any big money goodbye." Jane tore the cuticle on her thumb until it bled. "Clearing multiple lawsuits or a class action takes years. Trust me, I know. Lawyers are fuckers, and fucking folks around is what they do."

"My head's 'bout to explode. And all of this is gonna fall on poor old Pops."

"'Fraid so. This morning I tried Googling 'Marianne Tanner' to see what I could find." Wrapping her thumb in her T-shirt, Jane pressed the cotton wad tight to staunch the bleeding. "I miss my old law enforcement database. It was more efficient."

"Did Google find anything?"

Should I tell her? Jane swallowed hard. "I found her high school yearbook photo."

Her head snapped as the Boat swerved into a parking spot.

Gee stared straight ahead. "I never thought to look that up." Shoving The Boat into park, she dropped her hands to her lap. "What did she look like?"

"She was pretty, like you. I saw a resemblance. Dark hair, brown eyes. Same chin. You have Ken's lips."

"What's Pops doin' without 'em?" She uneasily joked.

"I can text you the link, if you want."

Gee shifted on her seat. "Do that. I'd like to see what she looked like. Did you find her obituary?"

"It hasn't posted yet, but that's another lead we should follow. The obit should come from the person acting as her executor. It might also list the names of other family members. And relatives post their condolences online these days. We might get more leads there." Jane unlatched her seatbelt. "Obits usually take at least a week once the executor gets the death certificate. So, right now, other than the yearbook photo, her WarBirds Wikipedia mention, and *The Times-Picayune* articles, that's pretty much all we have to go on."

"That's pathetic." Gee slumped. "Her whole life comes down to a yearbook picture and a couple of headlines."

"And you, don't forget. And her songs. She left us those."

"True dat." Stepping out of The Boat, Gee brightened. "And I'm gonna make her famous one day by singing them."

Chapter Nineteen

Same Day
10:36 AM

Jane thumbed the security call button. *This feels like déjà vu.* The Orleans Parish Coroner's Office door double clicked with a sound like a rifle's bolt action. Following Gee into the lobby, she chanced a tentative sniff. *No cadaverine, no methanethiol. No worries.* She relaxed. *Smells like balsam pine.*

"We just did this." Gee's face grew pinched. "And now we're back again."

"I was thinking the same thing. How're you holding up?"

"Shaky. But I gotta get through this if this is what we need to do."

Professional Death Investigator Dr. Tamerlane Sabatier stood waiting at the front desk, talking with a male receptionist. The strikingly tall woman still wore a wide, colorfully beaded headband to hold her natural hair off her face. Both hands were deeply buried in the pockets of her powder blue smock worn over sensible washable slacks and bright yellow rubber clogs. As they crossed the lobby, she turned. Jane noted the Crescent City Coroner's Office badge prominently clipped to a pocket filled with cheap ballpoint pens.

"Why am I not surprised to see you two again." She briskly crossed the tiled floor. "I can give you twenty minutes. I've got a mandatory holiday overtime meeting at eleven. Let's use Conference Room A."

Pulling out one of the four commercial plastic chairs arranged around a Formica-topped table, the PDI sat.

"Ms. Pascoe, your text wasn't completely clear. You had some questions about one of our Coroner's cases? Concerning your mother?"

"That's right." Gee scooted her chair closer. "Marianne Tanner."

"I remember that case." The PDI tapped her fingertips together. "Suspected homicide, undetermined cause of death. Working with skeletal remains is particularly difficult. Results can take months. You were lucky it got completed before Mardi Gras season. We're very short staffed, which is why we're working on a Saturday." She clicked her nails against the table. "Your mother's case was particularly complex, requiring multiple inter-departmental resources. NOPD homicide detectives, crime scene techs, our own PDI team and forensic pathologists. There's never any guarantee that we can determine a cause of death ..."

"That's not why we're here," Gee interrupted.

The PDI pulled up short. "Then why are you here?"

"I'm my mother's only child, but I think another family member is acting as Executor for her estate. I don't have any information on who that person is." She confessed. "I'm hoping you can tell me that."

"I'd like to help you." The PDI shifted uncomfortably. "But I can only share public information. Private information is strictly protected by law. I can't go down that path even if I wanted to. If word got out it could cost me my career."

Jane rested her elbows on the table. "What can you tell us? What public information can you share?"

Dr. Sabatier carefully considered the question before pulling out her phone. "Let me check."

Tapping the screen with her index finger, she swiped it twice. "Yes, I've still got the paperwork on the server. This much is public information, filed with the court." She looked up. "Does the name 'Steve Tanner of Leawood, Kansas,' ring a bell?"

"Never heard of him." Gee looked blank.

"Sounds like a family member," Jane said. "Same last name."

"According to the authorizing documents, he's the named executor for Marianne Tanner's estate and officially listed as her next of kin." The PDI checked her phone again. "In any case, NOPD notified us, the Coroner's Office about Marianne Tanner's decease. We reached out to Mr. Tanner through the Social Security Administration and notified him of her decease so he could claim her remains. Good thing he responded so quickly. Generally, homeless and unclaimed bodies get incinerated and placed in a pauper's grave paid for by the State of Louisiana."

"But who is he?" Gee demanded.

"Marianne Tanner's brother." She glanced up. "Wait, half-brother. Half siblings hold the same rights as full siblings under Kansas and Louisiana probate law."

"But I'm her daughter. Why didn't y'all reach out to me?"

"Because you're not listed as a relative or next of kin." The PDI blinked before defensively tucking her chin. "Hold on. If you're not listed on the probate documents, then how are you related to Marianne Tanner?" She angrily pushed away from the table. "*Merde*. I shouldn't be telling you any of this."

"Shit, Gee. I know what's happened." Jane rapped the table. "Who's listed on your birth certificate, as your parents?"

"You know this. Maman and Pops."

"Exactly. You're off the radar. There's no official record anywhere saying that you're Marianne Tanner's child."

"It's complicated." Gee pressed her hands against the table as her Adam's apple bobbed. "I'm Marianne Tanner's natural daughter. A love child. I'm adopted."

Dr. Sabatier laced her hands together. "Can you prove it?"

"We could," Jane said. "With a DNA sample from the skeleton, off a bone or from a tooth."

"Not to be difficult, but an official DNA request needs to come from the executor. And you'd need to send the sample out to be tested. NOPD hasn't had an in-house DNA lab since Katrina." Her gaze grew unfocused. "I may regret this, but I do want to help. Let me see what I can find out. I hope this doesn't come back to bite me."

Picking up her phone, she swiped the screen. "Mr. Steve Tanner delivered a notarized affidavit appointing him as Marianne Tanner's executor under Kansas Intestate Succession Law." She swiped the screen again. "That's a public record filed with the Kansas probate court. Judging from the timing, he must've used a summary probate procedure very similar to ours. Probably because her estate fell under the small estate limit, I'm guessing. Lucky man. Formal probate can take up to a year."

"What about her songs?" Gee asked. "Those are assets, right? Jane, am I off base?"

"He must not know about them."

"Songs?" The PDI squinted.

"Nothing. Never mind." Gee sat back. "What about her remains?"

"Mr. Tanner has already claimed them," Dr. Sabatier flatly stated. "Once they were released by NOPD, he claimed them under notarized Letters Testamentary on ... February fifteenth. Perfectly legal. Let me check something else. Yes, he provided her obit and chose cremation. He intends on taking the cremains home to Kansas for burial. We're still waiting on him to name the crematorium he wants to use. We're not expecting that information until Monday, close of business day."

"Cremated?" Gee rose, trembling. "She was *my* mother. I wasn't even asked if I wanted to keep her in NOLA, in the cemetery with me."

"It's more than that, Gee," Jane quickly inserted. "If she's cremated, you'll never get a DNA sample proving you're her daughter."

"This is fucked up!" Gee shouted. "Monday is two days away. How do I stop the cremation?"

"Please, lower your voice." Dr. Sabatier glanced at the closed door. "You can't. Yes, this is problematic, but as of right now you don't have the legal right to dispute Mr. Tanner's decisions. You'll need to get his permission to act on anything related to Marianne Tanner's estate." Rising to her feet, she smoothed her lab coat. "I wish you luck. I've seen this kind of family trouble before. If you can't reach an agreement with Mr. Tanner, you'll need to go to court. Ultimately, though, he has the right and the duty to dispose of the corpse 'with respect and without delay,' which is exactly what he's doing."

"Wait a second, Dr. Sabatier," Jane temporized. "A death certificate was issued, right?"

"Yes. My boss, the Deputy Coroner completed the medical certification and issued one on the fifteenth, the day the homicide investigation closed."

"I want a copy of that death certificate," Gee demanded.

"You'll need to ask the executor for it." The PDI stepped back. "It's out of our control."

"This is a fucking circus." Gee started pacing. "We need to get ahold of this Steve Tanner dude. Is he in NOLA?"

"He is as far as I know, but I can't share his contact information or his address of record." Reaching for the door, she paused. "What I can do, with your permission, is send him your contact information, mentioning who you say you are and that you'd like to talk with him about Marianne Tanner's estate. I could comfortably do that."

"Permission granted," Gee fiercely stated. "How long will that take?"

"That's entirely up to Mr. Tanner." Speaking over her shoulder, the PDI stepped into the hall. "He'll need to be the one reaching out to you."

Chapter Twenty

Same Day
11:32 AM

"This is insane." Gee swerved The Boat into the passing lane on Earhart Boulevard, ignoring a blaring car horn and obviously still steamed. "We need to find Steve Tanner."

Jane checked her seatbelt. "We can start by searching social media sites like Facebook and Twitter. See if 'Steve Tanner from Leawood, Kansas' posted anything about visiting NOLA." She double-checked the lock on her door. "People are idiots about protecting their online privacy. We might see where he's staying in a post or an Instagram pic."

"I'd love to show up on his doorstep." Gee's hand trembled as she pressed the cigarette lighter. "I've got a shitload of questions I want to ask him."

"Like?"

"Like who's your mother?" Gripping the lit cigar between her eyeteeth, she flattened the gas pedal, increasing their speed. "Pops said Marianne's mother died when she was in grade school. Her dad was in prison. I've never heard of Steve Tanner and suddenly I've got an uncle. I mean, how does that play? Where'd this 'bro come from?"

"He provided official documentation."

"Maybe." She inhaled. "Maybe not." She cut her eyes. "Can court documents be faked?"

"I'm sure they can be, Gee, but Crissakes! Forgery earns you federal prison time. If her estate isn't worth anything, why would he buy into that?"

"Her WarBirds songs are worth money."

"True, but he may not know about them. He's here to claim her remains."

"Fuck." Gee's fingers traced the steering wheel. "He ever finds out about the royalty money Frankie said Pops might get, he'll be climbing all over us claiming his share."

"It's more than that. We need his permission to get Marianne's DNA to prove you're her biological child and clear the copyright. Without that proof, you'll have no legal right to any part of Marianne's estate including her songs. Steve Tanner will inherit everything as next of kin. Goodbye big money. Goodbye Ken's new album. Goodbye sweet dream." Jane studied the passing buildings. "Out of curiosity, where are we going?"

Gee pointed at the built-in dashboard clock. "It's almost noon. I promised Cleo, we'd pick her up and carry her to Fancy's house."

Jane pushed her tense shoulder blades into the upholstery as she fought a ripple of unease. "Gee? Are you sure you've thought this through? I know you're trying to do the right thing. Have you considered what might happen if you let those two street kids live in Fancy's house?"

Gee raised her chin. "I believe I have."

"What if they trash the place? Cook meth in the kitchen? Tear out the sheetrock and sell the copper plumbing for scrap."

"You really think they're gonna do that?"

"They might. People steal the weirdest shit. I had to file criminal mischief reports on Nantucket rentals every season." Jane tapped the passenger door. "You still have time to reconsider. We could take Cleo to a homeless shelter like Graceland Cuddy suggested and drop her off."

"I'm not taking Cleo to a shelter. She's not a lost dog."

"I'm not saying she is, but what if she's playing you for a fool?"

"So, what if she is? Maybe she is playing me. Or maybe she's just a kid who needs a hand up. You and me, Jane, we were lucky. We came up all strong and independent. Cleo and Rex never had that. They never got that chance." Gee stroked her Adam's apple. "I know what it's like living outside the system. How hard it is when everything is stacked against you."

Turning the wheel, Gee followed the circular rotary. "I was lucky. I had Pops and Maman and Aunt Babette watching out for me. Cleo and Rex have nothing and nobody. Maybe with this I can give them a decent shot at a re-do." Her knuckles turned white as she tightened her grip. "Maman and Pops gave you a chance letting you in the family when you showed up homeless on our doorstep."

"I was never homeless. I had a roof over my head that I paid for."

"That didn't make it a home." Gee drummed the wheel with her thumbs. "Home is about being around people who give a damn. Who care. One thing I've learned chilling with Krewdio-54 is that sometimes family are the people you choose and not the ones you were born with."

She's right. "Gee, you're a better person than I am."

"Not true. Deep down you care, or you wouldn't be looking for Rex like you are."

"Investigation is what I was trained to do. It's what I do best. I can't turn it off." Jane studied her hands in her lap. "I wonder about that sometimes. Do I investigate things because I care or because I can see something is wrong and I need to set it right." She lifted her head. "But that's based on personal judgment. What if my judgment is wrong?"

"Then you change your mind. Nobody's right all the time. C'mon. We're just doing the best we can going off what we know day by day." Gee pointed at a bronze statue perched atop a limestone pillar. "Speaking of changing your mind, you heard they're removing General Lee?"

"I heard City Council approved it." Jane looked up as they circled the monument. "How do you feel about that, as a southerner?"

"NOLA's not really the south." Gee looked perturbed. "We prefer to do our own thing."

"Granted. But how do you feel about getting rid of Confederate generals? Renaming military bases. Does that stuff bother you?"

"Dee-Dee cared more about that than I do. I'm not political. But it seems to me they're trying to whitewash history. San-i-tize it." She drawled. "Make it all pretty and nice. Taking down a statue ain't gonna change what happened. I think they should keep the statues up." Straightening the wheel, she sped up, heading deeper into the Warehouse District. "Why not add a plaque or another statue explaining why things changed. That way, we can learn from our mistakes. Lord knows we've made plenty of them. Still do."

Jane sat back, impressed. "That's not a half-bad idea."

"I know." Slowing, she righteously pulled to the curb. "It's a damn shame no one ever asks for my opinion."

"Something's taped to the door." Jane's boots crunched on broken glass as she crossed the sidewalk. She pressed the flyer flat with her fingertips. "It's a Notice to Vacate from the Constable's Office. Says anyone squatting here has five days to move before they get cleared."

"Typical. Homeless people getting pushed out again." Gee looked over Jane's shoulder. "Does it give them a number, someone to call? Tell them where else to go live?"

"No. But you're doing your bit, giving Cleo a new home."

"And Rex." Putting her shoulder to the door, Gee shoved it open. "Don't forget him."

Cleo stepped from the shadows. She wore baggy gray sweatpants and a sleeveless wife-beater T-shirt. "Seen you from the window. You seen Rex around?"

UP JUMPED THE DEVIL

"Not since the last time," Jane said. "Any ideas where else he might be?"

"I know a couple of other places to look." She hefted a black plastic garbage bag. "Tol' my friends I was going with you. Gave them your license plate in case something bad happens."

Gee looked puzzled. "Why would something bad happen?"

"Because it sometimes do," she replied, as if speaking to an idiot.

Jane peered up the concrete staircase. "Anyone else still in here?"

"No. They moved out. Wanted to stay ahead of the cleaning crew." Cleo slung the garbage bag over her shoulder. "Those creeps are *entimide*. Sometimes street folks get hurt."

"Need a hand carrying your stuff?" Gee offered.

"This is it." Cleo slapped the plastic bag. "Everything I got."

Turning to the door, Jane noticed a message chalked above an elaborate symbol spray painted on the brick wall.

Rex: find T-Bone and follow me.

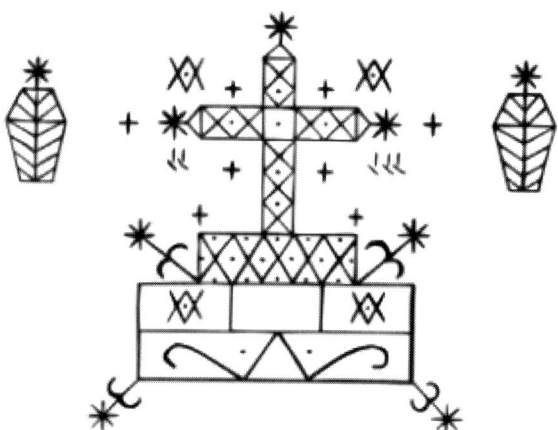

Gee followed Jane's glance before looking at Cleo. "You write that message above the *veve*?"

"Yes. In case Rex comes back."

"*Veve*?" Jane stammered, suddenly at a complete loss.

"It's a symbol used to summon a voodoo loa," Gee explained. "That one belongs to Baron Samedi. Ask Aunt Babette. She'll fill you in more than you ever wanted to know."

Crissakes! Gee knows I hate this voodoo shit. "Isn't Baron Samedi the god of death?"

"He's the loa of the dead, but he guards the past." Cleo swung the garbage bag to her opposite shoulder. "I wrote that hoping he'll keep Rex on this side." Fearful sorrow filled her eyes. Stepping through the doorway, she raised one hand to block the streaming sunlight. "Rex is still alive. I know it. If he was dead, I'd feel it."

"We're sure he is," Gee fibbed. "And we're gonna help you find him." She pointed at The Boat. "Set your stuff on the floorboards, and hop in."

"Floorboards." Cleo scowled. "You afraid my stuff's carrying bugs? Afraid my street shoes gonna mess up your fine leather seats?"

"Listen, little bitch. Let's get one thing straight right outta the gate. Cut the thug." Gee leaned against the fender. "The Boat is older than you are. She deserves respect."

"Whatever." Ignoring the request, Cleo heaved the garbage bag onto the leather bench seat. Lithely hopping on the doorframe, she spun a 180 and slid down next to it, clutching an ornate brass key strung on a ball chain around her neck. "Free ride to me. I'm gonna assume big white girl sits up front." Releasing the key, she stretched out her whipcord slim arms. "Got smokes?"

"Cigarillos." Gee passed her pack over her shoulder. "Help yourself."

"Thank you. I do believe I will." Tapping one out, Cleo bit the cigar before slipping the packet into her pocket.

Gee eyed her in the rearview mirror. "I want those back."

"You're the boss." Flipping the cigars at the console like a frisbee, Cleo thumb-flicked a cheap plastic lighter.

"Bye-bye, y'all," she grandly announced, settling back, and waving to an imaginary crowd of friends like a passing queen. "Got me a handsome chauffeur, a white lady bodyguard, and this fine, free limousine." Tapping cigar ash to the floorboards, she happily laughed. "This is me, moving on. I am on my way."

Chapter Twenty-One

Same Day
12:42 PM

"Don't waste your minutes," Jane warned. "You go through what I paid for, and you'll need to buy more minutes out of your own pocket."

Cleo studied her new cherry red pre-paid phone. "I do like having a phone. Feels like I'm in touch instead of watching the world go by."

"Don't forget they can watch you now. Track you through your apps."

"So says our reigning queen of security," Gee teased.

"Who cares where I am." Cleo scornfully rolled her eyes. Reaching over the seat, she lightly tapped Gee's shoulder. "Mister? What's the address of this new place we're going to."

"I'm not a mister, my name is Gigi, and it's 1562 Dauphine."

"Boujee address." Cleo eagerly started pressing buttons.

"Need help?" Jane offered.

"I got this." Cleo focused on her phone, intent. "I want to figure this out myself."

"Put Jane and me on your contact list." Gee turned left on Poydras Street before rattling off both numbers like a circus side show mind reader.

"How do you do that?" Jane studied the faint haze of dark stubble shadowing Gee's cheek as they turned right on Carondelet. "How do you remember numbers and addresses so easily?"

"Just do. Phone numbers, grade schoolteacher's names, song lyrics. Comes natural."

UP JUMPED THE DEVIL

"Wish I had your talent." Jane's head bobbed as The Boat bumped over the streetcar's neutral ground on Canal Street. "My brain's turned to mush. Lived here almost a year and I still get turned around." She flicked a finger at the passing businesses. "I grew up using the cardinal points, north, south, east, and west. Here you've got lakeside, riverside, downriver, and upriver. No wonder I'm confused."

"North, south, east, and west don't do us no good," Cleo stated from the back seat. "It'd be better if you learned it our way."

"Honest to God. I don't know how you keep it straight."

"Only thing in my life I do keep straight." Gee joked, turning right on N. Rampart St. "Lakeside is north, riverside is south, downriver means east, and upriver is west. Memorize that and you'll be golden."

"I remember locations easy," Cleo bragged, carefully slipping the phone into her hoodie pocket. "Me and Rex play this game called 'Never Get Lost.' We know every back-alley shortcut there is." She hunched her shoulders. "This city's easy s'long as you keep your ass riverside. Rex gets confused over Iberville, but he's okay again once he gets to Congo Square." She pointed at the upcoming intersection. "Too bad it's Saturday. Tomorrow it'd really be something to see."

"Congo Square?" Jane asked.

"A drum circle in Louis Armstrong Park," Gee explained. "Live music and dancing all day long."

"Plenty lively, too. Rex loves every kind of music there is. I can't keep him away from it. Lucky all day is free."

Gee turned right on Esplanade Avenue. "Back in the day Congo Square was where free Blacks and slaves met up. Sunday was their day off when they could enjoy life and have some fun. Folks say jazz music was born in Congo Square."

"Got every kinda beat you could ever want to hear."

Jane felt surprised. "Since when did slaves get a day off? I've never heard of that before."

"They did in NOLA." Gee smiled, turning left on Dauphine. "We got our own laws and traditions, don't you know."

"There's a spot." Jane pointed.

"Parking karma." Gee smoothly pulled The Boat to the curb. "It's a sign."

Cleo released a long sigh. "Rex and me gonna live here?"

"Like it?" Gee shut off the ignition. Stepping into the street, she admired the colorful facade with a connoisseur's eye, scanning the mango orange porch supports and the wooden shutters on either side of the lemon-yellow front door. "This was my friend Fancy's home." She turned. "Now it's yours."

"What happened to your friend?" Cleo swung her garbage bag.

"She ... died." Gee stared at the sidewalk. "She was murdered," she stated more forcefully. "And I miss her every day."

"We got her killers off the street, Gee. They'll never hurt anyone else."

"Yeah. We did do that." Filling her lungs, Gee clapped her hands together with a concussive sound like a gunshot. "Private sorrow." She unlatched the wrought-iron gate. "Fancy'd be the first one telling me to move on. She'd hate seeing us sad. That was not her way."

Jane flinched as the gate squealed. "Remind me to bring some WD-40 next time. I'll fix that gate."

"Don't touch it." Gee politely waved Cleo up the steps. "That's Fancy's cheap ass built-in burglar alarm system. You hear that squeak you know someone's coming up the steps. Every time I hear it, I think of her. It makes me laugh."

"I'm not sure me and Rex can live here." Cleo hunched her slim shoulders again. "These neighbors ain't gonna want us living near them. It's too nice."

"Sunshine, you can put that thought right outta your head." Gee unlocked the sticky bolt. "Fancy tamed this whole neighborhood, plus," she pointed her chin at the rundown house next door, "Miz Thibideaux will be watching out for you. No one's gonna mess with her. She's a voodoo queen."

Cleo seemed to shrink inside herself. "A voodoo lady?"

"*Bona fide*," Jane confirmed. "And she'll take every dime you have selling you fake spells and magic charms you don't need."

"Ignore her, Cleo." Gee shoved the door open. "Respect Miz T for what she is, and you'll get along fine." Removing one key from her ring, she offered it to Cleo on her open palm. "This is a good house. A safe place. I want you and Rex to think of it as your new home."

Cleo carefully plucked the key as if it might be hot, turning it over between her slim fingers. "This is my key. The key to my own door. I door I can lock whenever I want."

"And no one gets a house key but me, you, and Rex." Gee's eyes crinkled with crow's feet as she smiled. "Don't you want to see inside?"

"One mo." Cleo hesitated on the threshold.

"Is there a problem?" Jane asked.

"No *problem*. Jus' never owned two keys before." Cleo polished the house key with her thumb. "Waiting to see how that feels."

Chapter Twenty-Two

Same Day
1:18 PM

Fancy's house reeked of male funk and stale sandalwood cologne. Jane sneezed as she followed Gee inside. Cleo remained in the doorway, clutching the garbage bag filled with her clothes. She looked like a spooked and wary doe.

"Come on in," Gee stated, all business. "Check out your new place."

The streetwise teen took one hesitant step inside.

Crossing the room, Gee opened the shutters, spilling sunlit tiger stripes across the golden heart pine floor. Resting her hands on her hips, she nodded with satisfaction.

"I don't like taking Fancy's money for myself, but this feels like the right thing to do. Houses shouldn't stay empty. They get lonely." She pointed. "It's simple enough. Hallway leads to the bedrooms and the kitchen. Shared bathroom is in the middle." She crossed the floor. "Water, gas, and electricity are turned on. Don't worry about paying for utilities. I'll cover them as executor for Fancy's estate." Dropping her chin, she blinked.

Jane stretched out her hand. "Gee? You alright?"

"I'm fine," she insisted, combing her hair with her fingers. "Everything is fine."

"You don't look fine."

"I'm still getting used to Fancy being gone. I know she is. It's not that. I know she and Dee-Dee are both gone." Gee looked up, her eyes fierce. "But I keep thinking of things I want to tell them. Jokes

I want to share. I'll read an old text, and it hits me again that I *can't*. It's not getting easier. It doesn't *heal*."

"It's like that with me missing Rex," Cleo softly agreed. "Not having him around feels like I'm missing a big piece of me."

Gee angrily swept away tears. "And that is why we're gonna find your brother because I don't ever want anyone feeling this way." Roughly clearing her throat, she blindly marched down the hall. "C'mon. I'll show you the ropes." She pushed the first bedroom door open. "Fancy used this as her dressing room. There's plenty of racks and hangers. Push her stuff to one side. I'll deal with it later."

Dropping the garbage bag, Cleo gazed in wide-eyed wonder at the overflowing collection of Styrofoam wig stands, bubble-wrapped shoes and boots, and the rolling racks of taffeta and sequined gowns. "This all belonged to your friend?"

"You see anything you like, take it. Consider it a gift. You'd be doin' me a favor. Anything you don't take will get donated to the women's shelter."

Cleo reached for a pair of metallic silver platform boots.

"Except for those." Gee snatched them up. "Those I need for my Mardi Gras krewe costume."

Cleo drew back, obviously stung. "I been meaning to ask. So, you a man who dresses like a woman? A she/male."

"No, I'm not a transvestite." Gee hugged the silvery boots to her chest. "Sometimes I dress in drag for a party or a ball, but that's a one-time costume. Like dressing up for Halloween. What I am every day is a transgender woman. I'm a woman in a male-gendered body. It's a different thing."

"I suppose." Cleo uncertainly toed her garbage bag. "Funny thing. I notice when a woman dresses like a man, everyone laughs. When a man dresses like a woman, folks get mad. Why is that?"

Gee snorted. "Sunshine, you figure that out, do let me know."

"And her?" Cleo pointed at Jane. "She your partner?"

"Business partner," Jane quickly inserted.

"Damn, Jane." Gee laughed. "That was a little quick outta the gate, doncha think?"

"Business partners," Cleo slowly repeated. "What's your business?"

"Private investigators," Jane said. "We're developing an agency idea."

"I think Pascoe Private Investigations sounds catchy." Gee rocked on her heels. "PPI."

"Nuts to that." Jane shifted uncomfortably. "I'm carrying the credentials."

"What credentials? You got disbarred."

"I resigned."

"We'll need a name. How 'bout Pascoe/Byrne Investigations. PBI."

"Sounds like cheap beer. Why not go alphabetic? Byrne/Pascoe."

"Sounds like a threat."

"We'll figure it out." Jane waved her off. "We both need to get licensed first."

"On the list." Tucking the silvery boots under one elbow, Gee pulled out her wallet. "Frenchmen Grocery is three blocks over." She handed Cleo a sawbuck. "Make some groceries. Get yourself in some food."

Cleo nervously wove the twenty dollar bill between her fingers as her brazen confidence evaporated. "You both leaving now?"

"Why?" Gee hesitated. "What're you gonna do this afternoon?"

"Go looking for Rex." Her fierce confidence returned. "I'm not gonna quit 'til I find him. What're y'all doin?"

"I need to find a location for the Krewdio-54 Mardi Gras after party." Gee jiggled her keys. "The parade committee's riding my ass. Mardi Gras is only six days off."

"Nothing like waiting until the last minute," Jane snarked.

"I'm not the only one out looking." Gee fanned her fingers. "And offering a surprise location only adds to the anticipation."

"You need me." Cleo perked up. "I know every rathole there is. How much you looking to spend?"

"Zero."

"Some place abandoned then." She looked sly. "I know just the place."

Chapter Twenty-Three

Same Day
1:53 PM

"Head for Tulane Avenue," Cleo confidently stated. "Take us 'bout ten minutes to get there."

Keying the ignition, Gee eyes suddenly widened. "I think I know where we're going. Solid pick."

"Where is this?" Jane's voice rose as she struggled with the seatbelt.

"No! Don't tell her. Keep it a surprise." Gee turned The Boat onto Barracks Street. "I want to see her reaction when she sees it."

"Entering private property without permission carries a trespassing charge," Jane primly stated. "We could get arrested. Even a misdemeanor charge would jeopardize my job."

"You hate that job," Gee insisted. "We'd be doing you a favor." The Boat swayed as she turned left on N. Rampart. Pressing the in-dash lighter, she reached for her cigars.

Leaning over the seat, Cleo snapped her fingers. "I'll take one of them."

"I hope this location works out." Gee handed her the pack. "Maybe next year we can use it for a Krewdio-54 Disco Ball."

"Got enough space for miles. Me and Rex explored most of it." Cleo paused. "Do we need to be queer to join your krewe?"

"Absolutely not." Gee slid the cigar pack into the console. "There are gay krewes like Petronius or Amon-Ra, but so long as you adore disco and house music Krewdio-54 will always welcome you in."

"Hip-hop is more my kick." Cleo lit the cigar. "Ain't disco dead?"

UP JUMPED THE DEVIL

"Shut your mouth! Disco is the music of life. It's like dancing to a heartbeat. Have you listened to Purple Disco Machine? He's a DJ, on the radio, from Germany. Download the app on your phone." Reaching over, Gee prodded Jane's shoulder. "Don't forget to send in your Krewdio-54 membership form before the deadline or you'll miss out on our Mardi Gras parade."

"I'm still making up my mind." Jane clutched the door as The Boat turned left on N. Claiborne Avenue. "I'm not really into joining social clubs."

"Krewdio-54 is not just a social club." Gee lit her cigar. "It's a way of life. A way to celebrate and support our LGBTQ community." She returned the lighter to the dash. "Weren't you ever part of a group like that at some point in your life?"

I felt like part of the Nantucket police force family until things got ugly. "Maybe once," Jane admitted. "It didn't pan out."

"Don't give up on the idea." Gee puffed. "There are hundreds of krewes. You just need to find the one that fits. It's a great way to meet new people. Make new friends." She slid the smoldering cigar into the ashtray. "You might like the Intergalactic Krewe of ChewBacchus for Star Wars fans. They have a Carrie Fisher/Princess Leia marching band."

"Crissakes!" Jane scoffed. "What's their parade unit like? A second line of drunk Ewoks and Wookies waving light sabers?"

"Funny." Gee grew serious. "It's easy to poke fun, but krewes do a lot of good volunteer work for charities." Her look darkened. "And they bring people together. That has to count for something during these crazy times. Anything that helps people feel less alone is a good thing."

Speeding up to catch a changing traffic light, Gee turned left on Tulane Avenue before quickly shifting The Boat into the right lane. Glancing at the rear-view mirror, she captured Cleo's eyes. "Are we getting warm? Right side of the road, up ahead?"

Crossing her arms, Cleo smiled with satisfaction. "Hard to miss."

Chapter Twenty-Four

Same Day
2:11 PM

"Holy heck." Craning her neck, Jane studied the massive twenty-story Art Deco building towering above Tulane Avenue. Her voice rose in disbelief. "What is this place? It looks like an air-raid bunker."

"Charity Hospital." Gee eased The Boat closer to the cyclone fence surrounding the site.

"You wanted a free, big open space," Cleo piped up. "About a million square feet with one security guard and no cameras that work. They got tore up doing construction. Rex and me have crashed here a time or two. When you really need a rack to lay your head, pay the guard five bucks and squat."

Gee scratched her chin. "This might work."

"Are you insane?" Jane sputtered, appalled. "You can't invite a rave party crowd into a derelict building. People will die."

"It's not derelict." Opening her door, Gee stepped into the street. "This building's safe. They only fenced it off for a clean out." Crossing the cracked sidewalk, she headed for the Emergency Room marquee entrance, talking it through out loud. "It's got electricity, running water. The bathrooms work. The main lobby is huge. String up some twinkly lights, set up a DJ. We'd be good to go."

Jabbing her fingers through the zig-zag chain-link fence, she shook the padlocked gate, releasing a thrashing metallic rattle that bounced off the hospital's limestone facade. Tugging on the gate with both hands, Gee pried it open a slim twenty inches, turning sideways and slipping through the gap before standing in obvious triumph on the other side.

"You two coming?"

"Gee, it's posted. This is criminal trespassing. If we get caught, we'll get arrested and fined."

"Only fools follow the rules."

Cleo followed Gee through the gap as lithely as an eel.

"BWG, you can always wait for us in the car." She smirked.

The hell you say. Squeezing through the gap, Jane trotted to catch up, shivering as she entered the cool shadow thrown by the marquee. "Is this place still occupied?"

"Not anymore." Cupping both hands, Gee checked a smudged and gritty window. "Place got swamped by Katrina in 2005. Governor Blanco permanently shut it down." Moving to her right, she checked the next window. "No reason to, the military had scrubbed it spotless." Shrugging, she moved to a third window. "Something to do with politics. Now it's owned by LSU."

"*L'Hôpital des Pauvres de la Charité* was supposed to be for poor people to use forever, for free," Cleo sourly snapped. "Been that way for three hundred years. Rex and me was both born here. Now poor people got nowhere to go when we get sick."

"Looks like it's still filled with furniture and medical equipment," Jane noted.

"They're finally getting around to cleaning it out." Gee headed for a windowless metal door propped open by a brick.

"Surprise! So they can turn it into rich people condos." Cleo scowled. "Poor folks getting screwed again."

"Follow me." Easing the door open, Gee slipped inside. Cleo blindly followed.

In for a penny, in for a pound. Sweat slipped down Jane's spine as she stepped into the dim hallway. Her heart rate leapt as she paused to give her eyes time to adjust. A painful two-stroke drumbeat started pounding her throat as her focus tightened. The hallway's walls were painted shoulder high with industrial khaki green paint. The overall atmosphere smelled like black mold and her nose involuntarily crinkled. *I do smell something else, something sharp. What is that? Ammonia? Industrial cleaner?* Scanning a quick 180 degrees, she noted the grimy acoustic tile ceiling as her boots crunched on broken glass.

"Notorious BWG, keep it down." Cleo hissed. "You're making too much noise."

"BWG?" Jane wondered.

"Big white girl. Your new tag." Cleo danced ahead. "You should'a worn kicks like me."

"That's racist and insensitive." *She's right. I should've worn sneakers.*

"Don't change the fact that it's true."

Whatever. Remember Rule Number Five: Ignore the drama, don't engage. It's a distraction. Flicking on the flashlight feature of her iPhone, Jane scanned the floor, looking for a clearer path.

"Good idea," Gee noted, pulling out her phone.

"That cheap ass phone you give me don't do that," Cleo complained.

The two light beams wavered, converged, and held steady as they turned right, illuminating the cavernous main lobby. Noting some disjointed lettering, Jane flicked her iPhone up and read:

WELCOME TO T E MEDIC L CEN ER OF L UISIANA
    Where the Unusual Occurs & Miracles Happen

"Look at this space!" Gee twirled on the floor's great tiled seal. "We could so hold the Krewdio-54 after party here. Can't you see it, Jane? What could be better?"

Pointing one finger, Cleo stared down her arm. "All I know is y'all don't wanna go in Room Four." Dropping her arm, she shivered. "A lotta folks died going into that room. Just saying."

"The old trauma center," Gee agreed, raising her chin, and optimistically cocking her head. "And a lotta people got saved."

Flicking her light toward Room Four, Jane noted a wavering line of red-black blots on the floor. "Gee? How long did you say this hospital's been out of service?"

"Twelve years, since Katrina."

"I don't think so." Jane knelt as a leaden lump of pure apprehension hit the pit of her stomach. She studied the blots. "See those crimson centers?" She looked up. "That's fresh blood splatter."

Chapter Twenty-Five

"Just what do you mean by fresh?"

"Recent," Jane conceded.

"It could'a come off one of the workmen cleaning out the place."

"Shhh." Cleo's slim shoulders rose to her ears. "Someone's coming."

Jane listened intently. "Two voices. One male, one female."

"*Merde*. Hide. It's the security guard."

"Take the stairwell." Pointing her iPhone at the floor, Jane sped across the lobby. "Look for an exit."

"I'm sorry to see this place go, Denis." A cultured female voice echoed from the darkened hallway over the steady tapping of high heels like castanets. "We did a lot of good here. Improved a lot of lives."

"Yes, ma'am. Certainly improved my early retirement account." He chuckled as his leather shoes slapped the floor. "I'm real sorry to see you and the doctor leave."

"I suppose it's time. We needed more space."

Despite Jane's best effort, the fire door groaned as it opened. She shoved Gee and Cleo through.

"Did you hear that, Denis?"

"Yes, ma'am, I did." An industrial level halogen flashlight erratically lit the lobby. "Best stay behind me while I check it out. Might be a hostile intruder."

Scanning the twenty-story stairwell, Gee gripped the metal railing. "Which way? Up or down?"

"Down." Cleo raced down the steps, taking them two at a time. Her wild brown curls unfurled behind her like a banner. "Up only goes to other floors." Rounding the half-landing, she headed lower. "We need to get past them to get out."

Jane flinched as the fire door groaned again.

"Sounds like kids, ma'am. Y'all need to come out." The guard called down the stairwell. "It's not safe." His halogen beam bounced off the concrete walls. "You're gonna get hurt."

"Keep going." Jane panted. "Look for an emergency exit."

"No need for you to stay, ma'am. I know you're busy with things."

"Shouldn't you call for backup? Denis, I don't like the idea of you doing this alone."

"No, ma'am. I've done this before." His voice sounded ghoulishly hollow. "Please, ma'am. I'll take care of this. Go. I've got my Glock."

"Very well. I'll leave you to it."

Leaping off the bottom step, Jane followed Gee's wavering cellphone light and their running shadowy figures down a dank corridor.

"This way." Gee's phone lit a set of double doors pierced by two round porthole windows. "Hurry up."

"I'm right with you." Following Gee through the swinging doors, Jane skidded to a stop. The hairs on the back of her neck rose as her iPhone highlighted a semi-circular amphitheater filled with rows of spectator seating behind seamless plate glass. Snaking electrical plug circuitry and X-ray lightboards lined the yellow tiled walls around a gleaming stainless steel operating table.

Gee gasped. "What is this place?"

"A surgical theatre." Jane's knees weakened as black blots blanketed her vision. *Oh, no. Not now.* Gripping her forehead, she fought to stay focused as she noted more fresh blood splatter dotting the floor. "Gee?" Jane cried, as the mental fog swarmed in, shrouding her mind with searing migraine pain. She stumbled, feeling like she was suddenly shouting from the bottom of a deep, dark well. "Someone's still using this arena. That table's been scrubbed. No dust."

"I see that." Gee grasped her arm. "Damn, you're clammy. Hang onto me. I've got you. Don't pass out."

"What's wrong with her?" Cleo hissed.

"PTSD." Gripping Jane around the waist, Gee bodily took her weight, dragging Jane forward as she groaned. "Leave if you need to, but I'm not leaving her behind."

"I didn't say I was leaving." Cleo sounded hurt.

The security guard's bright halogen beam turned both porthole windows opaque.

"I know every inch of this complex," he crooned, his voice carrying a teasing lilt. "And when I catch you girls, we're gonna have some fun before I call the po-lice." He laughed, an echoing menacing sound. "Hell, those boys might even wanna get in on it. Hope y'all ready for that. But three of you sounds just 'bout right for me."

"Fucker means it." Cleo opened the door.

Rage at his obvious rape threat lit Jane's PTSD fog on fire. *Rule number one: Protect your family, protect your friends.* Pushing free of Gee's support, she raised her fists to face the oncoming menace. "You two go. He's not getting past me."

"Wrong answer." Gee grabbed Jane's arm. "He's got a gun."

"Give me her phone." Cleo repeatedly snapped her fingers. "I'll use her flashlight to lead him away." Stooping, she picked up a clanking section of lead pipe, sliding it sideways between both chrome handles and effectively creating a barricade. "Get BWG to the car. I'll meet you there."

"Can't let you do that," Jane retched, her hands on her knees.

"Give me your damn phone." Cleo held out her hand. Pointing toward a hallway split, she skittered left into the half-light. "Follow that ramp to Room Four. Don't stop moving 'til y'all see daylight."

Chapter Twenty-Six

Same Day
3:14 PM

Jane puked bitter ropy bile into the gutter before wiping her mouth on the back of her hand. The black blots had dissolved, her vision had cleared, and the searing migraine pain was lifting.

"Sorry to be like this."

Gee proffered a half-filled water bottle, bouncing back and forth off her toes. "Do what you gotta do. Feeling better?"

"Some."

"Good." She worriedly scanned the hospital doors. "I need to go back in and help her."

"I'll go with you." Jane's head swam as she pushed off The Boat.

"Like hell you will."

Jane flinched as a chrome chair shattered a second-story window. A shower of shattered glass mushroomed on the Emergency Room canopy as sixty feet of tan fire hose spiraled to the street.

"We may not need to." Gee breathed in awe.

"She is not going to do that."

"Oh, yes, she is." Gee trotted forward. "Step on the nozzle. Hold it flat so she can shimmy down." She grunted as she knelt on the hose, pulling it taut. "Help me."

"Tampering with fire equipment is a felony."

"Where is your head at?"

"She might fall."

"I ain't gonna fall," Cleo shouted. Swinging both legs over the windowsill, she looped the fire hose between her crossed feet, rapidly rappelling down hand-over-hand like a Cirque du Soliel superstar.

"*Merde.*" Gee stared with obvious admiration. "She could do real damage working a pole."

"Start the car!" Hanging by both hands, Cleo released her feet. "He's right behind me. Trying to bust in the door and pissed as hell." Exertion flushed her face, but her eyes held no fear. Pumping both arms, she raced to The Boat, sliding over the fender before diving headfirst into the rear seat.

"Go! Go! Go! Light a fire under this bucket." Clutching her side, she shrieked with laughter. "No catching a case with me, sucker!"

"That was epic." Gee smoked The Boat's tires as she peeled away. "I can't believe you did that."

"They's a whole bunch of things you don't know 'bout me," Cleo shouted. "People been underestimating me my entire life."

She's right. Jane blushed. *I'm really seeing Cleo for the first time. I let my bias override my perception. Who is this person?*

"You're gonna need a new location for your party." Cleo rested against the front seat. "That one ain't gonna work unless you're saving it for Halloween."

"She's enjoying her adrenaline high," Jane drily noted, "and so are you, Gee. Slow down, please. Speed limit's thirty-five. If we get stopped, they'd arrest us on suspicion."

Cleo patted Jane's shoulder. "You feeling better now, BWG?"

Jane raised her palm. "Better enough to ask for my phone back."

"You are feeling better." Nodding with satisfaction, she slapped the iPhone into Jane's hand. "That happen often? You getting sick?"

Jane felt ruffled. *I don't want to talk about it, but why not? Cleo deserves to know what to expect. She's part of the team.* "More often than I like."

"You should get medicine."

"I have Zoloft. I don't like taking it. Makes me feel logy for days."

"Rex gets stupid when he drinks lean." Cleo sat back. "Makes me crazy when he goes daft."

Jane turned sideways. "I meant to ask you about that. Where's Rex getting his syrup from? Codeine requires a prescription. Who's his source?"

"He never told me." Cleo stared down a side street. "Said he wanted to keep me from it. He do get it regular, though. Seems like whenever he wants."

"You ever see one of his bottles?"

"I may have." She squinted. "Why?"

"The label should list the prescribing doctor's name on it."

"Rex's bottles don't come with labels."

"He's getting it illegally. Off the street." Jane paused. "Syrup's not cheap. How's Rex paying for it?"

"I just said I don't know," Cleo snapped. "When I axed him, he bumped me off." She poked Jane's shoulder. "Let me axe you something. What was you saying in there before you freaked?"

Jane blinked uncertainly. "I don't remember."

Gee pressed the cigarette lighter. "Something about the operating table."

"That was it." Cleo agreed.

"Operating table." Closing her eyes, Jane dove into the murky depths of her battle scarred memory, trying to seek out and grasp the foggy details that darted just beyond her reach like a school of frightened minnows. She recalled the operating theater, the gleaming surgical table, and the blood splattered floor. Each flashing image hit her in the gut like a body blow. "Got it." She opened her eyes with a rush of satisfaction. "Someone's still using Charity Hospital for surgeries. We need to notify NOPD."

"You cain't do that!" Cleo yelled. "That security guard saw my face. You tell them and they'll lock me up." She pounded the headrest. "If you're gonna do that, stop this car right now, and let me out."

She's right. If we tell NOPD we'll all get tagged for criminal trespassing. "Simmer down." Jane's dormant detective instinct quivered as her mind lined up a host of new unanswered questions.

The dashboard lighter popped as Gee's cellphone trilled.

"Shouldn't text and drive," Jane warned, keeping a wary eye on the cross town traffic.

"I'm not texting, I'm reading." Gee's eyes widened as she shared her screen. "You're gonna die."

Noon, okay? Looking forward to meeting you.

"Who's that from?"

Gee slid her phone into the console. "Steve Tanner wants to meet the whole family, tomorrow after Mass."

Jane sat back, impressed. "How'd you locate him?"

"I do listen to you." She spoke around a mouthful of smoke from her cigar. "Took your advice. Searched Tinder last night during my break. Messaged him after his profile popped up. Not bad, yah?" She grinned like an imp. "How'd I do?"

Chapter Twenty-Seven

Sunday, February 19, 2017
1:52 PM

Leslie Pascoe wrung her hands as a city bus rumbled by on St. Claude Avenue. Standing at a front window, she still wore her Sunday best, a muted floral dress with neutral low-heeled pumps. Her silvery hair was neatly coiled in a braided crown around her head.

"Be right back." Ken heaved himself out of his easy chair. "Going to step outside for a quick second."

"Wait for me, Pops." Gee moved to join him.

Leslie's hem fluttered as she whirled. "Don't you two dare go get stoned. I need both of you clear-headed today."

"Sure thing, sweetheart." Ken tapped his pockets. "Whatever you say."

"Of course, Maman." Gee looked abashed.

Aunt Babette slid her hand down the ebony banister. "Any sign of him?"

"Not yet." Leslie returned to her perch, nervously fingering her cobalt blue glass beaded necklace. "I hope he can eat sandwiches. I covered them in cling wrap before we left. Wrapped them double so the bread stayed fresh."

"Leslie?" Ken worriedly frowned. "Why wouldn't a man eat sandwiches?"

"You never know." Her forehead creased to match his. "I made tuna salad. He might be vegan or allergic to eggs."

"Sweetheart, it'll be fine. If he is vegan or allergic, he would've said so." Ken gently took her hand between his two giant paws. "You're not poisoning anyone. No one's going to starve."

"I hope you're right." She pulled her hand free.

"Just so you know," Jane interrupted. "I searched public records for 'Steve Tanner'. If he's the same guy, he was charged once with simple assault in Kansas City, Missouri."

Aunt Babette looked up, startled. "He attacked someone?"

"No, the physical act is battery. He threatened to attack someone. It's a Class C misdemeanor. He got thirty days of jail time and a fine."

"Hush." Leslie spun around. "This might be him coming now."

They all moved to the window as a white Mitsubishi Mirage slowed.

Gee pushed aside the curtain. "You think that's him?"

"Could be," Jane stated. "It's a rental car. Look at the tag. There's a Best Budget Rental frame around the license plate."

"Help me, Lord." Leslie shook out her hands. "Give me the strength for this."

Tugging his shirt straight, Ken turned for the door.

"Ken?" Jane warned. "Make sure you ask to see his ID."

"Really?" He pulled up short. "How do I ask him for that?"

"It's simple. Just ask. It's a reasonable request to make before you let anyone into your home."

"Jane's right." Aunt Babette sat. "He's a stranger. We don't really know who he is."

"Alright," Ken grumbled. "Nothing like making a man feel welcome."

Turning back to the window, Jane observed the man stepping from the sub-compact rental car. *Approximately 25 years old. Roughly six foot tall. Remarkably square jaw. Trimmed black beard. He looks to be solid muscle. Forearms and neck tattooed with black gamer type designs. Untucked light blue short sleeved shirt, slim cut jeans, and those obnoxious white bottomed lace-up fake deck shoes the guys are wearing now.* Reaching back into the car, he retrieved a dark green binder.

"*Merde,*" Gee exclaimed. "He's younger than I am."

"I can already sense his negative energy." Aunt Babette shuddered. "He doesn't look clean. I'll need to burn a white sage wand after he leaves."

Leslie shared a pointed look. "Whatever he is, he is our guest, and he will be treated like one while he is in our home."

"Everyone ready?" Straightening his shoulders, Ken pulled the door open. "It's showtime."

Chapter Twenty-Eight

"G.G.? I believe you're expecting me." The stranger stood uncertainly in the dirt yard. "Steve Tanner. Marianne Tanner's brother."

"I'm Ken Pascoe," he boomed. "Gigi's my daughter. Come on up." Stretching out his hand, Ken glanced uneasily at the house. "Nice to meet you. Hate to do this, but I need to see some ID."

"Of course." Awkwardly tucking the binder under his left arm, Steve pulled out his wallet as he trotted up the steps. "I've got my Kansas driver's license."

"1732 Old Shawnee Trail, Leawood, Kansas." Flicking the ID with his index finger, Ken stared at the sky. "I remember that address. A lot of water under that damn bridge."

"It was our parent's house. I still live there. Never moved."

"Come on inside." Ken returned the license. "My wife's fixed lunch."

"She didn't need to do that. I don't want to be any trouble." Steve hunched as he returned his wallet to his back pocket. "But thanks."

Ken pulled up short as he noted the focused family circle waiting inside. "Okay, folks. It's official. Meet Steve Tanner." He pointedly glowered at Jane. "Says so on his ID. This is my wife, Leslie, our Aunt Babette, my daughter Gigi, and her friend, Jane."

"Nice to meet you." Steve looked flustered. "I'll do my best to remember everyone."

"Please, sit down." Leslie indicated the couch. "Make yourself comfortable. Have a seat."

"I'll get the sandwiches." Aunt Babette regarded him suspiciously. "Would you like sweet tea? Lemon?"

"Anything is fine, ma'am. I'm not picky." Steve sat, setting the binder on the coffee table before drying his palms on his knees. "Okay, well, this is awkward. I don't really know how to start this conversation other than to just jump in."

"It is for us, too." Ken commiserated.

"Here goes." Steve rubbed his hands together. "I'm in New Orleans to pick up my sister's cremains. The mortuary is taking care of things as we speak." He swallowed. "I'm not looking for a place to stay. I've got a room at Maison St. Jacques B&B." He stumbled a bit over the French pronunciation. "Lucky room number seven. I'm going to take Marianne home in a few days to be buried with the rest of the family. We have a nice Tanner family plot in the Leawood Pioneer Cemetery." His head bobbed repeatedly. "Marianne died intestate. That means she didn't leave a Will." He repeatedly tapped the binder. "I brought the court papers with me. I didn't even know about you people before yesterday. I hope that's okay."

"I think that sounds very nice," Leslie emphatically agreed.

I'll just bet it does. Jane repressed a snort. *Since it keeps Marianne out of the Broussard family tomb with you.*

"Here we go." Aunt Babette pushed through the swinging door backwards, carrying a loaded wicker tray. "Leslie, *sha*, this looks nice."

Carefully sliding the tray onto the coffee table, she handed out glasses of ice and mismatched plates. Tearing the cling wrap off the crust trimmed sandwiches, she balled it up before stuffing it into her pocket. "Please make a good meal everyone. I see that Leslie made plenty."

Selecting one triangle half, Steve took a polite bite before returning it to his plate. "The Coroner's Office said one of you is claiming to be Marianne's daughter." He glanced at Jane. "Is that you?"

"No." Gee pointed to her chest. "I'm Gigi. It's me."

"I'm confused." He paused, blinking repeatedly. "How are you her daughter? I mean, you're a man."

"I'm a transgender woman, but yes, Marianne Tanner was my birth mother."

"Okay." He swallowed again. "Let's go with that. So, if my sister Marianne was your mother, then who was your dad?"

"Me, I was. I mean, I am." Ken nervously glanced at his wife. "Marianne and I had a … relationship when we were kids. Before Leslie and I got married."

Steve carefully studied his iced tea. "Family is very important where I come from." He looked up. "If that's right, then I'm your uncle."

"Let's talk about that." Ken settled in. "Marianne didn't have any brothers or sisters when I knew her. How does that work?"

"I brought the papers with me." Flipping the binder open, Steve fanned out a set of official looking documents. "Marriage certificates, birth certificates, court orders. Everything's been notarized." He tapped an embossed gilt seal. "Marianne was my half-sister. We had the same father, Frank Tanner. Dad married Marianne's mom Sue Ellen when they were just out of high school." He frowned. "I never met Sue Ellen. I heard she died young. Dad married my mom, Charlene in 1991, and they had me."

Gee folded her arms. "It's strange you're my uncle and you're younger than me."

Steve shrugged. "Luck of the generations. When were you born?"

"Some time in 1984," Leslie inserted, looking troubled. "We don't know the exact month and date."

"As I recall." Ken harrumphed. "Frank Tanner got sent to prison."

"Yes. Dad served twelve years," Steve easily agreed. "He stayed clean once he got out. He credits my mom with helping him do that."

I should've brought notepaper. Jane intently listened. *I'm Googling all of this later.*

Gee spread the court documents. "Can I get a copy of these?"

"Sure. Email, or text? Dropbox? What works?"

"Text works best. You have my contact info."

"I'll send you PDFs." Steve tapped the pile of paperwork. "These documents prove I'm Marianne's Executor. I inherited her estate as her half-brother under Kansas inheritance law. I'm sorry to say that you and me are the last two Tanners left."

"She's a Pascoe," Ken barked.

Leslie straightened the tray. "Your sister went missing for thirty years." Looking uncomfortable, she cleared her throat. "How did they know where to find you?"

"The Coroner's Office here sent a letter to the Leawood address saying they had identified her remains. Once they supplied her death certificate, I filed as Executor." He pushed a document forward. "This Letters Testamentary makes it official. Marianne didn't leave a Will or a list of assigns. You can see my name is listed, making me her legal heir."

Leslie nervously glanced at Ken.

"I did have a couple of questions." Steve looked up. "Did my sister die in this house?"

Chapter Twenty-Nine

Looking guilt stricken, Leslie paled. "She did."

"I read what information I could find." Steve slowly slid the documents back into the binder. "It's not clear to me exactly how she died."

Aunt Babette adjusted her bracelets. "That's because we don't know how she died."

"What happened?" Steve raised both eyebrows. "The *Times-Picayune* said you both were arrested."

"That's right." Leslie linked her hands. "We were."

"Where does that stand? Is there going to be a trial?"

"No," Jane interrupted. "Formal charges weren't filed. The coroner couldn't determine Marianne's cause of death. Under Louisiana law, they're both free."

"But one of you did it, right? One of you killed her?"

"It was an accident, a horrible accident." Leslie fluttered her hands. "A tragedy."

"Leslie hit her with a shovel," Aunt Babette offered. "And I thought she was dead."

"We're both very sorry it happened."

"So, that's the end of it?" Steve massaged his forehead. "You folks in New Orleans sure do things differently than we do in Kansas."

"Better get used to it," Ken muttered.

Steve turned. "And you played with The WarBirds rock band?"

"Bass master and founding member, back in the day." Ken swigged his iced tea.

"My dad," Steve started slowly. "Said Marianne hung out with The WarBirds at Shawnee Mission East high school. He said Marianne sang with you guys. He said she had a real musical gift."

Leslie coughed.

"Oh, hell, no." Ken chuckled, obviously amused. "Marianne might've helped out on a few tracks, but she was never part of the band." He selected another sandwich. "The good news is Gigi inherited her voice, not mine. Gigi's got her vocal range."

"So, that was Marianne singing female lead on 'Love Power'?"

"That's her." Ken chuckled again. "All ninety-five decibels."

"What happened to the royalties from 'Love Power'?" Steve sat back. "It was a huge hit. Sold millions of copies. Still does."

"Oh, son. Poof! Those royalties are long gone. They got sold to a New York agency thirty-five years ago."

"Really?" Steve rubbed his thumb and fingers together. "Forty years' worth of royalties would add up to real money."

"We've never seen a dime of it," Leslie sourly chimed.

"Sad, but true," Ken agreed. "At least Marianne's voice will live on in her new songs, when Gigi sings them."

"New songs?" Steve pounced. "Marianne wrote more than just 'Love Power,' didn't she. My dad said she filled whole notebooks." He sat up. "Where are her other songs now? Do you have them?"

"I didn't say that." Ken looked white-eyed.

"Yes, you just did." Setting down his glass, Steve stood. "If you have my sister's notebooks, I want them. They belong to me. I inherited her estate."

"Like hell they do." Leslie unsteadily swayed upright. "They belong to Gigi. They're her inheritance as Marianne's daughter."

"She's not even a daughter." Steve sneered. "And you have no proof that's who she is."

"We can prove she's Marianne's daughter," Jane quickly inserted. "Easy enough if we get a DNA sample from her … remains."

"That's not going to happen." Stooping, Steve snatched up his binder. "You people are crooks. I'm not giving you permission for anything."

"Why not?" Gee cried. "Don't you want to know if we're related?"

"No, I don't want to know. I don't need to know. Besides, it's too late. She's being cremated as we speak."

Leslie jabbed her finger. "We took Gigi in after your sister abandoned her. We loved her. We gave Gigi a safe home to grow up in. Your sister was raising an infant in the gutter."

"Did my sister abandon her child?" Steve sputtered. "Or did you just keep him ... her because she left a baby behind after you murdered her?"

"Say what?" Silence fell over the room as Gee stood. "Pops? Maman?" Gee's knuckles turned white as she gripped the back of a chair. "You've been saying Marianne abandoned me my whole life. What if that's not true? What if she died before she could come back for me. What if that's why she left me behind." She blindly stared at the floor. "What if she loved me?"

"Gigi." Leslie reached out her trembling hand. "None of that matters anymore. It happened so long ago."

"Of course, it matters." Gee snatched back her arm. "It changes everything."

"This is all very nice." Steve hustled clear of the coffee table. "But I want Marianne's songs. Give them to me. Now."

"Never." Leslie spiritedly raised her chin. "You'll get them over my dead body."

"I said," Steve raised his hand to strike her. "Give them to me, bitch."

Jane leapt up to block his swing. "Back it down or I will take you out."

"You sonofabitch," Ken shouted. "Get the hell outta my house!"

"I'm not through with this." Jerking his arm down, Steve backed toward the door. "I'm calling my lawyer. Those songs belong to me. If you publish any of them, I'll sue your ass for every penny you've got."

"I said, GET OUT."

The Big House shook as Steve slammed the door.

"Gigi?" Leslie murmured. "Honey? You okay?"

"I'm so confused." Feeling for the chair, Gee sat. "I don't know where to start."

"It's a lot to unpack," Jane agreed.

"I have an idea." Aunt Babette hopefully pointed to the dirty plates. "Can we get his DNA off his glass? Like they do on TV?"

Give her credit. She is trying. "His DNA won't help prove Gee is related to Marianne."

"Why not?" Gee looked up. "If he's my uncle like he says he is."

"His DNA would prove that he and Marianne shared the same father, but his mitochondrial DNA won't match yours because they had different mothers. We need Marianne's DNA to prove you're related to her."

"And he just cremated her." Gee looked shattered. "Now I'll never be able to prove who I am."

"Kiddo?" Moving to Leslie's side, Ken linked their arms. "Like your mother said, we know who you are. You're our daughter. That's the only thing that really matters."

"I'm sorry, Pops. It's more than that." Gee awkwardly rose. "I need to go someplace and think." She stumbled toward the kitchen. Dropping her car keys, she scooped them up. "I'm gonna stay at Fancy's house until I figure this out."

"Gigi! Sweetheart, wait," Leslie cried.

"Let her go," Jane said. *I get why Gee's upset. Losing your identity is a game changer. She's doubting everything she knows about herself.* A sickening flutter of anxiety rippled through Jane's chest, stealing her breath. *Just like I did.*

"Ken, I don't care what that man said." Leslie looked haggard. "Those songs belong to Gigi." Flattening her fingers against her temples, she paced the floor. "What did Serena say? We've got possession. Possession is nine-tenths of the law, right?" She dropped both hands. "My God, if we lose that royalty money again, I will lose my cotton-picking mind."

"Leslie, *sha,* please. Stop." Aunt Babette clutched her necklace. "You're sounding *demente.*"

"I've never been saner in my life." Spinning around, Leslie marched for the staircase. "I'm going to hide those songs where he will *never* find them."

"Leslie..."

"No, Ken. Don't stop me. I'm right about this."

Ken winced. "I've said it before. Those WarBirds' songs are cursed."

"*Problem malveillant,*" Aunt Babette viciously agreed.

Chapter Thirty

Monday, February 20, 2017

Jane looked up from the laptop.

12:01 AM. Time for the midnight patrol.

Bolting the sticky security office door, she pocketed her iPhone and the key ring. Double-checking her duty belt for the expandable baton, she flicked on the powerful halogen flashlight.

I wonder how Gee's doing. It would be nice to know, but I get why she's ghosting me. I'm not going to bug her. I'll hear from her when she's ready to talk.

Walking to the Basin Street main gate, she tested the padlock. As usual, the nearby French Quarter's blazing neon bar signs projected a brightly lit dome high into the blue-black sky.

All secure. Considering the drama and excitement of the past few days, Jane paused, and her tense shoulders relaxed. *There's something to be said for tranquility.*

Feeling recentered, she started down St. Louis Alley, her steadily measured tread making the only sound that marred the silence. Smiling, she remembered her dad's favorite joke about the benefit of living next to a graveyard: *At least you get quiet neighbors.*

Her footsteps slowed as she recalled meeting with Mose Gallier before her shift. *That certainly didn't turn out the way I expected.* Jane had come to the meeting loaded for bear and anticipating rebukes and even dismissal. To her surprise, her boss had started out by offering her flattering words and a commendation.

"The Board was delighted to see the cemetery vandalism has ceased, Jane." Mose had risen on his toes to meet her at eye level. "They especially directed me to congratulate you on a job well done."

Sharing an oily smile, he had winked. "Nice work. Keep making me look good."

"Thank you, sir." Jane had felt an uneasy gut ripple. *I don't like Mose any better when he's being friendly. And the cemetery's sketchy security conditions did not get resolved simply because Rex Duchamp is MIA.*

"Now we need to gear up for Carnival season." Mose had smoothed his mustache. "Have you experienced Mardi Gras before?"

"No, sir. This'll be my first time."

"You're in for a treat." He'd sarcastically ticked the points off his fingers. "Our normal population doubles. Public drunkenness triples. Police response gets patchy because they're focused on crowd control. That puts increased pressure on us. We'll start seeing even more trespassing from the homeless riffraff climbing over the walls to find a place to sleep."

"Got it, sir. I've heard that the Mardi Gras balls and parades run for more than a week."

"That's correct. It's chaos, Jane, a madhouse. Here's how we'll respond." He had plowed ahead. "Starting on Saturday the 18th, we'll close the cemetery gates early. All Catholic cemeteries are closed on Mardi Gras Day."

"Will you be contracting a temporary partner to help me, sir? I have contacts at SecureForce if you need them."

"No need." Mose had quickly backpedaled. "The cemeteries are secure once the gates are padlocked. We're only adding temporary front office staff." He'd had the grace to look discomfited. "Actually, Jane, we'll be temporarily trimming your hours. Your shift will run from 10:00 PM to 2:00 AM during those ten days. And you'll want to take an unpaid vacation day for Fat Tuesday to enjoy yourself."

Typical. Jane acidly reviewed Mose's strategic cemetery coverage. *Expand the public facing front office and leave the already limited security response unchanged. Plus, I lose a full day's pay.* She rapped the flashlight against her palm. *Cheap bastid. Another shining example of intelligent middle management thinking.*

Quickly flicking the light beam left and right, Jane turned down Conti Alley heading for her favorite tomb.

Chapter Thirty-One

Jane studied the marble avenging angel perched above the bronze door on the Gaspard family tomb. Although the angel had lost her nose, both hands, and her flaming gilt bronze sword to vandals and scrap dealers decades ago, she had retained her intricately feathered wings. Even without her nose or her hands, Jane thought she looked serene.

She angel? Or he angel? Do angels have genders? Maybe both? Looking up, Jane considered Gee's situation as a woman living in a male gendered body. *Gee's certainly no angel, and she can be devilish when she wants to be, but there's not an evil bone in her body. I don't get how anyone could judge her because she's a transgender person. It would be like saying I shouldn't be a detective because I'm a woman. Who still believes in that ridiculous hoo-ha these days?*

Leaning her shoulder against the tomb wall, she tucked the flashlight into her armpit and checked her phone. *C'mon, Gee. Nothing new.* Jane felt stifled by frustration and prickly impatience. *Dr. Wacky said losing a 'relational identity' can really mess you up, and it sure did a number on me, but I need to know where we stand.*

Pushing off the wall, Jane continued down the alley, her flashlight sweeping the chipped slate pavement ahead, her mind a whirlwind of intriguing loose-end investigative possibilities. *What if Marianne Tanner didn't abandon Gee. That's gotta be blowing her mind, because it changes the whole dynamic between Gee and Leslie and Ken, and even Aunt Babette. Sure, Gee knew that either Leslie or AB was responsible for Marianne's death, but that was accidental manslaughter. But now, with this new information, what if Marianne never meant to leave Gee behind. That suggests missed options and different life choices, something deeper, something ... fundamental. Even though Leslie and Ken and AB have given Gee a wonderful home, they may have robbed her of her birth mother's love. The hitch is Gee will never know the truth of it. How about living with that uncertainty gnawing at your guts for the rest of your life.*

"Fuck." Tapping her lips, Jane gave herself a sheepish shake. "Detective to the bone. I'm working Logic Tree again. Feels good." *There's always unintended collateral damage when shit gets stirred up. Maybe Ken and Leslie should've reached out to the Tanner family back in Kansas thirty-odd years ago. Ken said he didn't think anyone was left, but they didn't even try. Anyway, how would they have explained to them where Marianne went?*

"Fuck." She repeated. *It's impossible to always make the best, wisest, right decision every single time, especially when a loved one is involved. You'll never get it absolutely right. That kind of perfection doesn't exist.*

Jane hesitated over a sudden insight. *I'm in the same boat as Gee, just as conflicted. Did I make the right call by not telling Trahan about the blood splatter we found at Charity Hospital?* Jane tugged her lip. *My gut is telling me that withholding intel from NOPD is the wrong move to make regardless of personal consequences. It's not too late to tell Trahan what we saw. Fuck!* Jane shook the tension from her hands. *Come on, Gee. Text me. I need to know our next move.*

She moved on. *Maybe it's my fault Gee's ghosting me.* The flashlight swept over the benevolent association mausoleum directly ahead. *Because as a friend I didn't reach out to her first.* Leaden uncertainty blanketed Jane's mind before a ripple of defensive protest bubbled to the surface. *I tried. I did. I swung by Fancy's place yesterday after work. True, I kept going because the house looked dark, and I didn't want to impose.* Jane's toxic self-doubt drilled her self-esteem like a shipworm as she warmed with shame. *Be honest. I didn't stop because I knew Gee was upset, and that level of emotional drama makes me twitch like a netted eel.*

Throwing her shoulders back, Jane straightened. *Suck it up, buttercup. Time to grow a pair and face the facts. I need to know that*

UP JUMPED THE DEVIL

Gee's okay, and I need a status update. I am stopping by Café Irene on my way home in the morning and I'm taking Gee café au lait and beignets for breakfast. There, decision made. Decided. Finished. Done. She picked up her pace. *How's that for a fucking action plan.*

Better. She immediately felt more in control of the situation. Gripping the flashlight, she strode toward the Conti Street entrance, her next patrol stop and her personal *bete noire*. Running the flashlight over the gate, Jane studied the padlocked and completely inadequate shoulder-high scroll-worked barrier in disgust. *I don't care how historic this gate is. Mose has got to convince the Board that I'm right about securing this cemetery access point. Any drunk could just roll right over the top of it.*

She glanced at the line of free-standing tombs stretching to her right. *At least these tombs back up to the solid Conti Street wall. It's not that much more secure, but it's something.* Catching a flickering movement from a nearby spear-pointed fence, she frowned. *What's that? Another offering?*

Reaching out, Jane plucked at the scrap of silvery metallic fabric before tugging it free. Balling it up, she shoved it into her breast pocket. *Another asshat tourist litterbug or more hoodoo voodoo?* She snorted, thinking of the growing collection of junky trinkets she had culled off tombs and arranged in a display on top of the filing cabinet in the security office. *Hotel shampoo bottles and mini perfumes left as gifts for Marie Laveau. Black plastic combs left on Nick Cage's pyramid tomb, supposed to make your hair regrow. Not sure how that works. Crissakes! He's not even in there yet.*

She froze. Cocking her head, Jane strained her hearing beyond the Basin Street city bus whining by. The hairs on the back of her neck ruffled and rose as she heard it again, the low, muted sound of a whimpering moan.

Chapter Thirty-Two

I heard that. I know I did.

Slapping the flashlight into her left hand, she popped the snap off the expandable baton on her duty belt. The flashlight's intense beam wavered and then steadied, casting into stark relief the elongated profile of the seated Italia statue on the marble mausoleum looming overhead.

This way. Inhaling a steadying breath, Jane tucked her chin, buckling her nerve against her galloping fear, her tongue suddenly feeling thick as it filled her parched mouth. Slipping sideways between two parapet tombs, she stepped into the shadows, cocking her head again. *What was that?*

She ran the flashlight over a row of ghostly tombs. The focused beam spotlighted a lumpy mass slumped behind the mausoleum's protective fence.

"Come on out of there." Jane tightened her grip on the baton. "No sudden moves."

She flinched as a hooded figure leapt to its feet.

"Help me! We need help."

Jane stared into the girl's terrified face. "Cleo?"

"It's Rex." She extended her blood-stained fingers. Dropping to her knees, she plucked at his sleeve. "He keeps passing out on me."

"Make some room. Let me see." Sliding the baton back into her belt loop, Jane clambered over the fence. "Is he stoned on lean?"

"Maybe. I ain't sure." Her voice quavered and cracked. "I don't know what this is."

Jane set the flashlight on the ground by her knee to illuminate the area. "How bad is it?"

"I don't know." Cleo wailed. "I only just found him."

Jane hesitated for a split second as her mind scrambled to high alert, trying to make sense of the crisis. Her previously dormant first responder training automatically rebooted so quickly Jane felt like she was having an out-of-body experience as a hyper-focused calm enveloped her senses, speeding through her nerve channels so completely it took robotic control.

What are we dealing with? Rex was limp, dressed in thin hospital scrubs, and barefoot. Every inch of his head above his nose was wrapped in layers of blood-spotted gauze. *I don't see active bleeding.* "Where's he hurt?"

"It's his head, cain't you see that?" Cleo cried.

"No, Sis." The slim teenager moaned. "Don't fuss. Jus' take me home."

"Why's he got that bandage wrapped around him?"

"Sissy, don't shout." He clutched her forearm. "They might find me. Why they do this to me, Sissy? I din't hurt nobody. Din't do nothing wrong."

He doesn't remember how he got injured. Post-event amnesia? Jane pulled out her iPhone. "I'm calling 911."

"No!" Rex's heels scrabbled curving grooves in the cemetery dirt. "No more doctors! I cain't go back there. I'll die."

"Doctors?" Jane paused.

"Them ones that give me the lean." Pressing his smudged fingers to his eyes, Rex yelped.

"Listen to me, 'bro." Cleo glanced around uncertainly. "We need to call an ambulance. Get you real help."

"Sissy?" His questing fingers scrabbled up her arm. "Who's this bitch you're trusting with my life?"

"A friend. A good friend. She's gonna help us."

"You know that, Sissy?" He beseeched. "You certain?"

"Yes, I'm certain."

"I trust you, Sissy." Rex collapsed against the marble tomb. "I trust you."

"Jane? You'll stay? You won't leave us?"

"As much as I can," she promised, sliding the flashlight closer to the two huddled teens as she stood. "Keep Rex calm while I'm gone."

"Why?" Cleo's panicked voice rose. "Where you goin'?"

"I need to unlock a gate for the EMTs." Jane paused, her imagination in grim overdrive. "Don't let Rex mess with that bandage. Whatever he's got going on underneath has scabbed over. Don't let him tear it open. I'll hurry. Be as quick as I can."

Climbing over the fence, Jane raced for the Conti Street entrance, dialing 911 on the fly. Turning a tight corner, her left knee cracked and popped with a sound like snapping celery. Jane limped on, the dial tone buzzing in her ear.

"City of New Orleans, 9-1-1. What's the address of your emergency?"

"St. Louis Cemetery." She panted. "421 Basin Street. One victim with an apparent head wound. I'll be waiting at the Conti Street gate, between Treme and Basin."

"Anyone in immediate danger?"

"No." Jane inhaled a shaky breath. "Seems to be stable at this red-hot second."

"Alright, ma'am. Stay on the line. Who am I speaking with?"

"Jane Byrne. B-y-r-n-e. I'm the cemetery's head security officer."

"Thank you. I'm getting this information out."

Jane heard the clicking of acrylic nails against a keyboard.

"Ma'am? I'm sending EMS to that location."

"10-4." Propping the cellphone between her shoulder and her chin, Jane fumbled the keyring, mentally kicking herself for not having the full emergency response protocol memorized. *I should already know how to do this. I've got to stop dialing shit in.* "You'll notify NOPD?"

"No need, ma'am. EMS, NOPD, and Fire Department response is consolidated." The dispatcher paused for a heartbeat. "Estimated response time for your district is eleven minutes."

"Eleven minutes?" Jane howled, appalled.

"Yes, ma'am." The dispatcher's voice turned coldly defensive. "It's a busy night. They've confirmed receipt."

"Out." Jane ended the call. *I should text Gee, let her know we found Rex, but I know she won't answer. She stores her phone in her locker. She'll be working the pole until two.*

Slipping her phone into her pocket, Jane struggled to stuff the recalcitrant key into the rusted padlock, twisting it savagely before pulling the freed chain link by stubborn link through the barred gate.

The gate screeched like a banshee as Jane wrenched it open, securing both sides with broken bricks. *I need to tell Trahan. Give her a status update.* Scrolling for her number, Jane initiated a text. *We found Rex Duchamp. Injured, but alive.*

The three bubble response was almost immediate. *Location?*

St. Louis Cemetery. Conti Street gate. NOPD notified.

On my way.

Reaching up, Jane massaged the painful tension cording her neck. *Feels good knowing I'm not alone in this response. Almost feels like my old law enforcement days.* She heard the high-pitched wailing of an approaching siren as red and white strobe lights bounced off the Basin Street buildings. *Fire truck or EMS ambulance. Ladies and gentlemen, place your bet. Which one gets here first.*

An EMS van bearing a green and gold fleur-de-lis logo swung through the intersection before sliding to a stop at the curb. The passenger door shot open, spilling light across the sidewalk as an EMS tech slid out.

"You called it in?" He drawled, noting Jane's uniform while tugging on a pair of nitrile gloves. "Where's the vic?"

"Thirty yards in." Jane pointed. "On the ground."

"He big sick?"

Jane blinked as she translated. "Yes, with an apparent head wound."

"Stay and play or load and go?"

"Load and go's my guess."

"Ricky?" He grabbed a flashlight and a MedTech trauma kit as the second EMT doubtfully eyed the gated entrance. "Grab the board and collar."

"Might have trouble fitting a gurney through, Jerome. Looks tight."

"I've seen tighter. Follow me. I'll show you how."

I'm still amazed how calm EMTs are. Jane led the way. *How stately. How slow. Is that EMS training or do the techs see so many emergencies they burn out over scrambling to get to the next one.*

She rounded the mausoleum. Cleo and Rex were still haloed by her flashlight. Hearing the gurney's metallic rattle, Cleo looked up.

"Rex passed out again." She cradled his bandaged head against her shoulder, struggling to hold her brother upright.

Pulling out a penlight, Jerome vaulted over the fence. "Need you to move out of the way now, miss." He knelt by her side. "We've got him." He cautiously checked the bloodied wrapping. "Get the neck collar on him, Ricky. Then the body board. We'll stabilize on the way to the hospital."

"Which hospital?" Jane leaned against the fence.

"DeltaCare Medical Center. You a family member?"

"I am." Cleo helplessly wrung her hands. "He's my brother."

"You can ride with us in the cab. Ricky? You ready? Lift on three."

Cleo followed them over the fence. "Jane? Will you follow us? Make sure we get there?"

"What do you mean make sure you get there?" Jerome efficiently tightened the bodyboard's bright orange straps to the gurney. "Why wouldn't you get to the hospital?"

UP JUMPED THE DEVIL

"Jane!" Cleo demanded. "I axed, will you go with us?"

"I can't." Jane choked as bright PTSD stars flared like falling comets around her peripheral vision. "I need to notify Mose. Coordinate backup security for the cemetery. NOPD will need a police report. Cleo, I can't abandon my post."

"So." Cleo shared a withering stare. "You spouted all those big fine words for nothing." Her slim arms clapped her sides. "I'm a stone-cold fool, and you're a lying bitch."

"Don't do her no good to go now anyhow." Pointing at the gate, Jerome maneuvered Rex and the gurney over the broken ground. "DeltaCare only allows one overnight visitor. You're it." He scanned the tight turn ahead. "She needs to wait until regular visiting hours open at six."

"Cleo, I swear I'll meet you when my shift is over." *It's not a weakness to ask for help.* Unlocking her iPhone, Jane hurriedly typed Gee a message. *Text me ASAP. We found Rex Duchamp.* She inhaled deeply. *I need your help.*

Chapter Thirty-Three

Same Day
8:16 AM

Loosely holding her iPhone in both hands, Jane stared at the vacant text screen as her reddening eyes watered and itched. Always hyper-sensitive to odors, the DeltaCare Medical Center's visitor waiting area presented a smoldering array of medicinal scents.

After completing her initial eyewitness NOPD report for Detective Trahan, Jane had raced the Ducati to her Bywater apartment to change out of uniform before heading to the hospital. Leaving Monster to idle, she'd noticed a shadowy shape shifting behind the Big House's rusting screened in back porch.

"Leslie? Have you heard anything from Gee?"

"Not a word." Leslie's saucer had clicked as she replaced her teacup. "It's been radio silence since the other day."

"Me neither. Should we be worried?"

"I naturally worry because I'm her mother." Leslie had sadly smiled.

"If you see her," Jane had bounced off her toes, "Will you give Gee a message? Tell her we found Rex Duchamp. He's at DeltaCare Medical Center. I'm heading over there as soon as I change."

"DeltaCare Medical Center," Leslie had carefully repeated. "And who is Rex Duchamp?"

"Remember Cleo, the homeless girl living in Fancy's place? Rex is her brother. He's been missing."

"I've got it." She had picked up her tea. "I'll give Gigi the message the next time I see her."

"Thanks." Jane had turned for her apartment.

"Jane? Don't fret." Leslie had called out. "Gigi will come back when she's ready. All we can do is love her and support her decisions."

UP JUMPED THE DEVIL

Don't fret. For the thousandth time that morning, Jane settled into the uncomfortable waiting room chair and checked her phone again.

The medical center's security door hissed open. Gee strode in, swinging two slim cans of sparkling cherry Hot Shot in her hands.

Speak of the devil, and there she is.

"Jesus, Jane. You look beat." Gee easily slid into the next seat as lithely as an otter. "You need a glow up. Your makeup's a mess."

"I'm not wearing makeup."

"My bad. Drink this." She proffered a chilly can. "It'll help."

"Gee?" Jane snapped the aluminum flip cap open with her thumbnail. "Where have you been?"

"Club Oz, working, but you knew that." Grimacing, she crooked her neck. "*Merde*, hospitals make me *fou*. Maman said Rex Duchamp's here." She sipped her neon pink drink. "Knew something was up when I got home, and Cleo was gone." She chugged a longer swallow. "Stopped by the Big House first. Maman and Pops were eating cush-cush. Looked delish, but I didn't want to stop. Took me this long to track you down."

Jane felt an unreasonable ripple of frustration. "Why didn't you text me? Or answer your phone."

"Couldn't. My phone died. Drowned in a tequila puddle. Bagged it in rice. Hope that works. May need to buy a new one." She peered down the hallway. "We waiting on Trahan?"

"Detective Trahan is in there now with Cleo and Rex. Taking preliminary statements."

"Got it." Gee settled back. "Okay. Fill me in. What'd I miss."

Collecting her thoughts, Jane sucked down the potent energy drink.

"During my midnight patrol, I found Cleo and Rex Duchamp near the Conti Street gate. Rex was injured. His head was bandaged. He was barefoot and wearing hospital scrubs."

"How did Cleo get him past you and inside St. Louis Cemetery?"

"I don't know that she did." Jane cast her memory back. "She just said she found him there." She set the empty can on the floor. "I called 911. EMS brought Rex in." She pointed at the tile floor. "I texted Trahan to keep her in the loop. She got to the cemetery just as EMS was leaving."

"What's wrong with Rex?" Gee squinted. "Why the bandage?"

"I don't know yet. They only let Cleo in the back. I haven't seen Trahan for an update."

"I was wrong." Gee crossed her arms. "My bet was Rex was dead. Maybe he had an accident."

"That doesn't explain him already wearing hospital scrubs."

"No, it does not. Is there a way to find out if he got admitted to another hospital before coming to this one?"

"I suppose we could call around, pretending to be a family member. Ask if he was admitted." Jane frowned. "These days, I'm not sure they'd give out patient information. Hospitals have gotten strict about protecting patient privacy. Crissakes! Try saying that three times, fast."

"Could Trahan get that information?"

"She might, but I doubt she'd share it. This is her investigation. Professional blue likes keeping intel on their side of the wall."

"Don't know 'bout you, but I think we're starting to sound like PIs." Gee picked at her blue nail polish. "If we did go full-time, is this the kinda thing we'd be doin'?"

"Pretty much. PIs generally work on police support, missing persons, divorce cases, insurance fraud. Speaking of which, have you heard from Steve Tanner?"

"Uncle Steve?" Gee tucked her hair behind her ears. "No. But I know Pops is bummed about the delay. He really wants to record that new album." She drummed her knees with her fingertips.

"Haven't heard from Frankie Malcolm or his lady lawyer either. This copyright bullshit is one hot mess. It's taking forever."

"Get used to it. This is how investigations work. We just need to keep gathering data and digging until we uncover the facts." Picking up her empty drink can, Jane crushed it as footsteps echoed from the hall.

Chapter Thirty-Four

Spotting them, NOPD Detective Shelli Trahan strode across the visitor's waiting room. "You two come with me," she ordered. "The Duchamp's are demanding to see you. Elevator's this way."

Gee trotted by her side. "What's up with Rex Duchamp?"

"I'd rather show you." Trahan looked deeply troubled. "Don't want to have to explain this twice."

Uh-oh. Jane fumbled her backpack as an apprehensive PTSD tremor shivered down both arms to her fingertips. *Cop speak for something grim.* "That bad?"

"Bad enough."

Trahan thumbed the elevator call button. The door slid open with a tinny ding. They piled in, shoulder-to-shoulder.

"Where's Dupree?" Gee wondered. "He on his way?"

"It's my case. He's homicide." Trahan pressed the fourth-floor button. "A man doesn't automatically need to lead every investigation."

"Sorry." Obviously stung, Gee turned aside. She traced her finger down a framed poster as the elevator shuddered and rose. "Looks like this place won a bunch of awards." She broke the awkward silence. "Heart and Vascular Unit. Urgent Care. Multi-Organ Transplants."

"Best medical center in NOLA," Trahan factually stated. "Now that Charity's closed."

Jane bit her lip. *Should I tell Trahan what we saw at Charity Hospital? It could still earn us a criminal trespassing charge.* She glanced at Gee, whose face remained stoically impassive. *Okay. Silence implies consent. Let's not.*

The elevator door slid open. Trahan marched toward a busy circular nurse's station where a male nurse conferred with a familiar-looking woman with shoulder-length bobbed hair, a business pantsuit, and sensible crepe shoes.

UP JUMPED THE DEVIL

Graceland Cuddy. From the Department of Children and Family Services. Crissakes! Jane blinked. *She's up early.*

"There you are, Shelli." Graceland tapped her clipboard with her pen. "I heard Rex Duchamp's been admitted. I've already shared my contact information with the nursing staff. I'd appreciate getting an updated NOPD report ASAP."

"Of course." Trahan looked affronted. "I'll need to write it, first."

The nurse checked his phone. "We'll need to be strict. Dr. Archer only gave you patient permission for twenty minutes."

"Let's not waste it," Jane said. "Which room?"

"447. Down the hallway, on the left."

"Follow me." Spinning on her heel, Trahan spoke over her shoulder. "I'm still not sure why the sister wanted to see you, but they won't talk to me unless you're in the room. Clue me in."

"We've been helping them get off the street," Gee drawled. "Build a better life."

Trahan scowled. "You do know the failure rate for that is like one hundred percent."

"Just because it's impossible doesn't mean we shouldn't try." Reaching past the detective, Gee pushed the half-opened door with her fingertips.

The sterile, boxy room offered a distant view of the Mercedes-Benz Superdome looking like a gigantic pewter clamshell. The sharply sweet, blended odor of chlorine bleach, urine, sour B.O., and apple juice smothered Jane's sinuses, bringing tears to her eyes as she faced the bed.

Rex Duchamp lay propped up by three pillows, his head swathed in purple adhesive Vet-Wrap. Surgical tape and fresh gauze pads covered the upper half of his face to his hairline. A limp clear bag of IV fluid hung from a tripod stand behind the bed, feeding antibiotic solution into a shunt taped to a bruised vein in the back of his right hand.

Cleo Duchamp sat hunched in a chair by her brother's side. She clasped Rex's free left hand between both of hers, interlinking their fingers. She looked wan with fatigue.

"I got here as fast as I could, Cleo," Jane murmured. "Like I promised."

Cleo studied Detective Trahan with swollen, red-rimmed eyes. "You tell them what they done to my brother yet?"

"I can't." Trahan looked abashed. "HIPPA regulations. He didn't give me permission to share that information. He needs to tell them himself."

"Tell us what?" Gee demanded.

"They stole my eyes!" Rex shrieked.

Chapter Thirty-Five

Vivisection. Jane shivered as morbid horror chilled her core. *Like those SS concentration camp experimental motherfuckers.*

Trahan unconsciously toyed with the badge on her belt. "We believe Rex Duchamp's a victim of live human organ harvesting."

"Don't talk 'bout me like I'm not in the room." Releasing Cleo's hand, Rex nervously folded the top sheet like a fan. "I ain't dead."

Cleo leaned closer. "Tell them what you told me, 'bro. Tell them who done this."

"It was them doctors that give me the sizzurp." He thrashed against the pillows. "Must've slipped me ruffie." He clutched the sheet. "Came to locked in a cement room. Cement walls, no windows. No way out except through the one steel door."

Time check. Jane pulled out her iPhone. *Second rule of investigation: Establish an event timeline.* "When was this?"

"I don't know. Cain't tell the days without daylight. How long I been gone?"

"Five days, maybe six," Jane interjected. "Do you think you were locked in that room for that long?"

"Maybe." Spent, Rex collapsed against the mattress. "All I did was sleep." He shuddered. "Didn't know what was going on," he wailed. "Didn't know what they wanted to take from me 'til it was too late."

Trahan settled in. "The men who took you, how many were there?"

"Wasn't jus' men. Was two men and a woman. I knowed she was there by her voice."

"Did you see their faces," Trahan stuttered. "I mean, before?"

"I never did. They wore masks when they opened the door to push the food in. Had to piss in a bucket." Reaching up, he massaged his shoulder. "Slept rough on the floor. They did give me a blanket."

"Any identifying marks on these people?" Jane pursued. "Any scars or tattoos?" *Always question all five senses. Touch, sight, hearing, taste, and smell.* "Did you hear or smell anything remarkable?"

"Tattoos?" He raised his fingers to his lips. "The bigger one, the man I seen the most had Baron Samedi tattooed right about his wrist. And she smelled like perfume and had a big diamond ring. Looked real to me. Sounded like a lady. You know, a snooty ass bitch."

"How about the other man? Anything more on him?"

"You mean the doctor?"

Trahan pushed off the wall. "He was a doctor?"

"That's what they called him. And then they laughed."

Jane felt a sudden chilling premonition as two unaffiliated ideas snapped together like magnets. *The security guard at Charity Hospital talked to a woman who mentioned a doctor. And we saw locked basement rooms and fresh blood splatter in the operating theater.* A leaden possibility hit the pit of her stomach with a bedrock certainty Jane hadn't felt since her active-duty detective days. *What are the odds. Wanna bet?*

"Detective Trahan, you need to interview the security officer at Charity Hospital."

Cleo gasped. "Why you telling her that?"

"Because it fits with everything Rex is saying. Charity Hospital has everything they'd need to perform illegal surgeries, except for victims. They could lure them in with promises of free meds or lean."

"I ain't no victim." Spittle flecked Rex's chin. "And I'm gonna kill those motherfuckers once I get outta here."

"Charity Hospital is closed." Detective Trahan's shoes squeaked as she turned. "And why do you know this?"

"We were in the lobby. Reason why doesn't matter." Folding her arms, Jane raised her chin. "We heard the security officer talking to a woman who mentioned working with a doctor. And we saw fresh blood splatter on the floor."

Trahan's eyes bulged until she nearly looked apoplectic. "How long have you known this? Kept this intel from NOPD?"

"A few days. I only just thought of it. Put two and two together."

"A few days." The detective's voice rose in disbelief. She looked betrayed. "When you know every hour in an investigation is critical."

"Don't do no good knowing if that's where we was kept," Rex interrupted. "We got moved. That's how I got away."

Jane's focus quivered to high alert. *ID a location and we might ID a person of interest.* "Rex, can you remember the new location? Could you find it again?"

"*Absolument.* Got this city memorized by my feet. Get me outta this bed and I'll show you the way, easy."

"Hold up." Raising her fingers to her lips, Gee looked horrified. "What did he mean by '*we* got moved'?"

"Them others." Rex blindly turned. "It wasn't just me they took."

Chapter Thirty-Six

"They screamed their names, so we'd remember," Rex said. "Some dude named Leo and a girl named Jaycee." His scrabbling heels crumpled the sheet. "But I know there was more, kept in other rooms. I could hear them."

"How many more?" Gee whispered. "How many others?"

"No way to tell." Rex shifted and flinched. "Never saw most of them in the new place. They moved us there, two at a time, shackled together in the back of a van. I only ever really saw Leo."

He moistened his cracked lips. "They kept coming back and taking pieces. They took Leo first. Nearly cut him in half taking his kidneys." Rex wiped runny snot with his fingers. "I had to listen to that man sobbing and praying until they came and took him away again. After that, he ... Leo never came back." His lips trembled. "That's when I knew they was gonna do the same thing to me."

Sweet Jesus! Jane felt paralyzed. *What have we uncovered?* She dug for her iPhone. "This is homicide. We need to tell Dupree."

"No! Stay out of it." Detective Trahan sliced the air with her flattened hand. "I'll notify Detective Dupree and NOPD."

"We need to stop this." Gee spat. "Rex? Where are these other people?"

"Somewhere's near Louis Armstrong Park." He fingered his bandaged head. "When I found the park, I knew how to get to the cemetery, to be safe."

"Cleo?" Jane turned as an unanswered Logic Tree possibility crossed her mind. "How did you know Rex was in the cemetery?"

"Came to me in a dream. An angel told me to look for Rex near the tomb. I did, and there he was."

Detective Trahan thumbed her badge again, an unconscious nervous tell. "Rex? How did you escape?"

"Nothing wrong with my ears," he snapped. "I listened. The food cart squeaked. When he opened the door, I could hear birds and a city bus. That tol' me they was bringing the food in from outside. I knew then I needed to get out that door."

He shifted uneasily. "The next time he come, I pretended to be asleep. When he took my bucket I slipped outside, quick, feeling my way down the wall until I found that door and then, zoom! I was gone."

"Brah, you took a real chance."

"Better than letting them keep coming at me taking pieces."

Everyone jumped as the door clicked. "Time's up." The nurse tapped his clipboard. "Non-family members need to leave."

"I'm not done," Detective Trahan protested.

"I'll check with the doctor about allowing an exception. I have your contact information. If she okay's it, I'll send a text."

"Do that. I'm staying on site. You two, come with me." Trahan pointed through the open door down the hallway. "I want details on what you saw at Charity Hospital." She strode ahead. "We can play catch-up in the cafeteria now, or I can pull you into the station for formal interviews."

Gee time-checked her phone. "I'm h'angry. Can we get breakfast?"

"The cafeteria should have something." Trahan pressed the elevator's call button. "Can't promise how good it'll be."

"Since this is your invite," Gee slyly cut her eyes. "You paying?"

Chapter Thirty-Seven

Jane rode the elevator to the ground floor facing forward in an uncomfortable silence, her mind offering a spinning vortex of competing snippets of investigative questions and suggestive follow-up leads. Logic Tree possibilities flashed off and on like high-intensity strobe lights, each one an individual laser blink of a suggestion that slipped through her mental grasp even as she tried to pin it down.

Did the woman we heard at Charity Hospital have anything to do with Rex's abduction? Who is the doctor she mentioned? The security guard who chased us would know. What about the holding cell location Rex mentioned? Could Rex really lead us to it? Are there more victims? Crissakes! How many people are we talking about? How long has this horror show been active?

She trailed Detective Trahan toward a chrome coffee service as Gee abandoned them to examine the pastry case.

Trahan handed Jane a cardboard cup. "I'm guessing you're ex-military or undercover law enforcement. Am I right?"

"Ex-detective." Jane trailed Trahan after she paid the cashier. "CSI. I'm a civilian now."

"I'd like to hear that story someday." The detective slid into a booth. Shaking four sugar packets, she poured the crystal sweetener into her cup. "Don't worry. You didn't give it away. I recognize the type. The thin blue line bleeds through no matter how hard you try to disguise it." She snorted. "Blue runs in my family. My dad, two uncles, and three brothers are NOPD. Grand-Pap was career Orleans Parish Sheriff."

Centering her phone on the Formica tabletop, she paused as Gee trotted over, carrying an iced cinnamon bun the size of The Boat's hubcap on a Styrofoam plate.

"Crissakes, Gee!" Jane sputtered. "That carb load will last you a month."

"Didn't say I was gonna eat it all." Gee slid onto the bench seat. "I'm willing to share. Want a piece?"

"Oh, hell no. If I ate that I'd need to take a nap from the insulin reaction."

"More for me." She licked her sticky fingertips. "This vanilla glaze is to die for. Like crack cocaine." She looked startled. "Not that I'd know what that is like. Just saying."

Trahan ignored her remark. "Do I have your permission to record our conversation? Easier than taking notes. I'd like to get what I can before I get back to Rex Duchamp, and finish taking his statement."

Jane carefully folded her hands. "Fine by me as long as we're protected by the Fifth Amendment Right against self-incrimination."

"What she said," Gee agreed around a chewy mouthful.

"As I've said, we're simply holding a conversation." Trahan pressed a button. "Detective Shelli Trahan, Monday, February 20, 2017. 9:22 a.m. Rex Duchamp abduction. Witnesses Jane Byrne and Gigi Pascoe." She unnecessarily rotated the phone 180 degrees. "Bring me up to speed. Let's start with you saying you overheard a woman talking to a security guard at Charity Hospital."

"And she mentioned working there with a doctor," Gee offered. "But we didn't catch their names."

Trahan frowned. "Step back. You were there because …?"

"An unrelated private investigation," Jane inserted before sipping her coffee. The cheap commercial brew tasted like mass produced coffee everywhere, bitter and burnt. *How badly do you want this information, Trahan? Are you willing to gloss over that little detail to get it?*

"Continue," Trahan said.

"We saw fresh blood splattered on the floor," Gee volunteered, unrolling the cinnamon bun until it looked like a broken fried snake. "And there were plenty of basement storage rooms to hold people in, like Rex said."

"Were you there alone?" Trahan looked troubled. "Was it just you two?"

No need to tell her that. Jane's natural caution flared.

"Just us two," Gee lied, looking wide-eyed and innocent.

Jane spun her cup. "You said you think Rex Duchamp's a victim of illegal human organ harvesting. Where'd you get that?"

"Since I got this assignment, I've been reviewing the stats." Trahan discarded her chewed-up plastic stirrer. "The NOLA demographic is just plain off when compared to the national average. Our missing homeless skew way too young, and too male. Why is that?" She stared out the window. "Sex trafficking might account for a 50/50 split, but what I'm seeing is not even close."

"You're a detective." Jane sat up. "Have you proposed an investigation? Sent a request up the line for review?"

"More than once." Trahan stared out a window. "My requests get torpedoed. Nobody cares about the homeless as long as they stay unseen." She thoughtfully scratched the table. "Rex Duchamp might be the ammunition I need to gain traction. Get some political focus. Grab social media." Her voice rang with suppressed passion. "If I can generate headlines, we might even see real change."

"If you think this has been goin' on for years." Gee sucked more glaze off her fingers. "Who's doin' it?"

Chapter Thirty-Eight

"Rich people." Trahan sneered. "Corneal transplants cost upwards of thirty-five thousand dollars, and there's a waiting list. Rich or influential people will pay double that off the dark web black market because they hate waiting for legally donated organs. They want it done now." She delicately shuddered. "God knows what they'd pay for a quick liver or for poor Leo's kidneys."

Jane spun her cup. "I thought donated organs only came from cadavers."

"Most do." Trahan acknowledged. "Most come from organ donors or from tissue banks."

Gee dropped her half-eaten section of cinnamon bun. "Don't mind me. I'm done eating. What's a tissue bank?"

Trahan cradled her coffee between both hands. "It's a private business that collects human cadaver tissue for medical research and for transplants."

She looked appalled. "Places make money off dead people?"

"They have operating costs like any other business." Trahan nonchalantly shrugged. "I'll bet you carry an organ donor card in your wallet."

"I've got one in my *purse* because I like helping people." Gee wiped her fingertips on a paper napkin. "Never really thought of what it meant." Her dark eyes sparkled mischievously. "They're welcome to any bits of me they can use after I'm gone. Not sure I'll be leaving them much. I'm running after it pretty hard."

"Voluntary donors like you are the known source." Trahan spun her phone again. "It's been estimated that ten percent of all U.S. tissue transplants come from undocumented sources."

"Undocumented." Jane tasted the word as an unsettling chill brushed her skin like a fine spray of sea mist.

"Ten percent?" Gee sputtered. "Check my math. That's like hundreds of people."

"Closer to thousands. And just in the U.S." Trahan drained her coffee. "The global percentage is probably higher." She looked discomfited. "I've read reports that China is harvesting its political prisoners. Reportedly, organs from Chinese inmates have been removed during executions before they're officially declared dead."

"Merde." Gee turned green. "How can they do that?"

"Sovereign borders," Trahan flatly stated. "We can't tell the Chinese, or anyone else what to do."

"Maybe we can't tell them." Leaning on her elbow, Gee stared down her finger. "But that shit needs to stop happening here."

"And that's exactly what I'm trying to do." Trahan crushed her cardboard cup. "I'm going to talk to my contact at the Coroner's Office. Pick her brain. See what she thinks happened to Rex Duchamp. Get her take on how he may have slipped through a donor system that's supposed to be regulated."

"Dr. Tamerlane Sabatier?" Jane asked.

Trahan blinked. "You know her?"

"We worked with her on our last case."

"This Medical Center specializes in organ transplants," Gee pointedly interrupted. "We should ask these people about that before we leave."

"Don't do that." Trahan held up her hand like a traffic cop. "Don't talk to anyone about this except me. I have a forty-eight-hour window to frame this investigation. I want to control every minute of it, so things don't drift."

Fair enough. I'd do the same thing in her shoes. "Is that how long the hospital's holding Rex?"

"Yes. Lucky break for me." Trahan scanned the nearly empty cafeteria. "This medical center has a security presence at every entrance with monitors in the hallways and the nurse's stations. He'll be secure."

Jane's spidey-sense tingled. "How about the stairwells?"

"Them, too." Raising one eyebrow, Trahan looked impressed. "Mounted hard-wired cameras including the roof. 24/7 closed circuit video loaded to the cloud."

"Why?" Gee looked puzzled. "You think someone might come after him?"

"I'd bet on it. Rex Duchamp's a key witness. Whoever did this won't want him walking around pointing fingers and naming names."

"What happens when the time is up?" Jane asked.

Trahan looked grimly determined. "That's being decided above my pay grade, but I want to have a voice in it."

"He could stay with his sister, Cleo and me, at Fancy's house," Gee offered. "That way, me and Jane could keep an eye on him." Looking appalled, she raised her fingers to her mouth. "OMG. That's so not what I meant to say."

"Nice offer though." Trahan looked intrigued. "What's the address?"

No, Gee. Don't give it up. Jane's reticence flared as Gee simply rattled it off.

"1562 Dauphine Street, Faubourg-Marigny."

"The FBI will probably want to hold Rex in their safe house location." Trahan's phone pinged. Glancing down, she checked her text window.

Jane felt a warning PTSD tingle. "FBI?"

"Yes. I've notified the local agency." Trahan slipped her phone into her pocket. "They're more interested in black market organ harvesting than anyone in NOLA or the State of Louisiana is." She rose. "I'll take any interest I can get. FYI: they'll want to interview the both of you."

Gee glanced down as her phone chimed.

"What's up?" Jane wondered. *More trouble? Bad news?*

"It's Pops. He's here." Sliding off the seat, she raced for an exit. "In Emergency."

Chapter Thirty-Nine

DeltaCare Medical Center's Emergency ward was U-shaped, curtained into 10-foot cubicles for privacy. Gee blew right past the busy nurse's station.

"Pops?" She shouted. "Where y'at?"

"Hush, Gee," Leslie called. "Over here."

Jane followed Ken Pascoe's groans. Ken was stretched out flat on a roll-away bed wearing a loose blue hospital gown. He was holding a sealed icepack to his head.

"Pops? What happened?" Gee breathlessly tucked the thin cotton blanket around her father's hairy bare knees. "Smoke too much?"

"No, I didn't smoke too much. Some street thug clocked me."

"I told you we needed to fix that sprung lock on the back door." Leslie wrung her hands. "I found him lying on the kitchen floor in a puddle of blood." Her voice trembled. "I thought he was dead."

"Scalp wounds do bleed like a motherfucker," Jane commiserated. *And don't I know it.*

"I'm fine," Ken growled. Adjusting the icepack, he winced. "Find the doctor who stitched me up and get me the fuck outta this hospital. I already told them I'm not filing a police report."

"Why not?" Jane asked.

"What's the use? I'm never gonna see my watch or my wallet again." Carefully pushing up on one elbow, he pointed at the chair. "Privacy, please. Hand me my pants. Will you two chuckleheads please turn around?"

"But Pops, what happened?"

Ken struggled to fasten his belt. "Your mother and Aunt Babette left the house this morning to make groceries …"

"Before attending noon Mass," Leslie nervously interrupted. "Like we always do."

"I went into the kitchen because Jane's fool dog was yapping its head off from her apartment."

Gee reached out to support him as Ken slipped his bare feet into his loafers.

"The kitchen door was propped open. I went to check on it ... and woke up on the floor with Leslie standing over me, hollering like a banshee, as only she can do."

"Don't you dare make a joke of this, Ken Pascoe." Leslie pressed both hands to her chest. "My heart skipped two beats when I saw you laying on the floor. You looked dead."

"Stop saying that woman. You'll bring down a jinx on me." He stiffly rose to his feet. "Some snatch-and-grab punk got the drop on me, that's all. My pride hurts worse than my head."

Jane frowned. "A home invasion in The Bywater? Since when?"

Balling up Ken's hospital gown, Leslie placed it on the blanket. "The neighborhood's changing. It's not nearly as safe as it used to be."

"Go find that lady doctor." Ken gestured. "I'm signing myself out."

Jane flinched as the privacy curtain hissed open.

"I heard that. And where do you think you're going, tough guy?"

"Home," Ken defiantly stated, buttoning his bloodied Hawaiian print shirt. He pointed his chin at Gee. "I've been sprung. She's my ride."

"There's no real reason to keep you." The doctor studied him carefully over the top of her thick, black-framed glasses. "You collected a pretty good goose egg, three small stitches, and a concussion."

Jane fingered her own fresh bumpy scalp scar. "I'm familiar with concussion watch protocol," she volunteered.

"Good thing. He's going to need it. Luckily, he has a thick skull."

"Love you, too, Doc." Reaching for Leslie's outstretched hand, Ken took one shaky step. "I just want to get home."

"Best place for you." The doctor smiled. "Take it easy. Get plenty of rest. Finest prescription I can give."

Pausing, Ken gazed at her hopefully. "Any chance at scoring pain meds? Oxy? Percocet? Vicodin, maybe?"

"Tylenol works best for the first twenty-four hours. Ibuprofen after that. Both are easily available over the counter at any pharmacy."

"You're no fun," Ken grumbled. Pulling the clipboard from her hands, he clicked the pen and signed the bottom sheet.

She resettled her glasses. "Check him tonight, when he sleeps, to make sure."

He returned the clipboard. "Make sure of what?"

"Someone needs to wake you every three hours to ensure you haven't slipped into a coma."

"Fuck that." Ken glowered. "Any of you pissants try waking me up every three hours tonight and I will personally toss you into the street."

"Thank you, doctor." Leslie apologetically smiled for Ken's coarse language. "We'll keep a good eye on him."

"It sounds like he has all the home care support that he needs." She co-signed the release form with a flourish. "Let's call an aide for a wheelchair, and you can be on your way."

"I don't need a goddamned wheelchair." Ken tottered toward the door. "Just show me the exit."

"I'm calling an aide anyway."

"Go ahead. Try and catch me."

"Quickly, Gee." Leslie gestured, trotting to stay by Ken's side. "Run ahead and bring the car around. Jane can help us to the door. One good thing, Jane," she said as an aside, "Aunt Babette was able to check on Piddles before the ambulance arrived. There's no need to worry. He's fine."

"Glad to know where I stand in her priorities." Ken shoved off a wall.

Leslie quickly swooped in to support him. "I can see I'm not going to win this no matter what I say." She looked up. "What would you prefer, Ken? Have the dog run into the street and get hit by an RTA bus?"

The exit door automatically opened just as Gee and The Boat swept up to the circular curb. Ken leaned on the fender as Jane fitted her thumb to the scooped chrome handle, unlatching the front seat and folding it forward as Leslie scooted into the back.

"Pops, you sit up front," Gee directed. "Jane can sit in back. We've got you. Take it easy."

"Take it easy, she said." Ken sank into the passenger seat so heavily the sprung upholstery pressed against Jane's knees. "Gigi, the way you drive, on the way home, do me one favor, please."

"Anything, Pops. Whatever you say."

"I've had enough for one day." Ken pressed his eyelids with his fingertips. "If you're gonna hit something on the way home, hit it hard. Next time, I don't want to survive."

"Humph." Leslie crossed her arms, looking nettled. "And I'm the one who gets blamed for jinxing him."

Chapter Forty

"Ken?" Jane leaned closer to the headrest. "You said you didn't see anyone. Did you hear anything? Smell anything?"

He started to protest before dropping his hands into his lap. "I did smell something funny in the kitchen. Like incense."

Gee turned. "Was it the white sage sticks Aunt Babette burns?"

"No. It wasn't herby. It was more sweet like ... honeysuckle."

"You also said you thought it was a snatch-and-grab because they took your watch and wallet," Jane pursued. "Was any other part of the house ransacked? Leslie, did they go through the bedrooms? The medicine cabinets?"

"I didn't have time to look. Ken needed my help."

"We could call and ask Aunt Babette," Gee suggested.

"She won't hear the landline if she's up in her room," Leslie said.

"Let's give it a try." Jane pulled out her iPhone. "It might be important."

"Why?"

Jane held the iPhone to her ear. "If this wasn't a random act, someone knew that you and Aunt Babette were out shopping. That Ken was alone."

"Sweet mother of God. What are you saying?" Leslie gripped the front seat. "Some prowler is watching our house?"

"It's one possibility."

"Speed up, Gigi." Leslie spoke into her ear. "Now Babette is alone."

Gee floored the accelerator.

"Three rings," Jane reported. "No answer."

The tires squealed as Gee turned left to catch a yellow traffic light.

"What are you saying?" Clutching his head, Ken groaned. "I can't follow this conversation. Someone's after me? Or after something in the house?"

"Maybe both. No answer." Jane ended the call.

"Ken?" Leslie raised her voice over the sound of the rushing wind. "Could this be Pied Stan sending you a message? You have kept up with his loan payments."

"Of course, I've kept up with his loan payments," Ken parroted harshly. "We're square. Whoever did this, it wasn't Pied Stan."

"If they weren't after Pops, then they were looking for something in the house." Gee savagely turned right. "Maman? Where did you hide Marianne's songs? We don't own anything else worth real money."

"That is not true," Leslie archly protested. "I inherited Grandmere Broussard's silver comb set and her genuine garnet ring." She stubbornly folded her arms. "And I'm not telling anyone, not even you where I put those songs until I see a royalty check with Ken Pascoe's name on it and that check clears the bank."

"Marianne's songs do sort of belong to me," Gee tentatively suggested.

"Two more possibilities," Jane said. "Steve Tanner wants them bad. So does Frankie Malcolm."

Ken cautiously turned. "You think one of them slugged me?"

"It's possible, as long as we're exploring persons of interest."

"Maman?" Gee scanned the rearview mirror. "Tell me you didn't hide those songs in the oven."

"Or in the dishwasher," Jane begged.

Leslie sat up. "It's no use giving me the third degree, girls. I've hidden them where no thief would ever think of looking." She bounced as Gee navigated The Boat onto the potholed driveway. "Gigi, stop the car. Let me out. Babette?" She called. "Where y'at?"

UP JUMPED THE DEVIL

Despite Piddle's high-pitched yips coming from inside Jane's apartment, the Big House remained eerily silent.

"Aunt Babette?" Slamming The Boat into park, Gee left the driver's side door hanging open as she sprinted up the back porch steps. "You here?"

Gooseflesh dappled Jane's forearms as she caught a shadowy flicker of movement behind the rusting screen.

"Aunt Babette?" Ducking her head into a patch of rooftop shadow, Gee paused, her voice sounding pinched. "You alright?"

Dragging both feet, the elderly woman pushed the screened door open.

Why is she walking like a zombie?

"Ken? You back? Still alive?" The elderly woman tottered forward. Her multiple bracelets jangled as she raised an immense handgun in her left hand.

Crissakes! Jane froze. *It's a Ruger Security-Six.* Her OCD instantly presented a scrolling list of subsequent and unnecessary details. *Double action revolver, six round cylinder, .357 Magnum. Where the hell did she get that gun?*

"Holy crap, Babette." Still standing by the car, Ken slowly raised both hands. "Careful where you point that thing." His forehead channeled into wrinkles. "When did you get a gun?"

"Bought it off a retired cop at the Three Fleas Market." She settled her weight on the top step. "Set me back three hundred dollars. He promised me it's reliable. Gave me the box of bullets for free."

"Babette!" Leslie looked shocked. "You know I don't allow guns in my house."

"It's my house, too, *sha*. And I'm not giving it up." Aunt Babette looked apologetic but unrepentant. "Home is the one place where we need to feel safe. My spellcasting is *puissant*, but I've conjured all the defensive protection I can. Someone evil is working red magic against us." She switched the revolver to her right hand. "I'll keep it locked in my room, same way Jane does. We can't be coming home with intruders running through our bedrooms."

Ken found his voice again. "I can't believe I'm going to say this, but she's right. We need to be able to defend ourselves." He pointed at the handgun. "But hell's bells, Babette. I'm calling you Dirty Harry from now on. That hog leg's bigger than you are."

"You go ahead and laugh, Ken Pascoe. Make my day." Her dark eyes shone. "I don't see no one sneaking up on me. You're the one sporting fresh stitches."

"Leslie? Sweetheart, I'm feeling dizzy." Ken suddenly wobbled. "Any chance I could move back into our bedroom? I'm nervous about climbing those stairs."

"Of course, Ken." She quickly moved to his side. "That's a sensible suggestion."

Finally. She's forgiven him. Forgotten her grudge.

"Let's get you settled in. I'll move my things upstairs."

Chapter Forty-One

Tuesday, February 21, 2017
1:34 PM

Barking a warning, Piddles leapt off his plaid dog bed. Turning the water tap off with a squeak, Jane grabbed a dishtowel, drying her hands as she walked toward the door.

"Good. You're up." Gee stood framed in the doorway. "I wasn't sure naptime was over."

"Come in. Want a water?"

"If it's handy." She ruffled Piddle's tasseled ears. "Hey, buddy. How you doin'?" Straightening, she smoothed her cropped top over her firm midriff. "Love what you've done with the place."

Jane tossed her a generic water bottle, confused. "I haven't done much."

"It's sarcasm." Plopping onto the lone upholstered chair, she crossed her bare legs at the knee. "Wouldn't hurt to buy a few pillows. Soften the place. You know, decorate."

"It's set up the way I like it."

Peering at a neat stack of self-defense and security manuals, Gee extended a finger, pushing them out of perfect alignment. "How's the OCD?"

"Stop that." Jane re-straightened the stack. "Don't be a brat."

"Can't help it." Gee linked her fingers. "I'm nervous about our FBI interview this afternoon."

"Don't be." Jane pulled a wooden chair away from the wall. "At this point, it's purely informational. It's not an arrest."

Gee rolled her heavily mascaraed eyes. "Maybe you're used to talking to the FBI, but I'm not." Scraping her turquoise painted nails against the plastic bottle, she peeled off the damp paper label, balling it between her fingers and her thumb. "I'm all for helping Cleo and Rex, but this thing with Pops getting attacked has me worried."

"Don't get confused. When I was on the force, I had more than one active investigation at one time. The trick is keeping them straight in your mind and not connecting the unrelated dots."

"So, teach me how to be an investigator. What do we do next?"

"M-O-M. I always start my investigations with motive, opportunity, and means." Jane ticked the three items off her fingertips. "Motive is the key. Figure out what the perp was doing and why, and you'll know who did it. We know Frankie Malcolm or Steve Tanner want Marianne's songs. Or that Ken lied about making the loan payments and the loan shark sent him a message, like Leslie suggested."

"There's an easy way to answer that last one. Pied Stan's office is on Tulane, on the way to FBI headquarters." Gee checked her phone. "We have time to swing by." She paused. "Are you packing any heat?"

"Heat?" Hiding her smile, Jane hefted her backpack. "No. Feel kinda naked without it."

"How did I sound?" Gee waggled both eyebrows. "Like a PI?"

"Keep working on it." Jane swept her keys off the counter. "Be a good boy, Pid." Closing the door, she double-checked the deadbolt before following Gee across the courtyard. "What do you know about this bail guy, Gee?" She slid onto the passenger seat. "Is Pied Stan legit? What's up with his name?"

"You'll see soon enough," Gee enigmatically replied. Resting her elbow on the seatback, she easily reversed onto St. Claude Avenue. "Have you ever needed a bail bondsman?"

"I did. Bunch of slimeball parasites. Like accident attorneys. Feeding off desperation."

"They're not all like that. One Stop has serious street cred. They've been around forever." As she rummaged through the dashboard searching for her cigars, a Ziploc baggie fell to the floor mat.

Scooping it up, Jane examined the red flannel bundle inside. "Another gift from Aunt Babette?"

"A sorrow *gris-gris*." Gee released a sigh that filled her cheeks. "I'm still missing Fancy and Dee-Dee. It's cool. I know they're still around. Doing what they can in their spirit forms, helping us from the other side."

More hoodoo voodoo. Jane turned the baggie over in her hands. "What's in this *gris-gris*?"

"Oh, hell. Anything Aunt Babette can find that makes it personal. Fingernails, gold teeth, hanks of hair, shells, sequins, beads. If it catches her eye and she thinks it might offer protective magic, she picks it up. She's like a crow that way." Gee turned. "You should ask to see her collection upstairs. She's got Tupperware bins filled with stuff."

The dashboard lighter popped. Gee lit her cigar. "I know you don't understand her magic or her belief, but voodoo is part of who we are. And don't take this the wrong way, but I don't think you understand our laws." She puffed. "The authorities are not the good guys. They are not on our side. We've bent the laws for three hundred years just to get along, to survive. And people still do stupid shit. They get into jams. Court dates take months." She flicked her fingers down the road. "Places like One Stop help. You don't want family members sitting in lockup, so we use them, like what Pops did with Maman and Aunt Babette."

"I'll try to keep an open mind."

"S'all I ask." Gee happily tapped the ash off her cigar. "Just look how much your life has changed since you started doing that."

"True, dat." Jane rested her elbow on the door. "I've nailed two hate-crime serial killers, I'm working on my second security assignment in ninety days, and I'm about to launch a private investigation agency with my new best friend, who's a transgender woman."

"Welcome to life." Gee laughed brightly as she resettled her tortoise shell sunglasses. "Is NOLA a great town, or what?"

Chapter Forty-Two

Same Day
2:19 PM

NOLA's gritty underbelly became more obvious the closer they got to the Broad Street intersection. Tulane Avenue was an aged thoroughfare lined with struggling independent small businesses, mostly Asian-themed massage studios, sketchy insurance agencies, and discount liquor stores. The nondescript two-story yellow brick storefronts they passed looked rabid with bad luck.

Jane felt cotton mouthed. "This is depressing."

"No reason to visit unless you need to." Gee pointed her cigar at a city block long colonnade of Corinthian columns. "Orleans Parish Criminal District Court. You ever get summoned for jury duty this is where you'll report."

"Don't wish that on me. I'm trying to fly under the radar." Jane grimly studied the courthouse. Its matching blocky Art Deco terminals looked like weather-stained concrete bunker holdouts from the last world war. "I swore I'd never step inside another courthouse."

"Welcome to One Stop." Gee bumped The Boat into a crumbling asphalt parking lot before swinging left, parking crooked, and taking two spaces.

The fifties' molded plastic sign hanging in front of the office was sun-faded with age, but a neon green fixture glared OPEN in the central plate glass window. Two smaller smoked glass windows on either side were plastered with shoe polished slogans: **One Stop Bail Bonds. Family Owned. 504-GET-FREE. Jesus is Lord. Your Friends in the Bail Bond Business.**

Jane scanned the street for loitering local interest and checked the sky for rain. "You putting the top up?"

"Should be good as it is." Gee tucked her cigars and the keys into her knock-off Chanel bag. "They've got security cameras."

Striding across the lot, she pressed the call button next to the door. The lock clicked and an alarm buzzed overhead until the door latched behind them.

Would you look at this. No bulletproof Plexiglas walls. Jane was surprised to see a sleek office environment. A streamlined row of desks projected from the left wall. Each desk was manned by two-person teams of youngish-looking associates wearing wireless Bluetooth headsets as they pecked away at laptop workstations. Soothing cool jazz classics floated from the ceiling-mounted speakers. A young woman in a navy polo shirt demurely folded her hands around her lengthy nail extensions as she approached.

"How can I help you?"

"Has Pied Stan got a minute?" Gee asked.

"This is in regards to a bond, or a loan?"

"Both."

"I'll see if he's available." Heading for a back room, she leaned into a doorway. "Stan? Someone's asking for you."

"Be right there."

Jane stepped back as Pied Stan filled the doorway. *Good Lord. He's six-six if he's an inch.* A Black male with a bald head and a face softened only by a seventies' porn star mustache, Pied Stan wore an impressive amount of gold jewelry including a diamond bezel Rolex watch strapped to his left wrist, two high-caret diamond pinky rings, and a rocking Cuban-link necklace bearing a weighty crucifix pendant showing suffering Jesus on the cross.

"You wanted to see me?"

What is on his face? Jane suddenly felt a profound loss for words. Skin pigment was missing from Pied Stan's jawline, resulting in a pale pink patch that completely encircled his mouth, his nose, and worked its way up both cheeks. Similar pinky patches covered most of his forearms and the back of his hands.

"I'm Gigi Pascoe." Gee stepped forward. "This is Jane Byrne. We wanted to ask you about a loan you made to Ken Pascoe, my dad."

"Take a seat." Pied Stan waved at a pair of chairs and a button upholstered couch. "I've heard of you, Gigi Pascoe." He spoke like he was counting his words.

"Call me Gee." She set her purse down neatly next to her feet.

"Hum." Narrowing his eyes, he studied her cropped midriff top, her fitted black mini skirt, her open toed sandals, and her turquoise nail polish. "And what are you supposed to be?"

"That's obvious." Gee didn't hesitate. "I'm fabulous."

"You certainly are." He guffawed, resting his hands on his stomach. "I've got a feeling you and me got something in common. People been looking at me funny all my life. I'm betting you know something 'bout that." He thumbed a pale patch on his forearm. "Your friend here, she's trying her best to hide it, but I can see she's wondering." The chair cracked as he stretched out his hand. "Boo! Watch out. Might be catching."

Chuckling, he sat back. "No, you can't. It's vitiligo. Had it since I was a kid. Runs in my family. We lose pigment in our skin. These patches keep getting bigger as I get older. I live long enough, I'm gonna die White."

He roared at his own joke. "There, my job is done. I made you uncomfortable. Now, what did you want to know?"

"The loan you made with my dad. Is he in trouble with it?"

"I can't tell you that. That loan was between me and him." He rubbed the crucifix pendant. "Confidentiality is my business. People trust me to keep certain private things private."

"Let me lay it out." Gee leaned in. "Pops got attacked yesterday, at home. Someone put him in the hospital."

"And you think it was me?"

"Was it?" Jane asked.

"That's insulting." He gave Jane a dead stare. "You think I'm that kinda thug?"

"Are you?" She persisted.

He studied Gee. "Who's this beyatch you're hanging with?"

"A friend, helping me sort through things."

"Some friend. I'll help you as much as I can." He tapped his knee. "My family's been in the bail bond and loan business for sixty-two years. Three generations." He pointed at the desk teams. "You see them kids? That's my personal community business training program. They work for me earning credits for their GREs."

He smoothed his sausage-sized fingers across the *Luke 18:7-8* printed on his tight T-shirt. "People come to One Stop because helping folks is my calling. I hear the Lord's Word every day. You ask anybody, and I mean anybody on the street if One Stop ever put a hit out over a loan. They're gonna say 'no,' because violence goes against my faith." He laid his hand over his heart. "I am my brother's keeper."

"I believe you," Gee stated.

"I know you're trying to do the right thing," he continued. "Let me ease your mind. Your father's loan is current. Whatever you got going on at your house, it wasn't me or mine."

"Thank you. One more thing." Gee quickly keyed some text into her phone. "Say for some reason Pops came into some money. Unexpected. Could he pay off his loan early?"

"I would love to see your father do that. Early payoff is a One Stop policy." Pied Stan sounded sincere. "I meant it when I said we're trying to help people. I know he wants that Fender back."

"Fender?" Gee gaped. "Pops gave you his guitar?"

"As collateral security. Nice piece." Pied Stan turned both hands palm side up. "Asked me to switch it out for the house on his note.

Not the smartest business decision I ever made, but I sleep good at night."

It must've killed Ken to hand over that guitar.

Gee looked enlightened. "That's why Pops wants the album advance. So he can un-hock his guitar."

"I've got it put up safe. Locked in storage."

"Climate controlled?" Jane pounced.

"That makes a difference?"

"I know something about it."

"This doesn't make sense." Gee looked confused. "If Pops swapped his guitar for the Big House on his note, why hasn't he told Maman? They're still fussin' over it."

"Stan?" The young woman shouted across the room. "It's getting on to three."

"I hear you." He rose like a sequoia. "Got a court date across the street. Stacking up like jets at Louis Armstrong Airport."

"It's a wise man who fights for justice." Gee reached for her purse. "Luke 18:7-8."

"Clever girl." Pied Stan resettled his watch. "Don't need to be a man to fight for freedom. 'All you have to do is be an intelligent human being.'"

"Who said that?" Jane wondered. "Jesus?"

"Another revolutionary." Pied Stan knowingly smiled. "Malcolm X."

Chapter Forty-Three

Same Day
3:13 PM

"What's your take?" Gee wondered. "Do we believe Pied Stan?"

"For now. He corroborated what Ken said about his loan." Jane studied the desolate landscape along Leon C. Simon Drive. The dead flat, empty city lots were dotted with cockeyed electric meter poles and scarred by deep waterlogged ruts. "Man, there is nothing out here."

"Katrina wiped this ward clean when the levees failed." Gee finished her Bigfoot Ultra Watermelon high energy drink. "Lakefront Airport was about the only place to survive." She grew grim. "You ever been through a Category Five hurricane?"

"No."

"You don't need to worry about what gets left behind because nothing *gets* left behind. Even this FBI field office is new. Katrina ripped the roof off the old one downtown." Her stomach growled. "We shoulda picked up some chicken when we stopped for gas. Now I'm hungry."

"I will never get used to the idea of buying fried chicken from a gas station. There's something fundamentally wrong with it."

"Don't be such a Yankee. Fuel Mart is a gas station *restaurant*. Their chicken is good eating. So are their oysters." Gee playfully shook her finger. "Your northerner prejudice is holding you back from enjoying some major deliciousness."

"Seriously, Gee. You would eat oysters you bought at a gas station."

"If they were fried," Gee happily replied. "S'part of our cuisine. Called a po'boy. Also made with shrimp. Sprinkle on some ghost pepper hot sauce and you got the best hangover remedy in the universe. White bread and hot grease soaks up all the leftover alcohol. Detoxifies your liver."

"I doubt that. Are you feeling hungover? You'll need to be on your toes during your interview."

"Why?" Gee suddenly looked worried. "Is this some kinda trap?"

"No. I think they're playing fair with us so far by asking us to come in voluntarily. They could've just as easily stopped by the Big House unannounced and talked to us there."

"Are they allowed to do that? What happened to 'my home is my castle'?"

"They have very broad powers. They can also swing by your place of employment and speak to you in front of your boss and your associates."

She snorted. "The girls at Club Oz would love that."

"It's a tactic they use to startle people into sharing information." Jane turned sideways as much as her seatbelt allowed. "Trust me, Gee. They know exactly what they're doing. They've got these interviews down to a science. Literally." She shifted. "Don't forget, once you get in there, you get to set the terms and conditions. Don't get spooked by any of their bullshit. You're not under arrest. If you feel like you're getting in too deep, back out. Demand an attorney and shut up. That'll drop an anchor on them. Full stop."

"Who pays for the attorney?"

"You'd need to. Just stick to the truth. You're simply being interviewed as a witness. You're not a criminal. And don't try to charm them or try to be funny. It might backfire."

"You're making this sound serious."

"It is serious. An agent's only goal is to secure the evidence they need for their investigation. They're not going to protect your rights or your interests. When you're in there, you need to act as your own best advocate. Special agents may act friendly, but they're not your friend. Remember that. Don't fall for it if they try."

"How do you know this?"

"I looked into working for the FBI once. *Five years and a lifetime ago.* "Seems like a dream." Jane toyed with her seatbelt. "When I was working with Cesar Mayas." *Should I ask her?* "Have you heard from him lately?"

Gee's face pinched shut. "He ghosted me."

"Sorry to hear that. I thought you two might have something special."

"We did have something special." She sounded brittle. "A one-night love affair. *C'est la vie. C'est la guerre.*" Reaching into the console, she shook a cigar from her pack. "I can't believe they scheduled our interviews for three-thirty. Who's awake at this time of day? I'm missing my disco nap."

Nice deflection. I'll play. "Disco nap?"

"It's the afternoon siesta I take so I can stay up all night dancing." The lighter popped and she lit her cigar. "Don't you take disco naps? With your vampire schedule at the cemetery?"

"Not really." Jane shifted uncomfortably. "I don't sleep much." *Panic attacks and PTSD see to it that I never do.*

"How much sleep do you get?"

"On average? About four hours." Jane picked at her nails. "Six if I'm lucky."

"Sounds 'bout right. Me, too." Gee stubbed out the cigar. "Feels like I could sleep for days. Never seem to get the chance."

"Slugging down those high energy drinks probably contributes to that."

"Better living through chemicals." Slowing The Boat, Gee turned into an access lane leading to a high-security gate. "Any idea of where to park?"

UP JUMPED THE DEVIL

"Ask him." Jane pointed to a stocky silhouette outlined against the bulletproof sentry box window. "He'll tell us where to go."

Chapter Forty-Four

Jane shivered. The air conditioned temperature in the NOLA FBI interview room was cranked so low the vents sounded like jet engines. Her metal chair sent a chill through her jeans into her thigh muscles, making her tailbone ache. *Clever ploy, rat bastids, but I know just what you're doing. Deliberately keep the room frigid and immediately split us up to increase my anxiety. Nice try, boys, but it won't work. I memorized your FBI training manual.*

Even expecting it, she jumped when the door clicked. Her sinuses immediately registered the amber aroma of his high-end designer cologne. She felt momentarily discomfited as the scent memory overrode her focus, triggering a pleasurable tingle that tickled her core.

"Jane. S'good to see you again."

FBI Special Agent Win Carter slid onto the opposite chair before sharing the world's greatest smile. Win's eyeteeth were slightly overlarge which made him appear wolfish but that did nothing to detract from his overall high-voltage appeal. *Crissakes!* Jane felt intoxicated. *I forgot Win was such a sex bomb.*

"Don't mind me." Setting down a legal pad, he repeatedly clicked a ballpoint pen. "I'm going to take notes. Old school. Tried using an iPad but I can't seem to stay organized. I'll incorporate my notes into a 302, later."

"302?" Jane asked, still feeling dazed.

"FBI Interview Report Form FD-302." Win repeated his killer smile. "That's the official term for it."

Win wore a slim gold neck chain, a status watch with an alligator leather strap, and no wedding band. The watch face read Piaget Altiplano, upside down. The rose gold bezel looked warm against his bronze skin. Jane tested her brakes. *Remember, he's an information broker, looking to gather evidence on possible violations of federal law. He is not a friend.*

"Thanks for agreeing to meet with me. I look forward to working with you again. How've you been?"

"I'm good," Jane started slowly, struggling to refocus. "Got a new position. Head of security for Catholic Cemeteries. It's a solid gig. Better than what I had before. More of a challenge."

"Guardian Self Storage. I remember. Still working nights?"

"Seems to come with the territory." She shrugged.

"Still living in The Bywater? Same apartment?"

"It suits me. I like the location, and the Pascoes. Nice folks."

"Still got the dog?" He hesitated for a split second. "A standard poodle, right?"

"Piddles? Yeah, he's still running around. Doing fine."

"Glad to hear it. That's a good report." Win squared the legal pad against the table. "I've already talked with NOPD Detective Shelli Trahan. I'm sure you know where I'm going with this. I've read her reports. I believe her preliminary investigation into the missing NOLA homeless persons has merit. Has legs."

He doodled a star on the paper. "We're getting involved because our bureau has a history partnering with local law enforcement agencies due to NOLA's nature as an active seaport." His shoulders relaxed. "Special Agent Billups Harris was in charge in 1911. F.C. Pendleton was special agent in charge in 1914. We go way back."

"Sounds like a final Jeopardy question." Jane smiled to remove any sting from her words. "I've heard about federal involvement in NOLA. Mostly when you Feds shut Storyville down."

"Ah, Storyville. The red-light birthplace of jazz." Win crooked his neck. "Just to be clear, that wasn't us. Technically, the U.S. Navy issued the order prohibiting prostitution within five miles of military sites although – to be fair we might have had some jurisdictional authority under The Mann Act if the bureau had decided to enforce it."

"In any case, it was the federal government."

"In any case, yes, it was." Win spun the pen through his fingers. "I can see you've done some homework."

"It came up during a private investigation. I've also talked with Detective Trahan about the missing homeless people, and I agree with her, and with you." *Why do I feel so defensive? Like Win needs to see I've been busy.* "Something is going on."

"Great." Leaning forward, Win looked alert. "Let's facilitate a mutual exchange of information. I'll go first. What do you think that is?"

Nice trick. Lobbing the focus back to me. "I think we're looking at a criminal conspiracy. A black market operation illegally harvesting human organs for transplants."

"Let's discuss that." He smoothly adjusted his cuffs. "Detective Trahan suggested that we should ask you and Ms. Pascoe about what you both overheard recently at Charity Hospital."

"I figured that was the trigger." Paranoia stole Jane's next breath. She throttled her anxiety. "You're asking me this in a conversational way, right? You're not formulating any charges for either one of us. Because if that's what you're doing, I want an attorney."

"Jane," Win protested. "Yes, I'm taking notes, but this is purely an informational conversation. We're friends, right? I asked you an open question. Just tell me why you were at Charity Hospital. What did you see or hear?"

Jane moistened her parched lips. *Tell the barebones truth.* "We were investigating potential sites for a Mardi Gras krewe party. Someone suggested using Charity Hospital. We went there to look."

"And?"

"While we were in the lobby, we heard a security guard talking to a woman. A lady. She sounded cultured. Educated. Classy."

UP JUMPED THE DEVIL

Win looked intent. "Any guess as to who this woman was?"

"Haven't a clue. We never saw them face to face." Jane scanned her battle scarred memory. "She called him 'Denis.' He mentioned working with a doctor. Then Denis chased us out of the building."

"He chased you out of a posted construction zone."

Are you testing me, Win? Trying to trip me up to get me flustered? Jane refused to surrender her focus. "While we were in Charity Hospital, we saw fresh blood splatter in the operating theater." Feeling a rising investigative excitement, Jane leaned in. "The room still had power. It looked recently scrubbed. Win, I'm telling you, it looked sketchy as hell. And Rex Duchamp seems to think he was originally held at Charity Hospital before he got moved to a new location."

Win scribbled a quick note.

"I know DeltaCare is releasing Rex tomorrow. I assume you're taking him into custody. What are your plans for Rex and his sister?"

Digging his pen into the legal pad, Win remained silent.

"Win, I need to know. These people are my concern." Jane stretched out both hands. "I come from law enforcement. I know how the game is played. I need to know what you're doing to protect them, so I can formulate my response. You need to trust me." *Don't say another word. Let him be the first one to break the silence. Don't even blink.*

Win's biceps stretched his sleeves as he folded his arms. "They're going into WITSEC. The application's been accepted by the U.S. Attorney General's Office."

"Good call." Jane sighed. *WITSEC. The Federal Witness Security Program.* "Does Rex know this?"

"Yes. We explained it to him very carefully. He seemed relieved."

"How did Cleo react?"

"Not as happy as Rex until we explained they'd be getting a combined subsistence stipend of sixty grand a year." Win's eyebrows nearly met as he frowned. "The sister seems more aware of the overall situation. More aware of the danger Rex is in as a key witness. It obviously weighs on her mind. Evidently, he's the only family she has left."

"I like that plan." Jane cracked a grin. "In the 'spirit of our ongoing mutual exchange of information,' what's your next step in the conspiracy investigation?"

Pressing both hands together, Win tapped his chin. "I'll continue to work closely with NOPD. Look into feeder labs, check them against transplant hospitals. See if anything jibes. Why? You got another suggestion?"

"Lean on Denis, the Charity Hospital security guard. Make him cough up the name of the woman we overheard. And get the name of that doctor."

"I would love to do that." Win studied his pen. "Just can't."

"Why are you ignoring such a great lead?"

Win double clicked the pen. "He's in the city morgue. Dead of a fentanyl overdose. His landlady called it in."

Chapter Forty-Five

Wednesday, February 22, 2017
1:17 PM

Cleo Duchamp sat huddled in The Boat's back seat, her knees tucked up under her chin. She looked red-eyed and miserable.

"Still not sure 'bout this," she muttered, resting one elbow on the glittery purple suitcase. "Feels like I'm stuck on train tracks, and I can't get off. What do y'all know about this witness protection program? It legit?"

"Win said they walked you through it," Jane said. "Why didn't you ask questions then?"

"They didn't want to hear from me." Cleo looked sullen. "They was mostly focused on Rex."

"He is the key witness to a potential federal felony." Jane threaded the seatbelt strap end through her fingers. "The prosecutor probably thinks his testimony is critical to the criminal case, not yours." *Play nice.* Her conscience stirred. Turning sideways, she softened her statement. "That said, both of you are high risk."

Cleo hugged herself tighter. "You're not helping."

"You both signed a Memorandum of Understanding going over the WITSEC rules though, right?"

"Yeah, they made us sign something. That FBI agent wasn't much help."

"Win Carter?" Jane felt irrationally defensive. "He's not affiliated with WITSEC. He's the case agent on the FBI investigation. It's two different things from two different agencies."

"Win?" Raising one eyebrow, Gee teased.

Jane refused the bait. "The FBI was only the requesting law enforcement agency. Special Agent Carter submitted your protection request to the OEO. After that, they turned your case over to the U.S. Marshals Service and the U.S. Attorney General's Office."

"Where's your phone?" Ignoring busy traffic, Gee scanned the passenger side of The Boat. "Are you Googling these answers?"

"All this information is in my head."

"Okay, Sherlock. I'm still learning. I'll bite. What's an OEO?"

"The Office of Enforcement Operations. Part of the U.S. Department of Justice." Jane rattled it off. "I used to get tested on this 'quiz jizz.' It's funny the things you remember."

"Too many strangers. Too much control." Cleo visibly wilted. "Starting to feel like I did 'bout foster care." She stared at the suitcase. "Rex and me hated that."

"WITSEC is a huge federal program," Jane commiserated. "At least you'll be safe. Once the hospital releases Rex, the Deputy Marshals will step in and off you'll go."

"They said they already had the other place ready for us. We'll be leaving NOLA right away."

Pulling into the DeltaCare parking lot, Gee searched for a spot. "Did they say where you're going?"

"She can't tell us that, Gee. They're getting totally anonymous new lives. New identities, new names, new documents."

"Maybe so." Gee shoved The Boat into park. "But you'll still have us."

"No, Gee, they won't." Releasing her seatbelt buckle, Jane stepped from the car. "They'll get cut off from all previous contacts, including us."

Cleo raised her red burner phone. "How'd they know if I sent you a text?"

"They'll know. First off, they'll confiscate that phone. Give you a new one." Jane grabbed the suitcase. "Once you enter WITSEC, you'll only be able to communicate through the Marshals Service."

"Not sure I like that." Cleo picked at her lower lip.

Jane rolled the suitcase toward the main entrance. "The Marshals Service is totally in charge. If something happens and they think your security's been compromised, they'll shift you and Rex to another location and give you fresh identities again."

Passing through a shady patch, Cleo slowed. "Wish we had another pick."

"You're up against the federal machine. Not to be harsh, but the Feds always win."

Gee thoughtfully juggled her car keys. "I don't think I could ever leave NOLA. Lose everyone I know. Leave everything behind."

"I need to be brave for Rex." Cleo firmed her lips. "He needs me to protect him." She took the suitcase. "Don't have a choice."

I'll play Devil's Advocate. Win should've explained this to her. "You do have a choice, Cleo. You and Rex can leave WITSEC if you ever decide you wanted to. You're not imprisoned, or under arrest. The only catch is that you'll lose federal protection the minute you two walk out the door." Jane felt an uneasy ripple. *As good as WITSEC is, it goes against human nature. Some witnesses can't stay gone. They can't resist returning to their old lives, their established habits, their family, and their friends.*

"I gotta do this." Cleo's shoulders slumped. She looked young, defenseless, and defeated. "We need to hole up someplace safe 'til Rex heals up."

Chapter Forty-Six

Pushing through DeltaCare's security door, Jane immediately noted Win Carter standing with a second FBI special agent near a cluster of barrel-backed chairs. Both agents wore good suits and status watches. Win's suit was more fashionably cut, showcasing slimmer trouser legs. His blazer was unbuttoned with his FBI agency badge prominently clipped to his black leather belt. *Looking dapper.* His bald head shone, and Jane's incurable curiosity flared. *How does he get his scalp looking buffed like that? Does he use wax?*

She also noticed two U.S. Deputy Marshals standing by the elevator bank. Both men looked irritated. *Their street uniform obviously represents the opposite end of the fashion spectrum.* The marshals wore khaki trousers under navy blue jackets emblazoned with the words U.S. MARSHAL in bold yellow letters across their backs. To underline their authority, they had MARSHAL printed sideways down both sleeves. Jane bit her lip. *Obviously overcompensating for something.* Star badge logos were embroidered over the brims on their ballcaps, and they carried handcuffs and service weapons on their duty belts. *Open carry in a medical center. Nice look.*

Catching sight of the marshals, Cleo froze. "This looks badong. Where's my brother?"

Jane pointed. "Special Agent Carter will know."

"Don't be nervous," Gee chorused. "We're not leaving you alone."

Seeing them, Win strode over trailed by the second special agent. "Good. You're here. This is Special Agent Abel Guidry from the NOLA bureau. He's assisting me. Listen, there's been a delay."

Cleo gasped. "Why? What's wrong?"

"Rex complained of a severe headache at breakfast. They took him downstairs for a CT scan."

"Rex had a stroke?" She trembled. "That's how MawMaw died."

"They're checking on it." Win offered a calming gesture using both hands. "An infection is also a possibility. They're running bloodwork tests. Remember, Rex came in rough."

Cleo danced in place. "I want to see him."

Special Agent Guidry stepped closer. "Not until they bring him back to his room. Don't worry, Ms. Duchamp. Your brother is in very capable hands. The aide will bring him up as soon as the scanning is over."

"How long does that ... CT scan take?"

"Less than an hour."

Win frowned. "The delay is that the lab needs twenty-four hours to process the results. Rex needs to stay in the Medical Center until he's stabilized and been released. Meaning," He massaged his left thumb. "The Deputy Marshals can't move you to the safe house until then."

"That's why they look pissed," Jane archly stated. "They'll need to come back tomorrow and do this all over again."

Special Agent Guidry snorted. "Don't worry 'bout them. They're getting paid."

Cleo suddenly squirmed. "Which ways the bathroom?"

Gee studied a lobby card. "Should be one by that emergency exit."

"Be right back." Cleo snatched her suitcase.

"Leave it," Gee kindly offered. "I'll watch it for you."

"Rather not. It's got my stuff plus I brought Rex Funyuns. They're his favorite." She quickly rolled away.

"Look how nervous she is." Jane stared at Win. "No wonder. Poor kid. They already mistrust the system and look what you're feeding them into." She flicked her fingers at the two rock solid Deputy Marshals. "Cleo's hiding it, but I bet she's terrified."

Chapter Forty-Seven

"They can reconsider their situation once the investigation is closed," Win temporized as his phone trilled. Glancing at the text message, he cocked his thumb at his fellow special agent. "Let's step over there. We need to take this."

"Gee, are we staying?" Picking at the dry skin on her palm, Jane glanced down the hallway. *No sign of Cleo yet.* "She'll need a ride home."

"I wasn't planning on sticking around. Could be a problem. Promised Krewdio-54 I'd help finish our parade costumes today. Big party weekend comin' up."

"You go do that. I'll stay. Call us an Uber when she's ready to go."

"Thanks, but no. I can spare another hour. Listen. Clue me in. What's our next step after they enter that witness protection program?"

"Win made a great suggestion at my interview. He's going to research feeder labs and transplant hospitals. See if anything looks off. We won't get any intel off that dead security guard, but Win might luck across names for that lady and the doctor we heard about."

"And he'll tell us that?"

"No. Absolutely not. He'll keep that intel to himself."

"No way you can worm it out of him using your feminine charms?"

"I'm not doing that, Gee. I'm a professional. That's not how I work. Make a note. That's not how we'll work."

"Fine. So, that's not gonna help us. What do we do?"

Jane considered their options. "I think we should talk to Dr. Sabatier at the Coroner's Office again. She's had time to think it over. She may have come up with something more. She helped us before. She might help us again."

UP JUMPED THE DEVIL

Gee looked eager. "When we're PIs, is this how it works? This is our day job?"

"As long as a client pays us to do it." Jane grimly kept her eye on the prize. "We'd talk to people, collect and check the facts. Figure out what really happened which is tricky because every witness has a different story, a different perspective, a different personal take. That can throw you at first." She started pacing. "And then, there's always that one goddamned question that nobody asks but when someone does ask it, it blows the investigation wide open."

Gee looked spellbound. "Snap. What's the question?"

Jane laughed. "That's the trick because it's a different question with every case. And nobody knows what the question is until it gets asked. But when that happens, Gee, it's the best goddamn feeling in the world because that's when you know you've got it on the run." A flutter of pure nostalgic memory briefly feathered her soul. "There's surveillance work, too, but that's not as exciting."

She paused as one of the marshals cocked his head to listen to his shoulder mic. Muttering something unintelligible, he clapped his partner's shoulder before urgently thumbing the elevator's call button.

"Gee? Look. Something's up."

Win Carter and Special Agent Guidry sped across the lobby toward them before skidding to a stop. Win looked furious. The veins stood out in his neck.

"Rex Duchamp is MIA. The aide went to get him. He's not in the CT center. Did you two have something to do with this?"

"Hell, no." Jane protested.

"Where'd he go?" Gee tucked her chin. "He's blind."

Win spun around. "Where's his sister? Where's Cleo Duchamp?"

"Still in the bathroom." Gee pointed down the hall.

"Secure all exits," Win ordered his junior partner. "Work with the marshals. Check the stairwells, the emergency doors. Find those kids."

He raced for the bathroom, Jane and Gee hard on his heels. They skidded to a stop before a door bearing an oblong blue silhouette of a cartoonish human wearing a dress. The door was clearly labeled WOMEN.

Win dropped his chin to his chest before heavily thumping the door with his fist.

"FBI." He bellowed. "I'm coming in." Placing his palm against the door, he shoved it open.

"I'm coming with you." Jane immediately followed him in.

"Me, too." Gee gleefully sidled in sideways. Rising onto her toes like a ballerina, she splayed both hands like starfish. "And I am *in*. I've wanted to shatter this glass ceiling for decades. Decades!"

Washing her hands at the sink, the single bathroom occupant shrieked. "Y'all can't come in here," she shouted, aghast. "This here's a ladies' room."

"FBI, ma'am," Win displayed his badge while refusing to meet her eyes. Striding down the stalls, he batted each unlocked door open, slamming it into the wall with a gunshot bang.

"Maybe you're FBI." The woman gave Gee a withering up-and-down stare. "But he's not a woman."

"Relax," Jane stated. "She's more of a girl than you are."

"Thank you kindly, Jane," Gee said as the affronted woman scurried by.

"Motherfucker. She's gone." Win angrily stabbed his phone with his index finger. Gritting his teeth, he looked betrayed. "If you two had anything to do with this, you are going down."

Clapping the phone to his ear, he turned and sprinted for the lobby.

"Going down?" Gee playfully tapped her chin. "I'm game. Jane? Any chance you think he meant it?"

"For fuck's sake, Gee. Please," Jane begged. "We are hip deep in canned shit. We need to find Rex and Cleo ASAP and prove we're not a part of this. We cannot fuck with the Feds."

"If we do find them, we're not giving them up." Gee stubbornly insisted. "They trust us. If they decided to leave, they need our help. I'll text Cleo. See what she says."

Tapping her keypad, Gee sent a text.

"*Merde.*" She gasped, surprised. "I'm blocked."

She tried again. "No. It's disabled."

"Let me see." Jane snatched the phone, looking up in wide-eyed wonder. "Cleo removed her SIM card. She knew they could use it to track her." Glittering golden sparkles melted along her peripheral vision as her blood pressure spiked. "She's way ahead of us. Where do we even look?"

Confidently unsnapping her purse, Gee pulled out her key ring. "I'd say we check Fancy's house. Faubourg-Marigny, don't you think?"

Chapter Forty-Eight

Same Day
3:06 PM

Gee leapt up the steps of Fancy Abellard's bungalow, taking them two at a time. The sheltering porch threw a triangle of dense shade over a coconut fiber doormat that read *Drink Up, Bitches*. Lifting the mat, she retrieved a house key.

"Yet another great security system," Jane tersely noted.

"Works for me." Unlocking the deadbolt, Gee shouldered the door open. "Hello, the house," she yelled, stepping into the parlor. "Where y'at?"

Golden dust motes spun in cascading spirals, stirred by the breeze.

"Check the bedroom." Gee disappeared into Fancy's dressing room. "And the back of the house."

Jane strode toward the kitchen, checking first to make sure the back door was still bolted from the inside and that the single double-hung window was latched. Everything appeared to be shipshape until she lifted the lid on the garbage can.

"Gee? When Cleo left this morning, she packed to go."

Gee slid into the doorway. "How do you know?"

"She took supplies." Fastidiously reaching past a mound of damp coffee grounds and cracked eggshells, Jane lifted a discarded plastic ring from a purified water six-pack that sat on top of an empty box of yogurt trail mix bars and the plastic overwrap off a pack of generic bathroom tissue.

"She knew she was leaving WITSEC." Jane dusted her hands. "She planned it. She probably had these supplies in her suitcase." She straightened. "You find anything?"

"The First Aid kit is missing, and she took every painkiller in the house." Gee opened the door to the refrigerator's freezer compartment. "*Merde*. She boosted my emergency vodka."

"You have emergency vodka?"

"Yes, for emergencies." Gee sounded defensive. "Jane? Back in the car? She was asking for help. We didn't listen."

Guilt sank its fangs into Jane's gut. "It's not too late. We can still help. We just need to find them."

"Think they'll use the warehouse?"

"That flops been cleared. They'll go somewhere new. Somewhere we don't know about."

"Like where?"

"They could be anywhere."

"Dead end." Lifting the garbage bag from the bin, Gee efficiently tied it off. "Does this happen a lot?"

"Dead ends?" Jane waited as Gee re-bolted the front door. "Nothing's over yet. We just need to switch gears. Investigate another thread, like figuring out who attacked Ken." She watched as Gee easily tossed the garbage into an alley dumpster. "Keep juggling different things."

"Is this how investigations work?"

"That's how it happened on the force." Jane slid into The Boat. "I used to work three, maybe four different investigative lines at the same time. The trick is doing just what we're doing today, making a tiny bit of progress on each case every day, and never putting it down until it gets resolved. Over time, the baby steps add up."

"Three or four different cases." Gee angled The Boat into the Marigny Street traffic. "You think we'll see that much PI work?"

"We will if we keep solving cases. Word'll hit the street. Word of mouth is the best way to grow the agency." Jane relaxed. "People love gossiping about their problems. Fix their problems and they'll find us."

"Like the bad ass street cred Pied Stan has." Gee turned left. "What's our next 'baby step'?"

"M-O-M on Ken. I think Pied Stan is in the clear. That leaves us with Frankie Malcolm or Steve Tanner, your new surprise uncle. They both want Marianne's songbooks. That makes them persons of interest under motivation."

"Or some street thug got lucky finding an unlocked back door, like Pops said."

"Leslie said nothing from the Big House got stolen." Jane suddenly felt satisfied. *Crissakes. I love discussing a case with a partner again. I've missed doing this.* "Do you recall where Frankie Malcolm was staying?"

"Frenchman's Inn. On Decatur. 212-836-7412."

"How do you remember that off the top of your head?"

"Just do." Gee shrugged. "Saw it on his business card same as you. Text him. See if he's available. I'd do it but I'm driving." Crow's feet crinkled her eyes as she shared a shit-eating grin. "And since I'm a full partner, not an Admin."

Chapter Forty-Nine

Same Day
3:54 PM

"This way." Gee opened an ornately carved wooden door leading into a sophisticated black and white marble-tiled lobby. "Frankie said he'd meet us in the inner courtyard."

Slowing, Jane admired an oil portrait of a Creole beauty wearing a daring off-the-shoulder black satin dress that highlighted her flawless creamy skin. The painting hung above a mottled porphyry mantlepiece, flanked by two bronze urns supported by plump gilded cupids.

"This place sure looks French." She trotted to catch up. "Was it a brothel?"

"Get your mind out of the gutter," Gee chided. "This ain't Storyville." She strode toward Reception. "It was a bakery. You know how serious the French are about baguettes. Back in the day, Old Man River was so close they heaved flour sacks straight off the steamboats through the front door."

"When did they move the river?"

"Nobody moves the river. The Mississippi moves itself. *Bonjour*." Gee slid her elbow onto the marble countertop. "Which way to the courtyard?"

"Yes, sir. Down the lobby, left at the French doors." The clerk gestured like he was guiding an airplane. "Then straight through to the pool."

"*Merci*." Gee slapped the counter with her palm. "Straight through to the pool," she repeated. Turning aside, she looked devilish. "We're deep in the *Vieux Carré*, Jane. Want to bet how many dead bodies they dug up putting in the pool?"

"I know they didn't dig up any live ones. And you can't scare me. I've seen *Poltergeist*."

Jane followed Gee into the slate-paved courtyard. Looking up, she scanned the two-story gingerbread style galleries. *They built those long windows way before air conditioning, to catch any available breeze.* Her nose tickled. *Imagine what that smelled like. No deodorant and everyone smoking and drinking nasty-ass swamp water. No wonder they died so young.* Feeling the pull of the city's history, she shivered. *Three hundred years of French, Spanish, French again, American, Creole, Cajun, you name it and all of it blending to make NOLA unique.* Jane shrugged off the uncomfortable prickling feeling between her shoulder blades. *And all of those ghosts are up there watching me. Eek! I hope they're friendly.*

"Ladies?" Sitting at a cast-iron café table, Frankie Malcolm raised his coffee cup. "How are you this fine day?"

"Excellent." Gee slid onto a chair. "Thanks for meeting with us."

"No problem."

His lime and balsam pine cologne rode the breeze. Jane sneezed.

"*Gesundheit*." Frankie pointed at a carafe. "Coffee?"

"I'd love a cup," Jane said.

"Help yourself. There's plenty. I don't usually drink coffee this late in the day, but NOLA coffee is the richest I've ever tasted. I can't seem to get enough."

"It's the chicory." Gee impatiently wiggled. "S'posed to help detoxify your liver."

"You'd certainly need that down here." Frankie shared a low-key chuckle. "This being the booze binging capital of the universe." He contentedly patted his belly. "I don't know how much longer I can afford to stay in NOLA. I'm up six, maybe seven pounds just from the boudin gravy and the shrimp and grits. I can't stop eating. Your cuisine is insane."

"Where's your partner?" Gee scanned the courtyard. "The lady lawyer?"

"Serena?" Frankie smoothed his patterned silk tie. "Flew back to New York. Sudden family emergency. Family first. One of the few unconventional business rules I insist on."

"Sorry to hear that." Jane picked up her cup. "When did she leave?"

"Monday afternoon. Right after she took the call." Picking up his cup, Frankie looked sly. "So, where do we stand? Did you bring me those songbooks? Any chance I'll be seeing those today?"

"No." Gee hesitated. "But that is partly why we're here."

"What's up?"

"Someone broke into the Pascoe's house." Jane sipped. "Ken was attacked."

"Oh my God." Frankie blanched. "Is he okay?"

"Pops is now. Got a concussion and some stitches."

"We're trying to figure out who attacked him."

"And you think it was me?" Frankie's face crumpled as his voice rose.

"Was it?"

"No!" His neck flushed an ugly mottled red. "I don't know what you two are playing at, but I've built my forty-year career working with creative artists with respect." His index finger drilled the table. "I wouldn't be where I am today if I did it any differently. I am a professional promoter. Ask anyone. My business practice is transparent."

Touched a nerve. "So, you say."

"I'll prove it. I'll tell you something you need to know." Turning sideways, he squarely faced Gee. "I've been approached by a guy named Steve Tanner. He claims he's Marianne Tanner's brother. That

The WarBirds' songs belong to him." His hands swept the table. "Said he wants to cut Ken out of the recording project. Wants to work with me on the new album, direct."

Gee's jaw dropped. "How did he find you?"

"I asked him that." The producer looked shaken. "Dude's a cyber stalker. World class. Saw that I produced 'Love Power' in The WarBirds' Wikipedia entry. Friended me on Facebook. Then when he saw me staying in this NOLA hotel in my Instagram posts, he just showed up asking me about recording his sister's songs. No heads-up. No email query. No warning. Nada. I walked into the lobby, and he was waiting for me."

Frankie circled his finger. "You people better watch your backs until the copyright issue gets sorted. I don't trust that dude one bit. You shouldn't either. He said he could get Marianne's songs for me, and I believed him. Now, with what you say happened to Ken, it sounds like maybe he's already tried."

"When did he say this?" Jane probed.

"Sunday afternoon. Planted his ass in a café chair and invited himself to a late lunch. Nice guy. Real sweetheart. Polished off a thirty-dollar pitcher of mimosas and a double Eggs Bennie. Put it on my room tab when I got up to use the washroom."

"Sunday afternoon," Gee slowly repeated. "The day before Pops got attacked."

Chapter Fifty

Same Day
5:17 PM

Crissakes. Look at all these damn people.

"You're right." Catching Jane's glance, Gee read her mind. "It's absolutely the wrong time of day to be heading uptown."

Jane felt awed by the sheer mass of costumed Mardi Gras revelers lining St. Charles Avenue. Strands of metallic green, silver, and purple toss bead necklaces already hung from the tree limbs and street signs. Families dressed in matching outfits and face paint trooped by carrying armloads of collapsed lawn chairs to claim their optimal parade viewing space. Jane hurriedly stepped aside for a man doggedly dragging a full-sized Weber charcoal grill. *Good Lord. And NOPD needs to police this madness.*

"The Krewe of Druids parade starts at six. If this goes late, we should stick around. The Ladies of Nyx toss hand-decorated purses. We should both grab one."

"I don't carry a purse," Jane said.

"Great! That means I'll get two," Gee retorted. She executed a twisty dance move in time to a thumping bass beat.

Jane's spirit lifted as more percussive music poured from every door, window, and street corner. *Music in NOLA is like a shared heartbeat. It's part of the city's collective soul.* "Excuse me." She avoided an amorous couple who had suddenly decided to get busy directly in her path. "Where is this place we're going? Maison St. Jacques."

"Three blocks over. Let's cut around the crowd."

"Love that idea." Gaining some elbow room, Jane breathed easier as she eyed the gracious Victorian Queen Anne-style mansions lining the parade route. These private homes had shaded gardens half-hidden behind the temporary Mardi Gras bleachers and barricades. Jane felt a surprising nostalgic pang. "This reminds me of Main Street on Nantucket, without the cobblestones."

"No surprise there." Gee marched along the gutter. "This whole neighborhood used to be plantations 'til Yankee carpetbaggers like you who didn't want to live in the Quarter with us Creoles built these houses." She pointed at a walled-off town block. "Even needed their own new cemetery. Like that hoo-ha makes a difference when you're dead."

"Lafayette Cemetery No. 1." The location clicked. "I'm sure it wasn't that grim."

"I'm sure it was." Gee laughed. "We just don't hold grudges."

"When is your Krewdio-54 parade?" Jane asked, realizing with a guilty start that she should already have known this detail.

"Noon on Friday. Thanks for asking." Gee trotted across the street to the opposite sidewalk, encouraging Jane to hurry. "We're just one unit. We're not big enough to have our own parade. We're walking behind the Krewe of Tucks, out of Loyola. They toss hand-decorated toilet brushes." She bypassed a gaggle of over-excited pre-teens. "I couldn't decide on which krewe to choose, but disco is my life, so I joined Krewdio-54. I'm qualified to join either krewe, disco or tucking." Looking over her shoulder, she grinned. "Jane, are you blushing?"

"No," Jane lied, quickly changing the subject. "Does Krewdio-54 have a float?"

"Not this year, but I'm so hoping for one next year." Gee rose on her toes. "I have the best idea ever. I want to use a giant silver shoe like the one from the movie *Priscilla, Queen of the Desert*."

"Let me guess. With you as the queen."

"I would be great!" Gee paused before a pillared mansion surrounded by azalea shrubbery. Reaching for the latch, she opened the wrought-iron gate. "Who else?"

"Gee, wait. Before we go in, let's refocus our PI strategy."

"Pied Stan is off the hook." She stepped into the garden. "What about Frankie Malcolm? You think he attacked Pops?"

"He genuinely went pale when he heard about it. He might be lying about the reason behind his reaction, but you can't fake an automatic physical response. My gut instinct says no."

"You're thinking it's Uncle Steve. So do I." Gee shook out her hands. "Do you ever get nervous interviewing suspects?"

Hell, yes, I got nervous. All the time at the Academy. "Call them 'persons of interest.' It sounds more professional. And yes, it gets easier the more you do it. You'll learn investigations aren't personal. You'll need to fly above the drama and not get sucked into them if that makes sense."

Gee still looked uncertain. "Got any tricks?"

"Just go in confidently, like you've been doing it for years."

"Fake it 'til you make it."

"Exactly." Jane laughed. "Remember if you start to feel an emotional pull or response, step away. We're looking for answers and direction, not engagement. I can go first, take the lead."

"No, I'm ready." Gee danced in place. "I want to see if I can do this."

"You're already halfway there." Jane followed her up the brick steps. "I've got your back if you need a safety net."

"This is exciting. Something new." Gee trembled. "Never needed a net before."

Chapter Fifty-One

"*Bonjour*." Gee confidently strode toward the reception desk. "Can you help me?"

Both B&B staffers looked up. The petite Asian woman hung up the landline phone. The balding White man had lifeless zombie eyes.

"Yes, sir?" He inquired his voice sepulchral.

"I'm looking for my uncle, Steve Tanner. Can you tell me, is he a guest?"

"Not without a subpoena," she replied.

"I'm sorry? What?" Gee blinked, looking shocked by the in-your-face unhelpful response. "You don't like my outfit?" She checked her shirtfront. "Something green stuck in my teeth?"

"Thank you. Never mind. We're good." Jane towed Gee toward the door. "Nice try but they can't share that information. It's illegal."

"That's *fou!* He's my uncle."

"They don't know that. And it wouldn't matter if they did."

"What are we supposed to do? Sit in the lobby and ambush him if he comes down?" Cocking her hip, she sounded miffed. "You may recall, last time we didn't part on the best of terms."

"Text him." Jane stepped outside. "Ask him to join us. This time, use finesse."

Gee giggled. "What's his number?"

"Fuck off."

"If you can't memorize numbers, Jane, at least add them to your Contacts. Use the technology." Pulling out her phone, Gee intently studied the screen. "He's not answering me. No dots."

"Too bad we don't know his room number."

"It's lucky number seven." Gee glanced up. "Remember?"

"Double fuck. Now you're showing off." Jane pulled out her iPhone. "I'll call the front desk and ask for his room by name. If they transfer the call, at least we'll know he's still registered."

Gee looked puzzled. "Why would they do that for you, and not for me?"

"Sometimes a front desk will do it if you specify the guest's name and room number. You never know. We might get lucky."

"Wait." Gee stopped. "We got dots. He's not here. He says he's home in Kansas City."

"Ask him, when did he leave NOLA?"

Gee typed. She looked up. "Flew home Sunday night."

"Crap. That's a solid alibi unless we want to argue with the TSA."

"He could be lying."

Activating Logic Tree, Jane started pacing. "He'd need to show at least one form of ID to get on a plane, even for a domestic flight. How far is NOLA from Kansas City?"

"I'll investigate." Gee refreshed her browser. "Eight hundred and fifty miles. Roughly ... thirteen hours. Even if he turned around and drove straight back, he couldn't have attacked Pops on Monday morning. There's not enough time."

Jane pointed her finger. "Ask which airline he took. He might've gotten off the plane early if he had a connecting flight and driven back."

"He'd need to use his credit card to rent a car," Gee argued. "I know that much. Car company's not just gonna give him one."

"Ask him which airline," Jane insisted. "Maybe he got off, paid cash, and caught a bus. The devil's in the details."

"You have a criminal mind." She typed the text. "I'll say in case I ever decide to visit." She studied the screen. "He says, 'AirBlue has direct flights to KC.'"

"Ask him when he's coming back."

"You're so needy," Gee griped, typing again while voicing an aside. "I'll bet he's talking to an estate attorney about owning Marianne's songs. What he doesn't know is that we know he's tried to cut us out of the deal with Frankie Malcolm." She looked up again. "He's not sure when he's coming back. I'll ask him to keep in touch."

"Good idea. He may not have had the opportunity or the means, but he sure had enough motive to attack Ken. That's one out of three."

"He gave me a thumbs up. Snap." Gee's face scrunched tight with concentration. "Another dead end. If it's not Pied Stan, or Frankie Malcolm, or Uncle Steve, then who attacked Pops?"

"Don't let it stress you out. Investigations do that sometimes before they crack open. Remember what I said. Let that line of investigation rest and switch gears. Send out another dog to hunt. We still need to interview Dr. Sabatier about tissue bank donations."

"Sounds dedicated as fuck, Jane, but listen." Gee pursed her lips. "I love doing this, I do, but it's Mardi Gras. I plan on partying my ass off, balls to the wall, pun intended this weekend." She ducked her chin. "Let's both take a break. Come with me to the Krewdio-54 party on Friday. Everyone will be there."

Should I go? Jane paused. *Mose reduced my hours at the cemetery. Do I really want to spend Mardi Gras holed up in my apartment with Mr. Piddles binge watching The Keepers?* "I don't think so, Gee," she dissembled. "It's not really my thing."

"How do you know? You've never tried it." Linking her fingers, Gee wheedled. "Please, Jane, I need a wingman. Don't make me party alone." She widened her eyes. "You're the only friend I have left."

"That is so not true." Jane pointed her finger. "And you're manipulating me."

Gee cocked her head. "Too much?"

"Ya think?" Jane snarked. *Maybe I should go.* Panic gripped her throat as her shoulders involuntarily rose to her ears. Swallowing hard she fought back. *I live in NOLA. I should give the full Mardi Gras experience a try, at least once.* She recalled her mother's repeated and familiar remonstrance. *All work and no play, makes Jane a dull girl.*

"I'll make you a deal. If we do the Dr. Sabatier interview, I'll go to your party. God knows I don't want you to stop loving life because of me."

"Huzzah!" Gee triumphantly raised her fists. "Jane gives in. It's a new personal best." She linked arms as Jane stiffened. "Not for nothing, Jane, I love you, I truly do, but you couldn't keep me from loving life if you tried."

Chapter Fifty-Two

Thursday, February 23, 2017
12:06 PM

"You're lucky to get me today." Professional Death Investigator Dr. Tamerlane Sabatier discarded her protective goggles before tossing her nitrile gloves into a hazardous waste bin. "I'm taking accrued time off for Mardi Gras. One more, and I'm done." She pointed. "Let's use my office. I've got my lunch."

"Lunch?" Gee turned sickly green. "One more?"

"Presumed accidental death." The PDI steadily marched ahead. "We see just about everything this time of year. Tox reports can be a real surprise. Witnesses saw this last guy slip on some toss beads, trip over his grill, and roll under a tandem float at the Krewe of Druids parade."

Tripped over his grill? Jane blinked. *I think I saw that guy.*

"We were at the Krewe of Druids parade." Gee whispered, aghast.

"You saw the accident?"

"No, but I heard sirens. Didn't think much of it. Sirens are always going off during Mardi Gras."

"I know they re-directed the Bonnebel marching band yesterday for another one. My niece plays snare drum." Soaping and rinsing her hands at the sink, she snatched three paper towels from the dispenser. "We average three, four ADs a year. Take a seat."

"ADs?" Gee wondered.

"Accidental deaths." She cocked her thumb at the closed door. "That poor fellow was killed instantly. Tires crushed his chest. Pronounced dead at the scene." Bending from the waist, the PDI reached into a minifridge, her voice sounding muffled. "I need to complete the autopsy today so we can notify the family, release his name. Get them a death cert." She straightened. "Bottled water?"

"Yes, please." Jane suddenly felt parched.

"I'll take one," Gee agreed.

"Catch. It's important to stay hydrated."

Reaching back into the fridge, the PDI pulled out a paper-wrapped sandwich, unwrapping it on the way to her desk. Jane's mouth watered as she caught an enticing whiff of marinated olive salad and garlic salami despite the oppressive morgue atmosphere.

Dr. Sabatier caught her stare. "Want a piece? There's plenty."

"No, thanks."

Gee waved her off. "I'm good."

"Sure? Okay. So, what is it now?" She asked around a chewy mouthful of thick muffaletta bread. "You two always bring me interesting lunchtime conversation."

Gee wiggled in her seat. "I guess what we really need to know," she glanced at Jane for confirmation, "is how donated organs get sent to transplant hospitals."

"What's the supply chain process?" Jane asked.

The PDI stopped chewing. She narrowed her eyes. "And you're asking me this because?"

"We're investigating a private case," Jane said, "that may involve live human organ harvesting."

"Click. I get it." Dr. Sabatier neatly wiped the corners of her mouth with her fingertips. "I just enjoyed this exact conversation with a smoking hot NOLA FBI special agent." She nibbled a bite of mortadella. "I can assure you two, same as I assured him that every organ donation processed through this Coroner's Office and our associated tissue bank is thoroughly documented."

"I'm sure they are." Jane pounced as her spidey sense tingled. *There's something off in her tone, the way she's emphasizing certain words.* She risked a shot in the dark. "But you think there may be some off-the-grid donations that aren't so properly documented?"

"Off the record?" The PDI toyed with the wrapper. "I have wondered. DeltaCare Medical Center does most of the transplant work now that Charity's shuttered." She wiped her mouth again. "Based on their volume, I can only assume they're getting some of their donor organs from other associated tissue banks. I know it's not us." Rolling her shoulders, she cracked her neck. "We can't meet their demand. Haven't done so for decades."

"How do you track your donations that come in, and where they go?" Jane leaned in. "Where can we find that information?"

"You can't." The ergonomic chair squeaked as the PDI sat back. "You'll never get access to that data. You'd hit a wall of HIPAA and personal privacy restrictions. I even wished that hot special agent *bonne chance*, and he's federal."

"Someone must sign off on the hospital-side supply chain," Jane insisted.

"Give us a name," Gee pleaded.

Dropping her half-eaten sandwich, Dr. Sabatier thoughtfully flicked crumbs off her smock. Steepling her fingers, she tapped her full lips before suddenly looking up, her eyes bright. "I'm not telling you anything you couldn't find on a public website. Dr. Beauford Hannity is DeltaCare's Chief Surgeon. His father, Dr. Gatewell Hannity was Chief Surgeon at Charity Hospital. It's a family affair. Always has been."

"And you think ..." Gee wondered.

"I'm not saying what I think. I'm only telling you what I know. This city's a political minefield. I've worked my ass off to become an Orleans Parish PDI. I won't risk my career." Balling the trash, she slid it into a waste can and stood. "I am suggesting that might be an interesting place to look." Checking the wall clock, she turned for the door. "And you didn't hear it from me."

Chapter Fifty-Three

Same Day
8:47 PM

Jane rapped on the bedroom door. "Gee? You decent?"

"Never been called that before." Came the tart reply. "Can't imagine why I'd want to start now. Come in. No peeking 'til I say so."

"Thought I'd give you an update on the Hannity family before I leave for my shift." Jane tentatively stepped over the threshold, unsure of what to expect. *This feels strange. I've never been inside Gee's bedroom before.* "This is nice."

"Suits me down to the ground." Gee stayed hidden behind a three-panel Victorian screen that divided the room in half.

"I'll bet." Jane felt a jealous twinge as she admired the French doors overlooking St. Claude Avenue. "No wonder you moved back home again. Fancy's place can't compete with this. Look at this space. You have a balcony, a private bathroom, and a working fireplace."

"No use in holding a grudge out of spite." Gee drawled, as the screen swayed dangerously. "I decided I'll never know what Marianne was thinking."

Who has Gee got back there with her, and what are they doing? "How did you score the master suite?"

"Maman and Pops like living on the ground floor. Or at least they did until Pops got booted upstairs. Maman avoids the staircase because arthritis hurts her knees."

"Leslie avoids that staircase because of Ken's drinking," an unseen Aunt Babette acidly stated. "Hard enough dragging that great lump down a hallway without needing to haul him upstairs to bed." She chuckled. "You should'a heard him caterwauling yesterday when I removed his stitches. Big baby."

Scooting an upholstered stool away from a mirrored Art Deco vanity, Jane sat. "You removed Ken's stitches?"

"Used my tweezers and cuticle scissors. One quick snip and a tug and we saved the co-pay." The screen trembled again. "Stop wiggling. You're not gonna like it if I stick this needle in your *derriere*. Would'a been a whole lot easier if you'd taken those shorts off so I could finish hemming without you in them."

"Custom tailoring is meant to be fitted," Gee archly stated. "Won't fit the same way coming off a hanger. The point is, Jane, yes, this is my bedroom. Sometimes I wonder if this *ensuite* isn't causing the problem with my love life."

"What problem?" Jane asked, confused.

"I simply must have my own private bathroom."

"That's an easy fix." Aunt Babette huffed as she shuffled around the screen, balling a loose thread between her palms. "Find you a sugar daddy rich enough to buy you a house with two bathrooms." She removed her wrist pin cushion. "You gonna do that, you better hurry up, *sha*. You're getting on in age. Might run outta sugar soon."

"Stay chill, Aunt Babette. I'm only thirty-two. Got plenty of sugar left."

Checking her iPhone, Jane kept her eye on the time. "Gee? Are you dancing tonight?"

"Called in sick. Need to finish this costume for the Krewdio-54 parade. Dress rehearsals at midnight."

Shorts. Seams. Jane steadily worked through a probability list. "I give up. What's your costume?"

"You're the big detective. Guess."

"No chance. I don't have enough data."

"Need a clue?" Gee reached one hand over the screen. "Hand me the blonde wig."

"Mae West," Jane snapped.

"Loser. Try someone born this millennium."

"Dolly Parton."

"Better. Don't have the tits. You could pull it off." She whisked the wig away. "Think of something that happened this month. *Merde*, where is your brain? We even watched it together."

Something we watched together this month.

"Obviously, Sherlock Holmes you are not. Give me the Hannity update while you puzzle it out."

"Fine. Both Hannity's went through Tulane University's School of Medicine. Hannity Senior is listed on the university's notable alumni donor list."

"No surprise there." Aunt Babette closed her wicker sewing basket. "The Hannity family donates folding money to charity."

"They're also clever about paying taxes. They registered a charitable non-profit foundation, a 501(c)3 in 1972."

"Tax evasion?" Gee wondered. "Is that what's going on?"

"No, it's legit. A lot of families with big money do it. They're also featured regularly in the *Seen* column in the social pages at most NOLA gala events. The family's high-profile. Especially the mother, Elaine Hannity. She makes Mr. Armond's annual Top Ten best dressed list."

"They got a big mansion on St. Charles Avenue in the Garden District." Aunt Babette smoothed the black wig. "And a gentlemen's horse farm in St. Tammany Parish north of Lake Pontchartrain."

Jane felt puzzled. "I didn't find any reference to a horse farm. How do you know that?"

"I know a lot of things about that family. Elaine Hannity's been sending a car for me since she was a Delta Tau sorority girl. She likes the way I read her Tarot cards. I made her a love *gris-gris* from her husband's pubic hair that one time when Gatewell strayed."

Jane winced as she processed the image. "Have you seen her recently?"

"No. And that is odd. Elaine usually sends a car for me twice a month. She must be busy."

"What do you know about her husband? And her son, Beauford?"

"They're non-believers. Too busy practicing medicine. Too busy gettin' themselves rich." She settled the black wig on its stand. "Elaine mostly hides me from them. Sneaks me in through the garage when I visit. She's very clever that way."

I've been blind. Aunt Babette is a valuable local resource. Jane considered a new idea. "Aunt Babette? You should join our private detective agency. We need you." *Only in NOLA would I want a voodoo priestess on my investigative team.*

"What's it pay?" Sly interest smoothed the wrinkles from the older woman's face. "What're my hours? Will I get benefits?"

"TBD. We need to find a paying client first."

"You two ready?" Gee proclaimed. "You both sittin' down? There is no shame in my game. You are about to die."

A single silvery knee-high stiletto boot teased its way from behind the screen, followed by a smooth stretch of hairless thigh. Gee's left hand snaked out next clutching a cordless white microphone. Planting her spiked heel on the floor, she spun around the screen looking coy, chin to her chest, like she was working a stripper's pole. Tossing her lustrous false blonde tresses, Gee pumped her buff arms as she strutted across the room wearing skin-tight silvery shorts, her firm six-pack abdomen bare under fake football shoulder pads strapped in place by elastic suspenders decorated with mirrored polka dots. She had exaggerated eyebrows penciled in over gray eyeshadow. Devil red lipstick plumped her mouth.

"Lady Gaga." Jane breathed. "*Bad Romance* at the Superbowl half-time show." She stood in open awe. "You look fabulous."

"Doesn't she?" Aunt Babette clasped her hands, obviously pleased.

Gee modestly lowered her exaggerated eyelash extensions. "I know."

Chapter Fifty-Four

Hunched over the handlebars and gripping the Ducati between her thighs, Jane roared along N. Rampart Street, her windbreaker snapping like a pennant as she risked a sharply angled turn onto Basin. Gee's cocky dead-on Lady Gaga impression had kept her so entertained she'd forgotten to watch the clock and was late for her shift.

Skidding Monster to a tire-popping stop, Jane's heart sank when she saw the cemetery's main gate standing open. Sliding off the bike, she removed her helmet. Her nose twitched as she smelled the minty cigarette smoke that reminded her of Tic-Tacs and peppermint patties. She reflexively sneezed as Mose Gallier, her supervisor, stepped out of the security office, backlit by an overhead light.

"Finally." He raised the intense hi-beam flashlight from her boots to her face, instantly robbing her of her night vision. "I stopped by to make sure the cemetery was secure. Guess what I found. No security." His left arm exaggeratedly swept the area. "I sent Rob Johnson home. Wondered if you were even bothering to report tonight."

"Blame Mardi Gras, sir." Blinking repeatedly to lessen the dense black blots before her eyes, Jane wheeled Monster against a wall. "The traffic, the barricades. Getting through the drunken mob."

"I'm not interested in hearing your excuses."

"It's not an excuse, sir. It's an observation."

"Semantics. I still don't care." Spinning on his heel, he trotted deeper into the cemetery. "While looking for you, I found something you need to see."

Checking her temper, Jane easily matched his stride. *I was only fifteen minutes late. How bad can it be?* Watching her footing, she followed Mose as he turned right at Alley 2R. The decrepit tombs they passed were the oldest in the cemetery, having been built haphazardly with no thought for the later organized grid pattern.

Zigzagging sideways into the random maze, Jane squeezed between two off-kilter crypts.

"Sir? Where are we going? What's happened?"

"Desecration. Sacrilege." Mose directed the flashlight at a chipped plastered wall. "Do you see what's been done? Do you know what this means?"

YO G + BWG + R

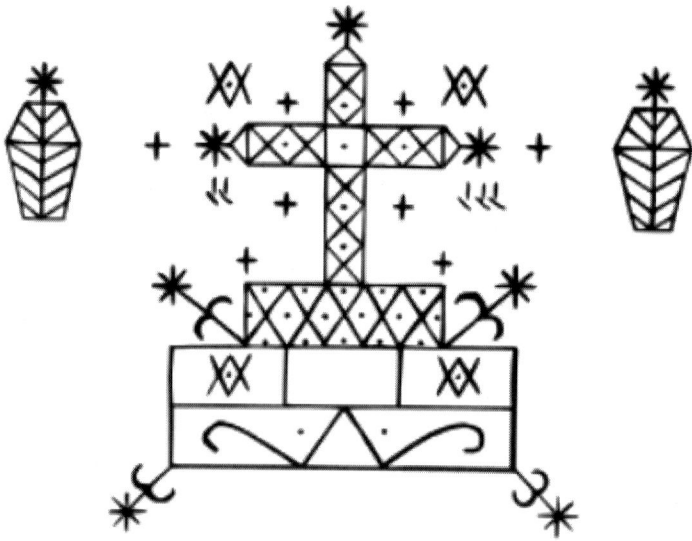

Jane's brain performed a mental handspring as she instantly translated the *veve*. *G + BWG = Big White Girl, Cleo's nicknames for us. +R means she's with Rex. And Baron Samedi is the patron loa of dead relatives and tombs.* A thrilling flicker of secret knowledge coursed through her veins as her dormant detective skillset kicked in. *Message received. Rex and Cleo are hiding in the cemetery. And they want us to find them.*

"Do you know what this means?" Mose repeated, his voice rising to a shrill crescendo.

UP JUMPED THE DEVIL

"Yes, sir, I do." *It means I need to ditch you ASAP.* "It's a voodoo *veve*."

"Voodoo being openly practiced in a Catholic cemetery." His finger shook. "I know we allow hoodoo offerings, shampoo, combs, and such to keep the tourists happy, but this is unacceptable. You were specifically hired to prevent this exact thing from happening. Your failure to protect Cemetery No. 1 is real."

My failure? Jane bit her lip, appreciating the irony of the situation. *You ignored every security precaution upgrade I suggested. I despised you for it at the time. Turns out that was a good thing. Trail cams would've recorded Cleo and Rex breaking in. Funny how things work out.*

Leaning forward, she swiped her palm across the *veve,* smearing the lettering and the Voodoo pictograph. "Should be easy enough to remove, sir." She displayed her grimy fingers. "It's blue chalk, not latex paint. Just needs a good scrub. Shouldn't take the maintenance guys more than half an hour."

"No! This needs to disappear tonight." Mose wiped his brow. "The Board of Governors will have my head if they learn about this."

Interesting visual. Jane hid her smile behind her smudged fingers, fighting an almost irresistibly devilish impulse to enter a complete nightly report including a high-res jpeg image into the cemetery's master core log just to see the resulting fallout. *High road. Take the high road.* "No worries, sir. I'll take care of it."

"See that you do." Mose marched for the security office like a bantam rooster. "And don't forget our reduced holiday schedule starts tomorrow. Don't make me fix your timesheet."

"Got it. Nightly four-hour shifts, 10:00 PM to 2:00 AM only, starting tomorrow. And Tuesday is Mardi Gras Day. You scheduled me off."

"All Catholic Cemeteries are closed on Tuesday." Wrenching the door open, Mose tossed the flashlight into a bin. Thoughtfully, he paused. "Maybe we should have some security at No. 1 on Mardi Gras Day after this." He looked up. "Are you free to work a shortened shift on Tuesday evening?"

"I may be able to, sir, at the holiday overtime pay scale rate outlined in my contract."

"Triple time?" His eyes bulged. "Forget it. Stay gone. Just make sure that voodoo symbol gets erased before you lock up in the morning."

"Roger that, sir." Escorting Mose to the main gate, Jane itched to retrieve the flashlight and commence her search.

Where do I begin? Where are Rex and Cleo hiding?

Chapter Fifty-Five

Raising the flashlight, Jane searched the moonlit tombs. *I need a tactical search strategy. Cleo is streetwise and sly. She wouldn't have posted that veve anywhere near their real hidey-hole. How does that intel help me.*

She recalled her police cadet motivational training. *What's driving Cleo's decision-making? Because that need is fueling her behavior. She snuck Rex out of the medical center. Now they're hiding from law enforcement. Her primary need then is to keep her brother safe. What would I do in her shoes?*

Find shelter. Find a secure place in the cemetery to hide. Jane considered the boneyard's irregular grid pattern. *The parapet tombs are bricked up tight. Some family mausoleums are big enough, but their gates are locked. To access one of them, they'd need a key.*

A sudden idea illuminated her mind. *I should search the cemetery's records. See if the name Duchamp is on the owner's list.* Jane felt a half-remembered flicker of accomplishment and pride. *That's developing an old school lead. Feels good. I've still got it.*

Stay on task. Jane refocused. *What do Rex and Cleo need?*

Access to prepared food and drinking water. She chewed her lip. *Rex is injured and blind. He's still recovering from his ordeal. Cleo will want easy access to Canal Street for their food and medical supplies.* Spinning quickly, Jane continued her search, angling southwest along Alley 3-L. *She'd avoid using the main gate. Too risky. They might be seen. Chances are they'd use the Conti Street gate for their access like they did before.*

Jogging a quick clockwise rotary, Jane checked the layered shadows around the blocky St. Vincent de Paul mausoleum without luck. Pulling up short before the Conti Street gate, she double-checked the padlock. *No signs of disturbance. Looks secure.*

Only a pair of shrill and distant sirens broke the silence.

Next guess. She shook the tension from her hands. *Use Logic Tree.* Recalling her first encounter with Rex when he scaled the Treme Street wall, Jane counted the number of days while feeling increasingly amazed. *Was that really only twelve days ago? Crissakes. Look how much has changed since then.*

Striding up Conti Alley, she considered the cemetery's layout. *Rex and Cleo both ran toward the Protestant section. Something keeps drawing them to that spot.* Heading for the entrance to the Thomas Layton memorials, Jane felt more confident and certain with each step. *Hiding in this corner of the cemetery makes sense. It's as far as you can get from the main gate. That would give them enough time to avoid contact with the maintenance crew or random tourist tour groups.* Turning right at Alley 10-L, Jane avoided the shattered marble angel before taking a sharp left into the open, grassy section. Suddenly, she froze.

Holding her breath, she cocked her head, switching the flashlight to her left hand. As she paused for a beat, her ears caught a whispery metallic squeal like the sound of someone furtively opening a dumpster.

Running the halogen beam across the Layton memorials, Jane peered into the darkness. Turning her head from side to side, she used her peripheral vision to detect the slightest movement. Her tongue suddenly felt thick, her mouth dust dry. A prickly thrill sparked her spine as the sibilant squeak was repeated.

It's behind me. Rising on her toes, Jane turned. *In the tombs.*

Chapter Fifty-Six

Jane slid her boots through the gravel to minimize any sound. Raising the flashlight to her left shoulder, she pointed the bright beam down the alley, squinting to catch any density changes, any sudden movement in the shadows.

Is it them? She cocked her ears to catch the slightest whisper, her thrumming nerves alert. Ungluing her tongue from the roof of her mouth, she decided to risk a verbal challenge.

"Security. Identify yourself."

Jane flinched as the metallic screeching was repeated near her hip. *So close?* Spinning around to face it, she focused the flashlight on the substantial family mausoleum on her left.

Creeping forward, she extended her right hand while ordering her leaden and protesting legs forward. Grasping a decorative fleur-de-lis, she pushed the swinging iron gate open, continuing up the two shallow marble steps toward the bricked up oven tomb, wildly unsure of what she would find.

"Cleo? Rex?"

That's odd. Jane ran the flashlight over the tomb's entrance. *These bricks aren't mortared.*

She shoved the bricked-up entrance with her fingertips. It swayed as a shower of red brick dust coated her boots. *A-ha.* Wedging the flashlight between two *fleur-de-lis*, Jane dug her fingers into a rough crumbling gap, wiggling a single brick loose until it came away in her hand.

Setting the brick by her boot, she straightened. Reaching into the cavity, Jane felt nothing but warmer air. *It's a sham. A false wall.* Using both hands, she quickly disassembled the coarse bricks, stacking them neatly and noticing for the first time the significant amount of powdery red dust that had already stained the white marble steps like pooled dried blood.

It's not the first time someone's done this.

Grabbing the flashlight, Jane scanned the tomb's interior, hesitant and leery of what she might find despite her extensive CSI de-sensitivity training. The halogen beam revealed a permanently installed marble slab that separated two brick-lined chambers stacked one on top of the other. Both chambers looked dry and empty. *Thank God for small mercies.*

Stepping back, she regrouped. *Corpses need to remain in an oven tomb for a year and one day. After that, they're dust and bones.* She probed the dim corners with the flashlight. *This tomb looks swept. No one dead has used it for years.* Kneeling to explore the lower crypt, a blue single-use Dollar Store bag caught her eye. *Someone alive has been sheltering here. Is it Cleo and Rex?*

I need to check that sack. Jane hesitated, petrified over feeling a sudden needle stick. *I should've brought gloves.* Reaching for her belt, she unsnapped her baton, using it to pull the plastic bag from the tomb. She found the bag stuffed with empty Funyuns wrappers and a box of blue billiard cue chalk cubes. *Bingo.* Jane acknowledged a momentary and supremely satisfying ripple of transcendent deduction. *Odds on its Cleo and Rex. But where are they?*

Straightening, she returned to Logic Tree to search for the answer. *Street parties, free food and drinks, and live jazz music on every street corner. They're out celebrating Mardi Gras in the Quarter like everyone else is.* Tucking the flashlight under her arm, Jane pulled out her iPhone. *I can't send Cleo a text to meet me. The U.S. Marshals Service confiscated her burner phone.* She suddenly felt blocked and helpless. *I need to call Gee, but she's out partying with her Krewdio-54 friends.* Jane tensed with frustration. *Doesn't anyone in this city besides me ever work?*

Shaking off the unproductive self-pity, she picked up a blue chalk cube. Peeling the paper wrapper off one corner, she scrawled a message across the tomb's mottled marble slab.

Chapter Fifty-Seven

Friday, February 24, 2017
12:17 AM

YO C+R. We're a team. Let us help. BWG+G
Stooping, Jane quickly rebricked the tomb's entrance. *Doesn't take long once you know the trick of it.* Dusting the brick dust from her hands, she trotted back to the security office, struggling with a tough decision as her previous law enforcement sensibility warred with her mutinous newly woke NOLA heart.

If I report what I found tonight to Mose, NOPD will arrest Rex and Cleo for criminal trespassing. Tack on the graffiti damage Rex did painting Marie Laveau's tomb and he wins a promotion to two Louisiana State felony charges.

If I skip telling Mose and tell Win Carter instead, he'll remand them to the U.S. Marshals Service and the WITSEC program. I already know Rex and Cleo don't want to do that.

But. Jane shivered as she felt the Devil's own temptation tap her shoulder. *At least that would be the end of it. I could send Win one quick text and then wash my hands of this whole fucking situation.*

Gee will never forgive me if I turn them in. Jane had never felt so divided. *Is there another option? What if I don't report Rex and Cleo to anyone and keep finding them a secret. I'd be risking my job and my reputation and violating my security employment contract. Fuck.* Her gut spasmed as she recognized an even greater risk. *I could be charged with aiding and abetting two federal fugitives. I'd be facing the same penalty as Rex and Cleo. Federal prison, up to five years. An unfriendly judge could tack on an additional harboring charge and extend my confinement.* Her mouth suddenly tasted as bitter as ashes. *And I've met unfriendly judges before.*

Am I comfortable risking this? Jane paused outside the security office door. *Do I follow the letter of the law? Or subvert the system to help Cleo and Rex.* Jane coughed as her gut instinct led her into a terrifying new direction. *I got fed into the criminal justice system. It chewed me up. I saw how it was stacked against me, from the inside. Everyone and everything are stacked against Cleo and Rex. They've never had a chance at building a decent life. Gee is all in for helping them. Am I?*

Jane swallowed past the leaden lump in her throat. *If we don't help them, no one will. Decision made. Silence it is.*

Despite her decision, Jane felt perversely anxious. *I'd feel better if I confirmed that Cleo and Rex are using that tomb. If it is someone else, someone random, all this worry is for nothing. How can I confirm that?* As she fumbled with her keychain, a fresh suggestion bloomed.

Setting the flashlight aside, Jane slid behind the gunmetal desk. Opening the cemetery's laptop, she typed in the five-digit passcode and launched the St. Louis Cemetery No. 1's Owner List spreadsheet.

Let's see if a Duchamp tomb is listed.

She ran her index finger down the screen scanning family names and their associated cemetery plot locations.

Ambrose - #32
Bienville - #117
Cage - #66
Clark - #12-B
Claiborne - #202
De Bore - #13, #17
Fontayne - #86
Fouquet - #03

UP JUMPED THE DEVIL

No Duchamp. Wait. Sometimes French Creole family names are hyphenated. Returning to the initial entry, she double-checked the report.

Lafon - #46
LaLaurie - #72
Leveau-Glapion - #23
Morial - #24
Morphy-Seguin - #56
Plessy – #43A, B
St. Jacques - #104
Thibideau - #91

Dead end. Jane slumped, defeated. *Nice try, Sherlock, but there's no record of a Duchamp family tomb.* Another amorphous idea briefly jelled. Just as quickly the suggestion evaporated through Jane's grasping mental fingers, leaving her with an unsatisfying image of its flickering forked tail. Try as she might, Jane couldn't even recall the essential gist of the idea, feeling that it was somehow vitally important, but it was gone.

Chapter Fifty-Eight

Mission accomplished. Jane slid the damp galvanized tin bucket back into the utility closet. *Veve be gone. That should make Mose happy. And if that message came from Cleo and Rex, they're as safe as I can make them.*

I'm guilty of concealing evidence. Jane clamped down on a vestigial twinge from her ingrained CSI collection protocol. *No regrets, dammit. I made my decision. I'm sticking to it.*

Looking up, she checked the wall clock. 6:01 a.m. Locking the security office door, Jane turned, zipping the windbreaker to her chin. The breeze off the Mississippi River felt brisk. Releasing the dial padlock, she rolled Monster onto the sidewalk before resecuring the gate. After buckling her helmet, she minutely re-adjusted the mirrors. *As much as Gee tries, she never puts these back exactly right. But she's almost ready for her first solo ride.*

Checking that Monster was in neutral, Jane started the motorcycle, reassured by its familiar electric whinny. Pointing the Ducati toward home, she paused, feeling edgy and restless. The somnolent and half-spent Mardi Gras energy surrounding the French Quarter was still palpable, merely dozing, as if waiting for the rosy-fingered dawn to yawn, stretch, and flare up again.

Releasing the clutch, she turned down Basin Street. *This time of day, NOLA is mine.* Jane shifted into second gear. *What a difference from patrolling Nantucket. There, I knew every little bend and bump in the road. My day-to-day life was mapped out. Life held less drama, but was living that way better than this? Or was I nestled in my comfort zone, bored to death and I didn't realize it.*

Leaning into a gravelly U-turn, she headed for the Chevron gas station. Monster's low fuel light had been glaring like a demonic red eye since Tuesday. She had counted on the Ducati's gallon and a half reserve to keep her mobile until payday, but the bike was riding ultralight. Her spidey sense kept warning her that it was time to either fill the tank or prepare for a long walk home.

Filling the tank with ten bucks' worth of gas, Jane returned to N. Rampart Street feeling fat and flush with a full fuel load, suddenly in the mood for a dawn patrol. Swooping left on Conti Street, she headed into the French Quarter, avoiding the concrete barricades, and scanning the side streets on the lookout for fresh Mardi Gras carnage.

Look at all the trash. That's gonna draw rats. It's disgusting. It's appalling. No, it's disgusting and appalling. I hope they recycle those Solo cups, the tiaras, and those toss beads. Pushing on, she peered ahead, trying to make sense of a shapeless hairy lump in the middle of the street. *Thank God. It's a wig. I thought it was somebody's dog.*

Popping out of the Quarter on Decatur, she slowed Monster to a stop, studying the slumped figure of a man passed out at the base of the Jean Baptiste le Moyne de Bienville statue in the triangle parklet. Costumed as a tuxedoed Voodoo loa, Baron Samedi, he wore full facial skeleton makeup. Even unconscious he maintained his grip on his black silk top hat. Jane laughed. *This is why I love NOLA. Being surrounded by crazy 24/7 helps me feel sane.*

Turning right, she aimlessly rode toward Canal Street as the sunrise increasingly warmed the blushing horizon. *If I think about it, if I'm really being honest, living with Gee and Leslie and Ken, and even Aunt Babette has been good for me. I found the new family I needed.* Noodling around, Jane turned right again at the stoplight. *I don't feel so anxious and alone anymore, the way I felt all last year. And the PTSD episodes aren't so grim.*

She burrowed deeper. *I need to stop being so self-critical. Stop beating myself up over every little thing. That's a defensive behavior I learned because of the trial. I need to un-learn it, pronto. It's holding me back.*

Shrugging the fierce tension from her shoulders, she followed the thought along a thrum of sudden insight. *I've cleared the fog. I'm over it. I'm ready to start risking some life changes again.*

Swooping Monster to the curb, Jane felt almost blind from dawning self-awareness. *What d'you know? I found my game.*

Chapter Fifty-Nine

Same Day
6:38 AM

Jane studied the slumbering neighborhood as a mango-colored dawn backlit the prestigious mansions and gigantic live oak trees. *Gee is right. The Garden District is sweet.*

After checking her text and email messages, she zipped her iPhone into her windbreaker. *Nothing. Even if Gee is home from the Krewdio-54 party with her pals, I won't hear from her until she wakes up this afternoon.* Shrugging, Jane still felt brittle and edgy. *No sense going home. I'd just stare at the TV. Goddamn insomnia. I know I won't sleep.*

Her ever-alert mental task master gave Jane a prod, reminding her of priority number one. *We need to find Cleo and Rex.* Logic Tree kicked in, automatically trying to connect the random dots. *Everything about this investigation points to Charity Hospital as ground zero. Win Carter said the security guard there died of a fentanyl overdose. Dr. Sabatier hinted that the two Hannity doctors might be involved in the black market organ transplant supply chain.* A fresh suggestion flared in Jane's mind like a fireworks finale on the Fourth of July. *Aunt Babette said the Hannitys live in the Garden District. I should check that out while I'm here.*

Retrieving her iPhone, she searched Google maps, snorting in derision as the internet irresponsibly confirmed the family's street address. *2508 Pyrtania Street. So much for personal privacy. There is none.* She pushed off the curb. *Let's take a look-see.*

On Nantucket, while patrolling the island's cobbled Main Street, Jane had seen plenty of high-end high-dollar mansions, but as she slowed Monster in front of the Hannity homestead, she had to admit their mansion smoked them all.

Radiating limitless prestige and elegant power, the red brick Federal style home modestly presented two pillared stories facing Prytania Street but mushroomed to a full three stories in the rear over its modern four-car garage addition. *Okay. I'm as impressed as I was meant to be. I feel sufficiently punked.*

Hitting Monster's kill switch, Jane settled the bike on its peg kickstand. *Interesting. The Hannity's humble abode takes up an entire city block. And every window is shuttered and dark.*

Hanging her helmet off the handlebars, Jane strolled across the street, recalling what she knew about the family. *Until he retired, Dr. Gatewell Hannity was Charity Hospital's Chief Surgeon. His wife, Elaine, is a big-time NOLA socialite. Their son, Dr. Beauford Hannity is Chief Surgeon with DeltaCare Medical Center.* She hopped over the curb.

Turning left on Third Street, Jane sauntered along the sidewalk, following an imposing security fence while scanning the roofline and the trees for surveillance cameras. Pausing in front of an automatic gate, she noted a silver Lexus IS 250C convertible parked inside the compound. Moving closer, she triggered an LED security floodlight. Scurrying into the shadows, Jane turned left on Coliseum and quickly hustled out of range.

The back of the Hannity mansion was as lifeless as the front had been. *Looks like they're still asleep. Or maybe they're staying at their horse farm to avoid the Mardi Gras chaos.* Turning left again, Jane started back for Prytania Street. *That was a dud.* Suddenly, she ducked into the dense shadow of a gnarled oak tree, feeling a frisson of familiar recognition. A window tinted four-door Ford Taurus sedan sat idling on Second Street. *Well, well, well. Maybe not such a dud after all. I can still recognize a surveillance team.*

UP JUMPED THE DEVIL

A globe streetlight shone into the passenger side of the parked vehicle highlighting the profiled silhouettes of the driver and the blocky bald man sitting in the passenger seat. Sticking to the shadows, Jane crept closer, memorizing the blue and white rear license tag.

U.S. GOVERNMENT
I411964
FOR OFFICIAL USE ONLY

It's the federal somebodies. Jane warmed with satisfaction. *If the NOLA FBI is interested in the Hannitys, then maybe we're on the right track with our investigation. Crissakes though, Win. Seriously? A tinted sedan displaying government plates.* Jane released a prickle of pure judgment. *Could you be any more obvious?*

I should sneak up on him. The Devil gave her a playful nudge. *Give him a scare.* She glided closer.

She froze as the passenger window emitted a low-pitched electronic whine. A cigarette butt hit the pavement, bursting into a spangle of orange sparks.

Now. Jane raced forward. *While his night vision is compromised.*

"Surprise, motherfucker!" She laughed, rapping the rear window with her knuckles. Her heart skipped a beat as the man in the passenger seat turned.

Fuck me. It's not Win.

Popping his door, the stranger stepped out of the sedan. Jane automatically cataloged his physical details. *Six foot tall, Asian, 240 pounds. Bald, gold eyetooth. No neck. Prominent scar on left side of chin.*

"Sorry." Jane defensively raised both fists. "Thought you were someone else."

Taking one step forward, he narrowed the gap.

"I can see that."

Jane couldn't pinpoint the accent, but his vowels were long and his consonants soft, as if talking hurt his mouth.

"Fuck off, Blondie. Unless you want to climb in the back and SMD."

Despite her shock, Jane recognized him as a professional. *Not FBI. Not U.S. Marshal Service. Who are these guys?*

"Get back in the car, Sid," the driver sourly stated. "We don't have time for this."

Stretching his arm across the seat, he flicked his fingers at Jane like he was shooing away a bug. *East Coast accent. New York? Sounds like Tony Soprano. Fills the seat behind the wheel. Gold pinkie ring, left hand, red stone. Acne scars on both cheeks.*

"Run along, Chickie," he said. "You got no business with us."

Sid doubtfully shook his head. "Unless maybe she does."

"No. You're right." Jane backed away. "My mistake. I'm gone."

Turning, she ran for Prytania Street, the space between her shoulder blades prickling a warning. *Keep going. Don't look back. They'll think I'm interested.* She heard the sedan pull away with a rubbery squeal. Running up to Monster, Jane grabbed the handlebars. Recognizing the key fob in her pocket, the automatic ignition fired up.

Crissakes! Jane swung aboard, her mind racing over fresh possibilities. *Government plates my ass.* Noticing that her hands were shaking, she repeatedly flexed her fingers until the trembling stopped. *Who was that. And why were they scoping out the Hannity's house?*

Create a record. Fighting the windbreaker, Jane pulled out her iPhone. *Time check: 7:14 a.m. Win gets up at six for his daily workout at the gym.* Hesitating for one second longer, Jane typed a text. *I need to see you ASAP. Up for coffee? Café Irene?*

A response bubble immediately popped up showing a thumbs-up emoji.

UP JUMPED THE DEVIL

What u know? See u then.

Chapter Sixty

Same Day
7:36 AM

FBI Special Agent Win Carter sat solo in a booth, his back against an interior wall. He gripped a white coffee mug between his long-fingered hands. Win looked freshly groomed and as the door closed behind her, Jane caught the mingled alpha male scent of his designer cologne and the dry cleaning solution that wafted from his buttoned-down broadcloth shirt. His smell tickled her nose and derailed her mental focus. Pressing her tongue against the roof of her mouth, Jane suppressed a sneeze.

Win quirked one eyebrow. "Do you know how trade you looked blowing in on your Ducati?"

Back at you. Jane slid onto the opposite bench seat.

"I ordered us cappuccino. Hope that's okay." He pointed to a second white mug. "Let me know if you want something more for breakfast. My treat."

"You had me at cappuccino," Jane quipped, wrapping her chilled fingers around the piping hot mug, and getting straight to business. "I need to pick your brain."

"And I thought you only wanted me for my looks."

Ignoring his playful suggestion, Jane honed her focus. "I stumbled onto a surveillance team this morning." She risked a tentative sip. "Thought it was you Feds at first. I was wrong."

Win lowered his mug. "Where was this?"

Jane hesitated. *How much intel do I want to share with the NOLA FBI?*

"Jane, you initiated this conversation. You should know by now you can trust me."

"Uptown." She blurted. "The Garden District." She clarified. "I was scouting a location as part of an ongoing private investigation."

Win frowned. "Does this 'ongoing private investigation' have anything to do with the human organ harvesting we've discussed?"

"Yes."

"Civilians." His frown turned into a hurtful scowl. "Jane, this is dangerous territory. I told you to leave it to the professionals."

She registered a core ripple of resentment. "Are you questioning my abilities?"

"No." Setting the mug down, he resettled his wristwatch. "I'm questioning your sanity."

"Win, investigation is what I do best." Jane leaned in, feeling the truth in her statement with bedrock certainty. "Investigation is my game."

"Your game could get you killed."

"My game is the best part of me. The best part of my life." Picking up her coffee, Jane took a bigger sip, scalding the tip of her tongue. "And I can use it to help people like Rex and Cleo Duchamp."

He tugged his earlobe. "Have you heard from either of the Duchamps since they bolted from DeltaCare?"

Define 'heard.' Jane wiggled uncomfortably. "Not a peep."

"Let me rephrase my question." Win studied her carefully. "Have you seen either one of them?"

She truthfully met his eyes. "I said, 'no'."

He spun his coffee mug with his index finger. "And you'd tell me if you did?"

"Of course," Jane lied, sitting up straight. "Win, what I need to know is if you and I are on the same track with this investigation or if the surveillance team I saw this morning was a random unrelated incident."

"Alright. Describe them to me. Describe what you saw."

Jane organized her thoughts. "At approximately 7:16 a.m., I spotted a late model Ford Taurus sedan parked near 2508 Pyrtania Street in the Garden District. The vehicle contained two individuals, male, in the front seat." She blindly recited from memory. "The passenger was six foot tall, Asian, approximately 240 pounds, built solid. Bald, gold front tooth. Prominent scar on his chin. The driver called him 'Sid.'" She paused for a breath. "The driver was Caucasian, and fatter. He sounded like Tony Soprano. Gold pinky ring. Acne scars on his face."

"Solid descriptions," Win admitted. "What made you think they were Federal agents?"

"Their sedan had a blue and white government car tag on it."

He raised one eyebrow again. "Did you get it?"

"I-411964. U.S. Government. For Official Use Only."

Reaching for his phone, Win quickly typed a text. "I'll check with FMVRS. My buddy works there." Pursing his lips, he looked puzzled. "The 'I' prefix indicates Department of the Interior. Can't imagine why they'd be involved unless that team reports to Biological Services."

Jane blinked, playing catch-up. "FMVRS?"

"Federal Motor Vehicle Registration System." Sharing his killer smile, Win hunched over his phone like a vulture. "Government vehicles are leased. FMVRS keeps a record of the plate until it's returned for destruction. Rick should be able to backtrack departmental ownership and find out who's using it. Cross-reference the internal team that way." He squinted. "Answer me this. What part of your private investigation took you to the Garden District at six in the morning?"

Careful. Jane hesitated. *I need to know if there's an FBI/Hannity connection, but I can't burn Dr. Sabatier as our source.* She moistened her lips. "DeltaCare Medical Center is a major player in national organ transplants. Dr. Beauford Hannity is the Center's Chief Surgeon. The Hannity family lives in the Garden District. We're investigating a possible connection to Rex Duchamp's abduction."

Win's phone buzzed. Looking down, he doubled tapped the screen. "Bad news. Rick says that specific plate was returned for destruction. That team you saw wasn't one of ours."

"I know what I saw."

"I'm not saying you're mistaken." Win looked sympathetic. "Each plate has a duplicate. Sometimes only one plate gets returned."

"What happens to the duplicate? It just floats around, getting used by anyone who needs fake government cover?"

"It happens. There's a dark web market for them. And counterfeits."

"Feds." Jane smirked. "You're sure your left hand knows what your right hand is doing?"

"The best I can do is report it outstanding." Win quickly typed another text. "Listen, you keep saying 'we.' Who are you working with?"

"A business associate." Jane risked another big sip.

"And you're both involved in the investigation?" Win's forehead furrowed. "Jane, the Hannity's are a very powerful, extremely well-connected family. They won't appreciate anyone poking around asking questions."

She leaned in. "Just tell me one thing, Win, straight up. Is the NOLA FBI investigating the Hannity family or its 501(c)(3) charitable foundation?"

Win's Adam's apple bobbed as he stared across the table. "I can tell you their foundation leases a private corporate jet. That's public information. It's a specific line item in their Annual Report's financial statement."

"Sorry?" Despite the caffeine thrumming her veins, Jane felt confused. "What am I missing? What's so key about the Hannity's leasing a jet?"

Win linked his fingers. "Some illegal donor organs are smuggled into the U.S. across international borders. International borders puts it on our radar." Checking his phone, he finished his coffee. "The Hannity's charitable foundation is very liberal about loaning their jet for compassionate global organ donation retrievals." Holding up one hand, he forestalled her unspoken protest. "And yes, we're working closely with U.S. Customs on tracking their overseas trips." Leaning sideways, he reached for his coat.

A horrific suggestion blossomed in Jane's mind. "'Compassionate global retrievals' like the organ donations coming from China?"

Win's eyes turned frosty. "Especially donations from Uyghurs, Tibetans, Christians, or anyone else Beijing classifies as political criminals. Those people have no say in making their donations, no voice."

Jane clasped his arm. "What about NOLA's missing homeless people. Are you investigating them?"

"Jane." He slid into his coat. "We're dealing with an *international* human rights abuse crisis. It takes precedence over anything local."

"But you're doing the same thing as the Chinese government." Scrambling up, she followed him toward the door. "Ghosting voiceless people while they disappear."

"Can we discuss this later?" He politely held the door open. "Over dinner? I'll text you. I really do need to go."

Wait! I wasn't finished. Jane felt strangely bereft as Win crossed the parking lot. *This is why law enforcement relationships never work out.* Looking both ways for approaching traffic, Win lankily strode for his car. *He needs to block out that part of his life that he can't share with me. And I'm doing the same thing to him. We have zero chance at a relationship.* She buckled her helmet under her chin. *We'll never be completely honest with each other because we're adversaries, not friends.*

Ignoring a blaring car horn, Jane merged Monster into the flowing downtown NOLA rush hour traffic. Bending low over the handlebars, she quick-shifted into sixth gear, heedlessly blasting through the intersection on a solid red light.

Chapter Sixty-One

Same Day
12:23 PM

Balancing the laptop on her knees, Jane settled into the couch, doom-scrolling Google news while she gently scratched the black standard poodle dozing by her side. Whining nasally, Piddles quivered as he chased a dream rabbit.

"Just don't fart," she muttered. *I should take Piddles for a run, grab a shower and a nap before I head to work.* With Mardi Gras week trimming her cemetery shift to four hours, the effort involved in getting clean hardly felt worth it, but Jane knew that her body would rebel if she tried slipping into a fresh uniform without exfoliating her skin first. *That's some high caliber OCD I got going on.* She glanced at the screen. *The habits we voluntarily make are the toughest ones to break.*

A headline from Google's Top Stories>Breaking Local News caught her eye. Gasping with disbelief, Jane sat up.

Prominent NOLA Family Members Found Murdered

This morning, February 24, 2017, at 9:47 a.m., a dispatcher with the St. Tammany Parish Sheriff's Office received a 911 call reporting two people were found dead at a remote horse farm near Folsom, St. Tammany Parish County, Louisiana, approximately one hour north of the city of New Orleans.

Sheriff's Office Major Crimes Detectives and Crime Scene Technicians were immediately called to the scene to begin an investigation. Local authorities are classifying the incident as multiple homicide.

Dr. Beauford Hannity, 45, Chief Surgeon with the DeltaCare Health Network was found dead in the vicinity of the stables. Dr. Gatewell Hannity, 72, retired former Chief Surgeon for Charity Hospital in New Orleans, was found shot in the head execution-style in the kitchen of the family's home.

There were no reported signs of a break-in or home invasion. No weapons were recovered on-site.

An unnamed source has alleged that certain members of the Hannity family were the subject of an on-going federal FBI investigation into public corruption.

Mrs. Elaine Reeves Hannity is asking members of the general public and the media to respect the family's need for privacy during the period of bereavement.

9:47 a.m. The Hannity's horse farm is one hour north of NOLA. That surveillance team I saw outside their house this morning could be the killers. Jane scrambled up, startling Piddles and nearly dropping the laptop she grasped. *I need to tell Gee.*

Running for the door, she dodged the over-excited and wildly barking poodle. "Get out of my way, dog, before I step on you." Tripping up the back porch steps, Jane noticed The Boat parked in the driveway. Throwing the screened door open, she piled into the kitchen.

"Jane! *Merde!*" Aunt Babette dropped a dripping spoon, splattering the stove with a greasy smear of the Holy Trinity sauce that was scenting the kitchen with onion and green bell pepper.

Jane skittered across the floor. "Is Gee upstairs?"

"She was making dodo last time I checked."

"Lower your voices, please. I'm here." Gee leaned against the doorframe of the servant's staircase. She blearily rubbed her eyes with one hand while clutching her embroidered Japanese kimono with the other. "Why the fire drill?"

"There's a break in our case." Jane panted. "Remember the two Hannity doctors from DeltaCare and Charity Hospital?"

"Yes. Dr. Sabatier told us about them." Pulling out a kitchen chair, Gee sat. "What of it?"

Sitting opposite, Jane opened the laptop. "They were both found shot dead at their horse farm in Folsom at 9:47 a.m."

"Shot dead?" Aunt Babette clutched the sink. "What of Elaine?"

Oh, fuck. Jane choked. *I forgot Elaine Hannity was Aunt Babette's client.* "She's alive. She's asking for privacy in the article."

"I can't imagine what this is doing to her." The older woman tottered.

Gee leapt up. "Sit down, Aunt Babette. Let me get you some water."

"Forget water." Shutting off the stove, she pointed at a high cabinet. "Fetch me a short glass and Ken's bourbon."

"AB, are you sure? It's barely noon."

"Do as I say, youngblood." She tapped her heart. "It's medicinal."

Gee poured a healthy slug into the glass before handing it to her. Aunt Babette handily tossed it back. "That's better." She wiped both eyes dry with her thumbs. "That poor woman. I'll need to call Elaine and send my condolences. See what I can do to help."

Jane studied the accompanying photograph showing Elaine Hannity dressed to the nines at some sumptuous gala. She had expected to see a bony X-ray trophy blonde, but Elaine Hannity was a statuesque brunette who looked a lot like the vintage actress Jane Russell. "She looks like a class act."

"She is. And smart as a whip." Aunt Babette pulled out a chair. "Alright, girls. Fill me in. I assume I'm part of the investigation now."

"She'd be great on our team," Gee eagerly agreed.

"True dat. As long as I'm not there to just answer phones." Aunt Babette's dark eyes gleamed. "I'd make a great detective. No one notices an old woman. I can sit on a park bench for hours with no never mind. I'm invisible."

She's right. "AB, you're in. Full partner. Starting now."

"*Bien*. Let's get started." Aunt Babette breathed fumes. "I'll call Elaine and find out what I can. Elaine may want to hold a séance. Remind me again. What's it say about her two men?"

Chapter Sixty-Two

Jane refreshed the article hoping for an update. "Beauford Hannity was found shot gunned near the stable. Gatewell was found in the kitchen. They're still saying he was killed execution-style." She paused. "What's important is that this new information tips their hand."

"Whose hand?" Aunt Babette asked.

"NOLA FBI." Jane scrolled the screen. "This 'unnamed source' mentioned public corruption. That must be the focus of the FBI investigation. I'll bet Win Carter wasn't thrilled when someone on his team leaked that detail."

"Clue me in." Gee re-tied her robe. "I'm still learning."

"Public corruption is a breach of public trust or an abuse of position by a federal, state, or local official. What makes it important is that it can include private sector accomplices."

"Accomplices ... like those two Hannity men?"

"That's my guess, AB."

Gee whistled. "Who d'you thinks the local official? Someone in the NOLA Coroner's Office? Jane, you're talking big city government."

"Bigger than we thought. And it means our investigation is on the right track because we're running parallel to the FBI. I suspected that much this morning when I rode past the Hannity mansion. I found a surveillance team parked outside. At first, I thought it was NOLA FBI. Now I'm thinking it was the killers."

"When was this?" Gee looked surprised.

"First thing this morning. Dawn."

"You saw the killers?" Aunt Babette squeaked.

"Yes. Two men, obvious pros. One Asian, one White. I gave Win the details."

"Special Agent Win Carter?" Tucking her chin, Gee looked askance. "When did you see him?"

"Earlier." Jane squirmed. "This morning."

Gee's eyes flared. "You two dating?"

"No. We met for coffee."

"And you talked with him about our case." Gee picked at the tablecloth.

"I just wanted to run the facts past him. Pick his brain."

"Before you talked to me." Gee pointed at Aunt Babette. "To us."

"Crissakes, Gee! You were still sleeping." Jane's temper flared. "What was I supposed to do? Is this a problem?"

"Hell, yes, it's a problem if we're partners. What am I supposed to think when I find out you're meeting – by yourself – with the FBI instead of me. How does that work?"

She has every right to be pissed. "I'm sorry. You're right." Jane rubbed her cropped hair. "I should've talked with you first. I didn't think it through. It's a bad habit left over from my old life. I automatically gravitate to a law enforcement environment."

"You need to automatically unlearn your old bad habit if we're going into business together." Gee raised her chin. "Tell me something. How much luck have you had lately working alone or with the FBI?"

"Not much."

"Tell the truth, now," Aunt Babette stated.

"None."

"*C'est exact*." Gee sighted down her index finger. "If working the way you used to do isn't working, you need to try something new." Gee folded her arms. "Anything else you haven't told us about?"

Shame warmed Jane's face. "I may have located Rex and Cleo Duchamp."

"On your own. Again." Gee slapped the table. "Where?"

"Hiding in a tomb in St. Louis Cemetery."

"Where did you say?" Aunt Babette turned from the stove. "Those two kids are living in a tomb?"

"It's been swept."

"I don't care how well a tomb's been swept." The skin on her neck wobbled. "No one alive should be sleeping with the dead. Baron Samedi will take notice. That's beggin' for possession."

"I didn't actually see them in it." Jane back pedaled. "I found their message chalked on a wall. Remember the *veve* we saw at the warehouse? It looked like that. I chalked them a message back. Said we were trying to help."

"*Problem malveillant.*" Aunt Babette tsk-tsked between her teeth. "Now the Baron will connect you with them."

More hoodoo voodoo. Jane bit her tongue. *Can we please keep this real.*

"I don't like the way this is going." Gee neatly tucked her hair behind her ears. "People are dying. First that hospital security guard, now those two Hannitys. Sounds like someone's cleaning up a mess."

"Eliminating witnesses," Jane agreed.

"And those two poor kids got everyone after them." Aunt Babette gently tapped her chest. "I'm worried they're next on the death list."

Gee cocked her head. "What's our next step?"

I don't know. Jane slumped, feeling drained. *I'm out of ideas. My well has run dry. I have decision fatigue.* "Got any ideas?"

"I do, but you're not gonna like it." Pushing back from the table, Gee stood, modestly refolding her robe. "It's Mardi Gras. We need to hit the street. Time to follow the call of the disco ball. Sittin' in this kitchen ain't doin' us no good." She exaggeratedly twanged before snapping her fingers. "The answers we want are out there, but first, you two need to come upstairs with me." She strode toward the servant's staircase. "Grab your sewing kit, Aunt B. Jane needs your expertise."

Chapter Sixty-Three

Saturday, February 25, 2017
12:10 PM

Help! I can't escape this. My brain is about to explode. Jane winced as surging waves of competing percussive sound pummeled her eardrums. The overwhelming background tsunami of snapping syncopated snare drums was being answered broadside by marching rows of brassy trumpets, oom-pah-pah tubas, and blatting trombones. This swirling noisome crescendo was underscored by the shrill staccato two-beat of tooting police whistles, shrieking crowd laughter, and roaring human cheers.

"Throw me somethin', mistah!"

She felt inebriated. Thumping kettle drums sounded like rounds of incoming mortar fire as the costumed Krewdio-54 dancers shimmied around her, mere steps ahead of the massively lurching tandem parade float built to look like a two-story Mississippi paddle-wheeler that dangerously loomed at their backs.

"How the fuck did I let you talk me into this?" Jane shouted. *White people in blackface. Black people in whiteface. This is insanity.* Reaching up, she adjusted her two-foot-tall, feathered headdress as she tripped along St. Charles Avenue in her platform boots. "I look like a Vegas showgirl. I'm going to get ticketed for public indecency dressed like this. And I should."

"Shut up. You're the bomb." Costumed again as Lady Gaga, Gee smoothly executed a side-step boogie move to The Crusaders hit 'Street Life' blasting from the portable Bluetooth speaker duct-taped to an Igloo cooler being hauled on a child's red Radio Flyer wagon by the Krewdio-54 dancer directly ahead.

"Cher! Stay in formation." The unit leader pointed her baton. "Try to keep up."

Spitting a long strand of black fake hair off her tongue, Jane took a giant step forward. "I'd feel better wearing my security uniform."

"Yah, you right." Gee shot her some sideways stink-eye. "As long as you don't mind representin' The Village People."

"Mistah! Mistah!" A pair of face-painted girls excitedly jumped on and off the curb under their mother's watchful eye. One girl already clutched a pair of gem-encrusted sunglasses. The smaller one waved a bejeweled toilet brush. "Throw me somethin'!"

Laughing, Gee slung them a handful of metallic green, gold, and purple toss bead necklaces. "Catch! Looks like you two already scored."

"Toilet brush?" Jane wondered."

"We're following Krewe of Tucks, remember?" Executing another spin turn, elbows held high, Gee shared a devilish grin. "Each krewe tosses their own souvenir." Next, she executed a funky crip walk dance step. "Gimme cups, doubloons, Moon Pies. Zulu krewe throws coconuts. Coconuts are rare. Real keepers."

Jane readjusted her headdress. "And you do this every year."

"Yes, to celebrate life." Gee winked. "Tell me you're not having fun. You need to join the krewe." Gee insisted. "You've been invited. You always say you're too busy, or no."

"I don't always say no."

"Prove it. Come with me to our Fat Monday Luncheon. You'll meet everyone there." Gee doubled down on her energetic dance moves. "Except for the ones who only come out at night."

"Alright. I will."

Delight lit Gee's face. "Did you really just say yes?"

"Yes." Jane shouted over the crowd noise. "Yes, I'll go with you to the luncheon." She stumbled as the Farmall tractor pulling the float behind them sputtered like a fully automatic AK-47. The street parade units and the wall-to-wall spectators swayed dangerously in response. *How in the hell does NOPD manage crowd control? This can't be safe.*

Gee caught her look. "I agree. Love Krewe of Tucks, love them, but we need to rethink our parade location next year." She cocked her thumb over her right shoulder. "Float Thirteen's behind us. Seriously bad juju with that one, the worst. It killed a man last year in the Endymion parade. Lurched forward and squashed him flat. That's why they moved it to this parade, in the daylight."

Jane felt flummoxed. "They let it back in a parade after it killed someone?"

"Po-po said it was his own fault." Gee spun a tight hip-wiggling circle. "Said he tripped trying to slip in-between the two hitched up parts." Quick stepping to a stop, she grabbed Jane's arm and pointed. "Look! Frankie Malcolm, and his lady lawyer, back in town."

"Where?"

"Standing at the barricade by the palm tree."

"That is Serena Melnyk." Jane avoided a crumbling asphalt pothole. *He did say they were staying to enjoy Mardi Gras.* "Any news about Ken's new album?"

"None that I've heard." Gee strutted around the curving Lee Circle rotary. "But I haven't seen Pops in like two days. We need to check."

Suddenly and unaccountably and with crystal-clear clarity, in the middle of the overwhelming Mardi Gras chaos, costumed as Cher, Jane felt her heart stir with a self-awareness that made her gasp. *I belong in the center of this madness, with Gee. Sure, there are day-to-day troubles to get through, but this is exactly where I'm supposed to be.*

After the sheer countless multitudes of alternate life decisions and choices she could've made, both spot-on and disastrous, and with each separate choice splintering off into millions of other related experiences that would've naturally occurred, the life she was living now was the best and most perfect on point result. Somehow, NOLA had erased her previous grievous mistakes as the city welcomed her in and absorbed her, enveloping her like a devoted and forgiving mother comforting a beloved and prodigal child. *Life isn't waiting in ambush to bite me anymore. This feels ... good. I'm someone new. And I like her.*

Gee gripped her elbow. "Jane? You okay?"

"I'm not sure. I think I'm tripping. Did you slip me a gummie?"

"Wasn't me." Gee laughed. "I would never do that. But I'd pay folding money to see you get high. Snap. I know what's goin' on. You're possessed. You caught the Mardi Gras magic. You've been de-zombified. You're feeling alive."

"Fuck that." Jane stretch-stepped over the streetcar tracks. "I'm feeling terrified."

"Same thing. Relax." Gee twirled as the Krewdio-54 soundtrack transitioned to Gloria Gaynor singing 'I Will Survive.' "It's good, it's bad, it is what it is. You're just scared 'cuz something new is starting. Like me learning to ride your bike." Gee adjusted her shoulder pads. "We all got to get through it. Meanwhile, kick back and enjoy the vibe. *Laissez les bons temps rouler.*"

Chapter Sixty-Four

"Throw me somethin', mistah!"

The roaring crowd noise kicked up another impossible notch as the high-stepping Krewdio-54 parade unit rounded Lee Circle. The front chorus line expanded like a surging sequined wave as krewe members shimmied and danced toward Canal Street to Grace Jones' pounding 'Pull Up to the Bumper.'

Jane ducked as a lime green strand of toss beads snared her feathered headdress. Bouncing off her nose, a golden plastic pendant dangled before her eyes.

"Let me get that." Gee quickly untangled the necklace from the black feather plumes. "Jane, look! Total score. You caught Thoth, the god of wisdom."

Pitching her voice lower to carry over the crowd's roar, Jane studied the ibis-headed Egyptian idol. "Good thing. I need all the wisdom I can get."

"Put it on. Wear it. It's terrific good luck."

"Yo, bitch!" A drunken frat boy wearing a court jester's cap shouted from behind a street-level steel barricade. "You got the beads." He nudged his equally hammered friends. "Show us your tits!"

Entitled sonofabitch. Clenching her fists, Jane searched for a nearby gap in the barricades. *Who the fuck do you think you're talking to.*

"No." Gee blocked her way. "Stay with the unit."

"They're being assholes!"

"Yes, they are." Gee herded her back into line. "Do like I do at Club Oz with my ass-hat clients. Ignore them. Don't engage."

"I'm shocked you're putting up with this."

"Why the surprise? Nothing we say is going to change them from being ignorant." Tucking her elbows to her ribs, Gee spun 360 degrees. "They need to woke their own damn selves."

"Y'all mind if we be right here?"

Stumbling in surprise, Jane barked her shin on the red wagon. "My brother's blind."

"Bless you, child. You two take that spot on the step, honey."

"Gee!" Wincing, Jane limped to catch up. "Cleo's in the crowd. I heard her."

Gee scanned the boisterous ten rows deep massed spectators. "Up the hill." She pointed. "By the monument. With Rex. Come on."

Arms akimbo, she dodged the final line of Krewdio-54 dancers before squeezing sideways between two of the concrete barricades enclosing the rotary, completely ignoring the official placard.

DANGER!
N.O.P.D. POLICE LINE
DO NOT CROSS

Jane followed as Gee raced up to the temporary eight-foot tall security fence walling the rotary spectators off from the street parade. Grasping a chain linked panel, Gee shook it in frustration.

"How do we get around this? Climb over?"

"We'd get shredded. I'm not climbing over anything dressed like this. Cleo!" Jane bellowed. "Cleo Duchamp. We need to talk."

Hearing the shout, Cleo turned, her eyes widening in surprise. Grabbing Rex's arm, she hauled her brother to his feet. "Bro, we gots to go. Them two bitches found us."

"Time to slip." Rex settled his knit cap lower over his grimy bandage. "Which way, Sis?'"

"Uphill." Clasping his hand, she led him up the slope.

Jane tracked them step-by-step along the street. "Cleo! We need to talk."

"Why would we do that?" She shepherded Rex further uphill. "Every time we see you something bad happens."

"We want to help," Gee pleaded.

"Leavin' us alone would be the best way to do that."

Tiny wire points pricked Jane's palms as she gripped the chain linked fence. "We have news. We know who hurt Rex."

Cleo slowed.

"Throw me somethin', mistah!"

Spectators shrieked as Float Thirteen loomed over the monument. Toss beads zipped through the air like sniper fire as the showboat float maneuvered around the curving Lee Circle rotary.

"Rex, you okay stayin' put? I need to talk to them. You stay here. They cain't get to you. They're on the other side of the fence."

Rex visibly shivered. "You leavin' me, Sissy?"

"Just for a 'mo. Sit on the step. You're safe in the crowd."

"I'll be alright." He released his grip on her sleeve. "I'll sit and listen to the jams 'til you get back."

Making sure Rex was settled, Cleo snaked downhill through the crowd. Drawing up before the fence, she threw her shoulders back, her eyes fierce with anger. "Give me the names of the ones who hurt my brother."

Gee rattled the fence. "Come back with us to Fancy's house. We can talk better. You'll be safe."

"No place is safe." She spat. "And I said, give me their names."

Gee glanced at Jane for confirmation. "We think it was a pair of doctors like Rex said."

"Think it was? You said you knew."

"We're still investigating," Jane said. "Looking for proof."

"Give me what you got. I said give me their motherfuckin' names."

"Sissy!" Rex's shrill cry sliced through the thumping sound of the marching band. He stood on the step, his arms outstretched as a damp stain darkened his crotch. "He's here! The doctor! He found me."

Cleo spun around. She started to shove her way uphill. "Rex! Don't move. I'm comin.'"

Hearing her voice, Rex slid down the grassy slope on his heels. "Sissy? Where y'at?" Windmilling both arms, he slammed into the security fence, feeling his way in the wrong direction before slipping through a loosely chained two panel gap.

"Watch it, little dude. You're steppin' into the parade."

A brawny spectator made a grab for him, but Rex jerked free. Tripping over a steel anchor plate, he stumbled into the street.

"Stay on the curb!" Cleo shrieked.

Rex blindly plowed headfirst into the plywood side of Float Thirteen. Pushing off and away, he rolled backwards as loose as a ragdoll as the tandem float surged ahead. His shoulders folded like angel's wings as he fell into the three-foot wide hitched gap.

Covering her eyes, Cleo screamed.

Chapter Sixty-Five

Sunday, February 26, 2017
8:32 AM

Jane set the empty takeout coffee cup on the tile floor between her boots. The unforgiving pre-formed plastic chair kept digging painfully into her hamstrings, but she was too drained to find a more comfortable seat. She looked up as two paramedics rushed past the plate glass window toward the Emergency entrance, pushing a screaming woman strapped to a gurney.

Gee flicked her fingers at the sterile waiting room. "We're spending a lot of time in this hospital. Think the universe is trying to tell us somethin'?"

"It's telling us too many people are getting hurt."

DeltaCare Medical Center's Plexiglas security door slid open. NOPD Detective Shelli Trahan marched in carrying an envelope. Spotting them, she veered away from the reception desk.

"Why am I not surprised to see you two here."

"We share a common interest in the situation," Jane snarked. Her eyes itched from the scent of hospital disinfectant and fatigue. "We are primary witnesses."

"You and a thousand other spectators at Lee Circle." Trahan tapped the envelope against her palm. "Between the parade coverage news teams and the Twitter videos, it's gone viral." She studied the floor. "I don't understand why people want to watch something so gruesome. When did accidents become entertainment?" She looked up. "It's disrespectful to the family, but I guess that doesn't matter anymore. Don't go anywhere, you two. I'll be back."

As Trahan left the envelope with the receptionist, Jane felt her energy lift. *There it is. Hello, caffeine.* She straightened. "Gee, yesterday, I know it all happened so fast, but did you catch anyone acting oddly?"

"Oddly?" She tasted the word. "You mean like people freaking out and screaming?"

"No. That's a normal response. But I'd love to know who Rex saw on that hill when he said, 'He's here. The doctor. He found me.'"

"He recognized someone by their voice. Someone he heard."

"And that's the disconnect that's tripping me up." Rubbing her hands, Jane raced through Logic Tree. "The 'doctor' he heard couldn't have been one of the Hannitys. They both died two days ago. That means Rex heard another doctor, someone else. Someone we haven't considered."

"You're sayin' instead of two doctors, we've got three."

"Yes. And Rex recognized the third doctor in the parade crowd yesterday."

"Dr. Sabatier?" Gee looked incredulous.

"No. It can't be her. Rex said, 'He's here. He found me.' The third doctor is a man."

"Some other doctor from the Coroner's Office, maybe?"

"Maybe. We need to go back to Dr. Sabatier. Warn her. She may be closer to this than she knows."

"You think the killer might go after her next?"

"He might."

"What about Cleo?"

"Her, too. Rex was the active witness, but the killer might think he told Cleo something. It depends on how far this killer wants to go to protect himself."

"This isn't goin' away, is it. Until we stop it." Gee chewed her lip. "Are we gonna tell Trahan or the FBI about the 'third doctor' idea?"

"Let's think about that. Sharing intel makes me nervous because I'm not sure who we can trust with it." Jane slowly ticked the points off her fingers. "The FBI may lose interest because Rex was their key witness. Without him, they're back to square one. The U.S. Marshals Service will sign off if the FBI doesn't need them for the WPP safe house escort. Without Rex, all of this falls back on Detective Trahan and the NOPD."

"So, what do we tell her?" Gee gestured with her chin. "Because she's comin' over."

"As little as possible." Jane shifted on her seat. "I don't like this setup. Not one bit. Local hospitals, Coroner's Office, hit team, NOPD. It smells like a conspiracy to me."

"With a killer hiding in the middle of it."

"Yep."

Scooting a chair closer, Detective Trahan sat. She expectantly rested her elbows on her knees. "I'd sure like to hear what you two have to say about Rex Duchamp's accident yesterday."

"Off the record?" Jane asked.

"For now." She shrugged. "If you want it that way."

"I never saw it coming," Gee volunteered, pointing at Jane. "We were dancing in the Krewdio-54 parade. Jane heard Cleo on the hill. We saw Cleo and Rex Duchamp sitting under the General Lee monument."

Looking surprised and irritated by Gee's brevity, Detective Trahan impatiently raised both hands. "And?"

"Cleo spotted us," Jane reported. "She came down to the street to talk. Rex followed her down the hill. He fell under the showboat float. Float Thirteen."

"That's it? That's all you saw."

"That was it," Jane lied. "What did the street security cams show?"

"They pretty much confirm what you've both said. No obvious signs of aggression from anyone in the crowd." Detective Trahan tapped her thumbs together. "It's preliminary and unofficial, but the Coroner's Office is pushing to label it an accident." She grimaced sourly. "It looks better on the City's Mardi Gras stats when it's reported that way."

Arching her eyebrows, Gee gave Jane a significant look.

"What does Rex's doctor say?" Jane asked.

"You'll need to ask Cleo Duchamp for that information. It can't come from me."

"Is she still upstairs?" Gee wondered.

"Yes. Sitting with her brother. She's been with him all night."

"Are you going to detain her?"

"Got no reason to. I took her statement." Trahan stood, looking dejected. "This 'accident' puts the final nail in my homeless NOLA investigation. I can see it coming at me like a train. Without Rex Duchamp as a witness, I'll get reassigned." Dropping her chin to her chest, she paused before looking up again. "You do know we're on the same team, right? Trying to make a difference. Trying to help?"

"Trying to help," Gee drawled.

"Damn, I hate quitting anything unfinished." Trahan blinked. "Keep me in mind if you hear anything more." Turning on her heel, she headed for the exit.

A tinny bell pinged as the lobby elevator door opened.

Chapter Sixty-Six

Cleo Duchamp stepped out of the elevator looking hunched, bedraggled, and defeated. Seeing them, she dried her eyes on her hoodie cuffs before crossing the lobby.

Oh, no. That poor kid. Jane's heart sank to her knees.

"I'm going to hell." Her lips trembled. "I just killed my own brother."

"Sit down, honey." Gee stood, offering her the chair. "He's gone?"

"I'd rather stand. I've been sittin' all night." She blindly stared out the door. "Rex's a zombie. They brung him in a coma, but this morning he got worse. Doctors say his brain won't stop bleeding. His body's still alive, but his brain is dead. How can that be?" She whispered with horror. "I know he's gonna die. I signed the papers sayin' they could stop his life support."

Gee tried reaching out before lowering her arm. "I don't have the words to say how sorry I am."

Cleo's shoulders dropped. "What do I do now? Rex's been with me my whole life. I don't ever remember him not bein' around." Her face tightened like a clenched fist. "This all started with that doctor that hooked him on lean. I'm gonna find that motherfucker and personally pop him myself." She choked as her slim shoulders shook. "I'm gonna need big help. That FBI fella sounded like he was checking out. Said from now on Rex's case is pending." She looked up. "What's that mean?"

"It means they may reexamine it later," Jane said.

"I know what pending means." Gee dragged her fingers through her hair. "Pending means that everyone in this investigation besides us has checked out. But not me. I'm not giving up on those other people who might still be out there, gettin' harvested. Your boy Win

Carter might walk away, but nothing about this is over. I'm not putting this down."

"He's not my boy." Jane's anger was replaced by a sagging disappointment that stole the wind from her sails. *Really, Win? Gee's right. That's the best you could do?*

Gee juggled her keys in one hand. "Let's start by getting you home. You're free to go?"

"That's what they told me." Cleo looked uncertain. "It's just I got no place to go to."

"You can stay at Fancy's house like you did before."

"I guess so." She hesitated.

"Why? What's wrong with it?"

Cleo shivered. "That place has haints. Things move around by themselves. I don't feel welcome, like the house wants me out."

"Fancy would never do that. She was the most welcoming person ever."

Let's keep this real. Jane glanced at the digital wall clock. "It's after nine. Let's go by E-Z-Mart and get her a new burner phone."

"One moment, Miss Duchamp. Could I have a word?"

Graceland Cuddy stood by the reception desk. Gripping a clipboard in both hands, the social worker strode over, her sensible rubber-soled shoes squeaking against the tiled floor.

"Miss Duchamp, I just heard. Please accept my condolences regarding your brother Rex. Such a tragedy for a young man. I'm sorry for your loss."

"Thank you," Cleo murmured.

"Miss Duchamp, before you go, I should ask, have you heard of the Sacred Heart Benevolent and Social Aid Society of Greater New Orleans?"

Cleo blinked. "The ... what?"

Graceland shared a gentle smile. "It's a group of very generous and socially minded citizens who work to provide funding for indigent cremations to lessen the financial burden that falls on families during their time of bereavement." She touched her chest. "I currently serve as Vice President."

Cleo looked askance. "What's that got to do with me?"

"I wanted to ask about your plans." Graceland cleared her throat. "What you'd like to do with your brother's remains."

"Seriously?" Gee trilled. "You're asking her this right now."

Shifting sideways, the social worker focused on Cleo. "I'm afraid we need to if we're going to initiate the paperwork in time. You see, internments are quite costly. Plain pine caskets start at eight hundred dollars and go up from there. Cremations average around sixteen hundred dollars." She frowned. "I'm surprised DeltaCare hasn't already mentioned these fees."

"They did say something about money." Cleo faltered. "But I don't have no sixteen hundred dollars."

Graceland efficiently switched the clipboard to her left hand. "There's another option. If you're willing to authorize organ donation as next-of-kin, the Society will work with Cuddy Mortuary to provide no-cost cremation or internment services in a timely and dignified manner." She dismissively shrugged. "You can also choose an anonymous pauper's grave provided by the State of Louisiana at no cost."

Cleo looked aghast. "Those are my choices?"

"I should also mention that if you work with the Benevolent Society, Cuddy Mortuary will transport your brother's remains from DeltaCare to the Coroner's Office and then to the mortuary or cemetery for free, once the remains have been released." She double clicked her pen. "Normally, that transportation service alone carries an additional thousand dollar expense."

"Cuddy Mortuary?" Gee stepped closer. "That's your cousin's place. Calhoun Cuddy, the fella we met at Café du Monde that one time." She squinted. "By chance is he a doctor?"

"No. Calhoun's not a physician." Graceland moistened her lips. "He does hold a degree in Mortuary Science. Why?"

"Just curious is all." Sinking her hands into her pockets, Gee settled back.

"Does this sound like something you'd like to pursue, Miss Duchamp? If we hurry, we should be able to finalize everything before the weekend."

"What do I need to do?" Cleo sounded defeated.

Graceland proffered the clipboard. "We just need your signature and your contact information on this release form."

"Why the rush?" Jane asked.

"Many shops, businesses, and cemeteries are closed on Wednesday and Thursday due to Lent. Never fear. We should be able to slip you in Tuesday morning. The Society and Cuddy Mortuary are both proficient in providing compassionate and detail oriented family care around Mardi Gras and other holidays."

"Such bitter choices." Cleo slumped. "Never thought in my life I'd be shopping for Rex's grave." She scrawled her name across the bottom of the form. "There. Take what you need. Rex don't need nothing no more." She snatched the clipboard back. "One thing. I want him placed in the tomb with the rest of the family for free or no deal."

"Of course," Graceland smoothly agreed. "Which cemetery?"

"St. Louis Number One."

"Which tomb?"

Cleo pointed at Jane. "Same one you almost caught us in. Bought and paid for by our great-great-*grandmere*." She proudly raised her chin. "All us Duchamps get buried in it."

"Cuddy Mortuary can easily accommodate your request." Graceland slipped the clipboard under her arm. "We've worked with the Catholic Diocese many times, placing cremains for other legacy NOLA families."

UP JUMPED THE DEVIL

"Then I guess we're done. At least Rex is outta his pain." Cleo's voice cracked. "He'll like it in heaven. It's got a lot of musicians. They got good jams. He can chill until I get there."

Chapter Sixty-Seven

Monday, February 27, 2017
Lundi Gras
AKA "Shrove Monday" or "Fat Monday"
3:20 PM

Clutching Fancy's sparkling purple suitcase, Cleo nervously stared at the Big House, her eyes hollow with fatigue. "You sure 'bout this?"

"Don't be scared." Gee lifted the hem of her borrowed sequined and feathered gown, already halfway up the back porch steps. "Maman'll be thrilled to have you stay with us."

You sure about that? Jane hid her significant doubt as she rounded the Cadillac's chrome bumper. Her stomach felt bloated as a basketball from her unusually too-big and too-rich lunch. *Leslie likes having things done her way. She doesn't like surprises, and it is her house.*

Cleo rested against the fender. "I didn't get a lick of sleep last night. Heard high heels clicking down the hall back and forth all night long. 'Fraid to shut my eyes. Sorry to trouble y'all 'bout this, but I didn't know who else to call."

Poor kid must be at the end of her rope. Empathy stirred Jane's heart. *Been there, done that. And I know she's tough. Crissakes! She slept in a tomb.*

"You wait while I go check. I promise you'll like it. It's a cute little bedroom on the third floor. Great place to stay so long as you don't mind the stairs."

"Or living next door to a voodoo queen," Jane warily added.

"Jus' did that," Cleo said. "Doesn't scare me."

"Gee, you still remember your dad's living up there, right?"

UP JUMPED THE DEVIL

"I've got a plan." Gee waved off Jane's remark. "And even if Maman "says 'no,' you can always stay with Jane." She reached for the screened door. "Hang tight, Cleo. This might take a mo.'"

Jane's OCD flared white-hot as she followed Gee across the porch. "You know I don't have a couch, and Piddles snores."

"Bet he says the same thing 'bout you." She pushed the unlocked kitchen door open. "Stop making roadblocks. We'll go to Walmart and buy an air mattress if we need to. Maman? Pops? Where y'at?"

"Careful where you step," Leslie warned.

"What's all this?" Jane pulled up short, pointing to a row of brown paper sacks running across the kitchen floor.

"We're sorting forbidden foods," Aunt Babette breathlessly explained, kneeling by the refrigerator. "Preparing for Lent."

"I love Lent." Ken raised a quart of Rocky Road ice cream. "Heathen that I am, I'm doing my Christian duty finishing this."

Leslie stiffly straightened. "You walk a mighty fine line, Ken Pascoe. Eating ice cream and smoking cigarettes."

"Story of my life. Can't stop now." Ken licked the spoon clean. "Ice cream, candy, and cigarettes aren't forbidden. I checked."

"They are indulgences, and you well know it. The very opposite of what Lent represents."

I'll need to hide my bag of Aunt Sally's Pralines. Jane bit her tongue. *Don't want to get in trouble with the Lent police.*

"Jane, you look nice." Aunt Babette tapped her chin. "I like seein' you gettin' into the Mardi Gras spirit."

"I wasn't sure about this outfit." Jane smoothed the vintage YSL gold mesh dress she scored from the Bridge House Thrift Store. "Feels strange being out of uniform."

"Babette's right, Jane," Leslie agreed. "You do look nice."

"Are you kidding? She looks smoking hot," Ken stated. "What?" He rolled his eyes. "I can't give her a compliment?"

"Girls, how was the Fat Monday Luncheon?" Ever the peacemaker, Aunt Babette changed the subject. "Did the alphabet community crown their new queens?"

"We did. National and local." Gee swept her hair off her shoulder. "Next year I'm running. Give me a rhinestone crown and I'll look just like Audrey Hepburn."

"It's not all party, Gigi." Leslie reached for another sack. "It takes hours of community service." She gazed, openly curious. "Did you enjoy yourself, Jane?"

"Unusual crowd." Jane considered the understatement. "Arnaud's is a wicked pissa of a restaurant. I can't remember the last time I ate a meal at a table with real linen tablecloths."

"Jane makes a great plus one." Gee swept her mermaid train aside. "I'm proud of you, Jane, for stepping up as my wingman." She muttered an obvious aside. "I'm still trying to make her admit she had fun."

Jane's nose twitched and she explosively sneezed. Unsatisfied, she sneezed again.

"Good heavens!" Leslie exclaimed.

"*Malchance*." Aunt Babette crossed her fingers on both hands. "Sneezing twice means trouble is coming."

"Is someone wearing perfume?" Jane repeatedly sniffed. "I smell something floral. Like gardenia."

"Not me," Leslie frowned. "Gigi, have you been vaping in the house again?"

"No, Maman. Not since you told me to stop."

"Now that you mention it," Aunt Babette slowly pushed up off her knees, "the energy flow feels disturbed, like a stranger has walked through the house. I thought I was being over-sensitive because of yesterday's new moon." She tested the air with her hand. "I still feel it."

"Ken? Did you leave the house today after we went to Mass?"

UP JUMPED THE DEVIL

"Maybe." Dropping the spoon into the empty quart container, Ken looked guilt stricken. "I might've stepped out for a quick second."

"To the E-Z-Mart for more cigarettes." Leslie scowled. "Did you remember to lock the back door when you left?"

"As much as I could do that," he defensively sputtered, "on a door with a bum lock."

Leslie scurried for the rear staircase. "I need to check something. Why does every single home repair fall on me to be fixed?"

"Quick, you two, while she's gone." Gee waved her hands like her nail polish was wet. "Pops, I need a big favor."

"Oh, no, you don't. Leave me out of it. I'm in enough hot water as it is."

"Listen," Gee heedlessly continued. "Pied Stan told us you swapped your guitar for the house on your bond note."

Ken gaped. "He had no right telling you that."

"Whatever. What I want to know is, why haven't you told Maman?"

Ken puffed up his chest. "Your mother needs to come back to me because she wants to, not just because she can."

"Typical." Aunt Babette thoughtfully wrapped a tea towel around her hand. "You're lettin' Leslie stay riled up because your pride got hurt."

"Maybe," Ken mumbled.

"Well, grow a pair and get over it." Gee checked the back stairs. "Because there's someone outside who needs a place to stay, and I want to give her that bedroom."

"Who is this person, Gigi?" Aunt Babette asked.

"Yes, who is this person?" Leslie repeated from the recessed staircase.

"Maman." Spinning around, Gee twined her fingers. "Remember I told you about the two homeless kids, Cleo and Rex? Rex died, and Cleo has nowhere to go. Maman, she's an orphan. Alone in the world. Sleeping in a tomb."

"And I suppose you want to move her into the Big House to live with us." Leslie's eyes filled with apprehension. "Rent-free."

"Please, Maman. Only for a few days. Until we sort things out."

"What's wrong with her staying at Fancy's place?"

"She thinks it's haunted."

"It probably is," Aunt Babette flatly said.

"Oh, Gigi. I don't know what to do with you." Gripping the handrail, Leslie stepped into the kitchen before hanging her head. "Your tender heart is going to get you into fearsome trouble one day." Sighing, she looked up. "But *sha*, that is what I do so love about you. Your generosity. The way you open your heart to help other people." She studied Ken. "It's a shame we don't have a spare room to offer her."

"But we do." Gee rose on her toes. "Time to 'fess up, Pops."

"Alright. I'll tell her, dammit. Leslie, after our ... disagreement, when I saw how upset you were, I went back to Stan, and I swapped my axe for the house on that promissory note."

Blindly reaching behind her, Leslie collapsed into a chair. "You gave Pied Stan your guitar."

"Yes. I told you, Stan's a decent fellow. He tore up my old note and wrote out a new one. Your house is safe. He'll never be able to take it from you."

"When did you do this?"

"Little more than a week ago."

"Why didn't you tell me?"

"Because it wouldn't have mended your trust." He gazed at her unblinking. "Sweetheart, I don't care about the axe, or the house, or anything except you. But I needed you to come back to me on your own. That way, I'll know you still trust me."

"You old homegrown fool." Wrapping both arms around Ken's neck, she planted a kiss on top of his head. "Let's move you back downstairs."

"That's my girl." Ken beamed.

Releasing Ken, Leslie turned. "Aunt Babette? This Cleo would be moving in next door to you. What do you have to say?"

"I'd love having some company, *sha*. It'd be like living in a girls' dorm." She hesitated. "Does Cleo throw late night parties? Will she get a key?"

"All parties off-site," Gee quickly inserted. "Same deal as with me. And a Big House key, yes, but not a key to your room. Your deadbolt will still keep your room secure, the same way it does now."

"Then I vote 'yes.'"

Leslie tucked her chin. "Ken?"

"Surprised I even get asked to vote, since you women will be making up my mind for me as usual," he groused. "Place is turning into a god-damned hen house, with me the only rooster."

"Technically," Gee sassed. "There will still be two cocks. Just saying."

"Honestly, Gigi!" Leslie sputtered. "The things that come out of your mouth."

"No. Please, don't say it." Holding up one hand, Jane stalled Gee's response. "Spare me."

Ken folded his arms, looking mulish. "I suppose I'd better agree. As I keep getting reminded, it's *your* house."

"Alright, Gigi, here's what we'll do." Leslie smoothed her hair off her brow. "We'll let this friend of yours – Cleo – live with us for forty days. It will be our family's Lenten sacrifice." She smugly raised her index finger. "But you're responsible for her and for anything she does. After Easter, we'll take another look at the situation and see where we stand."

"Maman! You darling! You're too good to live." Treading on her feathered hem, Gee clasped and kissed her mother's hands as Leslie girlishly giggled. "You're divine!"

Chapter Sixty-Eight

Same Day
5:12 PM

Time-checking her phone, Jane shouted up the main staircase. "Last call, Gee. If we're going to do this, we need to go."

"Hush, Jane!" Leslie hissed from the living room couch. "Cleo's sleeping."

"Lundi Gras used to be a day of rest." Aunt Babette sipped her wine. "Now it's a party day like all the others." Reaching behind her, she prodded the pillow at her back. "I doubt that girl would want to celebrate so soon after what happened to her brother. I peeked in on her before I came down. She was curled up on the bed, sound asleep like a cat in a patch of sunshine. I snuck in," she confessed, "and tucked her under a coverlet. Sleep is exactly what that poor girl needs."

"Sleep? Give me a break." Ken rattled his ice cubes. "Passed flat out is more like it. After taking a forty-minute shower that emptied our hot water tank. Can't begin to imagine her raid on our refrigerator when she wakes up."

"A cold shower would do you good, Ken," Leslie teased. "As penance for your many sins."

"Only if you joined me in it, sweetheart."

Gee clattered down the staircase. She had changed into a tie-dyed LGBTQ Proud T-shirt tied into a knot, baring her midriff over the silvery shorts from her Lady Gaga costume and the matching spiked heel boots.

"Gigi." Leslie warned. "I'll tell you right now you'll regret wearing those boots."

"I'm willing to suffer for my art." Gee slid her arms into a silvery mesh Bolero jacket. "Last chance to come with us. We could take The Boat. Don't you want to see Mayor Landrieu give Rex the key to the city? See Rex proclaim Carnival this year?"

Leslie visibly shuddered. "You two go right ahead. I'm not goin' anywhere near Spanish Plaza or those bean parades."

"Standing that long on concrete is too hard on my bunions," Aunt Babette sadly agreed.

"And I'll say it again." Ken set down his drink. Grasping Leslie's hands, he pulled her off the couch before sweeping her, protesting, into his arms. "You're all the Mardi Gras I need." Slipping easily into a waltz, he tunelessly began to sing as they danced across the heart pine floor.

"For all the money in Wall Street,
All the stocks of a railroad line,
I wouldn't exchange the girl I love,
She's good as a silver mine."

"Jane doesn't know *If Ever I Cease to Love*." Gee zipped her jacket. "It's the royal anthem that gets played when Rex appears. He's the King of the Carnival."

"Which is why he's called Rex," Ken explained over Leslie's shoulder.

"Maybe Rex Duchamp was named after him," Jane suggested.

"Maybe. This year, Rex is coming in on a train. He usually enters NOLA off a riverboat. Either way, it's a huge festival. Huge! Jane, you'll love it."

"You girls sure about doin' this? I'm sensing something odd." Aunt Babette looked uncertain. "Finding parking anywhere near Spanish Plaza will be a nightmare."

"We'll be okay." Gee grinned like a gargoyle. "We're taking Jane's Ducati. She's letting me drive."

Ken stopped dancing. "You got a motorcycle license?"

"No, Pops, it's dope. My regular Louisiana driver's license covers it."

"She's road ready." Jane settled her backpack. "She passed my test."

"Wear a helmet, Gigi." Leslie looked worried. "Remember what happened to Jane."

"Protect your dome, kiddo," Ken added. "Keep the rubber side down."

"Check, parents. Thanks for your concern. ATGATT. All the gear, all the time."

"Oh!" Ken blinked. "One more thing before you go. Steve Tanner's back in town. Said he wants to talk to me 'one last time' about Marianne's songs. Sounded a little like a threat. Said this was my last chance to work a deal before he hires an attorney."

"When did he call you?" Leslie pulled back.

"While you were at church."

"You're going to meet him?"

"I need to, sweetheart. Can't record a thing as it stands now without tripping into a lawsuit." Ken looked sheepish. "He wants to stop by the house on Wednesday."

"Ash Wednesday?" Leslie's voice rose. "Make sure he stops by after Noon Mass." She eyed the group. "I'd like to see all of us attend Ash Wednesday service. And Gigi, don't forget. You promised you wouldn't work that night as your Lenten sacrifice."

"Givin' up the cash to Jesus. I won't forget, Maman."

"Jane? Will you be sharing our pew?"

Quick. Think of an excuse. "I should probably stay home and watch the Big House."

Leslie blinked. "Why d'you need to watch the house?"

"For security. It's something I learned on Nantucket. Thieves like to ransack houses when they know the families are attending church services like funerals, or weddings, or Mass. That's why posting that information on social media or in the newspaper is such a bad idea. Someone should stay behind to stand guard. I volunteer."

"Damn," Gee muttered. "Nice save."

"I hadn't considered that." Glancing upstairs, Leslie uncertainly picked at her lips. "Maybe I should skip church and stay behind."

"Sweetheart." Ken patted his wife's arm. "Don't get your knickers in a twist. You know how much you enjoy going to Mass. Hell, you're the only reason I go."

"And Ash Wednesday Mass is important, *sha*," Aunt Babette insisted. "Lent focuses the heart on repentance."

"You're right," Leslie decisively stated. "I trust Jane. I'll go."

Lent focuses the heart on repentance. Jane reconsidered Mason Hollister's shooting, her excessive use of force charge, and the subsequent destruction of her entire personal life. *I repent nothing. And it's the perfect opportunity to set a trap to catch our prowler.*

Chapter Sixty-Nine

Same Day
5:48 PM

"You said I could drive," Gee complained over the brassy festival band. "I want my turn."

"Crissakes, Gee. I did you a solid." Jane locked their helmets to Monster's frame. Her temples pounded from suppressed tension. "That idiot cager on Decatur almost nailed us."

"Fine, but I'm driving home." She slid her credit card through the parking meter. "Three hours should be plenty, don't ya think?"

Three hours. A trickle of sweat slid down Jane's spine as she scanned the jostling mass of revelers heading for the stationary train near the Riverwalk a half mile away. *Am I sure I want to do this?* She gulped. *Spanish Plaza looks like a human stampede waiting to happen.*

"Let's go." Gee's feet were already tapping to the insistent percussive beat. Tucking her wallet into her cross-body purse, she pulled out her lighter and lit a rolled spliff as fat as a mummy's finger. "Welcome to the Lundi Gras Festival." Her voice squeaked as she exhaled. "I grew up on it. Want some of this?"

"None for me, thanks." Jane felt slightly queasy. "I've never partied a Mardi Gras season before."

"Unbelievable. Thank God you finally crawled out of your cave. Why would anyone want to miss this?" Mindless of the cannabis-scented trail she was spreading, Gee joined the massed and moving throng. "Excuse me." Bumping into a huddled couple, she adjusted her jacket and raised her voice. "Tonight's the Rex celebration. Tomorrow's the big parade. The Rex parade has something crazy like thirty floats and five hundred riders. It's insane."

"Sounds like a big deal." Jane's tongue felt swollen. She swallowed thickly.

"It is a big deal. The biggest," Gee continued like a carnival barker. Pinching the fiery cherry off the spliff, she tucked the butt in her purse, elbowing her way through a group of hooting teenagers. "The Zulu Social Aid and Pleasure Club hosts this festival. The food, the concerts, they pay for everything." She excitedly hurried into a tight gap as a blast of silvery trumpets sounded. "Hurry up! We'll miss the proclamation."

Jane's guts spasmed as she eyed the even denser wall of spectators packed around the gaily decorated railcar. *Steady on.* She released a ragged breath. *Focus on maintaining my personal space. What little there is. I can survive this.*

"Hail, Rex!"

The crowd shrieked with approval as the blonde bearded King of Carnival stepped onto the rear platform. Rex wore a magnificent green and purple striped tunic with a metallic gold belt. Ermine sleeves peeped from under his stiff high-collared gold lamé cape. Reaching up, he adjusted his bejeweled crown with his free hand before regally waving his golden scepter over his enthralled audience in magnificent benediction.

"Hail citizens of New Orleans," he grandly announced, sounding like the Wizard of Oz. "I loved arriving by train to visit my majesty's winter capital."

Jane stiffened as three equally and ornately costumed men bracketed Rex. Each bodyguard wore a fitted feather-plumed cap and a fully face-covering silk mask. *That's full on creepy.* Jane shivered. *They look like the KKK.* The only human features she could see were their alertly glittering eyes.

"Rex's lieutenants." Gee gave her a nudge. "Part of his royal entourage. It's a huge honor." She boogied in place as a tuba and the spiraling notes of a clarinet joined the musical mix. "Hail, Rex!"

UP JUMPED THE DEVIL

"Stay safe, citizens." Rex raised both arms. "Mardi Gras brings us together to celebrate our love of life. Have fun and remember the *joie de vivre* that makes NOLA great. *Laissez les bon temps rouler.*"

Gripping a handrail, he stepped off the platform, theatrically waving to the adoring crowd before leading his entourage through a uniformed military escort toward a well-lit viewing stage.

"Now he meets King and Queen Zulu and Mayor Mitch," Gee bellowed in Jane's ear. "The mayor gives him the key and control of the city for one day."

"For only one day? Let me guess. On Mardi Gras."

"*Petit malin*," Gee muttered darkly. "That's the sass I get for trying to correct your ignorance."

"Ten-nine-eight ..." The cheering spectators chanted.

Talk about a cross-section of society. Nervously clutching both elbows, Jane scanned the exuberant crowd as the remaining daylight faded to an opaque dusk. *Everyone's represented. Hard-partying hipsters next to families with kids. Those kids are cute. Already in their pajamas.*

"Seven-six ..."

A dozen anonymous men strolled by wearing floor-length crimson academic gowns and strangely beaked masks. Their apex leader steadily tolled a clanging brass bell with a tone so sharp it pierced Jane's eardrums.

"Gee, what's up with the men dressed like birds?"

"The krewe of Asclepius. Savage downers. They're not birds, they're physicians. Those are plague masks."

"Five-four-three ..."

"They're anticipating a plague this year?"

She snorted. "They anticipate a plague every year."

"Mose said the last plague swamped the cemeteries." Jane recalled the data. "Yellow fever in 1905."

"Sounds 'bout right. They'll never give up."

"Give what up? The idea of a fresh plague epidemic or wearing those masks?"

"Both!"

"Two-one ..."

BOOM!

Jane's knees buckled. Her shoulders met her ears as shrill whistling erupted directly overhead. A nuclear bright yellow sunburst illuminated the sky, reflecting an expanse of rippling golden rays across the Mississippi River bend.

"Yes!" Gee shrieked with childish delight. "Fireworks! My favorite part!"

BOOM. Crackle, whistle, sizzle, pop. BOOM!

Jane's panicked heartbeat doubled. Clapping her hands over her ears, she spun around, seeking an escape route through the jostling mob. Tripping over the uneven pavement, she fell to her knees, struggling upright again and blindly stumbling for the open street. Using her elbows, she fought to create gaps, searching for an exit or any access point that might offer an escape from the triggering explosions.

"Jane!" Gee shouted. "Where you goin'?"

BOOM. Sizzle, pop. BOOM.

Stumbling, flying forward out of control she careened off a hip-high barricade. Rolling sideways, she found a narrow gap. Slipping through, Jane raced on, desperate to outrun the nauseating PTSD migraine pain she knew was coming.

"Fuck!" She screamed. Her spiking blood pressure narrowed her vision to tubular tunnels. Protectively stretching out both hands, her stomach lurched as everything Jane saw suddenly reversed like a film negative. Black became white, white became black. She blinked as everything blurred and dissolved until her vision became as grainy as pepper.

UP JUMPED THE DEVIL

Falling to the ground, she clutched her ribcage, spitting acidic bile as the hellishly remembered hallucinatory slideshow began. Gasping, Jane stared up the golden staircase, seeing each gleaming step rising before her seeking eyes. Next came the individual ebony bannisters as rigid as cellblock bars. "Stop. Please stop," she begged, suddenly drenched in a sour sweat that reeked of spoiled meat. "I can't take this anymore." Jane sobbed as she heard the unforgiving and immutable sound of Sarah's pain-racked screams, the repeated percussive gunshots, and John's voice roaring 'No!'"

"Mason Hollister deserved to die." Jane repeatedly slammed her fists against the concrete until the pain of her shredded skin forced her to stop. "I repent nothing."

Suddenly spent, she felt observed by a watchful presence as an eerie silence blanketed her ears. Breathing harshly, Jane looked up and saw him.

Chapter Seventy

"Hello, Jane." He knowingly chuckled, resting both hands on the ivory skull-shaped head of an ebony cane. "I've been wanting to meet you."

Struggling to refocus her eyes, Jane fell hard on her left hip. Her senses blared a warning like a firehouse klaxon. The man – for he had lankily walked like a man was dressed in slim fitting black jeans, a WarBirds band T-shirt, a tailed tuxedo coat, and motorcycle boots with ankle chains. His clothes were smudged with powdery gray dust. He wore heavy silver rings on his fingers, an incisor pendant necklace on a lengthy cabled chain, and beaded bracelets on both wrists. His spade shaped fingernails were coal-black, and he was as rail thin as a whip. Every inch of his exposed skin was inked with blurry tattoos that looked like purpling bruises.

Snatching up his cane, he strolled closer with the self-aware charisma of a mega-watt rock star. Jane's nose automatically crinkled, and her mind swam. Even though he stank of putrescine and sandalwood, she felt an inexplicably magnetic attraction.

"Allow me." Tucking the cane under his right armpit, he politely raised his silk top hat spangled with metal studs and charms before extending his left hand to help her up. "Baron Samedi, patron LOA of this fine historic city of New Orleans."

Trembling to the marrow of her bones, Jane refused his offer. *He has no pupils.* She struggled for a rational answer. *White contact lenses.* Pushing off the pavement, she scrambled up.

"That's impolite." He mocked her rebuff.

She wobbled, and her knees threatened to give out as she straightened. "You're not real." She stammered from between her chattering teeth. "You're a hallucination. A delusion. PTSD."

"Oh no, Jane. I'm real." He chuckled again. Resting the cane against one knee, he resettled his top hat before reaching into his breast pocket. Pulling out a stubby cigar, he hypnotically flipped it back and forth through his bony fingers like a cardsharp working an ace of spades. "I may be the Lord of Death – and my domain is death, resurrection, black magic, and debauchery but I assure you I'm as real in this realm as I can be." He nonchalantly shrugged. "NOLA needs me. And *cherie*, I've been keeping my eye on you."

Jane's parched mouth held no words.

"Nothing to say? *Rarrisime*. A silent woman. Hopefully, you have learned what your mouth was truly meant for." Pulling out a kitchen match, he scraped it against his zipper, lighting the cigar and popping a smoke ring that shimmied in the air. Tsk-tsking his tongue against his rotten teeth, he coyly cocked his head. "Working all night in my cemetery, right outside the first gate of Guinee. Were you trying to catch my attention, Jane Byrne? Because you've succeeded. Watching you is more entertaining than binge-watching *The Deuce*. You're a genuine headcase. My very favorite busy little bee."

"Leave me alone." Pressing her throbbing temples, Jane moaned. "What do you want?"

"Oh, Jane. Don't play *stupide*." Rocking on his heels, he squinted one opaque white eye. "Mason Hollister seeks justice. He seeks *remediation*. There's time to repent before you die."

Jane began to weep as a brutally strong hand gripped her upper arm.

"What the fuck, Jane?" Gee shouted. "Why did you run away?"

"Help me, Gee." Jane's fingers desperately scrabbled up Gee's mesh jacket. "Did you see him? I think I'm seeing things."

Gripping both arms, Gee pulled Jane to her feet. "See who?"

"Satan, the Devil, M'sieur Diablo, Baron Samedi." Jane panted. "Whatever the fuck you call him."

"Are you tripping?" Ducking her head, Gee checked her eyes. "Did you eat a tab and not tell me?"

"No! He's after me," Jane insistently yelled. "Walked out of the crowd. Said I needed to repent. Said my turn to die was coming."

"I don't know what this is." Gee scanned the festival. "Throw your weight on me. I've got you. Let's get you home."

"He said Mason Hollister is seeking justice," Jane persisted. Pushing away, she bounced off a gritty brick wall and staggered solo down the sidewalk. "How did he know that." She wept fat tears. "I'm losing my mind. I've never had PTSD this bad before. I thought I was getting better."

"You are getting better." Catching Jane up, and firmly gripping her around the waist, Gee helped Jane limp toward the parking lot. "But something fucked up. You did this before at Charity Hospital, remember? Do you want me to take you to DeltaCare Emergency?"

"No! No. Just get me home."

"Lean on me." Gee searched for a gap in the bumper-to-bumper traffic. "Aunt Babette will know what to do."

Chapter Seventy-One

"Aunt Babette!" Gee braced the kitchen door open with her foot. "Maman! Pops! Help!"

"What is it, *sha*?" Aunt Babette clattered down the rear staircase.

"Something's wrong with Jane. She's gone *fou*."

"Get her to the couch." Clutching her robe, the elderly woman held the swinging door open. "Leslie!" She called down the hallway. "*Assistance*."

"I feel dizzy," Jane mumbled over the shuffle of slippered feet.

"What's wrong?" Leslie scurried into the living room. "Something's wrong with Gigi?"

"It's Jane."

"She freaked at the festival." Dumping Jane on the couch, Gee stepped back. "She's wobbly as hell. We barely made it home on her bike. Been shaking like that since I found her."

Leslie knelt. "What's she done to her hands?"

"She kept pounding them on the sidewalk."

"Leslie, fetch a dishtowel with some ice." Aunt Babette felt Jane's forehead. "It's not a fever." She looked up. "Gigi, did you girls take anything? Drink from someone's cup?"

"No." Gee paced like a caged animal. "I smoked a little cheeb. Just a puff. Jane didn't do anything, not even a beer."

"What's going on?" Ken trotted into the room, cinching the belt on his plaid bathrobe.

"Jane's ill. Thank you, *sha*." Aunt Babette gently wrapped Jane's hands in the chilly damp towel. "Let's work on these poor hands first."

Leslie glanced at the landline phone. "Should I call 911?"

"Not yet. Gigi, fetch a blanket. We need to wrap Jane up, keep her warm. Jane?" She peered up into her face. "What triggered this? Do you know?"

"Fireworks." Jane gasped as flashes of searing pain split her head. "Didn't know. Wasn't prepared. And then," her teeth chattered, "I saw him, saw something stalking me."

"Is that right?" Reaching for the blanket, Aunt Babette tucked Jane in. "There. That's better. I have an idea about what's happening. There are ways to check." Rising slowly, she pulled out her keyring. "Gigi, run up to my room. Fetch my special Black Pearl rum, the peppered bottle with the red 'X' on the label." Snapping her knobby fingers, she pointed. "And bring my ivory dice."

"Wassup?" Cleo stood blinking on the landing as Gee raced by. "Y'all are making a racket."

"I believe Jane has had a *visite*. Ken?" Aunt Babette snapped her fingers. "Smoke a cigarette."

"In the house?"

"Yes. In this very room, as near to Jane as you can get. Blow the smoke right on her."

"Sweetheart? You okay with that?"

"Babette, is this really *necessaire*?"

"Please. Do as I say. We need to smell the tobacco. It will help with my diagnosis."

"Aunt Babette?" Pausing on the landing, Gee raised an opaque flat-bottomed bottle. "Is this the right rum?"

"Yes, *sha*. Bring it here."

Cleo followed Gee down the staircase. "Is she working voodoo?"

"Yes. White magic. Don't be afraid. You're a part of this now."

Gesturing impatiently, Aunt Babette uncorked the rum with a pop before cupping Jane's chin. "Open your mouth, Jane. Take a healthy swig."

"No." Jane turned away. "I don't want any."

"Doesn't matter what you want. This isn't for you, it's for me. I need to see you taste it."

UP JUMPED THE DEVIL

Fucking hoodoo voodoo. Laying the dripping towel aside, Jane raised the bottle to her lips, anticipating the worst. Filling her mouth, she swallowed. The spiced rum coated her tongue like corn syrup before it slid down her throat as smooth and tasteless as iced spring water.

"Feel any heat?"

Jane sputtered with surprise. "There's no taste at all."

"*Bien*. Ken? Blow smoke on her. Give her a lungful."

He released a streaming jet of cigarette smoke like a dragon's breath.

"Smell that?"

Jane repeatedly sniffed. "Not a thing."

"Good. That's helping." Tossing the ivory dice on the coffee table, Aunt Babette flipped them face up to reveal a four and a five for a nine before patting them gently. "Now, Jane, when you had your vision, what did you see?"

"A man." Jane tightened the blanket around her neck as the trembling started again. "Dressed in black. He felt as hollow as death."

Aunt Babette pursed her wrinkled lips. "What did he look like?"

"Keith Richards on a bad day." Jane plucked at the buttons on her shirt. "His clothes were covered with baby powder."

"Grave dust. Go on."

"He wore a bunch of big rings with dirty tattoos everywhere like bruises." She gulped. "His eyes were white. Solid white. No pupils."

"This is my fault." Aunt Babette rotated her jangling bracelets. "I never should've let you take that cemetery job. I had my doubts at the time, but you were so thrilled to get it. I should've stopped you."

The blanket fell away as Jane straightened, her temples still throbbing. "What has my job got to do with this?"

"You're a beautiful woman. Working in the cemetery, you've attracted Baron Samedi's attention." She patted Jane's knee. "The

Baron likes human women. Yes, he can be rude and crude but he's also charming. When you saw him, didn't you feel the attraction?"

"I may have felt something," Jane admitted, resettling the blanket.

"The Baron stands at the crossroads between the world of death and the living. He leads the Ghede family, the spirits of the dead. These spirits are free and fearless, beyond all mortal dangers and social taboos."

"Better watch out, Gigi." Ken looked troubled. "Sounds more like your kind of people."

"Don't disrespect the Ghede," Aunt Babette declared. "And Jane, don't fear the shadows. It means you're moving closer to the light."

Jane rubbed her rubbery face with both hands. "Some of what he said didn't even make sense. St. Louis Cemetery is the 'first gate of Guinee.'"

"It is, and that's just one gate. The Vieux Carré has seven portals to the Voodoo underworld." Scooping up the dice, Aunt Babette dropped them into her pocket. "St. Louis Cemetery is the Baron's personal gate. Marie Laveau's tomb represents the highest point of the star on his *veve*."

"I've heard about the seven gates," Leslie said. "Some Tulane students went missing searching for them years ago, remember?"

"The seven gates are not to be toyed with. They must be opened in exactly the correct order. Approached incorrectly, they can permit dangerous spirits to enter the world of the living."

"Seven nights," Gee suddenly recited. "Seven moons, seven gates, seven tombs."

"You remembered!" Aunt Babette delightedly clapped her hands. "I wasn't sure that you would. You were so young."

"Babette!" Leslie went stiff. "You taught Gigi an incantation as a nursery rhyme!"

"It does no harm. Gigi, *sha,* you have a new responsibility. Now that we know the Baron is interested in Jane, you must stay alert. Protect her. Keep her safe. Jane, when you saw him, did he say anything more?"

She slumped against a cushion. "He said the man I shot, Mason Hollister is seeking remediation."

"That sounds correct. The Baron also delivers justice."

Cleo raised her fingers to her mouth. "Will she see him again?"

"That's up to him. But, if he's troublesome, we can ask Maman Brigette or St. Expedite for assistance." Stooping, Aunt Babette picked up the rum bottle. "Jane, you might want to think about making the Baron a friend."

"And how do I do that?"

"The Baron loves riddles and filthy jokes. Have one ready for him the next time."

"I don't want there to be a next time," Jane vehemently insisted. "And humor's not my thing."

Aunt Babette looked severe. "Then you better study up some."

"I've got one," Gee eagerly volunteered. "Why does eating raw oysters improve your sex life?"

"I'm afraid of this answer." Ken looked wary. "Why?"

"Because if you'll eat them, you'll eat anything."

"Shoot me now." Jane pressed her bruised fingertips to her eyes. "I'm still not sure I believe any of this is real."

"*Sha.*" Carrying the rum bottle and cupping the dripping towel, Aunt Babette headed for the kitchen. "What you believe in might be about to change."

Chapter Seventy-Two

Tuesday, February 28, 2017
Mardi Gras
AKA "Fat Tuesday" or "Shrove Tuesday"
10:17 AM

"I 'preciate you both comin' with me." Cleo sat in the back seat, tearing her nails. "It's a lot to get through."

"For what it's worth, I've been there." Gee pulled The Boat into the Cuddy Mortuary driveway. "Spent too much time in funeral parlors lately, losing friends. I bet it sucks losing a brother."

"Rex was the last family I had." Cleo blinked away tears.

Poor kid. I know what it's like to lose everyone you loved. It punches a hole in your soul that never fills back up. Jane squirmed. Squinting through the windshield, she studied a tri-lingual sign posted in French, English, and Spanish.

**WARNING
TRESPASSING IS A CRIME
TRESPASSERS WILL BE PROSECUTED
TO THE FULLEST EXTENT OF THE LAW.**

Rotating the wheel, Gee followed a handmade florescent orange DETOUR – VISITOR PARKING IN BACK sign spray painted on a sheet of plywood propped against a live oak tree.

After yesterday's eerie Rex festival experience, Jane still felt untethered and adrift. Her hands were bruised and sore, but her internal confidence and certainty felt battered. *How much of that did I imagine.* Her fading recollection felt surreally out of sequence. *I hate that this makes me doubt myself.* She kept checking the many tree-thrown shadows for a slim man wearing a top hat. Taking a deep breath, she clamped down on her anxiety. *Can't live my life being afraid.* She exhaled. *Sumbitch, if you want me, here I am.*

"Surprised a construction crew is working today," Gee noted.

"I did like you ast." Cleo prodded Jane's shoulder. "Called and checked. The lady said, 'Yes, that's right. Come on in.'"

They passed a fleet of spotless black Cadillac limousines including two matching hearses before the driveway split. The left fork led to a shady asphalted lot clearly labeled EMPLOYEES ONLY. ALL OTHERS WILL BE TOWED. Jane noted two Mercedes C-Class sedans, three BMW 4 Series convertibles, a black Ford Shelby GT500, and a silver convertible Lexus IS 250C.

"Look at those cars." She shrugged off a serious prickle of muscle car envy. "Someone's making real money. I'm in the wrong business."

"You can buy any car you want once we get our PI business going."

Continuing straight, they entered the construction site. A new cement block building was going up on their left next to an expansive vacant city lot surrounded by a sagging chain linked fence clearly posted with DANGER – KEEP OUT – SINKHOLE signs prominently displayed every twenty feet. Reaching the back lot, Gee slipped The Boat into a diagonal slot next to another branching live oak tree.

Opening the passenger door, Jane unlatched the front seat.

"Thanks." Slinging her new backpack over her shoulder, Cleo plodded toward Cuddy Mortuary's main entrance. Two HVAC installers wearing hardhats and neon yellow safety vests stopped cutting the shrink wrap off six palleted commercial air conditioning units.

"I'd tap the blonde for sure," the bearded one said. "You can do the spinner."

"Brah, that blonde's bigger than you are." His co-worker sniggered. "I'm thinking the she-male's more your type."

Cleo cut her eyes at Gee. "You hear smack talk like that often?"

"Only every day." Gee marched past the turquoise Port-A-Loo. "At least they're saying it. Most folks only think it."

"Still?"

"Still."

"How does that make you feel?"

"Sometimes it pisses me off. Mostly I ignore it. Can't change people's minds for them. They're gonna think what they think, even when it's ignorant and wrong."

"Like with me and Rex bein' homeless." Cleo glanced at Jane. "Some folks look at us and that's all they see."

"That used to be me." Jane cleared a frog from her throat. "But not anymore in a whole bunch of ways. I've changed."

Following Cleo and Gee around a muddy puddle and a snaking line of reflective orange traffic cones, Jane studied the substantial cinder block walls being assembled on the sturdy poured concrete pad. A windowless steel door had already been installed near one corner. Precariously perched on the top step of a yellow ladder, an electrician reached above his head to wire what looked to eventually be an automatic door for a drive through entrance. "What's this going to be? Looks like a bunker."

"A new crematorium, maybe?" Gee suggested. "No windows."

"Crematorium?" Cleo stuttered over the word. "Ain't that supposed to be what happens natural in the tomb?"

"That's cremation," Jane said. "Not everyone in NOLA has a family tomb to go into."

"Don't see no chimneys going up." Cleo archly protested. "How d'you figure they're gonna use this then? Microwave?"

"Maybe they haven't gotten there yet. It's still under construction." Jane shivered as she walked into the mortuary building's cooler shadow.

UP JUMPED THE DEVIL

Cuddy Mortuary had an elegant port cochere main entrance with six Doric pillars supporting a classical pediment. Oval windows ran the length of the pink brick facade behind meticulously trimmed shrubbery. A tiered fountain gently splashed to the right of the mahogany double door. Grasping an ornate bronze handle, Gee pulled the door open.

Pausing on the threshold, Cleo blinked to adjust her eyes to the interior dimness. "Last time I visited a funeral parlor was for my granny." She rubbed her arms. "Even the air feels dead."

"Miss Duchamp. And friends." Calhoun Cuddy strolled across the vestibule, extending his right hand. "My condolences on your loss. Let's go back to my office. It's more private." His gesture swept the hall. "Please, this way."

Chapter Seventy-Three

"Take a seat." Cuddy gestured toward four tapestried chairs.

"I'm sorry." Cleo gripped her backpack. "Can I use the bathroom?"

"Of course." He unbuttoned his suit coat. "Down the hall. The ladies' room is on the right."

"I'll just be a minute."

"Take all the time you need." He sat. Narrowing his eyes, he cocked his head, openly curious. "We've met before. At the Café du Monde. You were helping Graceland with the Duchamps if I'm remembering right."

"You have a good memory." Jane settled in.

He tapped his temple. "It helps with this business. It's critical we get the family names right." His shoulders hunched as he folded his hands, resting them on the leather blotter. "So, how are you and the Duchamps related?"

"Just interested friends." Gee elegantly crossed her legs at the knee.

"It's very Christian of you to take such an interest."

"I'll try anything once," Gee sassed. "Might get me into heaven."

"I'm surprised you're open on Mardi Gras Day," Jane inserted.

Cuddy sat back. "We're always open for families in need. I'd keep us open 365 days a year, but we do close on Ash Wednesday, Easter Sunday, Thanksgiving, and Christmas Day out of consideration for our employees."

"Business must be good." Jane cocked a thumb at an oval window. "We noticed the new construction."

"It was time to modernize and expand our facility to bring it up to the highest modern and professional mortuary standards. Cuddy Mortuary has been in business since 1854." He looked smug. "We must be doing something right. Our dedicated team of loyal staff members have been with us for decades – if not generations. We're a vital part of the overall community. We're committed to assisting NOLA's grieving families."

Jane flinched as a shadow filled the doorway.

"Sorry 'bout that." Cleo scurried to a chair.

"Miss Duchamp." Cuddy smiled sympathetically before clearing his throat. "First things, first. We're here to support you during this difficult time. We've worked with many NOLA families like yours to exceed expectations for your loved one's final rest. Cuddy Mortuary is here to provide a range of compassionate services." Reaching forward, he handed out bespoke business cards. "We're always available, 24/7. Don't hesitate to call or send me a personal email at Cuddy.Mortuary@hotmail.com."

Gee sniggered.

"What?" Jane asked.

"Hotmail. It's a crematorium. Get it?"

"Behave," Jane said severely.

"I 'preciate that." Cleo sniffed. "What's left for me to do for Rex?"

Opening a binder, Cuddy picked up a document. "The Coroner's Office has released your brother's remains. This is your certified copy of his death certificate. Make sure you keep this somewhere safe." He slid the certificate across the blotter. "We need to determine what you'd like in the way of a funeral service at a slight additional cost. Would you prefer a subdued chapel memorial, or a celebration of life? We also offer a jazz funeral with a second line parade."

"Rex didn't leave much reason to celebrate." Carefully folding the death certificate in half, Cleo sadly slid it into her backpack. "I guess I'd just like to put him in the family tomb in St. Louis Cemetery. Number eighty-six."

"Certainly." Cuddy double-checked his paperwork. "We'll need to work with the Catholic Cemeteries schedule to prepare the tomb ahead of time, but that shouldn't be an issue."

Gripping the armchair, Cleo turned sideways. "You'll both come to Rex's funeral? You'll be there with me?"

"Of course, we will," Gee easily agreed.

"The earliest we can schedule internment for is Friday." Cuddy toyed with a paper clip. "Of course, we'll handle any necessary permitting."

"One thing." Cleo looked hesitant and uncertain. "The hospital lady said the cost was paid. That right?"

"That's correct." He snapped the paper clip against the blotter. "As long as we keep to a simple internment, all costs will be covered by the Sacred Heart Benevolent and Social Aid Society."

Cleo slumped. "Then I guess that sounds like what we should do."

"Very good." Pulling another document from the binder, Cuddy handed Cleo a ballpoint pen. "I'll need your final authorization as Rex Duchamp's next-of-kin."

Pausing for a moment, Cleo scribbled her signature across the form.

"Very good." Cuddy repeated, rapping the desk with his knuckles. He closed the binder. "A trusted member of our mortuary staff will take custody of your brother's remains from the DeltaCare Medical Center. We'll deliver his remains to the St. Louis Cemetery tomb number eighty-six on Friday. How does an eleven o'clock internment sound?"

"Fine, I guess." Cleo sounded listless.

"Can we make it earlier, say ten-thirty?" Gee asked. "Maman and Aunt Babette will want to come. They'll want to go to the cathedral afterwards to offer a Mass intention and light some candles."

"They'd do that?" Cleo squeaked. "They care that much?"

UP JUMPED THE DEVIL

"Maman's heart's as big as a wheel." Gee stood before slipping her hands in her pockets. "I can already see she's taken you into the family the same way she did for me when I was a baby."

Jane blinked with a sudden realization. *The same thing Leslie did for me.*

"Too late to change her now." Gee sheepishly shrugged before draping her arm over Cleo's shoulders and whispering conspiratorially in her ear. "Let Maman do it. It's what she does best."

Chapter Seventy-Four

Wednesday, March 1, 2017
Ash Wednesday, Lent Begins
12:21 PM

Jane caught Piddles' preliminary questioning yip coming from her courtyard apartment. Pressing both palms against the ceramic tile in the Big House's second floor bathroom, she closed her eyes, listening intently for the slightest whisper of sound.

Come on in, said the spider to the fly. Jane smiled. *Come join my game.*

The kitchen door creaked. Jane automatically checked the Taser's holster clipped to her belt as footsteps padded down the hallway past Ken and Leslie's first floor bedroom. She held her breath for a momentary silence before the warped third step on the main staircase cracked.

I know the sounds of this house. I know exactly where you are.

"Jane?" Gee whispered through the Bluetooth headset. "Where y'at?"

"Welcome home. Second floor bathroom. Behind the door."

"Anything yet?"

"No one but you."

Gee breathed. "I'll hide behind the screen in my bedroom."

"Perfect." Jane resettled her earpiece. "No one saw you sneak back in?"

"Not a soul. Cut through the Burrow's side yard and hopped the fence."

"Neat trick."

UP JUMPED THE DEVIL

"I know how to sneak back into the Big House without getting caught. I was a teenager once. So, is this what a stakeout feels like?"

"Close enough. It's mostly watching and waiting." Jane settled back behind the door. "If our prowler's coming, the timing's right. Give the family an hour for Mass. Another hour if they stay for the Stations of the Cross. Either way, he gets a fat fifty minutes to ransack the house."

"You'd've made a good thief."

"I made a better detective, until I didn't." Jane scoffed. "Surprised to see Cleo go with them."

"She wants to pray for Rex. Pops will bring them home in The Boat."

"I'm still sorry about the way that whole thing with Rex Duchamp went down. I feel like I fumbled the ball."

"Me, too. But we're not giving up on it, right?"

"No. We're not giving up. We just need to keep at it." Jane considered her previous cases. "Sometimes investigations get hinky. Rex's case crimped because of the dead security guard and the Hannity murders. Maybe the perp's feeling safe enough to lay low. We may need to wait until the next thing triggers him into becoming visible and active again." Gee's raspy breathing filled her ears. "Lower your mouthpiece. All I can hear is your breathing."

"S'that better? Won't your boss miss these headsets?"

"The cemetery's closed. I'll return everything to the storage locker before Mose notices they're gone." Jane paused as a city bus rumbled down St. Claude Avenue. "Did Leslie ever say where she hid Marianne's songs?"

"Not to me. Maman just said they're put up somewhere safe."

Piddles lonesome howling suddenly shifted into an urgent bark.

"Hush." Jane's heartbeat doubled as her senses tuned to high alert. "Someone's here." She dried her palms on her slacks as the intruder shuffled across the kitchen linoleum floor and began to climb the rear stairs. *Must be wearing kicks. I can barely hear him.*

Reaching down, she unsnapped the holstered Taser as stealthy footsteps passed the bathroom door. Peering through the door jamb gap, Jane saw a tallish silhouette hesitate in front of the linen closet.

The knit capped prowler reached for the brass knob with a black gloved hand. As the closet door swung open, it blocked the intruder from Jane's view. *Crap! Didn't consider that.* Clean sheet sets and towels began to tumble to the floor.

"Yesss!" Clutching a tattered sheaf of legal pads, the prowler kicked the sheets aside. "Bingo!"

Jane threw the door open. Cupping the Taser with her left palm, she centered the unwavering red laser sight on the intruder's central body mass. "Don't move."

In a blur of movement, the intruder snatched and tossed a stack of folded towels. Jane sneezed as a vapor cloud of bitterly sharp chlorine bleach hit her squarely in the face. Throwing her left shoulder against the wall, she blindly blocked the rear exit as her eyes watered and her vision swam.

"Gee!" She swiped her streaming eyes with her sleeve. "He found the songs. Main staircase. He's coming at you."

"On it!" Gee howled. A rattling clatter echoed through the headset.

Tucking Marianne's songs under one arm like a Saints' running back, the prowler sped across the oak landing heading for the front door.

"Oh no, you didn't." Running from her bedroom, Gee launched like a panther. "I don't think so."

The Big House shook, and the windows rattled in their sashes as their bodies slammed against the hardwood floor. Wrestling for control of Marianne Tanner's songs, they slid across the polished oak boards toward the main staircase.

Fuck no. Jane raced toward the landing, gripping the Taser with both hands, and blinking her eyes clear. *If Gee rolls down that staircase, she'll break her neck.*

"Gee! Roll away." Jane shouted. "Give me a shot."

Yanking the legal pads from the prowler's grip, Gee rolled off her hip and leapt up like a ninja. "Motherfucker, those songs are mine."

Jane skidded to a stop. "Hands where I can see them. I will shoot."

"Don't shoot." Supporting her ribs, the prowler grimaced. "No need."

"Kyah." Gee exclaimed in disbelief. "It's that lawyer."

"Gee, call 911."

"Don't." Serena's sneakers scrabbled against the floor as she shakily rose to her feet. "I'll get disbarred." She gestured with both hands. "Let's work this out. I was only looking for the songs."

"For Frankie Malcolm," Gee raged.

"Frankie knows nothing about this." Removing her knit cap, she raked the hair off her face. "This was for me. I'll admit it was a mistake. Lapse in judgment. No harm, no foul. You've got the songs. Let me go. I'll catch a plane. You'll never see me again."

"You attacked my father, bitch."

"It wasn't personal." She splayed both hands. "He got between me and the door."

"I don't fucking care about the reason." Gee pulled out her phone. "I'm calling NOPD."

"No!" Fear contorted Serena's face. "Listen. I've got information about Ken Pascoe you need to hear."

"What information?" Gee hesitated.

"If I tell you, can I go?"

"Jane, what d'you think?"

"It's your call." Jane kept the laser sight centered on Serena's gut. "Up to me, I say we call Trahan and charge her with B&E. She might enjoy the Louisiana Correctional Institute for Women."

"My information is critically important," the lawyer vehemently argued. "I know it for a fact."

Gee uncertainly chewed her lip. "Let's hear it. Spill the tea."

"Frankie and Steve Tanner are working together. They signed an LLC." Serena quirked a sly knowing smile. "I know they did because I drafted it."

"What's an 'LLC'?" Jane asked.

"A limited partnership agreement. Once they get their hands on those songs and clear the copyright, they're cutting Ken Pascoe out of The WarBirds' record deal."

Lowering her fists, Gee pointed down the staircase. "Git."

Chapter Seventy-Five

Same Day
3:22 PM

"Gee? They're home." Jane dropped the living room curtain as The Boat pulled into the driveway.

"Any fresh dents?" She trotted for the kitchen.

"Should we tell them about Serena and the LLC?"

She slowed. "I think they need to know. Don't you?"

"Yes. Of course. I'm not used to sharing case details with civilians. I need to unlearn that, pronto."

"Hey, I'm still learning this PI game. Let me know if I'm doin' it wrong."

"No, you're doing great. You're a natural."

"Thanks." Opening the kitchen door, she shared a crooked grin. "I needed to hear that."

"Gigi?" Ken looked up from the courtyard. "All clear?"

"It is now, Pops."

"See?" Ken crowed, helping Leslie from The Boat. "I told you. All that worry over nothing."

"Leslie, hold my purse." Aunt Babette pressed her lavender hat to her head. "Give me your hand, Ken. I'm gonna need some help gettin' outta this rear seat."

Ken underhandedly tossed Gee the car keys. "Today we felt the need to pray all fourteen Stations of the Cross. There's two hours of my life I'll never get back."

"Heathen," Aunt Babette muttered.

"Where's Cleo?" Jane asked.

"That poor girl wanted some time to herself." Leslie straightened her belted church suit. "Said she'd walk home or catch the bus."

Grasping the handrail, Aunt Babette climbed the porch steps. "I'm going upstairs to change before our guest arrives."

"Lay my crown on my bed as you go by, Babette, will you please?" Removing her hat, Leslie smoothed her neatly braided hair. "I'll start making sandwiches."

"Don't forget my bowl of Hurricane fruit salad is chillin' in the fridge."

"You didn't put any rum in it, did you?"

"Me? During Lent?"

"Wait, before you go, we need to tell you something. While y'all were gone, we caught our prowler."

"You did?" Ken froze.

"In our house again?" Leslie squeaked.

Aunt Babette looked intent. "Who was it?"

"Serena, Frankie Malcolm's lady lawyer. We caught her upstairs by the linen cupboard."

"Upstairs?" Leslie paled. "Did she get the songs?"

"No, Maman. They're safe. I hid them in my pillowcase."

Ken gently touched his fresh pink scar. "Did you call the police?"

"We considered it," Jane said. "But we let her go."

"Let her go?" Ken fell into a chair, looking flummoxed. "Why?"

"We cut a deal. She swapped us insider information."

"She said she didn't mean to hurt you, Pops. She just wanted the songs. You got in the way."

"I can't believe Frankie put her up to it." Ken looked betrayed.

"She said it was all her idea, Pops. That Frankie wasn't involved."

He looked relieved. "I always said Frankie was a good egg."

"Not so fast. There's more," Jane stated. "She said Frankie Malcolm and Steve Tanner made some kind of partnership deal."

Gee eagerly agreed. "And once they get the songs and clear the copyright, Pops, they're cutting you out of the new album."

"I knew it!" Leslie stomped her foot.

"So, the question is," Aunt Babette calmly settled her bracelets. "What do we do when Steve Tanner arrives for lunch? Do we confront him, or do we pretend that we don't know any of this, and set him up, so to say, like a trap?"

"I suggest we keep this intel to ourselves for now." Jane cleared her throat as her habitual interrogation instinct kicked in. "There's no need to tip our hand. Trust but verify."

"I'm with Jane." Leslie angrily refolded a dishtowel. "I can't wait to hear what that crook has to say."

"He's due any minute." Ken stood. "I'll go wait for him outside."

"We'll go with you, Pops." Gee scooted for the front door.

"Shit." Ken mumbled as he stepped onto the front porch. Tipping a clay flowerpot, he retrieved his pack of cigarettes. His fingers shook as he repeatedly flicked a cheap neon green lighter. "Frankie. What the fuck." He inhaled deeply. "Leslie's counting on me to close this deal."

He flicked his half-smoked cigarette into the bushes as a Honda Accord slowed to the curb, a purple LED Lyft sign illuminated on the dashboard. The right rear door opened. Ken sucked in his breath as Steve Tanner stepped out. The left rear passenger door popped open directly into the St. Claude Avenue bus lane. Looking hesitant and uncertain, Frankie Malcolm walked around the rear bumper swinging his briefcase. He joined Steve on the sidewalk.

"Goddammit, Frankie." Ken leaned on the railing. "I didn't want to believe it. Had to see this with my own eyes."

"Stay chill, Kenny." Frankie's gold linked bracelet slid down his forearm as he raised his hand. "We need to break this stalemate. You need to be reasonable."

"Reasonable?" Ken sputtered. "I have nothing to say to that sonofabitch. He's a grifter, Frankie. A con. A fucking crook. I can't believe you're working with him. What happened to you, man?"

Steve Tanner followed the producer up the driveway. "We all want the same thing. We shouldn't be fighting over my sister's songs."

Gee tapped her chest. "They're my songs."

"Prove it."

"Stop this!" Frankie ordered. "We're not getting anywhere this way."

The front door swung open. "Ken? What's going on? I could hear y'all yellin' from the kitchen."

"Gigi was right." He stabbed a finger at the two men. "Look who showed up together."

"Ma'am?" Steve Tanner stepped closer. "We need to sit down and talk this out like adults. Those songs aren't doing any good sitting in a drawer."

"Nice guess, but wrong." Leslie sent them a scathing look. Defiantly raising her chin, she scanned St. Claude Avenue. "May as well bring them inside, Ken. No need keeping them in the yard and entertaining the neighbors."

Chapter Seventy-Six

"Sweet tea?" Aunt Babette held the dripping glass pitcher over the couch.

Steve Tanner nervously glanced up. "Any chance at a beer?"

"Not in this house until after Easter Sunday," Ken growled. "You're lucky enough to get sugar."

Gee crossed her arms. "It's Lent."

"Sandwich?" Leslie proffered a platter. "Homemade egg salad."

"Thank you." Frankie delicately selected a crustless triangle half.

"Where's your lady lawyer?" Gee asked.

"She got called back to New York for another family emergency. Sent me a text."

He looks clueless. Jane carefully studied the producer as her gut instinct executed a judgment. *He's telling the truth.*

Setting the vintage metallic tumbler on the coffee table, Steve cleared his throat. "Let's discuss the elephant in the room. Marianne's songs. Enough is enough. What's it going to take for you to give them to me?"

Leslie settled her hands in her lap. "We've already said we need to see a check with Ken or Gigi's name on it." She held up her finger. "And that check needs to clear the bank."

"That's not going to happen." Frankie quickly swallowed. "Not until after the album is produced, once a royalty stream is established." He wiped his fingers on a paper serviette. "No one in the music industry advances money on a flyer album. I'm risking my personal funds paying for the studio time and the session musicians we're going to need."

"Ken? It's your album." Leslie visibly wavered. "What do you think?"

"I need to ask you something, Frankie." Ken massaged his forehead with his fingertips. "I'm playing square with you, man. We heard you made some kind of agreement with this dude. That you're trying to cut me out of the new album deal."

Frankie sat back. "Where did you hear that?"

Gee gripped the armchair. "From Serena Melnyk. We caught your lawyer trespassin' in the house this morning searching for Marianne's songs."

Oh, Gee. Jane bit her tongue. *We need to work on that. So much for protecting intel.*

Looking desperate, Frankie unsnapped the locks on his briefcase. "It's true we have an agreement, Kenny, but Serena lied." He glanced at Steve for confirmation. "I did create an LLC to help Steve with his personal wealth management plan, but it had nothing to do with your new album contract. Those are two different things."

Reaching inside, he grasped a red binder, dropping it on the table with a thump. Flipping it open, he riffled through the pages with his thumb, making a sibilant shuffling sound like money spilling from an ATM. "I brought this draft contract for you to review. Let me assure you that the LLC is not the same as this, and effective immediately Serena Melnyk is no longer an associate member of my firm."

"People!" He scanned the silent circle of intent faces. "We've invested so much in this. Don't let it fall apart now. Are you open to discussing a royalty split?"

Aunt Babette crossed herself. "Here we go. Time to deal with the Devil."

Steve rattled the ice in his tumbler. "I might be open to an eighty/twenty split just to get this done."

"Who gets the eighty percent?" Ken shouted. "You?"

"Twenty percent is generous." Steve repeatedly prodded the contract. "Since you don't have one speck of proof that Gigi is my sister's daughter."

"We could've tested the DNA." Jane massaged her thumbs. "Until you cremated Marianne Tanner's remains."

"Woulda, coulda, shoulda." Steve smirked.

Aunt Babette suddenly perked up. "What do y'all need for a DNA test?"

"Bone samples, fingernails, hair," Jane automatically replied.

"Gigi?" The elderly woman turned sideways. "Where's the protective *gris-gris* I made for you?"

"In my purse."

"Fetch it for me, *sha*."

Glancing uncertainly over her shoulder, Gee walked to the hall table. Digging through her purse, she pulled out the thread-wrapped red flannel bundle. Juggling it from hand to hand she returned to her chair.

"*J'aurais dû m'en douter.*" Rolling her eyes to heaven, Aunt Babette chuckled as she untied the knotted *gris-gris* with her bony fingers. "This may have what you need."

Chapter Seventy-Seven

"Labs can't pull human DNA off shells or glass beads," Jane warned.

"Patience." The voodoo queen carefully poured the contents of the *gris-gris* into her cupped hand. "How 'bout a tooth?"

Jane held her breath as time stood still. "You have one of Marianne Tanner's teeth."

"Yes. Found it in the chicken yard when the men backfilled her grave."

"I've been carrying her tooth around with me this whole time?" Gee looked horrified. "That's disgusting."

"It's fantastic." Gently accepting the unwrapped cloth bundle, Jane cautiously examined the incisor, careful not to come in contact. "Dental enamel protects pulp tissue beautifully. Labs DNA test teeth all the time. It's just about the best type of sample there is."

Steve Tanner leapt up. "What kind of scam is this? That could be a tooth off anyone. Besides, it doesn't matter. I've already said you're not getting a DNA sample from me to compare it to."

"Sit down." Jane carefully rewrapped the *gris-gris*. "We don't need your DNA. If this is Marianne Tanner's tooth, it will match Gee's mitochondrial DNA sequence. The DNA she inherited from her biological mother." Smiling beatifically, Jane loved herself some forensic science Logic Tree. "It works both ways. Gee's DNA can prove it's Marianne's tooth, and the tooth can prove that Gee is Marianne Tanner's biological daughter. The lab testing might take a while, but there are plenty of independent labs who do that kind of work."

Leslie looked hopeful. "And a match will prove Marianne's songs belong to Gigi."

"No." Jane hesitated. *How do I explain this without hurting her feelings.* "A match will prove that Gee is Marianne's natural legal heir in Louisiana. You'd still need to go to court, but a conclusive DNA match would give you some high caliber ammunition for a judge or a jury to consider."

"Fuck!" Tugging his hair, Ken stretched the profanity into a drawn-out groan. "More lawyers."

"Please, people," Frankie begged. "Can't we compromise?"

Steve placed his hands on his knees. "I'd consider a fifty/fifty split from net album sales and the mechanical royalty."

"Never!" Leslie declared. "Marianne had nothing to do with creating Ken's new album. That royalty is off the table. Eighty/twenty on the mechanical royalty, with the eighty percent going to Gigi for her future."

"Hey!" Ken thumped his chest. "How about me? I'm the talent."

Leslie doggedly dug in. "Ken keeps the artist royalty, with fifty percent of the mechanical royalty going to Gigi, twenty-five percent to Ken, and twenty-five percent to him."

"Sweetheart." Ken turned to Leslie, looking astounded. "Look at you doing the math."

"Why are you surprised?" She looked ruffled. "I've always been good with money. You know that."

"Steve?" Frankie raised one eyebrow. "We've gone over the numbers. Twenty-five percent of a mechanical royalty is still a bucket load of money. And you won't need to produce anything."

Steve slowly rubbed his fingers against his thumbs. "Agreed."

"Deal!" Frankie beamed. "Kenny, don't forget you can still earn a third income stream with a performance royalty if you decide to tour in support of the new album."

Jane felt her spirit lift. *And Marianne Tanner will finally get recognized for her music. Postmortem, true, but it rights that long-time injustice.* She felt washed by a refreshing sense of payback satisfaction. *Even small justice tips the scale in the right direction.*

"Frankie?" Ken held his fingers to his lips. "Is this really going to happen?"

"Looks like the stars are in alignment this time, buddy. It's your turn to shine."

Pausing for a heartbeat, Ken and Gee stared at each other, their close kinship clearly stamped on their profiles.

"What d'you think, kiddo?" Ken whispered. "You ready to rock 'n roll?"

Throwing her head back, Gee howled. "Agreed."

Chapter Seventy-Eight

Same Day
11:23 PM

The rocker rhythmically creaked as Gee pushed off her toes. "I can't sort everything out that happened today." She sipped her chilled prosecco. "I feel like I should go to bed and start over again tomorrow."

"Ha!" Cleo laughed, leaning against the dodgy porch railing. "Give you a hint. You 'bout to get rich."

Jane ran the bubbly club soda and lime over her tongue. "I hope you remember your friends."

"'Specially any new poor ones."

Jane held her fingers under the raindrops pattering off the gutter. "What will you do with your energy when you stop dancing at Club Oz."

"I'll spend it working on our PI agency." Gee reached for her cigars. The flame from her lighter ghoulishly highlighted the angles in her face. "If you're still game."

Could I do that again for real? Jane felt a flicker of ambivalence and fear. *Quit my steady job at St. Louis Cemetery and rejoin my old investigative world?* She wrestled with the snaky coil of profound doubt before losing patience. *Crissakes. Stop picking at that scar. It's healed. Why not go pro? Just look at the last six months of my life. I've already been solving cases for free.* She firmly set her glass down. *Stop the personal uncertainty, dammit. The only person stopping me is me.* "I'd be willing to try with a partner."

Cleo sprang up. "Two partners. I need work."

"I am so digging this new vibe." Gee popped a perfect smoke ring. "We've already solved our first case. As soon as we get the lab report on the tooth, I'll know if I'm Marianne Tanner's daughter. Second mystery solved. That's two for two."

Cleo cleared her throat. "We still don't know who hurt Rex."

"True." Jane thoughtfully chewed an ice cube. "That's going to be tough with the organ donor supply chain disrupted and the Hannity trail dead."

Gee stopped rocking. "We could talk to Dr. Sabatier again."

"We could, but I'm not hopeful. Last time, she sounded checked out."

"How 'bout asking your FBI boyfriend."

"Our last conversation didn't end great." Jane cracked the ice cube between her molars. "If they've cold filed the case, Win's already been reassigned."

"Detective Trahan?" Gee sounded peeved. "NOPD?"

"Po-po don't care nothin' 'bout homeless," Cleo interjected. "We're invisible. Walking meat." She pushed off the railing. "We need to figure out who's doin' this. They killed Rex. Other folks might still be locked up."

She's right. Instead of backing away, I need to lean in. "There's no law that says we can't investigate on our own as private citizens." She paused as the RTA 11:40 PM No. 8 bus rumbled by. "We need to reconsider what we already know. Look for something we've missed or overlooked."

"I've got one." Gee refilled her crystal flute. "Who spooked Rex at the Krewdio-54 parade. Someone scared him into the street."

"It was a man." Cleo squinted with concentration. "Rex said 'doctor.' Said it was a 'he.'"

"There were hundreds of men at that rotary." Jane's heart quailed at the amount of sheer effort and man hours researching the parade route security video would take. *Lean in, dammit. Stop whining.*

UP JUMPED THE DEVIL

Offer a solution instead of a roadblock. "We could ask the city and NOPD about reviewing street video." She crossed her arms. "It'll be a fight. They're not going to just hand it over. We'd need to hire an attorney and have Cleo file a wrongful death lawsuit to get it."

"You're not listening to me," Cleo shrilly complained. "We can't fight the city. They're too big. We need our answer now."

"Where are all the missing homeless' bodies?" Gee stared into the night.

Jane's heart thumped as she slowly turned. "What did you say?"

"The bodies. The missing homeless people's bodies." Gee dropped the cigar. Rocking forward, she picked it up, flicking the gray ash off her knees. "Rex was homeless. They took him from DeltaCare Medical Center to the Coroner's Office and then to Cuddy Mortuary, right?"

"That's right," Cleo sadly agreed.

"Gee, where are you going with this?"

"There's a path, a right way to do things." She swiped her mouth. "For the missing homeless people gettin' harvested, where do their bodies end up? Trahan said we're talking 'bout enough missing people to fill St. Louis Cathedral."

"Don't you remember? Dr. Sabatier said indigent bodies get incinerated into pauper's graves by the state."

"Those are the homeless people who go through the Coroner's Office, the 'proper channel.'" Gee shut her eyes. "None of the harvested homeless people go through the Coroner's Office or Dr. Sabatier would've noticed."

Jane sat up. "They're not going into the Catholic cemeteries. Mose would've said so during orientation."

"So where are the harvested homeless people's bodies going?" Gee stubbed out the cigar. "Someone is doin' *improper* cremations. Oh, fuck." Her eyes shot open. Pushing off the rocker, she rose. "We saw Cuddy Mortuary installing air conditioners on their new

311

building yesterday." She staggered forward a step. "What do they need air conditioning on a crematorium for? Isn't gettin' it hot the whole fucking point?"

"What's that new building for then?" Cleo looked perplexed. "Didn't have no windows. Storage?"

Gee's palms clapped together with a gunshot crack. "Storage! It's not a crematorium. They're building holding cells because they can't lock folks up inside Charity Hospital anymore."

"Motive, opportunity, and means. It fits." Jane rose as her brain fired up like a jet engine. "And Calhoun Cuddy has his loyal staff members policing it."

"We need to tell the po-lice."

"Won't do any good. Everything we think is speculative. Trahan needs probable cause to execute a search warrant." Jane quickly time-checked her phone. "It's almost midnight. She'd never rouse a judge at this hour to get one."

"More people like Rex might be dying," Cleo wailed.

She's right. Jane's investigative instinct bayed like a hound. *Lean in. If they're not being held at Charity Hospital, where are they?* A Logic Tree answer chilled her core. "We need to go check Cuddy Mortuary. Now."

"Think of what you're saying." Gee blocked the door. "It's midnight. We'd be walking into a house of the dead at the high witching hour on one of the sacred holidays." Studying Jane, she purposefully lowered her chin. "Have you considered who we might meet?"

More hoodoo voodoo nonsense. Jane fought to stay rational. "We won't meet anyone. Cuddy Mortuary is closed for Ash Wednesday. Cuddy said so himself. The employees are home asleep."

"That's not who I meant, and you know it." Gee planted both hands on her hips. "And if not him, then how 'bout regular security or a mean ass pack of guard dogs?"

UP JUMPED THE DEVIL

"It's just a drive by, Gee. An in-and-out." Jane ignored the PTSD tension spiraling up her spine. "A quick look-see."

"Uh-huh. Famous last words. A quick look-see." She gazed at Cleo. "I suppose you're comin' with us?"

"Just you try and stop me." Cleo's eyes blazed.

Looking devilish, Gee pulled out her keys.

Chapter Seventy-Nine

Thursday, March 2, 2017
12:32 AM

Jane sat hunched on The Boat's passenger seat as they passed the shuttered warehouses in the Treme/Lafitte neighborhood heading for Mid-City. Midnight cross-town NOLA traffic was sparse. She felt exposed.

"I'm cold." She studied the waxing crescent moon, a comma in the sky. "Can we put the top up?"

"No need. It stopped raining." Gee adjusted a dashboard lever. "I'll turn up the heat."

"I'm with BWG." Cleo sat in the back seat, her purple hoodie pulled so low over her brow that only her nose, mouth, and chin showed. With her dark curls surrounding her face, she looked like a lion.

Jane turned. "Cleo, if you're working with us, you should update your contact list."

"Whatever you say, BWG." She pulled out her phone. "Hit me."

"Who do you think, Gee?" Jane shouted over the whistling windscreen. "The usual suspects? Detective Trahan, Dr. Sabatier."

"Yes, them. She's already got us. Maman, Pops, and Aunt Babette all use the landline. How 'bout your FBI buddy and the child welfare lady?"

"Win Carter, and Graceland Cuddy."

"Them." Speeding through a yellow caution light, Gee rattled off their phone numbers from memory. Slowing abruptly, she peered at the mortuary's parking lot. "Either of you two notice a gate when we were here before? They might be strict 'bout locking up."

"None that I saw," Jane noted. "Security looked lax for an active construction site. The only surveillance cameras I saw were mounted on the port cochere pointed at the street."

Gee slowed even more. Cuddy Mortuary appeared deserted. The blinds on the oval windows were lowered, looking like ethereal cobwebs when lit by the angled streetlights. The flickering and garish orange gaslights on either side of the main entrance offered the only signs of life.

A beer bottle popped under The Boat's tires like a rocket. Gee grimaced.

"Heads up," Jane reported. "They've chained the driveway."

"I'll drive around the corner and park on the side street."

"Good idea. The construction lane will be a mud pit after the rain. I don't want to explain what we're doing if you get The Boat stuck and need a tow."

"No law against using the sidewalk," Cleo agreed.

Pulling over between two streetlamps, Gee shifted The Boat into park. Sliding her hands between her knees, she hid the keys under the front seat.

"That's some high caliber security system you got going on," Jane snarked.

"I don't want them tearing The Boat up if they're going to steal her. Parts are gettin' hard to find." Gee stepped from the car. "Don't forget your phones."

"Got mine." Cleo slipped to Gee's side.

"Mute them." Jane slid her phone into her hoodie's wide belly pocket as her ever-present OCD flipped a warning flag. *Next time, wear something with a pocket that zips. Crissakes!* She felt unreasonably annoyed. *Trespassing charges on the radar and that's what I'm worrying about.*

"Yes, mother," Gee sassed, eagerly bouncing off her toes. "Let's go."

Fuck around and find out. Jane hesitated, filled with queasy second thoughts and doubts. *This is the difference between thinking about doing something stupid and actually doing it.* She felt a pressing need to offer a final admonition. "Just a reminder, stepping onto a construction site is considered criminal trespassing."

Gee crow hopped easily over the swinging chain. "Good to know."

"I'll remember to tell the judge this was your idea then." Cleo trailed Gee's streetlamp cast silhouette, slinking through the elongated shadow like a feral cat. "What are we looking for?"

"Anything suspicious," Jane said sharply, stung by Cleo's sarcasm.

"Like body parts?"

"Those would qualify."

"Let's check the dumpsters." Gee delicately picked mushy footholds through the sloppy ruts. "I am ruining my shoes."

Cleo shared some obvious stink-eye. "I know I ain't looking in no dumpster."

Jane shivered as a whisper of cooler air ruffled the hair on the nape of her neck like an unexpected kiss. The ragged ends of the construction area hazard tape snapped in a breeze that carried with it an overly sweet scent of a burning wild cherry cigar. The yellow hazard tape was woven in and around upright parallel rows of steel rebar reinforcement rods grounded into freshly poured concrete.

"Shoddy work." Jane slowed, feeling a frisson of fearsome *déjà vu.* "Every bit of that rebar should be capped. Fall on that and you'll get impaled."

Gee turned. "What's this you're saying?"

"Saw an accident happen like that on Nantucket once." Jane recalled the gruesome visual memory. "Horrible thing. A worker tripped and fell on open rebar. Speared him like a harpoon."

Cleo froze, wide-eyed. "Did he die?"

"No. But he kept screaming he wanted to until the EMTs cut him free using an acetylene torch borrowed off Simpson's Marina."

"Fuck, Jane. TMI. The things you remember." A patch of pea gravel crunched like poker chips as Gee strode past three red shipping containers. "C'mon, Motormouth. You said a quick look-see."

Pausing before one of the two green industrial dumpsters, Gee ran her fingers over an arching spray of rusting holes before bracing her palms under the black plastic lid. "Help me lift this. On three."

Am I ready for this? Pressing her tongue against the roof of her mouth, Jane blocked her over-sensitive sinuses against the coming anticipated stink. Extending both arms, she helped shove the lid open. Rising on her toes, she peered inside.

"It's empty." Gee gaped in surprise. "Let's check the other one."

Jane lifted and lowered the second lid. "Empty, too." She tentatively sniffed her hands. *My nose feels numb. I can't smell anything.*

"Is that suspicious?" Cleo wondered. "Not finding trash in a bin?"

"Maybe they empty 'em out every day," Gee suggested. "Bein' hazardous waste and all."

"Even on a holiday?" Jane countered.

A halogen spotlight snapped on, casting their shadows across the asphalt lot.

"Jane?" Gee froze. "They got spotlights."

"Run for The Boat." Jane skidded to a halt as a second halogen beam lit the construction site, severing their access to the street.

"This way." Cleo lithely slipped between two shipping containers. "Follow me."

"You said they didn't have lights," Gee fumed.

"I said I didn't see cameras." Jane flattened against the container's corrugated steel wall. "Don't panic. Give it a minute." Cautiously peering around a corner, she sought any human or canine security response. "They could be wired to motion sensors. Something they hooked up to discourage raccoons."

Looking up, she noticed a spiderweb of looping black cables. *They're running electricity.* Investigative data points began to snap like castanets as she turned. "Gee?" Jane pressed her sweating palms against the clammy metal. "It's cold."

"Sure as fuck is. I'm freezing my ass off," Gee complained. "Shoulda worn a hoodie like you and Cleo did. Next time we do this, I'll know better."

"No, Gee." Jane laid her cheek against the chilled steel. "This container is air conditioned. Or refrigerated."

"BWG's right." Cleo excitedly felt the container hand over hand. "Maybe this is where they're storing the dead homeless bodies."

"Winner, winner. Chicken dinner." Jane rapped the metal wall with a knuckle. "Or spare body parts."

Her heart contracted as someone inside tapped back.

Chapter Eighty

Even lit by the wan streetlight, Gee paled. "Tell me that was an echo."

"Poo-yie." Cleo's fingers scrabbled across the container. "Someone's in there. They need let out."

The hesitant tapping turned to insistent pounding and pitifully muted shrieks. "Help me! Don't leave."

"It's a girl." Jane frantically searched for an access point as her despised PTSD slideshow began to flicker. *She sounds like Sarah screaming.* Gritting her teeth, she throttled the vision. "Look for an opening. A sliding door, or a hatch."

Gee hauled Cleo into deeper shadow as a mortuary side door swung open. She hissed as a triangle of bright light spilled across the parking lot. Calhoun Cuddy stepped over the threshold. He gripped a 12 gauge pump action shotgun in his hands.

Tucking the buttstock against his right shoulder, Cuddy aimed the shotgun at the industrial dumpsters. "Goddamn homeless. Keep outta my recycle bin!"

"Don't shoot that shotgun inside city limits, Cal." A woman called out. "It's still loaded with dragon's breath rounds from the farm. Fire that, and you'll bring the NOPD down on us."

From the farm. Jane sucked in her breath as a woman holding a handgun stepped under the spotlight. Pausing in the doorway, Elaine Hannity looked as elegantly poised as a Parisian catwalk model.

Jane felt gut punched. Stretching out both arms, she herded Gee and Cleo toward the opposite end of the container. "That's it. Time to go."

"We can't leave her locked in there." Gee dug in her heels.

"We'll come back. With Trahan and a SWAT team. We're outgunned. Move it, Gee."

"BWG's right." Cleo hunched low. "Won't do us no good gettin' shot. This way." She insistently gestured.

Running toward the vacant lot and the sagging chain link fence, Cleo slipped through a bent section. "Hurry up." Throwing her full weight behind it, she widened the gap.

Gripping the horizontal top rail, Gee swung through the gap like she was working a pole. Trying to follow her lead, Jane swore as her hoodie snagged a razor-sharp steel connector. Her hoodie ripped as she wrestled it free.

Rolling through the gap and scrambling up to stand, Jane flinched as her left knee twinged a preliminary warning. "Fuck!" Wincing, she limped to catch up, her footfalls softened to sibilant silence by the underlying layer of decades old oak leaf mould. Still racing ahead, Cleo and Gee skirted a cluster of fifty-five gallon plastic drums. One blue drum had tipped over. It rested on its side, losing its black snap on cover among the dead leaves.

"Watch the sand," Gee warned.

Jane limped to a halt, growing more certain and horrified with each half-step. "It's not sand. It's ash."

Gee turned. "Say again?"

"Ash, Gee. Human ash."

Gee's horrified look swept the lot. "There must be fifty barrels out here."

"Thousands of missing people." Jane's nose insistently tickled. Without warning, she explosively sneezed.

"Calhoun!" Elaine shouted from their left. "They're in the side yard. Among the trees."

"I'll get 'em with my shotgun."

"Oh, for God's sake. I'll handle it. I've got my .22. No one will notice the pops."

Jane hurried Gee along. "You need to go. Catch up with Cleo."

"She's calling the cops." Gee paused. "Why? What's wrong with you?"

"My left knee's locked." Jane panted, almost blind with pain. "I can't walk."

Gee reached out. "Grab onto me."

"No. That doesn't make sense. You're mobile. Get Cleo to safety." Jane pointed at the distant streetlamp. "Lead them away. I'll circle around and meet you at The Boat. Move the car if you need to until NOPD arrives. Hurry, now." She insisted. "They're coming. I can see them moving through the trees."

"I hate this."

"So do I. Just do it. You're wasting time."

Gee took off like an Olympic sprinter out of the starting blocks. Moving like a blur she made a beeline for the distant side street before disappearing under the trees.

Using the mossy overhanging branches as cover, Jane hobbled along the chain link fence line, doing her best to stay silent and unseen. Her off kilter limp triggered a sciatic nerve spasm that detonated a lightning bolt of pain through the top of her skull. Gritting her teeth until they crunched, Jane bit back her cry, struggling to stay upright through a wobbling level of dizzying pain.

I am not going out like this. Drying her eyes on her sleeve, she spotted two bony white starfish under a gnarled exposed root. Holding her left leg straight, Jane carefully lowered herself to the ground. Rolling onto her good hip, she tugged her sleeves over her fingers and gently scraped the leaf litter aside. A moldy ulna and a rotten radius led her to the ribcage, and then to the empty eye sockets in the grinning death's head skull. Looking across the vacant lot, she noted dozens more lumps and bumps between twisted tree roots and mounds of dead leaves.

Leaning back against the tree trunk, Jane pressed her throbbing head against the channeled bark as investigative data points satisfyingly snapped together. *Thousands of missing homeless people over decades. Enough to fill St. Louis Cathedral. Dissected alive like lab rats.* She sighed with comprehension. *Cuddy Mortuary is a killing field.*

Tugging on her pant leg, Jane reached for her left ankle. *Someone needs to pay.* Her ragged fingernails scrabbled against the neoprene holster as she ripped open the securing Velcro strap. *No regrets.*

Chapter Eighty-One

The steadily crunching dried oak leaves were a dead giveaway. *Whoever it is knows the ground and isn't afraid. Yet.* Gripping Lucy, Jane controlled her breath, guessing the owner and the direction of the approaching footsteps.

Ducking her head, staying low and tightly pressed against the tree, she rolled onto her left shoulder using the trunk for cover. Her Ruger LC9 semi-automatic pistol fit snuggly in her hand. *Seven rounds in the magazine plus one in the chamber.* She felt the threat behind their pursuit tip in her favor.

Peering around the trunk, Jane silently released her pent-up breath as Calhoun Cuddy marched by on a narrow trodden path. He was still carrying the shotgun, casually sweeping it from side to side.

Okay. Gee and Cleo are clear. I've got Cuddy and Elaine on either side of me. Time to text Trahan. The risk factor is off the scale. Switching Lucy to her left hand, she reached into her hoodie pocket, searching for the square lump of her phone. Her seeking fingers only felt woolly fabric until they poked out the opposite side. *Fuck! Fuck! Fuck!* Jane's heart hammered. Setting Lucy on her outstretched knees, she repeatedly kneaded the pocket. *Where's my goddamn phone.*

"You sound like a chicken."

The slimly elongated shadow of a man wearing a top hat spilled over the leaves. The scent of his lit cigar scorched her nostrils.

"Did you want to live forever, Jane Byrne? I'm ready when you are."

"Not today." She snarled. "I'm busy."

"Riddle me this." The Baron softly chuckled. "If not you, then who? Who? Who?"

"You sound like a fucking owl." *On your feet, soldier. Can't stay put. I need to move.* Pushing off the dirt, Jane struggled upright, gripping Lucy in her right hand. "Here's one: What do you get when you cross an owl with a rooster?" She limped toward the dim streetlamp. "A cock that stays up all night."

Her sciatic nerve spasmed again. Jane fell hard, protecting Lucy and taking the brunt of the body slam on her right triceps. Rolling onto her belly with a grunt, she stared into the hollow depths of a two-meter wide sinkhole. Her eyes teared up as a blast of dank sulfurous air assaulted her face. Pressing her palms into the ground, she rolled away from the crumbling edge as her overactive OCD unnecessarily riffled through her ancient Police Academy vocabulary. *It's an oubliette. Did I really see human skulls down there?*

"Where are the others?"

Elaine Hannity stood stock-still under a tree, shrouded in Spanish moss like a lace mantilla. Stepping closer she aimed the deadly accurate Walther P22 at Jane's head.

Jane raised Lucy. "They're gone. For NOPD."

"Calhoun?" Elaine called over her shoulder. "We got ourselves a situation."

Jane braced herself as racing footsteps rustled the brush at her back.

"Jane? Where y'at?" Gee skittered to a halt, triggering a cascading shower of tumbling leaves.

"Watch the sinkhole!"

"I see it." Raising both hands, she challenged Elaine. "What you gonna do? Kill us both?"

"Calhoun!" Elaine's gun wavered. "Get over here. I mean it."

"No. It's over." Jane tensed. "This ends now. You hurt a lot of people."

"People." Elaine Hannity sneered. "They're not people. They're feral animals. Subhuman trash. I did the world a favor by getting rid of them."

UP JUMPED THE DEVIL

She looked up as a sudden breeze whistled through the trees. The wind shook the gnarled extended branches, upsetting a roosting flock of ravens. Cawing their protest, the black birds fluttered out of the live oaks in a dark swarm backlit by the moon. Closer to the ground, gray-green beards of Spanish moss swayed as crimson lightning strobe-lit the sky.

Staring at her feet, Elaine Hannity wobbled as an opaque silhouette fell over her like an opera cape. The ground beneath her abruptly funneled open with a sandy rush as a new sinkhole expanded like a greedily seeking mouth. Already trapped by the landslide up to her knees, Elaine clawed at the rapidly shifting soil, pulling the trigger on the .22 and firing a wild shot before sliding out of sight with a suddenly silenced scream.

Deafened by the gunshot, Jane's ears rang like tinny cymbals. Sitting up, she repeatedly blinked trying to clear her vision of the insistent red flashes that kept spotlighting the crooked veins in her eyeballs. *If not you, then who? Who? Who?* Scanning the killing field, she searched for Gee, only seeing the brittle scrubby brush and the solitary trees.

"Gee!" Jane shrieked. "Where y'at? Gee!"

Chapter Eighty-Two

"Don't take her, Baron Samedi," Jane begged. Clutching Lucy in her flattened hand, she snaked through the dirt, digging in with her elbows and dragging her bum left leg. "Take me."

The oak branches rustled overhead as the ravens settled in.

"*Merde.*" Gee coughed. "This *hurts.*"

Jane barked a laugh, almost swooning with relief. "Gee, I'm here. I've got you." Setting Lucy on the ground, she stripped off her hoodie.

"What are you doin'?" Gee hissed. Arching onto her heels, she rolled left, trying to escape the pain.

"Lay still. You took a hit." Quickly folding the hoodie into thirds, Jane worked the layered fabric under Gee's elbow to immobilize the joint. Gee hissed again as Jane knotted the sleeves into a compression bandage to slow the bleeding.

"You almost look like you know what you're doin'." Gee looked surprised, then remorseful. "Sorry 'bout things, Jane. This was a bad idea." Shifting again, she groaned. "We're in terrible trouble."

"Hush. We're not done yet." Hearing a brittle snapping approaching through the undergrowth, Jane curled into protective cover. Reaching for Lucy, she steadied the Ruger before sighting down the blued-steel barrel. *Come and get it, you sonofabitch. You want us you'll need to go through me.*

"Elaine!" Cuddy staggered to a stop. "Who'd you shoot?"

"Stay back!" Jane shouted. "I'm armed. This is the only warning you'll get."

"Elaine?" Cuddy repeated, hovering indistinctly in the trees.

"She fell down a sinkhole."

"You killed her." His voice softened as he raised the shotgun. "You bitch."

"Nobody move!" Detective Trahan ordered. "Weapons on the ground by your feet. Sir! Lower your weapon. Now!"

Calhoun Cuddy hesitated as an NOPD SWAT Tac 3 response team swarmed across the vacant lot as intently focused as ninjas. He froze as their tactical red laser sights spiderwebbed his chest.

"Listen to me, sir. Lower your weapon now. Place both hands behind your head. Sir! Final warning. Do it. I'm as serious as a train wreck."

Staring down their combined firepower, Cuddy slumped in defeat. Lowering the shotgun's butt end to his knees, he suddenly fit the barrel under his chin and pulled the trigger.

Jane winced as the booming thunderclap echoed off the mortuary.

"Goddamn it." Detective Trahan grabbed her shoulder mic. "Send a SWAT medic, stat. Your turn," she ordered. "Lower your handgun to the ground and raise both hands – higher where I can see them. Do it now."

Carefully placing Lucy on dry leaves, Jane linked her fingers behind her head. "There are two more victims. One with a gunshot wound fracture, here. Another one down a sinkhole. Status, unknown. There may be hydrogen sulfide venting near the sinkholes. Detective Trahan, we're not the threat."

"I'll determine the threat level." Trahan angrily sidestepped closer. "Officer Fontenot, detain 'em all. Make sure they're Mirandized. I don't want any blowback in court." She tugged her shoulder mic again. "Area secured. Call the Coroner. Send in EMS."

"Call for EMS backup." Jane glanced at the red shipping containers. "We have multiple unknown victims."

"Stop telling me how to do my job." Trahan tucked her chin. "Tac 3, walk EMS in. Stay alert for sinkholes. This ground is rotten. And ask them to please try not to contaminate my crime scene."

Pointing her service weapon at the ground, she strode closer. "Officer Fontenot? Handcuff this one."

"Is that necessary? I'm not a flight risk. I can't run."

"One more word and I'll consider a gag." She halted six feet away. "Are you willing to surrender your weapon?"

"I want it back. I have a CHP concealed carry permit in my wallet. In the car."

"It'll be returned." Studying Gee's rough hoodie bandage, she knelt. "How you doin'?"

"Been better." Shifting, Gee groaned.

"Let's get you some help. EMS, send a gurney based on my GPS."

The oak trees danced with their shifting shadows as the killing field filled with the strobing flashlight beams of the multiple response teams. *Going by what I'm hearing, they sound both shocked and disgusted.* Jane forced her shoulders down. *Hang on, campers. You haven't seen anything yet. Wait until you open those containers.*

Pressing the fleshy heels of her hands against her throbbing temples, she noticed that the red flashes blinding her were coming from the rooftop light bars on the half dozen blue and white NOPD Ford Interceptors filling the mortuary's parking lot and lining the intersecting cross street. *How much of this is real. Did I imagine Baron Samedi helping me?*

"Jane?" Gee weakly asked. "You alright?"

Looking up, Jane noticed Cleo slipping past the searchers along the chain linked fence line. "Yes. We're going to be fine."

"I waited by the car." Sounding breathless, Cleo dropped to her knees. "Called the po-lice from the numbers you gave me."

Detective Trahan spun around. "Officer Fontenot! Who let her in?"

"Sorry, ma'am. Don't know where she came from."

Cleo's eyes widened. "You got shot?" She tentatively reached out her hand.

UP JUMPED THE DEVIL

"Broke my arm." Gee groaned as an EMS team approached bouncing a wide-tired gurney over the lumpy soil. "Ma'am? Could I get some Tramadol?"

"Not likely." The lead EMS tech snorted. "Until you're admitted to ER."

Her partner flipped a bodyboard. "At least he seems alert, Alma."

"She's a 'she,'" Jane corrected.

"Sure thing, snowflake." His tone grew sarcastic. "If you don't mind, I'll keep using the pronouns I grew up with."

"Not everything they taught us as kids was right," Gee anxiously chattered as the techs fitted her with a cervical collar. "Things change. Pluto's not a planet. It's not Smokey the Bear. It's okay to change your mind."

Alma looked at Jane. "She on anything we should know about?"

"No. This is natural."

Cleo gripped the gurney. "Can we go with her to the hospital?"

"You family?"

"No." She slowly let go. "Not really."

"Only family in the ambulance. Ready to lift, Ronny? On three."

"Cleo, help me up." Jane wobbled to her feet. "We'll take The Boat. Detective Trahan, are we under arrest?"

"Not currently. I might change my mind later."

"Trahan?" Gee called, as Jane limped by her side. "Those people in the shipping containers need let out."

"How many?"

"All of them." Noticing the container hatches being raised, Gee visibly relaxed. Turning her head, she studied Cleo. "Something good will come from this, I swear. The city can't ignore being homeless anymore."

"Maybe something will finally be done to help those people," Jane agreed.

"You still don't get it, BWG." Cleo sturdily marched ahead. "They're not 'those people.' Maybe *we'll* finally do something about helping *us*."

Chapter Eighty-Three

Friday, March 3, 2017
10:21 AM

St. Louis Cemetery No. 1's familiar gravel crunched beneath Jane's boots. "That sling is a real work of art."

"*Tres chic*." Gee proudly stroked the sparkling display of vintage rhinestone brooches. "I raided Fancy's jewelry boxes. Aunt Babette helped me pin it. Can you believe Dr. Taab said I'll need to wear a sling for six months? I told him I'm not wearing a cast. Plaster ruins your skin."

"Sounds like your pole dancing career is over."

"Better open that PI agency. I need a new paycheck." Reaching up with her free hand, she straightened her black polka-dotted veil. "The Paracetamol's messin' with my memory. They never recovered Elaine Hannity's body, or did they? Did I dream that?"

"No, she's gone. They may never find her. That new sinkhole is still growing." Jane slowed to give Leslie and Aunt Babette time to catch up. "The St. Tammany Parish Sheriff's Office matched Cuddy's shotgun shells to the two homicides at the Hannity farm."

"You're sayin' Calhoun Cuddy killed Gatewell and Beauford Hannity."

"Or Elaine Hannity murdered her own family."

Gee looked troubled. "And one of them killed the security guard."

"We may never know. It's the most complex criminal conspiracy I've ever investigated. They used Graceland's Family Services connection to feed the organ donor pipeline to the receiving hospitals. Calhoun Cuddy performed the harvesting operations, first at Charity Hospital and later inside the mortuary."

Gee shuddered. "I remember hearin' that part."

"The people in the containers confirmed it. Then they used Cuddy Mortuary to dispose of the remains."

"At least Dr. Sabatier is in the clear."

"Yes, they completely bypassed the NOLA Coroner's Office. Internal investigation confirmed it."

"How did nobody notice this was goin' on?"

"It's like cooking a lobster in a pot. You start out small with cold water and you keep turning up the heat. Elaine and Cuddy started small at Charity Hospital until they built up the whole supply chain process."

Gee paused for a breather. "How many people are they sayin' they killed?"

"That's another thing we'll never know. Forensic labs can DNA test bone fragments, but those ash barrels were too degraded for a decent result."

"Wait up, girls. We can't keep up," Leslie protested. "There's something to be said for the Broussard tomb being so close to Basin Street." She glared. "Didn't know we were invited to take such a hike."

"Yes, *sha*, you right." Aunt Babette grimaced. "These Sunday pumps are killing my bunions."

"We're almost there. It's just up ahead." Jane returned to mulling over Elaine Hannity's bizarre demise. Her curiosity kept rehashing the event with its inexplicable features revolving like an out-of-control carousel. *Sinkholes exist. There's no such thing as red lightning. Everything I saw can be rationally explained.* She clung to Logic Tree. *Baron Samedi did not save me.*

Gooseflesh peppered her arms as she smelled smoldering tobacco. A shadowy man stepped from between two tombs.

"Pops!" Gee sounded scandalized. "You can't smoke in the cemetery."

"Why not?" Ken took one long final drag. "Who am I offending with my second-hand smoke. Everyone's dead."

"Gigi's right, Ken," Leslie scolded. "Show some respect. You're standing beside Marie Laveau's grave."

"I bet she liked smoking a good cigar or a pipe."

"She's gonna like this." Reaching into her voluminous handbag, Aunt Babette pulled out a travel-sized bottle of Prell Shampoo. Bending low, she placed it on the tomb's single marble step. "Gettin' hard to find but I know she likes it because it's so green."

"My turn." Kneeling, Jane unfastened her backpack. Tucking her ragged hair behind both ears, she laid two nip-sized bottles of Black Pearl Rum next to the shampoo. *One for her, and one for The Baron. Just in case.*

"Jane!" Leslie gasped. "I thought you didn't believe in voodoo."

"Can't hurt." Jane rose, scanning the nearby rooftops for clustered ravens.

Gee pulled her buzzing phone from her sling. "We'd better hurry. Cleo's says they're ready."

Crossing Center Alley, they found Cleo Duchamp waiting by the open tomb. She looked neat in the new black dress Aunt Babette had kindly purchased for her.

"Thanks for coming." She sniffled. "Rex would've appreciated it. I know I do."

A starkly simple pine casket filled the upper half of the vault. Off to one side, Mose Gallier and Rob Johnson, the cemetery's sexton stood next to a stack of time-worn bricks and a chalky five-gallon bucket of white lime mortar.

"Strange to think," Jane muttered. "Cuddy Mortuary held up their end of the deal."

Using her chin, Cleo gestured at the shattered marble angel lying in pieces on the ground. "Wish I had the money to get that fixed. Guess it's not important now." She blinked back unshed tears. "People think leavin' things behind to remember them by is important, but it's not. Things don't count. The only thing that really counts is family. Family feelings last because they're real."

She tapped her chest. "I know the people who came before us are watchin' to make sure we do it right. In a way, they're still here. Not here, I mean, but they're still with us." She studied the casket. "Like Rex."

"Love is love," Ken sang off-key. "It don't fade away."

"It's just 'specially sad when you're the last one in a family." Cleo dried her eyes on her cuffs. "Like me bein' the last Duchamp-Fontaine."

"You're still young, child." Leslie sympathized. "Your family's not over. You may have your own children someday."

"I'm sorry, *sha*," Aunt Babette interrupted. "What name did you say?"

"Duchamp-Fontayne." Cleo pointed to the incised script on the crypt. "They spelt it different back in the day. Daddy was a Duchamp, but Mama was a Fontaine."

Aunt Babette hissed. "Any relation to Arsène Fontayne?"

Cleo proudly raised her chin. "She was my great-great-*grandmere*. The most beautiful Storyville madam that ever lived."

"Oh, *sha! Perfaitment.*" Aunt Babette clasped her hands. "I knew somethin' was up. I felt our two souls connect the second we met." She laughed with obvious delight. "I should've trusted the spirit guides. There's always a reason."

Cleo looked wary. "Huh?"

"We're kin. Arsène Fontayne was my *grand-mere*." Her dark eyes twinkled. "I should've known. Everyone in N'awlins is related."

About the Author

Martha Reed is a multi-award-winning crime fiction author. Her short story, "The Honor Thief," was included in *This Time For Sure*, the Anthony Award-winning Bouchercon 2021 anthology. Her first Crescent City NOLA Mystery, *Love Power* won a 2021 Killer Nashville Silver Falchion Award. Martha is also the author of the Independent Publisher IPPY Book Award-winning John and Sarah Jarad Nantucket Mystery series. Visit her website www.reedmenow.com for more.